Voices Under Berlin

The Tale of a Monterey Mary

by

Thomas Heinrich Edward Hill

T.H.E. Hill

HOLLYWOOD BOOK FESTIVAL
2008 Award Winner

T.H.E. Hill
        Voices Under Berlin: The Tale of a Monterey Mary
Subject headings:
        Cold War — Fiction
        Intelligence service | Espionage | Spies
PS3608.I44 V65 2008
OCLC: 268677512
ISBN-10: 1434839737
ISBN-13: 978-1434839732

Published January 2008
Printed in the United States of America.
www.VoicesUnderBerlin.com
info@VoicesUnderBerlin.com

4 5 6 7 8 9 0

Dedicated to all the countless Kevins and Gabbies, Fast Eddies and Megs—not just in Berlin, but around the world—who for over forty years fought the secret Cold War for one tour and then went home.

Acknowledgments

Thanks to Kevin's daughter; to Gary E. Ahern, a Berlin veteran from the 1970s; to Jerry, an Air Force veteran of almost everywhere; to Wolf, a veteran of two tours in Berlin; to James W. Dunning, a veteran of the real army in Germany in the 1970s; to Ray Wenzel, who experienced many of the same pranks in the Air Force; to Bruce Ford, an ASA German linguist at Field Station Berlin in the 1960s, and currently the webmaster of the Field Station Berlin Veterans Group website <http://fsbvg.org>; and to Frank P. Galiani, the author of *Cello Music*; for reading drafts of the novel and making valuable comments on them.

Thanks also to all the members of the *Writer's On-line Workshops* January 2007 iteration of the *Writing the Novel Proposal*, who took the time to read and comment on the beginning of this novel: AnnNoE, Besu, Della, Edeana, Forda, Hannah, James, Jamie, Jay, Mo, and last, but hardly least, Instructor Alice.

They have all, in their own way, contributed to making this a better work of literature, but since I did not always take their advice, any shortcomings that it may still have remain those of my own invention.

YOU ARE ENTERING THE AMERICAN SECTOR
CARRYING WEAPONS OFF DUTY FORBIDDEN
OBEY TRAFFIC RULES

ВЫ ВЪЕЗЖАЕТЕ В АМЕРИКАНСКИЙ СЕКТОР
НОСИТЬ ОРУЖИЕ ЗАПРЕЩЕНО В НЕСЛУЖЕБНОЕ
ВРЕМЯ
ПОВИНУЙТЕСЬ ДОРОЖНЫМ ПРАВИЛАМ

VOUS ENTREZ DANS LE SECTEUR AMÉRICAIN
DÉFENSE DE PORTER DES ARMES EN DÉHORS DU
SERVICE
OBÉISSEZ AUX RÈGLES DE CIRCULATION

SIE BETRETEN DEN AMERIKANISCHEN SEKTOR

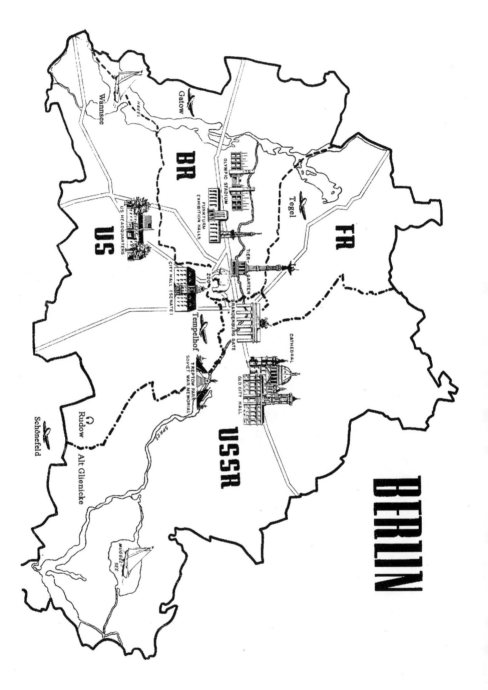

BERLIN

Contents

Guide to the Jargon

Voices Under Berlin is set in a time period and social milieu that had a very distinct jargon of its own which is incomprehensible to many present-day readers. This glossary is provided to help modern readers feel more "at home" in the text. The alphabetical arrangement makes it easy to look up the jargon the second time it occurs, because it is only glossed "in line" the first time it is used.

ABD
: *All But Dissertation.* An academic distinction that reminds everyone that you have not completed all the requirements for your Ph.D.

AFN
: *The Armed Forces Network.* AFN provides radio and (later) TV broadcasting to the U.S. Armed Forces overseas.

Ami
: German slang for *American*.

APO
: *Army Post Office.*

BAFS
: *British Armed Forces Script.* A sort of monopoly money that you can only spend in the **NAAFI** (see) and in British military clubs. Intended to prevent black market activities.

beat feet
: *To beat feet* means to leave, usually on foot, but not necessarily.

black
: In the jargon of case officers, to be *black* is to be free of surveillance.

book	*To book* is GI slang for *to leave*.
Bruderschaft	A German loan word used in Russian. It means *brotherhood*. Drinking to 'Bruderschaft' signifies agreement to switch from the formal 'you' to the informal 'you' in both German and Russian.
burn, the	The destruction of the classified paper trash by burning.
CG	*Commanding General.*
civies	Civilian clothes as opposed to a uniform.
Club 48	The NCO club in Berlin, located at the corner of Clay-Allee and Saargemuender Strasse. It was named for the number of states that made up the United States at that time.
Class VI	The military designation of a liquor store.
crash	*To crash* is to fall into a deep sleep when one is very tired.
Days	The shift from 08:00 to 16:00.
ditty	A *manual morse operator*. The term is derived from the way that spoken morse represents *dots* and *dashes*. There they are known as *dits* and *das*. At some Sites they were referred to as *ditty boppers*.
DMZ	*Demilitarized Zone.*
double-digit midget	A short-timer with less than 100 days left to go before discharge from the service.
Deuce and a half	A two and a half ton truck found in units all through the army.
Duty Train	The daily train run by the American and British Forces between Berlin and their Zones in Germany.
Dynamo Moscow	The soccer team made up of players from the KGB.
Eden, The	A night club popular with GIs in Berlin.
early-in	Taking off from work early, usually at the beginning of a shift. Normally done when the work load was light on the previous shift.
fish	GI slang for a *gullible soul*.
first shirt	Senior enlisted man in a company.

Flag Orders Travel orders for members of the American forces transiting East Germany to the **Zone** (see) by train or by car. The orders had a large flag printed at the top, hence the name.

FUBAR *F...ed-up Beyond All Recognition.*

Gator(s) Member of the U.S. 6th Infantry Regiment, Berlin, popularly referred to as such because of the alligator on their unit shoulder patch.

Gehlen Lieutenant General Reinhard Gehlen (1902-1979) directed German military intelligence operations against the Soviets during World War II. At the end of the war, Gehlen and his staff surrendered to the Americans, and were soon put back into action against the Soviets under American sponsorship. In 1956, he became the chief of the West-German intelligence service.

GI A *soldier.* See **O.D. green**.

GosBank The abbreviation for *Soviet State Bank*: Gosudarstvennyj bank.

GSFG *Group of Soviet Forces, Germany.*

goldbricking *Goofing off.*

Harnack House The American Officers' and Civilians' Open Mess, located at 16 Ihnestrasse.

Head Shed *Headquarters.*

Herm *German* in the jargon of military linguists (see **Monterey Mary**).

honey-trap The use of a member of the opposite sex to secure vital information from the target of the operation via an amorous liaison. See **Mata Hari**.

HQs *Headquarters.*

IG The *Inspector General*. The man who comes around to make sure that you are not only giving the appearance of doing things "by the book," but are also actually doing things according to regulations.

intel *Intelligence,* as in Military Intelligence.

Kidnapping   In 1951, the Bowman Gum Company issued a series of trading cards with the title "Fight the Red Menace: Children's Crusade Against Communism." There were 48 cards in the series, and card number 33 was "Berlin Kidnapping." In the foreground, the card shows an American PFC (Private First Class) in the grip of three Red Army soldiers (recognizable by their uniforms), and, in the background, a military sedan with uniformed Russian driver can be seen waiting. According to *The Secret War for Europe: A Dossier of Espionage,* by Louis Hagen (Stein and Day, 1969), between the end of World War II and 1959, there had been 255 kidnappings and 340 attempted kidnappings in West Berlin.

Kilroy   World War II slang for *a soldier.*

Kartoffelsalat   German for *potato salad.*

Kneipe   German for *pub*(lic house).

KP   *Kitchen Police.* Peeling potatoes, washing dishes, pots and pans for 300+ people in the mess hall. A dirty, tiring detail that usually lasted over 12 hours. See also **police.**

L   See **Time.**

lingie   *Linguist.* See **Monterey Mary.**

M   See **Time.**

Mary   See **Monterey Mary.**

Mata Hari   The prototype of a seductive female spy. Mata Hari was the pseudonym of the most renowned woman spy in World War I. Her real name was Margaretha Gertruida Zelle (1876-1917). Her mother was Indonesian and her cover story was that she was a Javanese princess. *Mata Hari* means *Eye of the dawn* in Malay. She was executed by firing squad for spying for the Germans. See **SWALLOW.**

Mids   The shift from 24:00 to 08:00.

mill   *Military typewriter.*

MOD	*Ministry of Defense.*
Monterey Mary	An Army linguist trained at the language school in Monterey, CA.
moose	GI slang for *girlfriend/mistress*. Originally the Japanese word for *daughter/girl* [musume].
MP	*Military Police.*
NAAFI	*The Navy Army & Air Force Institutes.* The British abbreviation for *PX*. In Berlin, the NAAFI was open to members of the American and French forces as well.
NCO	*Non-Commissioned Officer.* An enlisted supervisor.
newk	GI slang for an *inexperienced newcomer*.
non-frat	*Non-fraternization.*
NTR	*Nothing to Report.*
OCS	*Officer Candidate School.* Where the Army turns young men into officers.
O.D. green	*Olive Drab* green. The standard camouflage color for military equipment and uniforms. Calling someone "O.D. green in color, unit of issue each" meant that they were Army to the core. Compare the term *GI*, which is really an abbreviation for *Government Issue*.
op	*Operation* or *operator*.
ops	*Operators.*
OSS	*Office of Strategic Services.* The forerunner of the CIA. It ran operations against Nazi Germany during World War II.
pavement artist	A specialist in foot surveillance, a tail.
PCS	*Permanent Change of Station*: military jargon for a reassignment.
perschat	*Personal chatter.* A conversation of an unofficial nature.
police	*To police* means to pick up all the trash strewn about the ground within a specified area. During *police call*, the sergeant in charge is likely to say: "If it moves, salute it, if it don't, pick it up!" The *state of police* is a description

	of how well the area has been cleaned up. See also **Kitchen Police (KP)**.
PX	*Post Exchange.* A department store run exclusively for members of the American Armed Forces. In Berlin, the PX was open to members of the British and French forces as well.
QC	*Quality control.*
QC'd	*Quality controlled.*
rabbit run	A type of counter-surveillance operation during which you do something unexpected to attract the attention of the opposition's counter-espionage team so that you can see if they think you are worth following.
rack	GI slang for *bed*.
red	In the jargon of case officers, to be *red* is to be under surveillance.
Resident, the	The KGB's term for the official-cover intelligence officer in charge of operations at the location where he resides.
RTO	*Rail Transportation Office.* The Office that ran the Military Duty Trains to and from Berlin.
SAS	The *Special Air Service.* Roughly the British equivalent of the Green Berets.
Schatzie	The German word for *sweetheart*. The more refined slang for **moose** (see).
scribe	A *transcriber* or the adjective *transcription*.
script	A *transcript*.
Shoss	GI slang for the German word *Chaussee* (highway).
SibTyazhMash	*The Siberian Heavy Machinery Factory* in Krasnoyarsk.
Site, the	Short for *the Operations Site.* The location of the signals collection activity.
SOP	*Standard Operating Procedure.* Written instructions that explain how things are supposed to be done.
Stars and Stripes	The English-language newspaper printed for the U.S. Armed Forces overseas.

straight leg infantry Non-mechanized infantry.

SWALLOW The Russian cover term for a female agent used in **honey-trap** (see) operations.

Swings The shift from 16:00 to 24:00.

TDY *Temporary Duty*. Military jargon for a business trip.

Time The military (and most of Europe) uses 24-hour time so that there will never be any confusion between 2 A.M. and 2 P.M.. In 24-hour time, all the P.M. times are the time plus 12, eg. 2 P.M. in civilian time is 14:00 in military time.

When used after a time the abbreviation 'L' means "local time." The Abbreviation 'Z' means "Zulu time." In civilian parlance, Zulu time is Greenwich Mean Time. When used after a time the abbreviation 'M' means "Moscow time," the Russian equivalent of "Zulu" time

TO & E *Table of Organization and Equipment.* The document that defines how many people and how much equipment a unit has.

top kick Senior enlisted man in a unit.

treads *Career soldiers.* A condensate of the word *retread* = someone who has re-enlisted. The Russian slang for tread is *makaronshchik*, with reference to all the macaroni that is served in Russian mess halls.

trick GI slang for the *teams* that worked rotating shift. There were four teams (A Trick, B Trick, C Trick and D Trick) that worked six days on with two days off, rotating from **Days** to **Swings** to **Mids** (see).

U-Bahn The German word for *subway*.

Uni German slang for *university*.

USAEUR *U.S. Army Europe.*

USO The *United Service Organizations*. The USO provides morale, welfare and recreation-type services to those in uniform. I spent many a

	pleasant hour in the USO Club, and I thank all who worked and work there.
Voentorg	The Russian word for *PX* (see).
Vopo	The East-German police, the *Volkspolizei*.
weeny	Someone with no useful purpose.
Weisse mit Schuss	A German white beer with a shot of raspberry syrup in it. Highly recommended. A Berlin specialty.
world, the	The world outside. Normally used to refer to the United States.
Würstelstand	German for *Hot Dog Stand*.
Z	See **Time**.
Zone, the	The American Zone of Occupation. Even though the occupation of Germany ended in 1949, Western Germany was still referred to as *"the Zone"* by GIs in Berlin. The city of Berlin itself was divided into *Sectors*.

A Note on How the Russians Address Each Other

In conversation, polite Russians address each other by their first name and patronymic (father's first name plus an ending (-vich) that means "son of"). For example: Boris Borisovich Badunov is Boris, son of Boris Badunov. To be polite, an interlocutor would address him as Boris Borisovich. The closest equivalent in English would be to address him as "Mr. Badunov." At the time that the action of this story takes place, the use of a first name alone was an indication of a close personal friendship. The Russians are becoming more "Americanized" in the twenty-first century, and now tend to the American-style use of first names.

1
Rain

Rain is the thing that you always remember about Berlin. It was raining on the twenty-second of July 1954, the day Kevin got there, and it was raining the day he left, three years later to the day. He liked to tell the story that one year he had taken a three-day pass to Munich in the American Zone of Germany and had missed what little summer there was altogether.

Most of those who participated in the operation still don't realize it, but the fate of Project PBJOINTLY hung in the balance on the eighth of September, and rain was the thing that tipped the scales to failure, and Kevin the person. That was the day that the tunnel they were digging hit water eight feet below the concrete of the basement floor in the warehouse that provided cover for what they were doing.

"If my mother could see me now," said Kevin, up to his ankles in the brown ooze that seemed to have stopped rising. "She thought that I had a nice safe spy job, where all I had to worry about was fighting off all those Mata Haris, trying to wring secrets out of me."

"Is that what I signed up for?" quipped Blackie. "My recruiter wouldn't tell me anything except that it was too secret to tell me about it. If I had known about the Mata Haris, I'd have signed up for four."

"Three years or four. It doesn't matter. Just help Kilroy there figure out where the water is coming from!" ordered Master-

Sergeant Laufflaecker. *You would have thought that neither one of them had ever handled a shovel before,* he said to himself. "You two clowns probably broke open a sewer drain. Now find out where the hole is so we can close it back up and get back to work!" continued the sergeant whose job it was to keep the tunnel moving forward.

It wasn't a sewer drain—it didn't smell bad. It didn't smell at all. It was just rain water, and there was always plenty of that in Berlin. It was trapped by a layer of clay that none of the geologists on the survey team had predicted. The geologists were reasonably intelligent and would have found it, if the project wasn't so secret that they had not been allowed to take core samples. The irascible Chief of Base, whose sarcasm was sometimes heavy enough to crush rocks, not to mention less-than-sturdy egos, had given their request short shrift.

"You want to what?" exclaimed the Chief of Base. "If you take core samples out in the compound enclosure, we might as well send an engraved announcement to the Russians to let them know that we are digging a tunnel under the Sector border to tap three of their communications cables. Why don't we do it up right, and put a neon sign on the roof and sell tickets!"

So the geologists, who recognized the space between a rock and a hard place when they saw one, looked in some old books, took some pictures, walked back and forth on the Operations-Site compound and wrote: "The prevailing soil type in the Rudow district of Berlin is dry sand to a depth of 32 feet below the surface, which is the prevailing level of the water table in the subject area." So much for prior planning. At a depth of 16 feet below the surface, Kevin was standing in a foot of water, wondering just how deep it would get.

"I don't think it is a drain," said Blackie in the direction of the tunnel opening in the basement of the warehouse.

"That's your problem all right, you don't think," yelled Sergeant Laufflaecker, whose parade-ground voice was almost as big a threat to the security of the project as having the geologists drill test holes. It was loud enough that you could hear it from one end of the compound to the other, and on a good day with the wind behind it, it would probably reach all the way to the East-German Vopo tower that kept an eye on the Site from across the

Schönefelder Chaussee on the other side of the Sector border in Alt Glienicke. Everybody hoped that the guards in the tower didn't speak English.

That voice, however, was part and parcel of Master-Sergeant Laufflaecker, Thomas E., O.D. green in color, unit of issue, each. He was from the old army, the one that had fought World War II, and he measured your worth by the sharpness of the crease in your uniform pants, the length of your hair and the depth of the shine of your shoes. On his scale of worth, Kevin and Blackie were the lowest of the low. He was about as thrilled to be in an intelligence unit as the 9539th Telecommunications Unit was to have him. *Now that's a joke, if I ever heard one: military intelligence. There ain't no such animal,* he thought to himself with great regularity.

There was a rumor that he had pissed off the assignments clerk in Personnel when he showed up to talk about his next tour of duty by telling the clerk what a slob he was.

"You ain't fit to wear this uniform, if you can't keep it clean and them creases razor sharp. If you was in my unit, you wouldn't look so sloppy. That's one thing I never put up with in my units. Who's your top sergeant?"

So much for Sergeant Laufflaecker's long sought-after assignment to headquarters, 7th Infantry. Both he and the 9539th TCU would have been much happier if he had gone there, but he didn't.

Kevin often wondered if the clerk had thought about the pain and suffering that he was inflicting on the 9539th when—with the stroke of a pen—he sent the blustering Master-Sergeant Laufflaecker to the 'hell' of an 'intelligence' unit instead of to the "seven steps to hell" of the 7th Infantry. Perhaps he was only focused on the pleasure of doing a job on Master-Sergeant Laufflaecker, a pleasure that did not last too long, and was accompanied by some very unpleasant consequences. Half an hour later, he was facing the music in his top kick's office. Sergeant Laufflaecker had dropped by to complain to an old buddy in Personnel, also from the old, World-War-II army, about that slovenly bum in a wrinkled uniform behind a desk, filling out papers, instead of on KP, doing pots and pans in the mess hall where he belonged.

He should have had more consideration for his fellow man, thought Kevin to himself. He had spent more than his share of time doing pots and pans in the mess hall, and was not sure if he preferred

KP to digging the tunnel or not. He would have to give it some more thought.

Damn weenies is just goldbricking, said Sergeant Laufflaecker, lightly under his breath. *I wish I had gone to 7th Army, where they got real men and not these 'Marys',* he complained.

"I'm comin' down there and that water had better be up to your assholes," said Sergeant Laufflaecker in his command voice, the one that made Blackie's and Kevin's blood run cold.

He came down and shot right back up like a yo-yo. Even though the water was not as deep as he had specified it needed to be, he chased Kevin and Blackie up the ladder ahead of him. That was the good side of Sergeant Laufflaecker. He hated the peacetime army, and when things were quiet and safe, he treated his troops like the lowest form of animal life, but when the going got tough, he was ready to put his life on the line to protect the imbeciles, whom the army, in its infinite wisdom, had placed under his care.

Sergeant Laufflaecker picked up the receiver of the field telephone that was on the crate that served as his desk in the basement of the warehouse with a hole in its floor. He spun the crank a couple of times, and waited for the distant end to answer.

"Yes," said the civilian duty officer on the other end of the line, who knew that this could only mean trouble.

"You'd better get the Chief of Base down here right away. We got a little problem," intoned Sergeant Laufflaecker in a calm, conversational voice that conveyed a greater sense of urgency than his usual loud-speaker-like pronouncements.

The duty officer—even though he was a civilian—knew better than to trifle with Sergeant Laufflaecker. He picked up the secure line to the Chief of Base, who dropped everything and started the counter-surveillance run that would take him 47 minutes to complete, before a closed panel truck dropped off some "supplies," consisting of the Chief of Base, inside the warehouse. The world could be ending, but cover had to be maintained at all costs. This was, after all, a covert project. It wouldn't do for the Chief of Base to be seen coming to the Site.

When he got there, he saw Kevin, Blackie and Sergeant Laufflaecker at the edge of the tunnel opening, watching the water rise. It was about three and a half feet deep by then.

"You mentioned a little problem, sergeant?" inquired the Chief of Base.

"We appear to have some ground water seepage, sir," replied Laufflaecker.

"Pumps?" asked the Chief of Base.

"Not a one to be had through normal channels," answered Laufflaecker, who had been on the phone for about twenty minutes.

"And through abnormal channels?"

"I can get you two small drainage pumps for four bottles of whiskey and eight cartons of cigs, but they'll only slow it down. We'll need something bigger to turn the tide."

The Chief of Base turned to the duty officer, who was following along behind him like a nervous dog. "Get him the whiskey and the cigarettes!" The duty officer disappeared.

"When can I have my pumps?"

"They'll be here in about ten minutes. I thought that it was a fair price, so I placed the order on approval."

"Tell the duty officer to make that six bottles of whiskey. The other two are for you. Since you'll be drinking it yourself, tell him I said to give you the 'Black and White.' My personal favorite," added the Chief of Base.

"Thank you, sir," responded Master-Sergeant Laufflaecker in a pleased voice. You could do a lot with two bottles of whiskey besides drink it, and Laufflaecker was going over the possibilities in his militarily efficient mind. If he went to Potsdamer Platz where the American, British and Soviet Sectors met, there was a brisk trade in deficit goods there, occasionally referred to as the "black market," where he could convert his two bottles of Scotch into something more useful. He eventually got two cuckoo clocks for them that would fetch him a hundred dollars back in the States. An August Schwer eight-day Leaf-and-Bird and an Anton Schneider chalet-style cuckoo clock with a moving chimney sweep!

"Once you get the small pumps running, you and your miners can take off till I can get the big pumps in from the Zone," continued the Chief of Base.

If the Chief of Base had known what was going to happen when the miners dispersed all over Berlin, he would have made them stay and bail out the tunnel by hand, but he wasn't clairvoyant, so he turned on his heel and was gone.

At about this time, another 1,356 feet east of the tunnel face, circuit 39 on cable A went active.

Circuit 39:   08:32-08:37Z 08 September 1954

FEMALE 1: MOSCOW, This is WUENSDORF in GERMANY.
    Please give me the GRU duty officer for my
    party.
FEMALE 2: Of course, WUENSDORF. Just a moment.
MALE 1: GRU Headquarters. Captain DEZHURNYJ
    speaking.
FEMALE 2: Your party is on the line, WUENSDORF.
MALE 2: General SERPOV, please.
MALE 1: May I say who's calling?
MALE 2: Colonel MOLOTOV from WUENSDORF.
MALE 1: I will see if he's in.
MALE 3: VYACHESLAV MIKHAJLOVICH! Good news on
    project JITNEY, I hope.
MALE 2: Yes, JITNEY is off to a good start,
    VLADLEN MARKOVICH. Captain SILNYAKOV and
    his team were efficient as usual. We have
    the subject in custody.
MALE 3: Is he cooperating?
MALE 2: No, but what else would you expect with
    an American. They're still working on him.
    He'll change his tune yet.
MALE 3: Change his tune or not, at least he's out
    of the game. He's been a thorn in our side
    for some time.
MALE 2: That he has. You said that there might be
    new instructions?
MALE 3: Yes. If he cooperates and we can double
    him so that he will work for us, you're not
    to harm him any more than is necessary to
    gain his cooperation. He needs to be able
    to go back under his own steam so that it
    will look as if nothing has happened.
MALE 2: There's nothing different in that. That's
    what we always do.
MALE 3: Yes. I am just making sure that we are

both reading from the same set of sheet
music.

MALE 2: Of course.

MALE 3: If he does not cooperate, then you are to
make sure that he cannot go back to work
against us ever again. You are authorized
to take any measures short of killing him
to achieve this goal. He has to be able to
take a message back with him when he goes.

MALE 2: We could just pin a note to the body and
drop it in the American Sector.

MALE 3: We want him to deliver the note, so that
he can convince them that we are serious.

MALE 2: Oh, you want him to be able to put the
contents of the note into context?

MALE 3: Yes, exactly.

MALE 2: I've seen him, and I don't think that we
have a messenger. I think that he'll make a
good double agent.

MALE 3: Don't underestimate these Americans. They
can be tougher than they look.

MALE 2: We'll see. How long do I have to work on
him before I have to decide how to send him
back?

MALE 3: You have until Monday the 13th.

MALE 2: Good thing I'm not superstitious.

MALE 3: He has to be found so that he can deliver
his message by 14:00 Local that day.

MALE 2: We'll have to work fast.

MALE 3: See that you do.

MALE 2: And the message he is to take back, if I
can't double him?

MALE 3: It is being finessed in both English and
German to convey just the right tone. We
will send it out to you on the teletype
when we've got it ready.

MALE 2: Give me a call when it goes, so that I
can be on the lookout for it.

MALE 3: I'll have the case officer call you as
soon as he has a file time for the message.

MALE 2: That should be fine. If he's to be found
in time to deliver the message by 14:00

Local, I will have to decide how to send
him back by 08:00 Local, that's 10:00 your
time. I'll give you a call when I decide.

MALE 3: Very good.

MALE 2: You have an alternate way of delivering
the message, in case I can turn him?

MALE 3: Yes. It is all laid on, ready to go at an
hour's notice.

MALE 2: I'll try to see that you have to make use
of it.

MALE 3: You do that, VYACHESLAV MIKHAJLOVICH.

MALE 2: I serve the Soviet Union, VLADLEN
MARKOVICH.

[Hang up]

2
Gabbie

Kevin showered, put on his civies, grabbed his new German NINO-Flex raincoat—better than the ones they had in the PX—and headed for the Dahlem Museum in Zehlendorf. He had been wanting to go, but had never been able to get any time off when it was opened. This was his chance.

By the time that the bus and the subway—better known to those in Germany as the U-Bahn—conveyed Kevin from Rudow to Zehlendorf, it was lunch time. That was OK by Kevin, since it gave him a chance to check out the cafeteria in the basement. It was crowded, which was a good sign. At least there was something to eat. He was pleased to find that it tasted good too. A definite improvement on the Mess Hall in his opinion.

When Kevin got to the end of the line with his food and paid the cashier, there was only one place left to sit. It was at a table for two, but Gabbie was occupying the other chair. Germans are very pragmatic people and realize that seating space is at a premium in places to eat, so sharing your table with a total stranger is a not an uncommon occurrence. You are entitled to a chair and a place for your dishes and silverware, but not to a whole table for yourself.

If the chair at her table had not been the only place to sit, Kevin never would have approached her. She was too pretty, and his people skills were somewhat underdeveloped, to say the least.

Kevin walked over to the table, and said in his very best Berliner accented German: "Darf ich?" Gabbie looked up, took in his new Herm raincoat, and said: "Bitte." Kevin sat down.

Her real name was Gabriele, but everybody called her "Gabbie," and she was certainly that. She could talk your ears off. It was her compulsion to talk got things started. "What do you think of the goulash? Isn't it better than last week's? It must have been made out of an old horse last week, don't you think?"

Kevin's taciturn response was Berlinerisch: "Ja." Her waterfall of German words continued while Kevin ate, and he was pleased to find that all the effort he had invested in that self-study German course had paid off. He could actually understand her, most of the time. His monosyllabic responses between mouthfuls sounded German enough not to break the illusion of being a German that his raincoat gave him.

It's a good thing goulash is eaten with a spoon, otherwise his knife and fork manners would have given him away immediately. It wasn't that he didn't know that Europeans hold their knives in their right hands, and their forks in their left. He had read the stories of the American OSS operatives who had parachuted into Nazi Germany and been rolled up by the Gestapo for holding their silverware in the wrong hands. It was because mechanical habits are hard to break. He had to concentrate really hard to keep his eating implements in the hands that European manners required, and right now his concentration was focused on Gabbie.

Having finished his goulash, Kevin decided to take the next chance she gave him to talk to ask her to go look at the South-Seas art and ethnography exhibit upstairs, which was what he had come for. Saying a sentence that long gave him away.

"You're an Ami! But you speak such good German. How did you manage that? Are your parents German? Your grandmother?"

Before Kevin could say anything, she continued, "Of course I'd love to see the exhibit again. It's one of my favorites." The waterfall of words had resumed.

They picked up their trays and took them to the window for the dishwashers. The chairs that they had been sitting in did not have a chance to get cold. They had hardly stood up, when another couple sat down.

They climbed the stairs to the ground floor, crossed the foyer and went down the hall to the *Abteilung Südsee,* where the Oceanic art and artifacts exhibits were. The collection at the Dahlem was impressive. "It dates back to the second voyage of Captain Cook in the eighteenth century," said Gabbie, translating out loud from the first sign in the exhibit into English.

"1772-1775," said Kevin in German. He noticed that her face lit up in a smile of surprise. "The numbers are easy to read," remarked Kevin. "It's things like *'enthalten diese kulturgeschichtlichen Sammlungen Objekte aus dem kultischen Bereich'* that tie my tongue up in knots."

"Your tongue doesn't seem to have suffered too much reading that one," observed Gabbie, pleased to have found a German-speaking American with a sense of humor. Most of the others she had met played a record that seemed to only have one track on it.

They walked over to the first of the display cases with the artifacts from the Sepik region of Papua New Guinea. Each had a caption card that told where the item was from, when it was collected, and what it was used for. "Apotropaic gable mask, collected by Captain Cook, used to frighten evil spirits away from a ceremonial house," read Gabbie out loud in English. "Spirit mask with clan images, collected by captain Cook, used to invoke the memory of honored ancestors," read Kevin in German. "Look, there's a crocodile coming out of its mouth! What's the German word for crocodile? It's not one of those words that you use every day," continued Kevin to his surprise. He hadn't yet figured out how to stop Gabbie's waterfall of words so that he could talk.

"*Krokodil,*" replied Gabbie, who was pleased to be asked a question like that by an Ami. It was much more pleasant to be asked that, than to get the questions that she usually heard from Amis.

"No wonder I couldn't remember what it was. It's too much like English. It's supposed to be different to be German," explained Kevin. He noticed that Gabbie smiled her bright smile again. She had just thought that Kevin was too much like a German. Amis were supposed to be different, and usually were.

Their tour of the exhibits came to an abrupt end. The museum guard for the exhibit, an older gentleman with graying hair in a clearly well-worn, but well-maintained uniform and an obviously military bearing, walked up behind them unobtrusively and cleared his throat. "I regret to have to inform you that the museum is closing. You will have to leave for today, but I do hope that you will come back again tomorrow to continue your tour of the exhibit." He really hated to tell them that. He had been watching them slowly reading the exhibit cards for hours, but he had a wife to get home to, whom he still looked at the way Kevin had been looking at Gabbie. He was sure that he would see the young lady and the young officer again. He was right and he was wrong. Kevin was not an officer.

They left the museum together. The rain had turned to a drizzle. She offered to share her umbrella. Kevin offered her a chocolate sundae at the PX, which was nearby, and the only thing he knew about in the area that would fit his budget. Gabbie was not sure what a 'chocolate Sunday' was, but was prepared to find out.

The PX

"I've never had anything like that before," she said as they left the PX, heading for the Oskar-Helene-Heim U-Bahn station. She had not planned on letting Kevin take her all the way home, but when he asked for her telephone number, she had to admit that she did not have one. The thought of giving him her address without letting him escort her home seemed strange, which—even though he was strange for an Ami—was not the way that she wanted to end their first date, so she did not protest when he got on the U-Bahn with her.

The U-Bahn deposited them in Steglitz, and they walked four blocks to an apartment building that still had visible war damage. Reconstruction was the priority. Making it look pretty would come later. It was one of those huge Berlin apartment buildings with an immense staircase and an after-thought elevator that did not work. She stopped at the outside door to the building.

"I've had a lovely time," she said. "I never imagined that Sunday could be such a tasty day of the week."

Actually, it was a Wednesday, September the eighth to be precise.

"I never thought of a sundae quite that way before," replied Kevin. "I had a wonderful time, too. Can I call on you again?"

"Yes."

"Tomorrow? We could go visit Sophie-Charlotte," said Kevin, referring to the royal museum in the British Sector. He had some British Armed Forces Script, and they could go to the NAAFI, the British PX. You had to pay for everything there in BAFS.

"All right. I'll meet you there at 13:00."

"I could collect you here at 11:30, and we could have lunch first."

"I've never been collected before. I'm not sure I'll like it."

"I hope you will. It means that I get to see you sooner and that I can keep you company on the U-Bahn on the way up there."

"In that case, 11:30 here," she said extending her right hand palm-down to signify the closing of the audience.

"Küss die Hand, gnädiges Fräulein," said Kevin, clicking his heels together, and kissing the extended hand lightly in an elegant bow.

Maybe the guard at the Dahlem had been right. All Kevin needed was a duelling scar on his right cheek and he would have looked like the Dahlem guard's military academy classmate Heinrich, who had been killed by the Americans in Normandy on D-day. Maybe that's why he had thought of Kevin as "the young officer."

If he had seen Kevin just now, a sense of déjà vu would have swept him back to a pre-war evening in front of just such a building, also in Steglitz, maybe even this very one, when he had waited at a discrete distance as Heinrich had bid good night to Liesl, before they returned to the barracks. Heinrich had kissed her hand and clicked his heels. It had been raining.

Gabbie was flabbergasted. She had been expecting a handshake—such typical American gaucherie—or an attempt to kiss her on the lips—perhaps more so typically American—but not that he would kiss her hand, and click his heels. Nobody did that anymore. Not even the Germans.

Circuit 53:   20:19-20:22Z 08 September 1954

FEMALE 1: MOSCOW, this is KARLSHORST. 6389 for my party, please.

FEMALE 2: It's ringing. Put your party on the line.

MALE 1: Finance. 6389.

MALE 2: Captain ULYANOV, please.

MALE 1: Speaking.

MALE 2: This is Colonel BORIS BORISOVICH BADUNOV in KARLSHORST, GERMANY. General BESSTRASHNYJ has recommended you for a vacant position here. I have already seen your file, but I had a few questions that I wanted to ask in person. The general said that I could not bring you out or come back myself, and would have to be satisfied with a phone interview. He said that he would tell you to expect my call.

MALE 1: Yes, comrade colonel. The general did inform me that you would be calling, and instructed me to answer all your questions to the best of my ability.

MALE 2: Very good, VLADIMIR IL'YICH. Is this a good time? Can we begin? I won't keep you long at all.

MALE 1: Yes, comrade colonel. You have my full attention.

MALE 2: What is your wife's favorite flower?
MALE 1: I'm sorry, comrade colonel. I did not
understand.
MALE 2: You're not deaf, I hope, comrade captain.
MALE 1: No, there was static on the line, comrade
colonel.
MALE 2: What is your wife's favorite flower?
MALE 1: Red roses, comrade colonel.
MALE 2: And when is your anniversary?
MALE 1: December the fifth.
MALE 2: And did you buy her flowers?
MALE 1: No, comrade colonel. There were none in
the shops.
MALE 2: What did you get her?
MALE 1: A pair of boots and a box of chocolates.
Imported.
MALE 2: The boots or the chocolates?
MALE 1: The chocolates. Imported boots are not
warm enough for MOSCOW winters.
MALE 2: A sensible decision. What was the score
of Saturday's match between Dynamo Moscow
and Spartak.
MALE 1: We won 2:0. ILJIN in the twenty-third and
POBEDONOSTSEV in the seventy-ninth.
MALE 2: When was the last time you took your wife
to the theater?
MALE 1: Thursday.
MALE 2: What is the weight of ten thousand
American Dollars in twenty-dollar bills?
MALE 1: Exactly half a kilo, comrade colonel.
MALE 2: And how big a package is this?
MALE 1: New bills form a package approximately
5.5 centimeters thick. Used bills increase
the thickness of the package by
approximately half a centimeter.
MALE 2: The same amount in West German Marks?
MALE 1: That is forty-thousand West German Marks.
In fifty-mark bills, it would weigh almost
900 grams and be 11.4 centimeters thick, if
the bills were new. Used bills would make
the package over 12 centimeters thick. I
would recommend a minimum of four packages

for convenience of transport, comrade
colonel.
MALE 2: Thank you, VLADIMIR IL'YICH. You should
have your orders by the end of the week.
MALE 1: Thank you, comrade colonel.
[Hang up]

[Transcriber note: Dynamo Moscow is the soccer
team made up of players from the KGB.
Dynamo won the match on September 4th 2:0.]

The Black Market

3
Blackie

Blackie was a manual morse operator who had trained at Fort Devens, Massachusetts. In the jargon of the Site, Blackie was a "ditty-bopper," a name that referred to how manual morse code is verbalized for training purposes. Fort Devens was full of people who walked around during their training courses saying things like "da-da-da-dit da-da-dit-da." Blackie was actually rather good at it, and as a reward, he had been sent to Berlin for this "cushy" special assignment in the 9539th.

While it may seem incongruous to have a manual morse operator assigned to a cable-tap operation—manual morse is, after all, a way of communication that is most widely employed on shortwave radio—there was a very good reason for it.

It was all the Russians' fault. They practiced a reasonable form of radio security. When their units were in garrison, they sent all their manual morse traffic via the cable so that it could not be intercepted. It was only when the units went on maneuvers that they actually used shortwave radio to transmit their messages. The three target cables carried a good bit of manual morse.

The powers that be who were trying to reward Blackie for his diligence during the course, however, were not aware that the "cushy" part of the assignment to the 9539th was months away. When Blackie arrived, the first thing that Master-Sergeant

Laufflaecker did was shove a pickax in his hands and tell him to get busy digging the tunnel.

"If you don't like that pickax, I can get you a shovel, or would you prefer to work in the mess hall? There's always room for another body on KP," said Sergeant Laufflaecker, sure of what Blackie's answer would be before he asked the question.

That was another disappointment for Blackie. While all the other army units in Berlin had hired local civilians to do the onerous chores of garrison life like KP, the 9539th hadn't, because the Chief of Base was afraid that they would compromise the operation. If the Chief of Base had had his way, the 9539th would have been a little self-contained island that kept its inhabitants isolated from the security threat that was represented by everything on the other side of the compound wire. Fortunately for the inhabitants of the 9539th he didn't get his way, but he had fought for it really hard, and KP was one of the concessions that had been made to him.

The fact that the reality of the "reward" Blackie had been given for good performance in school did not match the patently positive prevarication of it painted for him back in the world gave him a slight attitude problem that would remain with him, even after the "cushy" part of the job started at the end of February.

There were several versions of the story of how Blackie got his nickname, and all of them had a certain amount of internal logic about them. One was that the first day that he had come up out of the tunnel, he was covered from head to toe in the black sealant that was used to make the sections of the tunnel liner watertight. Legend had it that Kevin had poured a whole can over his head in revenge for Blackie dropping a steel tunnel segment on his toe. There was a big black blotch of sealant at the twenty-foot marker to back up this legend, but Kevin, who should have known the real truth of the tale, denied everything.

One of the other versions of the origin of Blackie's nickname was that it reflected his status as the biggest blackmarketeer in the 9539th, but he didn't become a powerhouse on the black market until after the tunnel was finished, and people who had been around from the beginning all knew that he had picked up his nickname before that.

Another story was that his nickname came from his predilection for giving other operators "black ears" with the carbon paper that Operations was awash in after the taps were turned on, but this explanation was also based on more recent history, which made it seem somewhat less credible than the story of the sealant.

With digging shut down while the Chief of Base waited for the big pumps from the Zone, Blackie went off in search of fun, excitement and female companionship, all of which he found, but not in that order.

His first stop was The Eden, a basement warren of rooms near the Kurfürstendamm that was popular with GIs. Blackie's fun, however, didn't arrive until after the excitement. The excitement started when, after putting himself on the outside of a fourth liter of beer, he spilled his fifth liter all over a member of the U.S. 6th Infantry Regiment, popularly referred to as the "Gators" because of the alligator on their unit shoulder patch. This particular Gator looked like he used to play professional football before he became a whole army platoon all by himself.

Blackie came to with his head in the lap of a very attractive blonde who seemed genuinely concerned for his well-being. He thought that he had died and gone to Heaven, but the pain in his left eye regained the attention of his reawakening consciousness about three seconds later, and he was brought down to earth. The attention of the blonde, whose name was Trudie, kept him from sinking any further in the hierarchy of locations described by Dante.

"The big brute," she said in English with a slight German accent. "He could have hurt you."

"Oh, it's nothing," mumbled Blackie, who came from a rough neighborhood in Chicago, and—contrary to what people might have been led to believe by his numerous stories of victories won in street battles against the toughs back home—had woken up in a lot worse shape than this a number of times.

She helped him regain his feet, and then righted the table that he had knocked over when the platoon of one had put him out for the count.

A waitress with an overfull bosom—even by German standards—seemed to materialize out of nowhere with two chairs. Blackie plopped down in one of them because it seemed easier than standing up.

"What'll it be?" said the German waitress in faultless GI-accented English.

"I think he'll have a Coke," said Trudie, "and some ice for his eye. I'll have the same, but without the ice." Germans always thought that drinking things with ice in them was too weird, but The Eden always had plenty of ice on hand. It served a lot of Americans.

Blackie wasn't used to having women order for him. In fact, he always ordered for them, but he thought that he would let her get away with it just this once. He tried to nod his accord with the order to the waitress, but it just made the room spin.

Four Cokes and six trips to the men's room later, Blackie was reasonably sober and back up on cloud nine, amazed that Trudie was still at the table with him. He climbed up onto cloud ten, when she agreed to let him take her home. He was hoping to make cloud eleven when they got to her front door, but she took him down a couple of notches, when he pushed his luck and tried to come in.

Trudie was left handed, so she hit him in the right eye.

"I'll see you tomorrow at 11:00 for lunch at Club 48," said Trudie after she smacked him. She knew that she had him right where she wanted him: in the palm of the hand that had just left its imprint on his right eye.

This second black eye got worked into the story of his fight with the Gator at The Eden, when he talked about his night on the town to the eager audience back in the barracks. He didn't say a word about Trudie to his listeners, or about the fact that she had invited herself to lunch with him at Club 48. He could never have lived it down if they had known that a girl had invited him out on a date.

Blackie was right on time for lunch. It was hamburgers like they never made in Hamburg. These were GI all the way, with plenty of ketchup, pickles and cheese. Blackie ordered this time. He left off the onions. He still had hopes of a kiss.

Circuit 53:   15:26-15:28Z 09 September 1954

FEMALE 1: MOSCOW operator? This is KARLSHORST,
        GERMANY. Please give me 5467.
FEMALE 2: It's ringing.
MALE 1: 5467.

FEMALE 1: Your party's on the line, KARLSHORST.
    Go ahead, please.
MALE 2: EVGENIJ! It's BORIS at Karl's.
MALE 1: BORIS! It's good to hear from you. What's
    important enough for you to call?
MALE 2: I wanted to catch you before you went
    home, EVGENIJ. One of my SWALLOWs, the
    pretty one with the big bright eyes that
    you could almost swim in, has met an EAGLE
    with access to something secret.
MALE 1: That's good news! You haven't been
    swimming in those big bright eyes yourself,
    have you, my dear brother-in-law?
MALE 2: How could you say such a thing?
MALE 1: We've known each other a long time. It
    would not be the first time.
MALE 2: Yes, it is tempting, you're right, but
    that was before I married NATASHA.
MALE 1: And how does your SWALLOW know that he
    knows something secret?
MALE 2: He told her that he could not tell her
    what he does. He might as well come right
    out and say that he does something
    classified.
MALE 1: You would think that they would give them
    a believable cover story.
MALE 2: Like we do?
MALE 1: No, better. But you are right. The ones
    who are only out to impress women just say
    that they are spies. Saying that he can't
    say what he does indicates that he could be
    a productive target. Have your SWALLOW get
    closer to this EAGLE. But be careful. If he
    really is a spy, he could compromise your
    SWALLOW. While she is working this EAGLE,
    isolate her from everything else, just in
    case.
MALE 2: I'll do that. You can't be too careful
    with the Americans.
MALE 1: What's her CODENAME?
MALE 2: PRIMROSE.
MALE 1: How very appropriate for a SWALLOW.

MALE 2: Yes, my admin officer has an overly
    developed sense of humor.
MALE 1: Did you get the cameras?
MALE 2: Yes, they will be in the next shipment of
    "documents."
MALE 1: Good. I'll keep an eye out for them.
MALE 2: I sent them EYES ONLY. We don't want some
    clerk opening them up. You'd have to shoot
    him.
MALE 1: And don't think that I wouldn't. Thanks
    for the heads up about PRIMROSE. When will
    I see the full report?
MALE 2: It should be on the wire in about an
    hour.
MALE 1: In that case, I think I'll go home and
    read it in the morning. I've been late
    every night this week and OLGA will get
    really mad if I am late again.
MALE 2: It'll keep. You don't want to get her
    mad. If mama's unhappy, everybody's
    unhappy. Give her my regards.
MALE 1: And the same to NATASHA.
MALE 2: Yes, of course. Good night.
[HANG UP]

4
Lieutenant Sherlock, Robert NMI

For some reason—some say it was the introduction of computers that sorted everything alphabetically—in Army parlance, people are identified by their last name first, first name and middle initial. Those who do not have a middle initial, are issued three by the Army so that they sound almost like British officers, who invariably seem to be introduced as Colonel Sackville hyphen Smith (pronounced Smyth and the hyphen is silent), O.B.E.. Lieutenant Sherlock, Robert N.M.I. was one of those people. His name even sounded slightly British, which added to the impression that N.M.I. was an honorific, and induced one British officer who ran into Lieutenant Sherlock in the Harnack House Officers' Club to guess at its meaning.

"Not Much Intelligence," quipped the officer in a fit of pique because Lieutenant Sherlock did not know that "O.B.E." stood for "Order of the British Empire."

"No, 'No Middle Initial'," replied Lieutenant Sherlock, who was tired of that joke.

Lieutenant Sherlock, however, was not known to the members of the 9539th as Lieutenant Sherlock. He was more widely referred to as Lieutenant Sheerluck, a nickname that rolled off the tongue almost of its own volition, after people had heard the tale of his short, but illustrious military career, which had been saved by the apotropaic quality of his first name, *lieutenant*.

Lieutenant Sheerluck came to the 9539th in a blaze of glory from a tactical unit that was commanded by an obviously intelligent man, who had more pull with officer assignments in Washington than the 9539th's colonel did. He managed to get Lieutenant Sheerluck reassigned out of his unit, a feat that it seemed beyond the power of the 9539th's colonel. It was naturally assumed that the nameless commanding officer of Lieutenant Sheerluck's previous unit had pictures or tapes of someone in Washington doing something he shouldn't have been doing and that he blackmailed them into "reassigning" Sheerluck to the Site.

The fact that Lieutenant Sheerluck was reassigned to another unit and not taken off in irons to the Army penitentiary at Fort Leavenworth was one of those ironies of ironclad military logic that only made sense when viewed from an officer's point of view. If any of the people who made the Site function had done what he did, they would have been in the military prison at Fort Leavenworth, but then they were not officers and gentlemen by act of Congress. They were only lowly enlisted men.

The tale that caused this logical distress came from reputedly reputable sources, but there were about five or six versions of it floating around the 9539th. There was, nonetheless, some substantiating evidence on Sheerluck's face: he did not have any eyebrows.

There was a common thread to all of them, however. Most of the differences were just embellishments. It seems that the battalion had set up operations on a hilltop inside the one-kilometer zone along the border between the Russian and American Zones of Germany. They had been there a day. Most of the equipment was functioning and Sheerluck, not having anything better to do, was happily inspecting the state of cleanliness in the compound, known in Army parlance as "the state of police."

Now electricity is an essential element of any signals collection operation. The battalion had set up a ten-kilowatt generator in the middle of the compound and it ran 24 hours a day. It was fed by a 250-gallon tank of gasoline that stood on stilts next to the generator. In typical military "I-don't-know-how-to-do-this-but-it's-got-to-be-done" fashion, the gas line ran from the left side of the generator to the right side where the carburetor of the motor that drove the generator was located.

As if to prove that the people who installed it did not know what they were doing, there was a loose fitting at the top of the gas line where it exited the tank. This fitting vibrated itself open just enough to let the gasoline in the tank begin to flow out onto the outside of the copper tubing. The gasoline on the outside of the tubing followed the tube down to the point just above the manifold of the generator motor, where the tubing started to climb back up to the second post that supported its traverse from the left side of the motor to the right. The liquid on the outside of the tubing could not climb back up to the next post like the gasoline on the inside could. Instead, in keeping with the laws of gravity, the gasoline on the outside of the tubing started to drip onto the hot engine manifold. It was at this time that Lieutenant Sheerluck discovered a cigarette butt—some say it was a candy bar wrapper—near the analysts' van and had pulled out his notebook to make a note of it.

An alert analyst in the van saw the flame, applied his keen analytical insight to what he had seen, recognized the impending disaster and took action. He grabbed a fire extinguisher, jumped out of the van onto the ground, and just as he was preparing to run to the generator to put out the fire, he was transfixed by Lieutenant Sheerluck's now famous line: "Hey, you, troop! Where's your headgear?"

The plucky, but nameless troop tried to explain, but Lieutenant Sheerluck brooked no insolence from his men. "Get back inside that van and get your headgear, soldier, and I mean *now!*" said Lieutenant Sheerluck with his arm raised to point the way. The dauntless analyst displayed his keen analytic insight yet again, by recognizing that the fire at the generator was now out of control. He set the extinguisher down where he stood. Saluted. Turned and ran back into the van, slamming the door shut after him, whereupon he and everybody else in the van assumed the fetal position and said a few Hail Marys. He wasn't Catholic, but figured he could use all the help he could get.

Lieutenant Sheerluck smiled, pleased at the instant and unquestioning obedience that his stern voice and imposing gold second-lieutenant's bars conveyed to his subordinates. He kept watching the door, waiting for the soldier to reemerge with his hat on and pick up his fire extinguisher. While he was waiting, the fire climbed up the gas line to the tank of flammable liquid, which, quite predictably, exploded with some considerable force, terminating the battalion's field operations and removing Lieutenant Sheerluck's eyebrows in the bargain.

When he was released from the hospital in Frankfurt three months later, his orders were not back to his beloved battalion, but to the 9539th, where he could apply his skills as a Russian linguist. He had an "All But Dissertation" doctorate in Russian. It said so in his 201 file, the repository of all such data in the Army. If it was in his 201 file, it had to be true.

That was not, however, what he was doing on the day of the flood. There were not any Russians for him to listen to yet, because the tunnel was just getting started. Since officers are exempt from physical labor, he could not be expected to help dig the tunnel, which suited Sergeant Laufflaecker just fine, because he could not stand junior officers, especially in peacetime.

The colonel did not really have anything for him to do either, so he made him the 'other duties as assigned' officer for the 9539th, which, on the day of the flood, meant that he was reviewing the mess-hall menu for the next week, and trying to decide if he wanted to eat lunch at the Harnack House or to taste-test the mess sergeant's version of southern-fried chicken, which he had some doubts about, since the mess sergeant had never been south of the Mason-Dixon Line in his life. He approved the menu and went off through the rain to keep a stool warm in the bar of the Harnack House until the kitchen opened for lunch.

By the time he actually got back from lunch, the flood was being held in check by the pumps that Sergeant Laufflaecker had obtained through abnormal channels, and the miners had all dispersed to whatever refuge they could find in Berlin. This meant that the warehouse was empty. Since Lieutenant Sheerluck did not actually have a job to begin with, he did not actually notice that there was nothing going on in the warehouse.

He was actually pleased to have a "do nothing" job. It gave him a chance to actually work on his dissertation: *The Socioeconomic Impacts of the Russian Spelling Reform of 1917 on the Publication of Lesser-known Provincial Futurist Poets.*

He could not actually go on being A.B.D. forever, that is unless his advisor did not actually retire at the end of the academic

year as planned, so Lieutenant Sheerluck had to hope that things
would actually work out for the best, which meant that he had to
actually keep working on his dissertation. By the time that the big
pumps came in and the digging resumed in the tunnel again, he
had actually written twenty pages of turgid academic prose of the
highest calibre, which meant that he had used the word *actually* at
least five times on every page. He was immensely pleased with
himself.

He did not in fact, however, notice that the digging had
started again. What he really noticed was that the mess hall had
started serving meals on the Swing and Mid shifts. Tunnel digging
went on round-the-clock, 24 hours a day, and the miners had to
eat, or as close an approximation to eating as the Army could
arrange.

Circuit 53:   14:09-14:15Z 07 October 1954

FEMALE 1: This is MOSCOW, KARLSHORST. I need 4371
    for my party, please.
FEMALE 2: Just a second. I'll ring them.
MALE 1: 4371.
FEMALE 2: Go ahead, your party's on the line.
MALE 2: BORIS! I wanted to get your unofficial
    opinion about that last PRIMROSE report.
MALE 1: Why my 'unofficial' opinion, EVGENIJ?
    What about the official one didn't you
    like?
MALE 2: You didn't suggest a reason for SPOTLIGHT
    going to 24-hour operations. What do you
    think is going on over there?
MALE 1: It's obviously not a warehouse. It does
    not have any local workers, and all the
    real warehouses use them so that the
    Americans won't have to lift a finger.
    Warehouses also don't run 24 hours a day.
    My guess is that it's a signals collection
    operation and that they are targeting the
    flight activity over at SCHÖNEFELD
    airfield.

MALE 2: That makes sense. Why didn't you put that in the report?

MALE 1: You're the one who taught me not to put speculation in field reports, and that's all this is: speculation.

MALE 2: Your speculation is better than some people's facts. You're close to the action and I trust your instincts.

MALE 1: Thank you, but that's not a reason to put it in a report.

MALE 2: It's frightening to hear my own words in someone else's mouth. Yes, of course, you're right. Next time, phone your speculation in to me. I want to know what you're thinking, even if it is not something that can go on paper.

MALE 1: Be happy to. While we're exchanging opinions, I'd like to hear yours on the LONDON communiqué.

[Transcriber Comment: The LONDON communiqué refers to the statement issued by Americans, the British and the French at the end of the Nine-Power Conference in LONDON (28 September - 3 October) that made certain security guarantees for the city of BERLIN. It said: "The security and welfare of BERLIN and the maintenance of the position of the Three Powers there are regarded by the Three Powers as essential elements of the peace of the free world in the present international situation. Accordingly they will maintain armed forces within the territory of Berlin as long as their responsibilities require it. They therefore reaffirm that they will treat any attack against BERLIN from any quarter as an attack upon their forces and themselves."]

MALE 2: It means that you and I will have an interesting job until we retire. It will only increase the Central Committee's feeling that they need our "services." It

will be good for promotions and for
funding.

MALE 1: But will it come to a shooting war?

MALE 2: I hardly think so. We got through the
Airlift without a shooting war. This is
just sabre rattling, but the sabres are
going to stay in their scabbards, as long
as you and I and our American and British
friends play by the rules and don't let
things get out of hand.

MALE 1: It's not so much the Americans or the
British that I'm worried about. They tend
to play by the rules, well, the British
more than the Americans. It's GEHLEN and
his people. I wonder if this will make them
think that they can take a more aggressive
stance.

MALE 2: They can hardly be more aggressive than
they are now. If they start to get too
uppity, we can send them a subtle message.

MALE 1: How subtle?

MALE 2: Not like we did in the old days with a
head in a hatbox. A couple of broken legs
and a message to take home that this is not
the way the game is played.

MALE 1: And if they don't take the hint?

MALE 2: Then we send them a hatbox. But it might
be a good idea to send a message directly
to the Americans first. They're the ones
funding and supplying GEHLEN. They can rein
him in, if they understand the necessity of
it.

MALE 1: It would have to be very direct. The
Americans don't like subtlety or hints.
With them you have to get right to the
point.

MALE 2: Yes, of course. Well, then just grab one
of their people, give him a message and
send him back. Without the broken legs.
You're right. The Americans wouldn't
understand the subtlety of a broken leg and
would want to go tit for tat.

MALE 1: We'd all end up on crutches.
MALE 2: It would make it easy on the surveillance
    teams.
MALE 1: They'd probably be on crutches too.
MALE 2: Oh, I can see it now. Every third person
    on the Kurfürstendamm with their leg in a
    cast. It would be hilarious. On second
    thought, just drop them a note tied around
    a brick, delivered through the Resident's
    window at home.
MALE 1: Yes, that sounds sensible. I've had my
    leg broken enough times as it is.
MALE 2: Anything else?
MALE 1: No. Give my best to OLGA.
MALE 2: Of course, and tell NATASHA that I asked
    about her. Good evening, BORIS.
MALE 1: I will. Good night, EVGENIJ.
[Hang up]

5
In the Swing of Things

It was all Sergeant Laufflaecker's fault. If Sergeant Laufflaecker had been able to find big enough pumps in Berlin, it would never have happened, but by the time the big pumps got in from the Zone and were installed, Gabbie had moved into the top ten of Kevin's favorite things in Berlin.

Gabbie was a student at the Freie Universität, which is near the Dahlem Museum, where she and Kevin had met. She was taking ethnography, specializing in the islands of the Pacific, which was why she was in the museum so often, and had just happened to meet Kevin there. Homework for classes kept her fairly busy. There were tons of books to read. Her professors thought nothing of assigning a book a week to read in each class, and did not hesitate to assign books that were only in English. She could read those all right, but it was much slower going than books in German.

Her heavy study schedule, and an eight-o'clock class that met every day, meant that she did not keep late hours. While Kevin was off, waiting for the pumps to come in, that was OK. He could spend a lot of time at the museum and on campus during the day. He realized that going back to work would put a big crimp on his ambition to spend more time with Gabbie. In the days of the antediluvian tunnel, Kevin had been assigned to the Day shift with Blackie at the tunnel face and never got off until long after Gabbie was back home with her nose in a book, prepping for her eight-o'clock. *That shouldn't be a problem though*, thought

Kevin to himself. *We dig 24 hours a day. All I need to do is to get moved to the Swing shift.*

The four-to-midnight shift suited him better than Mids. He always felt queasy on Mids at around 03:00 Local time, no matter what time he went to bed. He knew better than to tell Sergeant Laufflaecker the real reason he wanted to go on Swings. He had heard Sergeant Laufflaecker's lecture on *"Fraud-leins,"* the word that he used to describe German women who were only looking for a ticket out of the desolation of post-war Germany to the land of the Big PX, better known in some circles as America. Most everybody else called them *PX Hounds,* but Sergeant Laufflaecker had his own special word for it.

As if that weren't enough, the Chief of Base had decreed that anybody who acquired a "moose"—the unflattering military slang for steady girlfriend—would be shipped out of Berlin to an infantry unit so fast that he'd there before he realized that he had left. Kevin had to be inventive. He had to be imaginative. He had to be economical with the truth.

"I need to go on Swings, sergeant, so I can have somebody to talk Russian to, otherwise I'm going to forget it all," lied Kevin to Sergeant Laufflaecker.

"Mike don't speak no Russian," replied Sergeant Laufflaecker, who was in a good mood and felt like giving Kevin a hard time.

"No, he doesn't, but Fast Eddie does," parried Kevin, recognizing this verbal two-step for what it was.

"OK," responded Sergeant Laufflaecker, "but none of that there Monterey Mary stuff," unable to resist giving Kevin another turn of the screw.

"Eddie's not my type," answered Kevin in tone. "And, besides, he's married."

Sergeant Laufflaecker made a note to move Kevin to Swings and Mike to Days, and the sergeant's fateful pencil, having writ, moved back to the pocket from whence it came, and not all the collective pomp and circumstance of the Site could lure it back to erase a word of it, though there were some who later came to think that it would have been a good idea.

Sergeant Edward Fastbinder was not one of them. He got along with Kevin well enough. They had been together in language school at Monterey. There he had learned that what others perceived as arrogance and condescension in Kevin's tone was not backed up by malice or spite. It was just Kevin's uncompromising principles, and, if you ignored them, Kevin was OK-enough company. Kevin's warped sense of humor also happened to match Eddie's just fine.

"Why do KGB guys always go around in threes?" asked Kevin.

"Beats me. Why do they go around in threes?" replied Eddie, knowing that he would be sorry that he had asked.

"There's one who can read and not write. One who can write and not read, and one who can neither write nor read to keep an eye on the two intellectuals."

Eddie didn't say anything, but he had a pained look on his face.

Fast Eddie was on Swings because the only job his wife Meg could get was as a cashier at the military movie theater, near the main PX. Whoever said that "two can live as cheaply as one" never tried it on sergeant's pay. The first showing at the Outpost was not until 18:30 Local. Meg started work at 18:00 Local and did not get off until 23:30 Local, so if Eddie had been on Days, they never would have seen each other.

Sergeant Laufflaecker had a sort of a soft spot for young couples in love, and he put Eddie on straight Swings so that Eddie and Meg could see each other once in a while. He thought that, after the war, if he had been in a cushy "intelligence" unit like this one, where somebody actually cared if you got to see your wife every now and again, instead of in a leg infantry unit that was out in the field all the time, then he might have still been married to Alice. He had really loved Alice, but she could not put up with him being gone all the time. Now he was just married to the Army. It wasn't as much fun as being married to Alice, and certainly not as soft and as warm.

Swings suited Eddie and Meg just fine. They were not all that fond of the Bar and Ballroom circuit anyway. Straight Swings gave them a different perspective on Berlin that most other GI couples did not get, because they were out of sync with most of the activities scheduled for Americans. If it was not raining, they could go to the American beach at the Wannsee during the week when it was not crowded. If it was, they could have lunch at the

British PX, with its egg-salad and cress sandwiches, listen to people speak the Queen's English, and pretend to be POSH. Actually, it did not all that much matter what they did, as long as they could do it together.

Circuit 53:   10:43-10:48Z 12 October 1954

FEMALE 1: MOSCOW, this is KARLSHORST, GERMANY calling. Can I have 6389 for my party, please?

FEMALE 2: I'll put you through. It's ringing. Put your party on the line.

MALE 1: Finance. 6389.

MALE 2: Captain BRONSHTEIN, please.

MALE 1: VLADIMIR IL'YICH! It's good to hear from you. How's life in GERMANY?

MALE 2: It's great, LEV DAVIDOVICH. We have a whole house to ourselves. There's plenty to buy in the shops. NADEZHDA is ecstatic. Of course, we can't go to the opera as often. It's too far away. But, other than that, taking this job was a great decision.

MALE 1: Some people have all the luck.

MALE 2: And best of all, I'm away from BESPOLEZNYJ.

MALE 1: Like I said: some people have all the luck. You missed his latest exploit.

MALE 2: What was that?

MALE 1: He had me calculate the average serial number of all the thousand-dollar packets being shipped to WASHINGTON.

MALE 2: He what?! You meant that old joke about being able to statistically determine all the serial numbers of a random stack of old bills unless the difference between the average and the top bill was more than the KROPOTKIN constant?

MALE 1: That's the one.

MALE 2: Are they still pulling that on first year students?

MALE 1: And apparently on the head of Finance, when nobody's looking.

MALE 2: Why didn't one of the instructors tell him what was going on?

MALE 1: Why do you think? Can you imagine what he would say?

MALE 2: Of course I can. He'd threaten to have them all shot, and reassigned to SIBERIA, in that order.

MALE 1: I can't understand how BESSTRASHNYJ lets him get away with it.

MALE 2: He's been a Party member since KHRUSHCHEV was a corporal, even though that shouldn't be a reason.

MALE 1: You know better than that. Your excellent Party record didn't hurt your chances for that plush job of yours in GERMANY.

MALE 2: I like to think that I got it on the merit of my accomplishments.

MALE 1: And I like to think that I'll make major on the next cycle, but both you and I know that that won't happen because of my 'political history,' despite my many accomplishments.

MALE 2: OK, you're right, but being a captain in MOSCOW is better than being dead in MEXICO with an ax planted in the middle of your skull.

MALE 1: There are times that I am not so sure about that, and most of them are when I have to deal with BESPOLEZNYJ. He gives me a splitting headache every time I have to talk to him.

MALE 2: If I hear of an opening out here, I'll put in a good word for you.

MALE 1: Please do. Did you just want to B.S., or did you have something official? Himself just walked into the office, and you know what he thinks about personal use of the phone.

MALE 2: It's the next currency shipment. One of the case officers just told me that his

source wants that whole thing in one-dollar
bills. It's 5,000. I told him I wasn't sure
that you would have that many lying around.

MALE 1: What's he going to do? Paper his living
room with them? I'll have to go to GosBank,
but I'll see what I can do, but only
because it's you. Anybody else, and I'd
have told them to go to hell.

MALE 2: You're a prince.

MALE 1: I'd rather be a Party hack.

MALE 2: Promotion'd be faster.

MALE 1: That it would.

MALE 2: Can I send you a little something from
out here? Me to you for the extra effort.

MALE 1: Coffee or American cigarettes.

MALE 2: I think that can be arranged.

MALE 1: Sure you don't want 10,000 in ones?

MALE 2: Only if I can keep 'em for personal use.

MALE 1: Dream on.

MALE 2: I will. Tell TATYANA that I asked after
her.

MALE 1: We broke up.

MALE 2: I'm sorry. I should have known.

MALE 1: That's why you're not a case officer.
Here he comes. I'll take care of that right
away for you, comrade captain. I serve the
Soviet Union!

[Hang up]

6

The Dead Man in the Tunnel

The last stretch of the tunnel before it reached the Schönefelder Chaussee ran beneath an open field that bordered on the Alt-Glienicke Cemetery. You could see the cemetery clearly from the Crow's Nest, where they kept an eye on the Vopos who had a tower on the other side of "the Shoss," as everybody called the big road just across the Sector border. Everybody knew about the cemetery, and talked about it. The question on everybody's mind was: "Are we going to have to dig through a grave to get to the cables?"

"You out of your ever-loving?! The cemetery is twenty feet south of the tunnel track," said the coldly logical surveyor, who worked straight Days and never went further into the tunnel than his theodolite at the opening.

"But what if the graveyard used to be bigger, and that field wasn't always a field, but part of the graveyard?" challenged Lefty, who had read *Tom Sawyer* and knew all about the dangers of graveyards at midnight, which was when he went on duty next. "There's a reason they call Mids the graveyard shift, you know."

The confines of the tunnel were especially conducive to macabre thoughts late on a Mid as you walked past the cemetery underground, on the same plane, so to speak, as its inhabitants.

Lefty, however, was not the first one to meet the dead man in the tunnel. He made his appearance during a Swing on the last

Sunday in October. Kevin and Fast Eddie had been at the face of the tunnel for about thirty minutes, when Kevin said, "This load?"

"OK," said Fast Eddie, who picked up the large burlap bag that they normally used to bring down loose materials like nuts and bolts and braces. He stuck in his hand and pulled out a tibia, a fibula and a femur.

"Get another one of those long ones," said Kevin.

"Where'd you get this stuff?" asked Fast Eddie, dropping the bones into the box where the dirt removed from the tunnel face went while it waited to be taken back to the warehouse basement and dumped in a pile with all the rest.

"At Potsdamer Platz. It cost me two cartons of cigarettes."

"That's pretty pricey. Who'd it used to belong to? Hitler?" asked Eddie.

"No, an old teaching buddy of the guy who sold it to me. They used to teach Basic Anatomy together at the university until he was denazified, he said."

"Ah, a professor. No wonder, but for that price you should have gotten a copy of his diploma as well."

"I'll remember that for next time. Let's get some dirt on 'em before Charlie gets back," replied Kevin.

They had the whole box full of dirt by the time Charlie got back with the forklift and the new tunnel segments. They wrestled the tunnel segments off the forklift, loaded the box on the forklift, and Charlie headed back out to dump the dirt.

As soon as he was out of sight, Kevin said: "Let's spread the rest of 'em around the face."

"What'd you say this guy's name was?"

"Von Friedhofen, Doctor Yorick von Friedhofen."

"Alas, poor Yorick, I knew him well," intoned Fast Eddie, holding the skull in the palm of his outstretched hand.

"A fellow of infinite jest, of most excellent fancy," added Kevin.

"What's his last name mean?"

"'Von Graveyard,'" responded Kevin.

"That's rich! Let's get a little dirt on 'em," said Eddie, throwing a shovel full of dirt on the bones scattered about the face of the tunnel.

"Charlie should be there by now. Ready?"

"Yeah."

Kevin and Fast Eddie took off toward the tunnel-staging area with a blood curdling scream. Before they got half way back, they ran into Master-Sergeant Laufflaecker, who was running full tilt in their direction.

"What happened? Was there a cave-in?" asked Sergeant Laufflaecker.

"Worse than that! There's a dead man in the tunnel. I'm not going back down there!" replied Eddie.

"He says his name is Von Friedhofen, Yorick von Friedhofen. I'm not going back down there either!" added Kevin.

"What do you mean 'his name is'? You said he was dead."

"He is. He's complaining that we disturbed his sleep," answered Kevin.

"You two are disturbed."

At about that time, the cry of "Mother of God!" made its way down the tunnel from the staging area to where Kevin, Fast Eddie and Sergeant Laufflaecker were standing. Reassured by the knowledge that Kevin and Fast Eddie were alive—but not for much longer, if he had anything to say about it—Sergeant Laufflaecker wheeled round and ran off down the tunnel toward the staging area. When he got there, Charlie, Detroit and Bama were fixed to the spot like fence posts on the perimeter of the dump pile where all the dirt from the tunnel went. They were all staring at the four bones that were on the top of the pile.

"Those must be Doctor Von Friedhofen's. I'll bet that's what he was talking about, when he said he wants his leg back," said Kevin from somewhere behind Sergeant Laufflaecker.

"Doctor von what are you talking about?" said Charlie, the first one to regain the power of speech.

"The dead man in the tunnel," answered Kevin slightly out of breath. "He's pissed because we woke him up and he wants his leg back."

"Charlie, you take it back down to him. Tell him we're sorry," said Eddie.

"Tell who you're sorry?" asked Charlie, unaware that he shouldn't be having this conversation at all.

"The dead man in the tunnel. And take him his leg back. He seemed really insistent about that," answered Kevin.

"I'm not going down no tunnel to talk to some dead Kraut. I can't talk Kraut anyway. Kevin's the only one here who can talk Kraut. He's the one with a long-haired dictionary. If anybody's going, it's going to be you, Kev!" said Charlie, displaying some indication of logical brain function.

"But I don't think he likes me," responded Kevin.

"All right, you clowns!" said Sergeant Laufflaecker, when the light bulb went on above his head as he recalled what day it was. "We're going back down to the face ..."

"But there's a dead man down there," objected Kevin.

"There'll be two dead men down there in a minute, and that's not countin' your Doctor von what's-his-name. Get moving!" intoned Sergeant Laufflaecker.

That night's Swing set a record for the most earth moved on a single shift, and Kevin and Fast Eddie did not take a break from the face the whole time. The dead man in the tunnel proved to be quite talkative, and it turns out that he spoke rather good English—he was, after all, a doctor. He kept turning up on Mids when someone had to go down the tunnel for something or other. The strange thing was that he never ever talked to Kevin or Fast Eddie again.

Circuit 53:   15:17-15:23Z 02 November 1954

FEMALE 1: KARLSHORST. This is MOSCOW. Please let
    me have 4371 for my party.
FEMALE 2: I'll connect you. It's ringing.
MALE 1: 4371.
FEMALE 2: Go ahead, your party's on the line.
MALE 2: BORIS! I'm calling about that last
    PRIMROSE report.
MALE 1: Yes, EVGENIJ? What about it?
MALE 2: I ran the check run that you wanted on
    that DR. YORIK VON FRIEDHOFEN and we can't
    find a thing on him.
MALE 1: I was hoping that you could find
    something there after all our local
    resources pulled a blank.

MALE 2: I can't understand it. It must be an
        alias. Maybe it's one of GEHLEN's men?
MALE 1: We thought of that too, and tapped our
        sources there as well.
MALE 2: Nothing from any of them?
MALE 1: Not a hint. It must be something that is
        being really closely held.
MALE 2: This German angle has me worried. If
        GEHLEN's not in on it, then maybe it's
        weapons related, one of their German
        scientists setting something up. It
        suggests a facet to SPOTLIGHT that makes me
        uncomfortable.
MALE 1: I see what you mean. I'll get in contact
        with PRIMROSE immediately.
MALE 2: If you get anything on VON FRIEDHOFEN,
        report directly to me and nothing in
        writing. Understand? If it is weapons
        related, we want to keep it out of the
        regular channels. If the Americans get wind
        of the fact that we know, it could spook
        them and make them take precipitous action.
MALE 1: I understand. Directly to you and nothing
        in writing.
MALE 2: Very good. Anything else on your end?
MALE 1: No, things are quiet as the grave.
MALE 2: That's good to hear. OLGA wonders if you
        could arrange for a cuckoo clock. She's
        plotting for my next star and needs it to
        grease the spousal skids, as it were. I
        think that she is going to give it to NINA
        PETROVNA.
[Transcriber note: NINA PETROVNA (KHRUSHCHEVA) is
the wife of Politburo member NIKITA
SERGEEVICH KHRUSHCHEV.]
MALE 1: Tell her to consider it done. Knowing
        her, I may as well congratulate you now.
MALE 2: Don't count my stars before they're
        hatched! That could be bad luck.
MALE 1: In that case, break a leg! Give NATASHA a
        call. Her birthday's coming up and you
        wouldn't want to miss it.

```
MALE 2: I will. But tell her we talked and I said
        'Happy birthday!' just in case.
MALE 1: I'll do that. And my best to OLGA.
MALE 2: Of course. Good evening, BORIS.
[Hang up]
```

At the tunnel face: Kevin (left) and Fast Eddie (right)
Second row: Charlie (left) and Blackie (right)
Foreground: Sergeant Laufflaecker

7
Snow

The rain had turned to snow, which was a good thing and a bad thing. It was a good thing, because the snow did not get you as damp as the rain. The snow flakes just sort of floated past you without sticking to your clothes. It was a bad thing, because the tunnel was heated, and that made the ground above it so warm that the snow would not stick there either. It just melted as soon as it hit the ground, unlike the snow on either side of the tunnel track, which just lay there, forming a soft white carpet on the otherwise barren compound enclosure. When seen from the Crow's Nest, it looked like the finger of God, pointing to the Heavens, well, to the Vopo tower across the Shoss in any event.

Kevin was in the Crow's Nest. It was cold, but it beat swinging a pick-ax at the tunnel face. He had earned this dubious privilege the week before, when he cut his right arm wide open on the edge of a tunnel segment that they were manhandling into place. They rushed him off—sort of—to the 279th Station Hospital, where they put 12 stitches in his right arm, a hypodermic full of antibiotics in his left arm, a tetanus shot into his buttocks, a sling around his left shoulder, and a light-duty slip into the right pocket of what was left of his uniform blouse, after they had cut it apart to get at the wound.

The whole thing had put Kevin in a bad mood. It was not so much the pain—there was a lot of it—or the blood—there was a lot of that too—or the screaming—Blackie could not stand the sight of blood—as it was maintaining the Site's cover while all of these things were going on, by delaying transporting him to the hospital, until they cleaned him up so he would not look like he had been digging a tunnel when it happened. They had taken off his dirty fatigue uniform, showered him down and dressed him up again in clean fatigues and boots—which did not fit, because they were Blackie's, and, of course, too tight—before loading him unceremoniously into a jeep, driven by Fast Eddie, whose uniform happened to be clean, for a whirlwind ride to the hospital.

They did not call Fast Eddie "fast" for nothing. When they got there, Kevin breathed a sigh of relief. He had thought that Fast Eddie was going to get them all killed in a traffic accident. Racing that tram with the clanging bell to that intersection was the point that Kevin had been sure that they were all dead, but they didn't even come close, according to Fast Eddie. "Missed him by a mile," said Fast Eddie to Sergeant Laufflaecker, who was in the back with Kevin. Sergeant Laufflaecker could have sworn that it was more like half an inch, but did not say that out loud.

The other high point of the breakneck ride to the hospital had been Sergeant Laufflaecker intoning that he had seen worse in the war, where people had real wounds, not just some namby-pamby little cut on the arm, and went on to describe some of them in vivid detail. What made it even worse, was that Sergeant Laufflaecker was trying to sound calm to reassure Kevin. His idea of calm was to speak slowly and clearly, which, in reality, made him sound like an undertaker whom Kevin had once seen in some horror movie that he could not recall the name of. This impression was helped by the fact that his uniform blouse was covered in blood, Kevin's. Kevin would have rather had him yell like he did all the time. The good thing about Sergeant Laufflaecker, however, was that he really had seen worse than that in the war, and knew the first aid for it. That, however, did not cross Kevin's mind until later.

Kevin picked up the handset of the field telephone in the Crow's Nest and spun the crank four times. This sent a surge of electricity down the wire to the field telephone on the crate that served as Sergeant Laufflaecker's desk in the basement of the warehouse. The phone rang. Sergeant Laufflaecker picked up with a line that made him sound like the butler in that same horror movie that Kevin could not remember the name of: "You rang?"

"I think that you need to come up here and see this," said Kevin cautiously to the disembodied Sergeant Laufflaecker.

"What? Floozies in the Vopo tower again?" replied Sergeant Laufflaecker, who did not always appreciate Kevin's jokes.

"Worse than that. Snow!"

"And what is worse about snow than floozies in the Vopo tower?" asked Sergeant Laufflaecker, who immediately regretted giving Kevin a straight line like that.

"Because it shows you where the tunnel is, and the floozies don't."

"I'll be right up," came the curt reply, and he was true to his word.

Sergeant Laufflaecker agreed with Kevin's assessment of the tactical situation. The tunnel was going to be blown before they made it across the Sector border.

"Ideas?" asked Sergeant Laufflaecker, who was slowly coming to realize that Kevin could occasionally put two and two together and get four.

"Turn off the heat in the tunnel," replied Kevin, who wished that they would just reroute it to the Crow's Nest, because it was cold up there.

"OK. That's a good strategic approach. We need something a bit more tactical."

"Put up a circus tent?" said Kevin, without an idea in the world of where they would get one.

Sergeant Laufflaecker did not know where they could get one either, but he did know where he could get a whole bunch of smaller tents. "Thanks. I'll take care of it," he said, and he was gone. All Kevin could do was shiver while he watched for the mythical floozies in the Vopo tower and watched the snow uncover the tunnel.

Once back downstairs, Sergeant Laufflaecker evacuated the tunnel and shut down the heating system. He picked up the field phone to the duty officer, and told him to call the Chief of Base on the secure line and get him out to the Site now. Fifty-three minutes later, the Chief of Base ended his counter-surveillance run by stepping out of the panel truck inside the warehouse dressed as a moustached American captain with quartermaster insignia.

He was greeted by a pleased Sergeant Laufflaecker, who had been on the phone for seven minutes to his old-army buddy at McNair Barracks in the 6th Infantry Regiment. He explained the problem of the snow as they climbed the ladder to the Crow's Nest. The Chief of Base surveyed the natural disaster that had descended on him with calm regard, and turned to Sergeant Laufflaecker.

"Is that smile on your face because you are thinking about your fair lady? Or because you've come up with a way out of this FUBAR situation?"

"I must give credit where credit is due. Kilroy here had the original idea, but I modified it for use in the field, so to speak. It's gonna cost you six bottles of whiskey, three bottles of your finest Russian tradin' vodka, 30 cartons of cigarettes and four cases of beer," said Sergeant Laufflaecker without blinking an eye.

"Cheap at half the price," replied the Chief of Base, "as long as it works. What do I get for it?"

"Headquarters company of the 3rd battalion of the 6th Infantry Regiment is going to set up all their command center tents out in our compound, right over the tunnel track. I know their top kick from the war."

"When'll they be here?"

"Any minute now. It was the three bottles of Stolichnaya that swung the deal. Larry said that he would treat it like an alert when I offered him those."

Six minutes later, a jeep leading five deuce-and-a-halves pulled up at the compound gate. The MP at the gate waved them into the compound enclosure. When Master-Sergeant Laufflaecker said "jump!", if you said anything, it was "How high?" And that was only after you were in the air. The MP had been told to expect them.

Sixteen minutes and thirty-seven seconds later, the compound enclosure and the tunnel track were covered in an array of army-green General Purpose tents.

"See what well-trained troops can do?" said Master-Sergeant Jones to Master-Sergeant Laufflaecker.

"Ain't it the truth," said Master-Sergeant Laufflaecker, beckoning in the direction of the warehouse. Six soldiers came out of the door and walked in his direction. They were carrying six obviously heavy boxes.

"Where do you want 'em?" asked Master-Sergeant Laufflaecker to his friend Larry.

"Back of the first truck."

Sergeant Laufflaecker signaled to his troops to put the boxes in the back of the first truck.

"It's a pleasure doing business with you," said Master-Sergeant Jones. "See you at Club 48 on Friday?"

"Sure thing. Thanks again. We'll need 'em for about a week."

The convoy pulled out. Sergeant Laufflaecker waved good-bye and walked back inside the warehouse. The Chief of Base was waiting for him, just out of sight of the open door.

"A very smooth operation, sergeant. When you retire, if you need a job, just let me know," said the Chief of Base. "Did you take a commission on that deal?"

"No, sir," replied Sergeant Laufflaecker.

"Take four bottles of ten-year-old Scotch out of petty cash," said the Chief of Base. "You deserve it."

"Thank you, sir!" replied Sergeant Laufflaecker. "Perhaps another for my idea man?" added Sergeant Laufflaecker, who recognized the sound of opportunity knocking when he heard it, and liked to spread the wealth around when it did.

"Why not?" said the Chief of Base, pleased to have had his pet project saved by Sergeant Laufflaecker's and Kilroy's quick thinking.

Circuit 53:   10:07-10:12Z 21 December 1954

```
FEMALE 1: KARLSHORST operator. This is MOSCOW.
     Can I have 4371 for my party?
FEMALE 2: Just a moment. It's ringing.
MALE 1: 4371.
FEMALE 2: Your party's on the line, MOSCOW. Go
     ahead, please.
MALE 2: BORIS! Merry Christmas! as the Americans
     say.
MALE 1: The same to you and to OLGA. But I
     suspect that you didn't call me at work,
     just to offer me the greetings of the
```

season for some bourgeois capitalist
holiday. What's important enough to get you
on the phone, EVGENIJ?

MALE 2: The last report you sent in on SPOTLIGHT.
The one from the comrades. What are all
those tents for?

MALE 1: It could be any number of things. They
could be just airing them.

MALE 2: Is that what <u>you</u> think?

MALE 1: Yes.

MALE 2: Why wasn't that in the report?

MALE 1: It's a liaison report. It's supposed to
be passed on without comment.

MALE 2: I've told you I want to hear your
comments. Next time, let me have them.
Under separate cover, of course.

MALE 1: Of course. Since you seem to want to know
more about these tents, I'll tell you
something that was left out of the last
PRIMROSE report about SPOTLIGHT. She says
that the tents are there for "Santa Claus'
deployment." They'll be there a week, until
Santa and his reindeer have come and gone.

MALE 2: I see why you left it out. Have the
comrades reported any activity in and
around the tents?

MALE 1: None.

MALE 2: Airing?

MALE 1: That's what I think.

MALE 2: All right. I just wanted to check with
you. Something doesn't feel right about
this, but I can't put my finger on it. I
wanted your input, because you are closer
to the source, and might have a better feel
for what it could be.

MALE 1: Airing.

MALE 2: If you say so. My best to NATASHA.

MALE 1: Of course, and mine to OLGA. Merry
Christmas!

MALE 2: Thank you, BORIS! And don't go American
on me.

[Hang up]

8
The Calm Before the Storm

On February the twenty-fifth, the tunnel diggers arrived at the terminus. They had gotten the tunnel where it needed to go.

"And now comes the hard part," said the Chief of Base, whose participation in digging the tunnel—ignoring the first shovelful of dirt that he had moved at the opening ceremony—had not included digging, developing blisters, getting dirt under his fingernails, having stitches taken in his arms, his legs or his head, cracking a rib, breaking a leg, being buried in a cave-in, or wading out of the flood.

What he meant to say was: "And now comes the most technically challenging part." The cables were located three feet below the far shoulder of the Schönefelder Chaussee, and digging up to the cables without dropping a part of the Shoss on your head would be far from a trivial exercise. For this part of the fun and games, the Chief of Base brought in some real experts at digging, and sent his impress gang of amateur miners who had brought the tunnel this far on a well-earned vacation.

"I don't care what you do, as long as you stay out of the way and out of trouble for a month. If you want to go back to the States, you have to take leave, but if you want to stay in the city, all you need to do is check in once a day," said the Chief of Base. "I can't give you bonus pay or pay you for all the overtime you've put in, but I can give you time off. So consider this a 'Bonus Month'. Have fun!'"

Kevin became an auditor at the Freie Universität, so that he could keep Gabbie company in some of her classes. When he went to the first professor to ask permission to register as a *Gasthörer*, Gabbie went with him and, as usual, had tried to do all the talking. The professor was in a hurry and wanted to get right to the point, so he cut Gabbie off in mid sentence, looked over his half-glasses and directed a question at Kevin.

"And what, kind sir, is the meaning of the names *Melanesien, Mikronesien* and *Polynesien*?" asked the professor in German, pointing a gangly arm at Kevin.

Kevin wondered how the professor had managed to create a break in Gabbie's waterfall of words. Kevin had still not been able to figure out how to do it. The wondering created a hesitation, which the professor began to interpret as Kevin not understanding his question, but that impression changed when Kevin finally did open his mouth.

"The Melanasian islands are the 'black islands,' named after their dark-skinned population. Micronesia is the area of 'small islands,' and Polynesia is the area of 'many islands'," replied Kevin in German. He and Gabbie had spent a lot of time in the South Seas exhibit in the Dahlem. "The names are all based on Greek roots."

Having discovered that, despite his American accent, Kevin's answers could be more coherent than those of some of his real students, the professor signed off on Kevin's form, and suggested that when they approached his colleagues, teaching the rest of Gabbie's classes, Kevin go alone. This was his first unofficial encounter with an American, and he began to see what some German girls saw in them. This one was polite and reasonably well-spoken.

Blackie became a full-time blackmarketeer and earned a small fortune, which made him even more insufferable than he had been when he was broke. It did, however, make his moose rather happy. Now he could keep her in the style to which she had hoped to become accustomed when she became a moose.

"Blackie, Liebling, I just can't choose between the red and the black," said Blackie's moose coyly.

"Get one of each, honey. It's only money," said Blackie with a flourish. She looked good in either color.

Fast Eddie and his wife Meg went on a second honeymoon. They went to The Armed Forces Recreation Center in Garmisch and did not look at the mountains. It didn't rain the whole time they were there and they didn't even notice. Their first daughter, Elizabeth, was born on Christmas day, 1955, which, as far as Elizabeth was concerned, was a swindle. She always felt that a summer birthday was much preferable to a Christmas birthday, because you got more presents, and they came twice a year. She never forgave the Chief of Base for giving her father a month off in March. Not even after she joined the Agency.

"When I have a kid, it's not going to be on Christmas day," she would say. "It's such a total gyp. You never get as many presents as children with birthdays in July. I just couldn't bear to do that to my own kid."

Elizabeth kept her word. Meg, named after her grandmother, was born on December the twenty-fourth.

Master-Sergeant Laufflaecker was the person with whom all the miners had to check in, but since he did not have to really deal with them for more than a minute at a time, it was a vacation for him too, most of the time.

"You say that you're at the corner of *Einbahnstrasse* and *Kein Einfahrt*! That means "One-way street" and No entry"! Call me back when you sober up!" said Sergeant Laufflaecker to Charlie who was checking in by phone from somewhere downtown.

Lieutenant Sheerluck had not been one of the miners, so he did not get any time off. He did not really mind, because his dissertation—the only part of his do-nothing job that really kept him busy—had to be revised for his new advisor, who wanted all instances of the word *actually* to be changed to read *really*. That kept him really busy, because he was a slow typist and his dissertation was 217 pages long.

"Damn typos!" he lamented as he ripped a page out of the aging machine that pretended it was really a typewriter, and threw crumpled page in the growing pile, overflowing the wastepaper basket. "They're really getting my goat!"

You could not have any typos or corrections in the final version of the dissertation, and he could not find a competent

English typist. He should have asked Meg. She could type 60 words a minute with no mistakes, and she and Eddie could have used the extra money with a baby on the way. Lieutenant Sheerluck did not know that, because his conversations with the enlisted men were limited to things like haircuts, shoe shines and military courtesy. Sergeant Laufflaecker could have told him, but he did not like lieutenants.

The expert miners were really pros imported from Wales, where mining was an art form. They were efficient and on time, which meant that the equipment installation crew began their work on April the sixth as planned. There was a lot of equipment, and much of it had to be set up in the tunnel near the cable, so the first tap did not go on-line until May third. The Chief of Base's 'Bonus Month' had turned into two.

Circuit 53:   11:42-11:47Z 15 April 1955

FEMALE 1: KARLSHORST. This is MOSCOW. Can I have 4371 for my party?

FEMALE 2: It was busy just a minute ago. Let me check. It's ringing.

MALE 1: 4371.

FEMALE 2: Go ahead, your party's on the line.

MALE 2: BORIS, what's happened to PRIMROSE? I haven't seen a report from her in a while.

MALE 1: It's all been Nothing To Report. She says that all the regular members of SPOTLIGHT have been given some time off, while they wait for a crew of specialists to do something.

MALE 2: That's not NTR! What kind of specialists? Could this have anything to do with Von FRIEDHOFEN?

MALE 1: Possibly, but there just isn't enough information to even base a good guess on. They are waiting, and PRIMROSE doesn't know what for. All her EAGLE knows is that they are from Wales.

MALE 2: Remember what I said about wanting to
        hear your guesses, especially about
        SPOTLIGHT. Don't keep me in the dark, even
        if all you've got is a faint glimmer of an
        idea.
MALE 1: Not a one. All I can say is that the
        regular crew is enjoying some time off.
MALE 2: I would enjoy a little time off. What
        would you do with some?
MALE 1: NATASHA and I would go to SOCHI.
MALE 2: Yes, that would be nice. OLGA and I would
        go to LONDON. There used to be this little
        fish and chips shop near Russell Square
        that we would go to after servicing a dead
        drop at the British Museum. I'd like to see
        if it is still there. You just can't get
        fish and chips like that anyplace else. It
        had a sign that said "The Best Fish and
        Chips in the Whole of London," and it was
        the truth.
MALE 1: NATASHA and I have a place like that
        here. It's a sort of snackbar called a
        "Wurstelstand," and it has the best potato
        salad we've ever tasted. The owner's wife
        makes it herself. It's at its best when you
        mix it with the curry sauce from the hot
        dog the Germans call a "wurst." We always
        go there after clearing a dead drop in the
        Sophie-Charlotte Museum.
MALE 2: LONDON. Those were the good old days.
        Playing hide-and-seek on the street with
        our British friends. I miss the excitement
        of the game.
MALE 1: Come out for a visit. I can get you back
        on the street for a round or two. At the
        very least we can do a rabbit run, and see
        who wants to follow us.
MALE 2: That's very tempting, BORIS. I just may
        do that.
MALE 1: NATASHA would be so very pleased to see
        you, and you could do a little shopping for
        OLGA. Or, better yet, bring OLGA. I could

arrange a representational function where wives are required.

MALE 2: Now you <u>are</u> tempting me, BORIS.

MALE 1: The invitation is genuine, EVGENIJ.

MALE 2: I'll see what I can do. I would like to see SPOTLIGHT myself, and you and NATASHA as well, and OLGA complains that I never take her anywhere.

MALE 1: Just give me a date, and I'll get the function lined up.

MALE 2: I'll check my calendar and get back to you. Tell NATASHA I asked after her.

MALE 1: I'll do that. And my best to OLGA.

MALE 2: Of course. Good evening, BORIS.

[Hang up]

9
The Tap Turns On

The real fun began in May. That was when the first tap came on line. The Chief of Base, disguised as a British captain with quartermaster insignia, was on Site to officially bring the first circuit on-line. The technicians were right on time. It was exactly 10:00 Zulu. Everything was in readiness for the Chief of Base to throw the power switch to turn on the first tape recorder. There was a small, select crowd, consisting mostly of the Day shift, the British cable technicians and three VIP guests who looked a little rumpled after being delivered to the Site by truck with the Chief of Base. The Chief of Base said a few, well-chosen words that boiled down to 'it's taken us a long time to get here, so now let's get the show on the road, and make hay while the sun shines.'

His metaphor was inappropriate, because, while it was spring, it was Berlin and it was raining. He turned the recorder on and nothing happened. This caused some consternation among the assembled multitude, mostly among the three VIPs, who had expected the recorder to start turning immediately and to be able to listen to some Russian or German whom they couldn't understand say something secret that they couldn't comprehend.

"OK. What's wrong with it?!" said the Chief of Base in a tone that showed he wanted an answer two minutes ago. He did not like to be made to look stupid in front of his VIP guests. They had appropriated a lot of money to make this moment possible.

"There's nothing wrong with it, sir," said the chief technician, deftly refusing delivery of the Chief of Base's implied insult. He had been tapping German phone lines since before the war. He had done the tap in Vienna for SILVER. On top of that, he was unimpressed by the Yank's "VIPs." He had briefed Churchill and Eisenhower. Now there were some VIPs for you. "It's a voice activated recorder. There's nobody on the line now."

They stood around silently for about five minutes staring at the recorder do nothing, its little green "ON" light glowing brightly. Then Sergeant Laufflaecker took charge of the situation.

"Perhaps the gentlemen would like to have a little light refreshment while we are waiting."

The senator had a bourbon and branch water. The congressman had the Irish whiskey. The Chief of Station had a Weisse mit Schuss, a white German beer with a shot of raspberry syrup in it.. He'd been to Berlin before, and knew what was good. There were some snacks, that Lieutenant Sheerluck had had the mess sergeant make up for the occasion, but luckily for him, none of the VIPs touched them.

"To those loose lips, that are going to help us sink those proverbial ships," said the Chief of Base, raising his glass for a toast.

The VIPs, together with the rest of the assemblage, raised their glasses high. The recorder, however, just sat there silently staring at them with its one green eye.

"Not overly talkative, these Roosians," said the senator.

"Mighty tight-lipped," said the congressman.

"We've been blown," said the Chief of Station.

"Have another drink," said Sergeant Laufflaecker.

Four toasts later—it was beginning to look like a reception at the Russian Embassy, where the toasts went on for hours, thought the Chief of Base—the recorder seemed to wink its eye, and started spinning its reels. A female voice could be heard through the loud speaker that had been plugged into the recorder especially for this occasion.

"*Карлсхорст, девушка. Это Москва. Можно 4371 для моего абонента?*" said the voice.

"It's in Russian, sir," said Lieutenant Sheerluck, displaying his keen linguistic skills. "It's an international call to Moscow."

"That's more like it," said the senator.

"Pretty interesting stuff," said the congressman.

"That's not intel," said the Chief of Station.

A male voice came on the line and was quickly joined by a second male voice. Lieutenant Sheerluck looked pensive as he tried to catch every word. The conversation was short. The recorder reels clicked to a stop. The first conversation of many was on tape.

"I have to agree with the COS," said Lieutenant Sheerluck. "It's not intel. Just two Russians named Boris and Evgenij talking about having lunch at the British Army Club. It's not important."

"Speaking of lunch, gentlemen, our reservation at the Harnack House is for 12:00, and the counter-surveillance run takes an hour. We should be leaving right about now, if you want to be on time," said the Chief of Base.

"Quite right," said the senator.

"But of course," said the congressman.

"Cover is for the inconvenience of the individual," said the Chief of Station, who had skipped breakfast and wisely passed on the mess sergeant's snacks. He was getting hungry.

The VIPs left. The technicians went back to work. Lieutenant Sheerluck went back to his dissertation. Sergeant Laufflaecker and the rest of the Day shift finished off what was left of the light refreshments. They ate in the mess hall all the time and were immune. The tape stayed on the recorder until Kevin came in with the Swing shift and took it down to scribe.

Circuit 53:   10:07-10:11Z 03 May 1955
             Reel 1

FEMALE 1: KARLSHORST, operator. This is MOSCOW.
     Can I have 4371 for my party?
FEMALE 2: It's ringing.
MALE 1: 4371.
FEMALE 2: Your party's on the line. Go ahead,
     please.
MALE 2: BORIS! How's life on the forward edge of
     Communism?
MALE 1: The barricades are still holding,
     EVGENIJ. It's good to hear from you. What's

important enough for you to call?

MALE 2: I was looking at the surveillance report for our main American friend, and could not understand what he was doing up on Reichskanzlerplatz yesterday around lunch.

MALE 1: Probably eating at the British Army Club. They say that the food there is better than in Harnack House.

MALE 2: Are you sure? Why didn't the pavement artist follow him inside?

MALE 1: About the food? I wouldn't mind confirming that personally, if you want. Will you authorize the hard currency expenditure for me to find out?

MALE 2: Don't be facetious, Boris.

MALE 1: I wasn't trying to be. The facilities are only for members of the forces and you have to pay in British Armed Forces Script. The tail didn't have any BAFS.

MALE 2: Why not?!

MALE 1: Your office would not authorize the expenditure of hard currency for a surveillance op.

MALE 2: My office? Who in my office!

MALE 1: Colonel BESPOLEZNYJ.

MALE 2: That idiot! You'll have your authorization in the morning. I want a full report on the food at the British Army Club. Have a Scotch egg for me. That was one of the things I enjoyed most during our tour in England. That and fish and chips. And have a bitter. And have our American friend followed inside next time.

MALE 1: Thank you, comrade General. And my kind regards to Colonel BESPOLEZNYJ.

MALE 2: He should live so long.

MALE 1: How's OLGA? Does she need more coffee?

MALE 2: Yes, as a matter of fact.

MALE 1: I'll see that she gets some more.

MALE 2: Yes, she'll appreciate that.

MALE 1: Give her my regards.

MALE 2: And mine to NATASHA.

```
MALE 1: I will, and thanks again for the BAFS.
[HANG UP]
```

Kevin pulled the transcript out of his mill, stood up and walked over to Fast Eddie.

"Here's a good one. The KGB is surveilling the Chief of Base and smuggling coffee," said Kevin enthusiastically.

"Right," answered Fast Eddie taking the transcript. He read the single page of text. "Just admit that you're making this up, so I can go back to sleep," groaned Fast Eddie.

"I don't make this stuff up. I just put down what they say."

"You expect me to report this to the Chief of Base with a straight face? I heard that Sheerluck was here when the call was recorded and he said it was NTR. That's what it says in the *Pass-on Book*," replied Eddie.

"I don't care what it says in the *Pass-on Book*. All I care about is what it says on tape."

"You can go to jail for faking stuff!"

"I'm not faking it, Eddie!'

"They'll send me to jail too for aiding and abetting."

"This is not nuclear science. It's just plain, everyday, ordinary spying. They want to know what the Chief of Base is doing, so they have him followed," explained Kevin.

"And I suppose that he does not know that?"

"Ask him."

"Ask him what? Did you go to the NAAFI yesterday, and were you followed when you went there?"

"Yes."

"I can't believe I'm having this conversation," groaned Fast Eddie.

"I can't believe *I'm* having this conversation! Where's your elan? Where's your sense of daring-do? Where's your patriotism? Where's your mom's apple pie?"

"Leave my mom out of this! I'm not going to do it. Let's just throw this in the burn bag and you can do the real script. The one that says 'Nothing To Report'."

"Now that's criminal. If they'd send you to jail for that, I'd applaud."

"You'd applaud them sending me to jail?"

"If you don't report my script," said Kevin, applauding.

"If I don't report this nonsense of the KGB trailing the Chief of Base? I wasn't born yesterday," yelled Fast Eddie, raising the conversation to a higher level, and attracting the attention of the Chief of Base, who was walking by the door of the scribe bay in one of the counter-surveillance disguises that he always wore when he visited the Site.

"Just when were you born?" asked the Chief of Base, who looked suspiciously like an army sergeant first class with tank corps insignia.

"Long enough ago to know that he's making this up," replied Eddie, turning to see who had asked the question. Kevin had already recognized the voice.

"Making what up?" asked the Chief of Base.

"That you went to the NAAFI yesterday, and that you were followed when you went there," said Eddie in resignation.

"I did go to the NAAFI yesterday," said the Chief of Base. "How did you know that?"

"General Besstrashnyj in Moscow told me so," replied Kevin, pleased to have had one of the facts of his script confirmed.

"And how did he come by this information?"

"From the surveillance report Karlshorst sent him."

"I was 'black' the whole way," intoned the Chief of Base.

"You had lunch there."

"Let me see this script," said the Chief of Base, reaching for the blue copy of the script on Eddie's desk.

The Chief of Base read the script slowly. He looked Kevin up and down. He looked Fast Eddie over.

"I don't see my name in there," said the Chief of Base.

"You're 'our main American Friend'. I suppose you never talk around stuff on the phone," replied Kevin.

"And I don't see Besstrashnyj," said the Chief of Base with somewhat less conviction than before.

"The second male speaker's name is Evgenij and he's a general, and his office is the one that got the surveillance report, and he can authorize hard currency expenditures, and he was stationed in England. Colonel-General Evgenij Petrovich Besstrashnyj is the head of European Operations at KGB Headquarters in Moscow.

He was stationed in London as a military attaché from 1948-1952. His wife's name is Olga. I looked in the bio book," said Kevin at a machine-gun pace.

"He's making it up," said Fast Eddie.

"I'll have the tape quality controlled," concluded the Chief of Base.

"Don't let Sheerluck touch it," said Kevin forcefully. "Get a real scribe."

"And why not Lieutenant *Sher*lock?"

"He couldn't scribe his way out of a wet paper bag. It says in the *Pass-on Book* that he NTR'd this call. It was the first one of the day."

"I see," said the Chief of Base. "Give me the tape!"

Kevin rewound the tape, put it in a jacket and handed it to the Chief of Base, who put the tape and the script in a big brown envelope. He looked Kevin over one more time and walked out of the bay.

"I thought that went well," said Fast Eddie. "He didn't have you shot."

"He didn't have a gun with him," replied Kevin.

Check Point "Tunnel"

10
Old-world Masters, Quality Assured

The NAAFI tape, as it came to be known, made its way across town in the van with the Chief of Base. It spent the night in a comfortably roomy safe in the Chief of Base's office, and rose early to be packed and wrapped before heading to the courier office at Gatow to be manifested on the next courier flight out of Berlin. Two days later, apparently unfatigued from its travels, the tape landed on the desk of the Site's Stateside Project Officer, where it promptly found its way to a tape recorder for play-back.

The tape had been accompanied by a hand-written note from the Chief of Base. The Project Officer took it out and looked it over. *His handwriting is worse than ever. He should have finished medical school,* thought the Project Officer to himself. Slowly he pieced the message together. It said:

> *"Congratulations! It's a bouncing baby tape. This is the first one out of the tap. There is a local difference of opinion about its significance. One opinion is that it is NTR. The other is that it has direct local impact. (A copy of the transcript and my write-up of the purported analysis is in the tape jacket.) I*

need to know which one I can trust for local support. Please Q.C. the tape and get back to me soonest EXCLUSIVE. I haven't figured out how I'm going to handle this yet, and I don't want your message getting wide distro. In your message, please do not indicate that there are two versions. Just tell me which one you like best."

Oh, what a tangled web we weave ... thought the Project Officer, who knew the Chief of Base from OSS days. *I wonder which of those military lingies we sent him is right? My money's on the one with the doctorate. Those Marys can be a mixed bag.*

He walked over to a huge desk, piled high with dictionaries and reference books. It had a sign on it that said:

𝕮𝔷𝔞𝔯𝔬𝔡𝔷𝔦𝔢𝔧, 𝔙𝔬𝔩𝔰𝔥𝔢𝔟𝔫𝔦𝔨 & 𝔐𝔞𝔤 𝔒𝔩𝔡-𝔚𝔬𝔯𝔩𝔡 𝔐𝔞𝔰𝔱𝔢𝔯𝔰. 𝔔𝔲𝔞𝔩𝔦𝔱𝔶 𝔄𝔰𝔰𝔲𝔯𝔢𝔡

The Quality Controller who sat at the desk was crusty, brusque and gruff, but he could pull words off a tape like nobody else. He had worked material from the bugs in the Embassy for years and from the Vienna taps. The Project Officer trusted his ear completely. If there was anything wrong with the NAAFI transcript, he would say so in no uncertain terms.

"Good, clear audio," said the Quality Controller as the tape started, and that was the last thing he said until it stopped. He looked up and said: "Nice piece of work. Whoever did this can come work for me anytime. Mind you, he put an extra comma in one sentence, but I can break him of those bad habits. Russian punctuation is not like English. You have to keep the two separate."

"And the analysis?" asked the Project Officer.

"Looks pretty good. The jargon's right. Let me check the names," said the Quality Controller, turning to a massive, oak 3X5 card file that was planted solidly next to his colossal desk, forming an 'L' with it. He yanked open a drawer, rifled the cards with a practiced hand, picked up one, studied it for a second, put it back and closed the drawer. He grabbed the drawer immediately above it, ran his finger down the row of cards to a tab, threw the tab back, picked out a card, and laughed.

"It's OK, I guess. He got Besstrashnyj dead to rights, but he missed the I.D. on Boris. That's Colonel Boris Borisovich Badunov, head of ops at the KGB Residency in Karlshorst. He's married to Besstrashnyj's sister, Natasha. He's got a lot more pull than his rank suggests, because of that. Boris isn't in the published working aid, so missing him isn't that bad."

"But the Chief of Base was being shadowed?" asked the Project Officer, somewhat taken aback by this uncustomarily glowing praise for some Army scribe in Berlin whom he had never seen before. The QC normally thought that everybody else's work was crap.

"Oh, yeah, and ol' Evgenij is really pissed that the tail couldn't follow him into the Brit Army Club, 'cause he didn't have any BAFS. I wouldn't want to be in Bespoleznyj's shoes. By the way, his name means "useless" and he probably is. I can look him up, if you want. He's probably some wheel in KGB finance. I'll bet Besstrashnyj's going to ream him a new asshole."

"Why don't you do that," said the Project Officer. "I'll be having someone put together a report, and I'll want them to have all the details. Thanks."

The Quality Controller turned back to his 3X5 card file. The Project Officer went back to his desk and typed a message to go EXCLUSIVE to the Chief of Base.

TO: CHIEF OF BASE (EXCLUSIVE)
FROM: PROJECT OFFICER
CONGRATULATIONS ON BOUNCING BABY TAPE. TAPE AND TRANSCRIPT ARE IN EXCELLENT HEALTH. CONFIRM THAT IT HAS SIGNIFICANT LOCAL IMPACT. YOU WERE RED. MY TRUSTED EAR, HOWEVER, COMPLAINS THAT IT COULD HAVE BEEN MORE COMPLETE. LACKS ID OF TWO OTHER PARTIES MENTIONED, BUT HE ADDS THAT THEY ARE NOT LISTED IN YOUR LOCAL WORKING AIDS. IDS WILL BE INCLUDED IN REPORT, WHICH WILL BE DISTRO IN HARD COPY ONLY. KUDOS TO THE SCRIBE WHO DID THE SCRIPT.

The message winged its way across the ocean, and apparently wearied by its long flight, it settled down in a sealed brown envelope to nap until the Chief of Base came in to work the next morning. It was awakened when the letter opener jostled it while cutting it out of the envelope. The message conveyed its contents to the Chief of Base, who said: "Well, I'll be damned!" and picked up the secure phone to call the colonel in charge of the 9539th.

Ignoring the usual pleasantries, the Chief of Base got right down to brass tacks.

"You remember our discussion about the first tape? Well, I got the feedback I asked for from the States. Find something for the lieutenant to do that will keep him away from my tapes," said the Chief of Base, cursing his luck that it was the lieutenant who was deaf.

"I could just issue an order that he is not to do any transcribing," suggested the colonel.

"No, I don't want to risk pissing him off with a direct confrontation about his language skills. That could create a threat to security. He could go off and tell the Russians what he knows out of spite," said the Chief of Base, thinking of a couple of successful ops he had run against the Germans that had started exactly that way.

The Chief of Base, having talked to the commander of Lieutenant Sherlock's previous unit, the ill-fated tactical battalion, suggested a transfer. The colonel countered that this was a special op, and people only get transferred out of a special op with a promotion, and everybody knew that, so the lieutenant would be expecting a promotion. The Chief of Base was prepared to promote him, but the colonel pointed out that the promotion would have to be to captain for Sherlock to become excess to the Table of Organization and Equipment, and that he was still only a second-lieutenant.

"Well then, promote him to first-lieutenant, and let me know when you can make him a captain," said the Chief of Base, demonstrating the kind of thinking that made him a good case officer.

"The average time in grade to captain is 30 months," said the colonel pointedly.

"Maybe we'll think of something that will shorten the cycle, or a way to rebalance the T.O. and E.," said the Chief of Base hopefully. "Promote him and give him a new job to go with it that does not have anything to do with Russian."

Lieutenant Sheerluck had earned his nickname once again.

Circuit 53:   14:57-15:01Z 06 May 1955
Reel 509

FEMALE 1: KARLSHORST, this is MOSCOW. I need 5298
    for my party, please.
FEMALE 2: Just a moment. It's ringing.
MALE 1: 5298. Finance.
FEMALE 2: Put your party on the line
MALE 2: Hello?
MALE 1: 5298. Finance.
MALE 2: Is that you, VLADIMIR IL'YICH?
MALE 1: LEV DAVIDOVICH! What did I do wrong this
    time?
MALE 2: You signed where you should have
    initialed, and BESPOLEZNYJ would have your
    head on a platter, if you were here, but I
    fixed it by putting an "Original Signature
    Required" stamp under the place where you
    signed instead of initialling.
MALE 1: Thank you. But don't you think that he'll
    figure it out eventually?
MALE 2: He never caught on to the KROPOTKIN
    constant, and he's been in a strange mood
    lately.
MALE 1: How so?
MALE 2: A couple of days ago he gets called up to
    BESSTRASHNYJ's office, and when he came
    down again, he was completely changed.
    MALENKOV came in from the GosBank run just
    before him and hadn't had a chance to wipe
    the dust off his shoes, and BESPOLEZNYJ
    didn't say a thing about it to him.
MALE 1: That is strange.
MALE 2: Rumor has it that he has been offered the
    residency in some banana republic; everyone
    you ask gives you a different country, so

you can just pick your own favorite Latin American hot spot rather than having me tell you one that's wrong.

MALE 1: He must have done something to really piss BESSTRASHNYJ off. I thought with those Party connections of his, he'd never get the boot.

MALE 2: This isn't the boot. It's a promotion, an offer of prestige that's unheard of for a finance officer.

MALE 1: Like I said: the boot. He's being kicked upstairs. You don't think that they'd ever offer you a residency anywhere, no matter how great a job you were doing, do you?

MALE 2: You've got a point there.

MALE 1: How are you and Katya getting on?

MALE 2: We broke up.

MALE 1: I should have known. And, if I'd known, I'd have been a case officer instead of a finance officer, right?

MALE 2: Right.

MALE 1: I'm sorry to hear it. Better luck next time.

MALE 2: Her name's VIOLETTA. It's the real thing this time.

MALE 1: That's your opinion.

MALE 2: No, it's hers too.

MALE 1: In that case, I'll be offended, if you don't send us an invitation to the wedding.

MALE 2: We hadn't gotten around to that yet. Oh, by the way, I had something else official to justify this call. Your most recent request to use BAFS on ops has been approved, but since we don't have access to them, we'll just up your shipment of Dollars, West Marks or Pounds, and you'll have to make your own arrangements.

MALE 1: That's good news, but it's bad news too. Having to fend for myself to get BAFS will mean a lot more work. Just up my shipment of West Marks. They're easier to move on the black market, which is where I'll have

to get the BAFS. I'll have to get one of
the German-speaking case officers to go out
for me.

MALE 2: There's more. BESSTRASHNYJ is coming out
to your place, and he wants to be sure that
you have enough BAFS for him to visit the
British Voentorg.

MALE 1: How many's that?

MALE 2: As many as he wants, and he's taking his
wife.

MALE 1: How much extra am I getting in my
shipment for his trip?

MALE 2: A thousand Dollars, four thousand West
Marks and sixteen thousand East Marks.

MALE 1: If that's not enough, can I juggle some
of the other accounts until you can send me
some more?

MALE 2: With BESSTRASHNYJ anything is possible.
He signs his own vouchers.

MALE 1: Thanks for the heads-up. Can I send you a
little something to show my appreciation?
Me to you for the extra effort.

MALE 2: American cigarettes.

MALE 1: I'll take care of it.

MALE 2: And I'll take care of you. Any hint of a
job out there?

MALE 1: Not a one, but if BESPOLEZNYJ leaves,
life will be better back there.

MALE 2: Dream on.

MALE 1: OK, well, at least it will be different.

MALE 2: I guess you're right. My best to
NADEZHDA.

MALE 1: And our best to ...?

MALE 2: VIOLETTA, comrade captain. I serve the
Soviet Union!

MALE 1: Sure you do. Bye.

[Hang up]

11
The Chad Count

The opening of the Tap unleashed a flood of new faces as the 9539th filled its previously empty operational slots. The miners who had been with the tunnel from the time before it was a hole in the basement of the warehouse felt a certain sense of superiority to the newcomers, and were sometimes inclined to demonstrate this energetically to the *newks*.

Corporal Neumann was eminently likeable, a fine, upstanding young man of good breeding, education and deportment. None of the morse or printer ops could stand him. They could not understand what he was doing in the Army, and if he had to be in the Army, why he wasn't an officer. His mother couldn't understand it either, which was exactly why he was in the Army and wasn't an officer. But Blackie didn't know about Corporal Neumann's mother, which was understandable, since Corporal Neumann did not like Blackie and would never have shared anything as personal with him as his relationship with his mother.

The main trouble with Corporal Neumann was that, having grown up in a family where no one played any practical jokes on anyone else, he was blind to the cunning artifices of people like Blackie, who had broken their funny bones on practical jokes and thought that everybody else should have an opportunity to do the same. Blackie's 'best' ideas for practical jokes seemed to coincide with the approach of the witching hour. There were some who said that the peak of his cycle occurred during the full moon, but the chad count took place on the twenty-eighth of May and the moon was in its first quarter.

"Corporal Neumann, sir," intoned Blackie in his best obsequiously straight-faced voice, "the Day ops dropped us in it. They mixed up the pink and the yellow chad, and we can't do the chad count before the classified burn, like it calls for in the SOP. What are we going to do?"

"What do you mean 'count the chad'?" said Corporal Neumann, exhibiting a modicum of common sense.

"Count the little round pieces of paper that are punched out of the paper tape when the teletype operators poke up the messages to send back to the world," said Blackie.

"I know what chad is. What I don't know is why anyone would want to count it," said Corporal Neumann, not realizing that just having this conversation was a mistake.

"Use your head for something other than keeping your ears apart," said Blackie, setting the hook before he started to reel his fish in. "If we don't destroy all the chad, and the Russkies get a hold of some of it, they can break the messages on the paper tape that the chad is from. That's why we have to count it, to make sure we got it all."

"You just count the pink and the yellow together then," responded Neumann condescendingly, oblivious to the trap that had just sprung closed on him.

"We can't. We have to have a separate count of each color. The destruction officer has to certify that we burned 127,386 pink chads and 358,931 yellow chads. If the numbers don't match the actual destruction, there'll be hell to pay when Lieutenant Sheerluck sees the report when he comes in in the morning."

"Then you'd better get busy," replied Corporal Neumann curtly.

"The count has to be done by an NCO and Sergeant Fastbinder took an early-in. That means you're the ranking man on the trick."

"Shit! When did Sergeant Fastbinder decide to take an early-in?!" said Corporal Neumann, uncustomarily swearing.

"About 30 seconds after he found out that the Day trick shafted him with the chad count. It's that kind of decisiveness that makes him a good sergeant."

Corporal Neumann took the chad bag decisively with a look of determination in his eye that disappeared when the yellow count got to 1,364. By the time that the pink count got to 2,813, he looked distraught. When the yellow count reached 3,196, he looked desperate. That was the point at which Kevin walked by. It was 19:23 Local.

"Chad count? News to me."

"Don't you ever read the Standard Operating Procedures?" said Corporal Neumann, who, at about the time that he said the word 'read,' replaced his look of despair with one of sheepishness, and went off in search of a copy of the SOP for the burn.

Kevin hadn't even broken stride on his way to the latrine. *Reading*, he said to himself, *is a prerequisite for success.*

Circuit 53:   **18:23-18:26Z 31 May 1955**
                Reel 3463

FEMALE 1: This is MOSCOW, KARLSHORST. I need a
    connection to 4371 for my party.
FEMALE 2: Just a moment. It's ringing.
MALE 1: 4371.
FEMALE 2: MOSCOW, your party's on the line.
MALE 2: BORIS! I just wanted to thank you
    personally for the way you handled our
    trip.
MALE 1: You're welcome, EVGENIJ? We were glad to
    see you.
MALE 2: It was fun to be out on the street again,
    playing the game with our British and
    American friends. I hadn't realized how
    much I missed it until I looked at the
    reflection in that plate glass window and
    saw that parade of pavement artists that
    our friends had provided for my
    entertainment.
MALE 1: That was very considerate of them, wasn't
    it? Should I send them a 'Thank you' note?
MALE 2: It's a shame we can't. I got the
    impression at the reception that you

arranged for OLGA that our American
friends' Resident would appreciate the
joke.

MALE 1: I'm sure that he would. It's too bad that
the game isn't played like that.

MALE 2: Yes, it is. I also enjoyed meeting
PRIMROSE. Beautiful, but also very
intelligent and highly motivated.

MALE 1: Yes, that's right. You can't buy
motivation like that.

MALE 2: Revenge. It's a powerful motivator. How
thoughtful of the Americans to kill her
father during the war so that she would
want to work for us against them. They seem
to be falling over themselves to be helpful
to us.

MALE 1: The Americans say "bending over
backwards".

MALE 2: Sounds rather uncomfortable, but if
they're willing to go to all that trouble,
then let them "bend over backwards." Too
bad that they won't bend over a little
further and give us some more info on
SPOTLIGHT. I'm curious about what all those
new faces are doing there.

MALE 1: I suspect that they went operational, and
we are about to go operational too. The
Wurstelstand goes in tomorrow. That should
be quite productive. The photos should be
better than the ones we get from the
Comrades in any event.

[Transcriber note: The "Comrades" are the East
Germans.]

MALE 2: I hope so. Where did you dig up that old
Nazi to run it? He's quite a character.

MALE 1: Yes, he is. One of his old subordinates
works for us, and happened onto him in
ROSTOCK, where, of all things, he was
running a Wurstelstand. We couldn't have
developed a better legend for him, if we'd
tried. A promise of amnesty, a few false
documents, some money and he's ours.

MALE 2: GERMANY has all the modern conveniences, it's almost like 'hot and cold running spies'. You just turn on a tap and out they come, right when you need them. And to think; OLGA's sister down on the farm doesn't even have indoor running water.

MALE 1: I just hope that the Americans are in the same boat when it comes to spies.

MALE 2: BORIS, you're too funny by half today. I can't imagine how NATASHA puts up with your jokes. By the way, tell her again what a good time we had.

MALE 1: She couldn't let her favorite brother and his wife stay in a hotel, when we have such a big house. She was glad to do it. She got to see more of you two that way.

MALE 2: You're right. It is a big house. It almost makes me feel jealous, but NATASHA deserves it 'for putting up with you'.

MALE 1: You're too kind, EVGENIJ. Give my best to OLGA. Tell her she deserves a medal for putting up with you.

MALE 2: Oh, you've heard about that, have you?

MALE 1: It's a small world, and I am a trained intelligence officer.

MALE 2: That you are.

MALE 1: Congratulations!

MALE 2: Thank you. Good evening, BORIS.

MALE 1: Good night, EVGENIJ.

[Hang up]

12
A Spring Outing

June the first was—for Berlin—a nice spring day. There was a light drizzle with patches of sun. Kevin was up early so that he could pick up Gabbie for a day at the beach on the Wannsee, the large lake on the western end of Berlin that ran along the edge of the Grünewald forest. A large part of the lake was only open to members of the American forces and "their guests."

Gabbie had been too busy for him to see her the day before, and starting early was Kevin's way of making up for that. Fast Eddie and Meg were meeting them there for lunch.

Sergeant Laufflaecker had been to the Wannsee twice, but he was not a beach sort of person, having lost his taste for beaches in Normandy, on Omaha. Lieutenant Sheerluck did not know that there was a beach in Berlin. Besides, both of them were on Days and they could not have gone, even if they had wanted to. Blackie was on Potsdamer Platz, trying to make enough money so that he could buy the beach.

It was not crowded at all. There was one group of officers' wives at a table on the veranda, laughing very loudly at some off-color joke. There was a couple renting a sailboat. Kevin recognized the man. He was the doctor who had sewn up his arm at the hospital. He must have been on nights or weekends at the emergency room. Doctors, nurses, MPs and intel people were the only ones who were off during the day during the week. That's what made the beach so attractive then. With everybody else at work, it was almost like a private club.

This was not their first time at the Wannsee beach. Gabbie had been favorably impressed the first time, and had hinted to Kevin that she would not be disappointed if they went again. A wink was as good as a nod to Kevin where Gabbie was concerned. Now that classes were out at the *Uni*, they had been to the Wannsee a number of times. Gabbie talked and Kevin listened. He liked listening, especially to Gabbie. The sound of the conversation at the table of officers' wives was not intrusive—except when they laughed—or even intelligible, but Kevin could imagine what they were saying.

"What's he doing out here with his Schatzie, when I don't get to see Jack for more than a couple of hours at a time? I haven't seen Jack during the day for a month, or at night either for most of that time. He can't be a doctor. I'd recognize him. Maybe he's an MP or one of those 'spooks'," said the colonel's wife with the large, garish hat, who didn't look a day over 40, even though she was. She was not too enthusiastic about Americans seeing German girls. The scowl on her face when she looked in Kevin and Gabbie's direction said so.

Kevin turned his attention back to Gabbie, who was imagining that they were on a beach on an island in the South Seas, and what she could do for her thesis project, while they were there. She could not really afford to go on a trip like that, and neither could Kevin, though he would have been happy to pay her way, if he had had the money, as long as he could go with her. All he could afford was a new American swimsuit for her from the PX. It looked good on her, but it did not keep the American wives from recognizing her as a German. She did not shave her legs like they did, but that was not a problem for Kevin. Kevin's problem was Gabbie's mother, Liesl, who was appalled at the idea of her daughter dating an American.

"I told Mutti that I was going to the library to study," said Gabbie in German with a wink.

"Don't you think that she'll notice that you have a suntan?" asked Kevin.

"I'll tell her I took my book outside and sat on a bench to enjoy the sun."

This train of thought was going nowhere fast, because neither of them was anxious to move it along to the confrontation that was inevitably waiting for them at the rail terminus. They were both relieved to be able to change the subject when Fast Eddie and Meg showed up for lunch. All four of them moved over to a table on the veranda, and ordered. The officers' wives had decided to go somewhere else for lunch. The food at the Wannsee was OK, but it was not as good as at the Harnack House or the Brit Army Club or the French Pavillon du Lac. It was mostly of the hamburger-and-french-fries variety. The tuna salad on toast was great.

Meg and Gabbie got on rather well, and it did not take long before they had their own private conversation going that more or less excluded the guys. The guys could either listen silently to the girls or could try to make some meaningless small talk that did not interest them. They wanted to talk about work, which was their main shared interest, but everything interesting that they had to say to each other was classified. Kevin told a joke.

"There were these three transcribers walking into work one day. The first one said: 'Mighty windy!' The second one replied: 'No, it's Thursday.' The third one added: 'Me, too. Let's all have a drink.'"

Fast Eddie groaned, and they decided to join the girls' conversation, which had turned to the movies.

Sabrina was going to be at the Outpost Theater where Meg worked that weekend. Gabbie had heard good things about the movie and wanted to see Audrey Hepburn in English.

"I can't imagine what she'll sound like. People never sound the same in English as they do in German," said Gabbie. "You know that the American movies shown in German theaters are all dubbed in German."

"Both Eddie and Kevin are off Sunday Swing, so that's settled," said Meg, who could make a decision in a heartbeat, and usually did, without consulting Eddie, who did not seem to mind. "We'll tell Gabbie's mother that I've invited her to the movies and not say a thing about Kevin."

Kevin and Fast Eddie both looked at each other, and then, because the thought was classified, each of them said silently to himself: *And I thought that I knew something about covert operations and cover stories!* They could not say that out loud because the girls were not cleared, and were not supposed to know what it was exactly that the guys did each day in uniform. That "supposed to," however, was just the forlorn hope of some security officer, who must not have been married or ever had a girlfriend.

The bad thing about working Swings is that you have to be at work at 16:00 Local. That meant that before the conversation progressed too much further, the guys had to leave for work. The girls, however, decided that they would go shopping. Meg was pleased to have a translator along who could explain to the saleslady what maternity clothes were. They grabbed the S-Bahn to a shopping area that Gabbie knew about that normally had things in Meg's size. The guys left to go change into uniform so they could make the Swing.

Fast Eddie got into work a few minutes behind Kevin, who was rummaging through the analysts' desk, looking for something.

"There's probably a good reason for you pillaging my desk?" asked Eddie, more than a little annoyed that Kevin was invading his territory. It was bad enough that he had to share the desk with the other two shifts' analysts.

"Hey, Eddie! When you came in, did you notice the new Wurstelstand out by the gate?" asked Kevin, hardly looking in his direction.

"Yeah, what of it?" grumbled Eddie.

"You mean you don't remember the tape from last night?!" said Kevin in amazement.

"Which tape? There were lots of them," growled Eddie.

"The one with the Wurstelstand!" said Kevin, who could not believe that Fast Eddie could not remember the Wurstelstand tape. He could play it back in his head, as clear as day.

"No."

"You know. My buddies Boris and Evgenij. Evgenij just back from his trip to Berlin. Thanks all around. More of this PRIMROSE stuff, and they were going to take the Wurstelstand operational tomorrow, that's today our time."

"Tell me again why you're so sure that Gabbie isn't PRIMROSE," said Fast Eddie who was a trained intelligence analyst, even if his Russian vocabulary couldn't keep up with all the stuff that Kevin kept coming up with in his scripts. It was his job to question everything until he understood it.

"Because Gabbie's father Heinrich was killed on the eastern front in the battle for Stalingrad, and in the tape we're looking for,

Besstrashnyj said that PRIMROSE's father was killed by the Americans," replied Kevin. "Now come on, Eddie! Help me find the script," implored Kevin. Kevin would be more than a little displeased when he eventually found out that Gabbie had been lying to him.

"If Days didn't throw it away, they probably packed it up for the courier run," said Eddie in resignation. "Get out of my way."

Fast Eddie sat down at his desk and looked through the stacks of paper that formed the filing system of the desk. They were all in date/time order, which made it easy for him to come to the conclusion that Days had indeed packed it up for shipment. There was nothing later than 07:00 Zulu of that morning.

Kevin was ready to re-do the script, but the tape had also been packed up for shipment. Days had been particularly efficient. Lieutenant Sheerluck had obviously been in charge of the courier run. No scrap of paper had been left unpacked, no tape unwrapped. Sheerluck's motto for the courier run was "If it moves, salute it, if it don't, pack it up!" He was hard to ignore.

Since Fast Eddie would not believe Kevin without either the tape or the transcript, all Kevin could do was pull the tape on the collection recorder and see if his friends Boris and Evgenij had something else to say to him. They didn't, but the last tape of the Swing did.

Circuit 173:   15:31-15:32Z 01 June 1955
Reel 4526

MALE 1: VOVA! VOVA, I know you're out there.
    Vovaaaaaaah!
MALE 2: Put a sock in it, VOLODYA! You're gonna
    get me in trouble. The lieutenant was just
    here. He'd have a cow, if he caught me
    BS-ing on-line with you.
MALE 1: I'm sorry, VOVA. I'm just bored shitless.
    With all of you out there in the field,
    there's nothing to do here. I'd even be
    glad to see the lieutenant and have him

bawl me out, that's how bad it is. It's
like being in a ghost town.

MALE 2: You must be in bad shape, if you miss the
lieutenant. I can't imagine being that
bored.

MALE 1: OK, next time, you stay here and I'll go
out with the deployment, and you see how
you like it.

MALE 2: It's a deal. I haven't been to bed since
we left. The food's worse than in garrison.
The lieutenant's in a worse mood than
normal. I think he had a fight with his
wife about being out in the field so much,
or something, 'cause here I am up to my
asshole in mud trying to dig the van out of
some swamp that his map says is a road and
he walks up and starts bitching about me
not having my hat on. Even the first shirt
isn't that big a prick, not even on his
worst days.

MALE 1: Well, maybe on second thought, I'll stay
here.

MALE 2: No, you don't. A deal's a deal. Next time
I'm staying in EBERSWALDE and you can come
out to the stinking field and play stupid
war games. I hope that you get VALERIJ's
van. At least I've been here tied into the
landline back to Headquarters and your
sorry-assed face. Compared to him, I'm in
the lap of luxury. He's set up and torn
down 20 times rushing from one side of the
LETZ to the other and crossing that stupid
river that I can't pronounce each time.
Yeah, that's where you belong, in VALERIJ's
van.

MALE 1: Even VALERIJ's van sounds better to me
right now than being back here and being
bored to death.

MALE 2: Shut up! Here comes the lieutenant again!
[Hang up]

13
Kitchen Counter Intelligence

Kevin ripped the script out of the mill with a flourish. He rushed over to Fast Eddie, waving the script around. Eddie was doing the crossword from the Sunday edition of *The Times* in pencil. Meg had gotten it special for him, because she knew what he thought about the crossword puzzles in *The Stars and Stripes*.

"OK, Eddie, here's one you've got to report. 20 Guards out of garrison, doing river crossings in the Letzlingerheide training area," said Kevin, bouncing off the walls.

Eddie had been concentrating really hard on 27 across, and Kevin's interruption made him testy. It was "ONMLKJIH back" in five letters. The fifth letter was an 'R'.

"It's almost trick change and I'm ready to go home to see how much money Gabbie helped Meg spend, which is all your fault, because she couldn't spend it without Gabbie, and here you come with some made-up script about river crossings. Let me see it!" said Eddie, who still couldn't believe that Kevin was really hearing all this stuff.

Fast Eddie looked the script over slowly. He turned the page upside down, left-side-up, right-side-up and looked at the back of the page. "I don't see any 20 Guards or any training area. I'm not going to report this! And quit bugging me with this made-up shit!" He was obviously not in a good mood.

Before Kevin could say anything else, Fast Eddie added: "I'm toast. I'm gonna book and take an earlier bus and see if I can meet Meg at the Outpost. See if you can get the Mids analyst to bite, but I'm outa here."

Eddie got to the Outpost just as the last show was letting out. His early arrival to pick her up surprised Meg, but it was a pleasant surprise. She was always glad to see him. Seeing her improved his mood too. He grabbed a broom to help her clean up so that she could get the theater closed and head for home.

They walked home hand in hand, and Eddie's mood improved even more when he found out how much she'd spent shopping with Gabbie.

"Gabbie took me to this marvelous maternity store over in the East, and I got four complete outfits for just 30 West Marks," said Meg as she climbed up to sit on the kitchen counter so that she'd be tall enough for Eddie to kiss her without bending his neck double, and her having to stand on her tippy toes.

"That's great," said Eddie, who had had desolate visions of her spending three times as much. Her kiss made him forget that he should have been mad about her shopping in the East.

When he came up for air and his normal brain function resumed, the idea of Gabbie in the East steered his thoughts back to the conversation that he had had with Kevin earlier that evening about why Kevin was sure that Gabbie wasn't PRIMROSE.

"What do you think that Gabbie sees in Kevin?" asked Eddie, who had not found Kevin's arguments against Gabbie being PRIMROSE entirely convincing.

"Well, he's not unpleasant to look at, in a disheveled sort of way," said Meg coyly, pausing for just a second before adding, "but not as good looking as you, tall, dark and handsome." That got Meg another kiss, which was what she had been fishing for with the compliment.

"But you hear all these stories about fraudleins who just want to get to the land of the big PX. Do you think that she's just after a ticket to the States or goodies from the PX?" continued Eddie to Meg's dismay.

"I don't think so," said Meg sternly. She wanted to get back to their kissing game. "The only thing she talks about from the PX is chocolate sundaes from the snack bar, and the way she talks about him doesn't make it sound like she's interested in the size of his wallet."

"What's she interested in then?" asked Eddie, pressing his luck.

"Why the third degree, Eddie? What's going on? You doing this for Kevin?"

"No, Kevin would strangle me with a patch cord if he knew I was asking. It's just something that came up at work."

"Oh, so you think she's a spy?"

"No, it's not that at all," mumbled Eddie.

"Oh, come on, lover. Do you actually believe that we don't know what it is you guys do at 'the Site'? You're some kind of spooks, and somebody at work, probably Sergeant Laufflaecker, told you to interrogate me to see what I know about Gabbie. He probably thinks that she's Mata Hari."

"OK, you got me," said Eddie, glad to have been reminded that one of the reasons he loved Meg was that the grey matter in her head was good for something other than just keeping her ears apart. He was also relieved that he didn't have to admit this was his own idea.

"That's more like it, big guy. Here's what she told me. She'd had her fill of American pick-up artists just looking to get laid. She made an exception for Kevin because she didn't know he was an American at first. He fooled her with his great German. He's shy, polite and didn't make a pass at her on their first date. He kissed her hand and clicked his heels. She couldn't believe it. She said she felt like she was in an old movie. She says he's witty, intelligent, and he makes her laugh."

"He makes her laugh? Nobody laughs at Kevin's jokes," said Eddie, interrupting her.

"She does. And she says he's a good kisser," replied Meg. "But I can't imagine that he's a better kisser than you," she added, which got her another kiss to prove the point.

"And what's this thing about her mother not wanting her to date Kevin?" asked Eddie, trying to keep his interrogation on track.

"It's not just Kevin. Her mom's pissed at all Americans, because they killed Gabbie's father in Normandy on D-day," replied Meg. "I'd be pissed too, but I don't think that she can hold that against Kevin personally. He couldn't have been ten years old at the time."

Fast Eddie didn't know what to say. That didn't quite jibe with what Kevin had told him earlier.

"OK, lover. Turnabout is fair play. What do you think Kevin

sees in Gabbie?" said Meg, taking over the initiative in their conversation.

"She's not unpleasant to look at in a German sort of way, but not as gorgeous as you are, five-foot-two, eyes of blue," said Eddie, who could play the kissing game almost as well as Meg could, but that was neither here nor there, because the way they played it they both always won.

"Come on, Eddie, there must be something else."

"I don't know. She's got the same kind of parts that you have, and they're put together the same sort of way. Maybe it's her hairy legs."

"Is that a turn on? If it is, I can let the hair on my legs grow."

"Maybe for Kevin, but not for me."

"And?" said Meg, who was determined to get as much information for Gabbie as she had given.

"He doesn't talk about her much, but when he does it's clear that she's at the top of his list of priorities. She's ahead of sleeping at any rate. He closes down the Swing and then gets up early to meet her at oh-dark-early-eight-hundred hours for a date almost every day."

"Tell me something she doesn't know," said Meg, who would have made a good interrogator.

"He's taking a risk going out with her at all. If the brass find out about her, they'll yank his clearance, and he'll be in the Zone in a leg infantry unit before he could say 'good-bye'. And it's a big risk, considering how much he enjoys his job, and how miserable I think he'd be in the real army."

"I'm not sure that I can tell her that. She might break up with him just to keep him from losing his job," said Meg a little taken back by this revelation.

"Then just tell her that she's got his attention, and that he doesn't talk about her the way that some guys talk about their mooses, bragging about how much they're getting. In fact, he gets mad if you call her a moose."

"Is that a roundabout way of saying he respects her?"

"I guess so."

"Does he have a girlfriend in the States?" asked Meg, getting down to brass tacks.

"I've never heard him mention one, and she's the only picture in his room."

"Now we're getting somewhere," said Meg. "Ask him straight out about a stateside girlfriend when you see him tomorrow, and call me before I have to leave for work with his answer. Gabbie's coming over for coffee after you two leave for the Swing. I'm helping her practice her English. Kevin always speaks German with her, but she figures that being better at speaking English might just come in handy some day."

"The things I do for you."

"You mean the things you do for these," said Meg, giving him another kiss.

Circuit 53:   **10:44-10:49Z 02 June 1955**
             Reel 4783

FEMALE 1: MOSCOW, I'd like 6389 for my party, please. This is this is KARLSHORST, GERMANY.

FEMALE 2: Just a moment. It's ringing. Put your party on the line.

MALE 1: Finance. 6389.

MALE 2: Captain BRONSHTEIN, please.

MALE 1: VLADIMIR IL'YICH! How's life on the forward edge of Communism?

MALE 2: Taking this job was a great decision, LEV DAVIDOVICH. NADEZHDA is expecting, you know.

MALE 1: Congratulations!

MALE 2: She keeps telling me how great the OB-GYN clinic is here. Much better even than in MOSCOW, except for the Party elite clinic there, of course.

MALE 1: Nothing's too good for the defenders of Communism. What can I do for you today, VLADIMIR IL'YICH? More wallpaper for that source who only wants one-dollar bills?

MALE 2: No, something more personal, LEV DAVIDOVICH.

MALE 1: You want me to be the godfather?

MALE 2: No, NADEZHDA's brother and his wife will
        be the godparents, but I have something
        even better for you.
MALE 1: What could be better than being a
        godfather?
MALE 2: Being in charge of the SWALLOWS here. The
        position just became vacant.
MALE 1: Being in charge of the women who are the
        bait in the honey traps?! Who do I have to
        kill to get the job?
MALE 2: Nobody. Colonel BADUNOV is back in MOSCOW
        on emergency leave. His mother just died.
        And he hasn't had time to start thinking
        about replacements yet. The incumbent
        reminds me of you, and I'm sure that you're
        what Colonel BADUNOV wants. He just needs
        to learn that you're available.
MALE 1: Why is the position open?
MALE 2: The incumbent was promoted, and given a
        new assignment, running the SWALLOWS in the
        other GERMANY.
MALE 1: Oh, so there's an upward career path for
        this job too. Sounds better all the time.
        What do I have to do?
MALE 2: Colonel BADUNOV will be staying with
        General BESSTRASHNYJ. The colonel's wife is
        the general's sister. Just drop into the
        general's office and leave a note for the
        colonel, saying that you've got wind of the
        job and would like to be considered for it.
MALE 1: That's all?
MALE 2: Once he sees you, that'll be all.
MALE 1: You sound confident of my success.
MALE 2: I've seen the incumbent. He could be your
        brother.
MALE 1: I don't have a brother.
MALE 2: I know. But if you did, he'd be VALERIJ.
        Get upstairs and leave a note. The colonel
        prefers them handwritten.
MALE 1: Thanks! I'll do it right now. Bye.
MALE 2: Bye.
[Hang up]

14
The Worst 'L' Stand

The Mids analyst would not report Kevin's 20-Guards script either, so Kevin went back to his room and crashed. The alarm clock went off at 06:30 Local. He had an early date with Gabbie. They took the boat up from Wannsee to Tegel, and Kevin miscalculated how long it would take to get back. When he finally got in, Fast Eddie was waiting for him with a Weisse mit Schuss. It was even cold. The guy in the new "Worst 'L' Stand," as the morse and printer ops had christened it, knew what Americans wanted.

"I don't care what it is. From now on, even if you say Hannibal is coming across Potsdamer Platz on elephant-back, I'm going to report it," said Fast Eddie holding out the beer to Kevin. "We got in a report from the world this morning that said 20 Guards is in the Letzlingerheide Training Area doing river crossings. I don't know where it came from, but it didn't come out of here. I checked all the logs. My apologies!"

"Accepted," said Kevin with a pleased smile.

"Now tell me where it says '20 Guards'," said Fast Eddie. "I want to believe it, but it'll help, if I understand it."

"Vova wants to stay in Eberswalde next time, so that's where Volodya is now. Volodya is at Headquarters, so Headquarters is also in Eberswalde. 20-Guards Head Shed is in Eberswalde, so this is 20 Guards. They're out in the field playing 'war games' in 'the Letz.' That's short for Letzlingerheide. Back and forth across the river that Vova can't pronounce says that they are doing forced river crossings. It's as simple as $1 + 1 + 1 + 1 + 1 + 1 = 6$. It's not nuclear science. It's just looking in the working aids. Like I always say: 'reading is a prerequisite for success in this endeavor'."

"Your explanation's got too much math in it," said Eddie, whose B.A. was in English Literature.

"Does this mean you're going to report the Wurstelstand?" asked Kevin hopefully.

"What do you got against Herman the German?" responded Fast Eddie, lamenting the fact that no good deed ever goes unpunished. "He serves a good beer, and it's even cold."

"That he's probably working for my buddy Boris over in KGB ops," replied Kevin, oblivious to the irony in Fast Eddie's question.

"You have a buddy in KGB ops?" inquired a new American voice that incongruously came out of a British captain with SAS insignia and an enormous handlebar moustache. It was the Chief of Base in disguise, making an evening tour of his dominions.

"Yes, he tells me everything," said Kevin with a certain amount of pride, recognizing the new speaker's voice.

"Tell me more," said the Chief of Base in a tone that made Fast Eddie cringe.

Kevin told him about the Wurstelstand tape that Eddie couldn't report because it had been couriered out to the world, and about 20 Guards, and about Eddie's promise to report his stuff, even if it was Hannibal crossing Potsdamer Platz by elephant. Fast Eddie was just starting to wonder how long it would take them to cut his orders to a straight leg infantry unit on the DMZ in Korea, when the Chief of Base turned to him and said: "Yes, you do that. Even if he says that Hannibal's Alps come out onto Potsdamer Platz."

You could have knocked Fast Eddie over with a feather.

"Have a beer. You look a little pea-ked," said Kevin holding out his Weisse to Eddie.

"Where'd you get that?" asked the Chief of Base, a tone higher than the one that made Eddie cringe.

"From the Wurstelstand?" said Kevin, looking to Fast Eddie for confirmation.

Eddie nodded. He was wondering how he was going to explain

being reassigned to Fort Leavenworth to Meg, and how often she would be able to visit him.

"It's cold. The condensation's probably messed up the fingerprints," growled the Chief of Base, looking at the beer. "Go get a warm one. Tell him it's to take home and not to drink now. I want fingerprints and not condensation. Got it?"

Fast Eddie nodded again. He swallowed hard before speaking. "You'd better send Kevin. I don't think that I could say all that in German," said Eddie, recovering some of his composure.

"I'll bet he speaks English," said Kevin. "Should I get you a Weisse to drink now, to go with your take-out order, *captain*?" said Kevin to the Chief of Base.

The Chief of Base tilted his head and looked at Kevin for a minute. "Why not? Get us all one, plus that one to go." He gave Kevin a five-mark coin. "My treat," he said.

Kevin was gone about five minutes. He got back just as Fast Eddie was finishing a joke. "... Me too, let's all have a drink." The Chief of Base laughed.

"His English is pretty good, just like I thought," said Kevin, handing round the beers. "I got 'em all 'mit Schuss.' I hope you like 'em that way," he said to the Chief of Base. "Your take-out order is in the bag. If that bottle doesn't have usable fingerprints on it, I'll eat it."

"Thanks! I may hold you to that. Prosit!" said the Chief of Base, raising his bottle. He took a swig out of the bottle. "Take it easy on the beers, OK? I like my scripts and my reports straight with no chaser."

"Only on special occasions. Eddie was apologizing for not reporting 20 Guards," said Kevin.

"Let's keep it that way, the beer I mean, not the not reporting," said the Chief of Base.

"Fine by me," said Kevin. "Let's see if I can find you something else to report, Eddie," added Kevin, heading for the collection recorder.

"And you say that he's a 'straight arrow'?" said the Chief of Base to Eddie.

"Straight as they come, just a little short on people skills."

"I see. Good evening," said the Chief of Base and left just as abruptly as he had arrived.

Circuit 158:   13:47-13:50Z 02 June 1955
                   Reel 4802

MALE 1: WUENSDORF, this is NORA. Channel check.
MALE 2: NORA, this is WUENSDORF. I read you
        fivers.
MALE 1: KONSTANTINYCH, is that you?
MALE 2: ALEKSANYCH! I didn't know you were down
        in 8 Guards.
MALE 1: I got here just a week ago. It's a hell
        of a lot better than PINSK.
MALE 2: You can say that again. I didn't know
        that they had any position vacancies down
        there. How'd you get the assignment?
MALE 1: You might say that it was an affair of
        the heart.
MALE 2: You and LENA didn't break up, did you?
MALE 1: No, it's an accompanied tour and she's
        here. She thinks it's better than PINSK
        too. How's MARUSYA?
MALE 2: Great. She agrees with LENA. We'll have
        to try and get together. I don't get to
        travel, but there's always some reason or
        other to come back here to the main
        flagpole, consultations, training, a
        courier run . . .
MALE 1: That sounds like a great idea. I'll ask
        around and see what I can come up with. You
        always on this circuit?
MALE 2: No, not always, but just ask whoever
        answers if I'm around. If you don't
        recognize 'em, just tell them that you have
        a multiplexer problem and have to talk to
        me about it. That always works. But what
        about this affair of the heart that got you
        to NORA?
MALE 1: The guy who had this job went and got
        himself killed by his moose.
MALE 2: What?
MALE 1: He'd apparently been having a great time
        with this moose, but she thought that he

```
            was getting serious, and when she found out
            that he had a wife back in the [SOVIET]
            UNION, she baked him an applestrudel with
            rat poison in it.
MALE 2: Yeah, I see what you mean. An affair of
            the heart. Even without the threat of being
            poisoned it's better not to mess around
            with these local women. The security goons
            will have you shipped off to SIBERIA in
            nothing flat if they find out.
MALE 1: Yeah, tell me about it. That's why the
            requisition for this vacancy said that the
            candidate had to be married and that the
            spouse had to accompany him.
MALE 2: Glad you made it out here. Whoops! Here
            comes the lieutenant. Keep in touch. [in a
            much louder voice, obviously for the
            benefit of the lieutenant] NORA, this is
            WUENSDORF. I read you fivers.
[Hang up]
```

"Hey, Kevin," said Fast Eddie when he had finished reading the script. "You don't have a wife or a girlfriend back in the States, do you?"

"No, Eddie. Why you asking? ... You just getting round to reading that perschat about the guy whose moose poisoned his applestrudel? I must have done that an hour ago."

"Yeah."

"No, I don't think that I've got anything to worry about with Gabbie," said Kevin who didn't realize that he was being remotely interrogated for Gabbie's benefit by Meg.

"You're probably right, but I'll have something to worry about with Meg if I don't call her before she leaves for work," said Fast Eddie, who, in the rush of discovering that Kevin's 20-Guards script was real, had forgotten that he needed to ask Kevin about stateside girlfriends until he read the "Affair of the Heart" script. "I'll be back in a flash," he said, as he beat a hasty retreat from the scribe bay in the direction of the only phone with an outside line.

YOU ARE LEAVING THE AMERICAN
SECTOR AT THE CENTER OF THE BRIDGE

ВЫ ОСТАВЛЯЕТЕ АМЕРИКАНСКИЙ
СЕКТОР НА СЕРЕДИНЕ МОСТА

AU MILIEU DU PONT VOUS
QUITTEZ LE SECTEUR AMÉRICAIN

SIE VERLASSEN DEN AMERIKANISCHEN SEKTOR

15
A Side Trip to Potsdam

Even though Berlin never had exactly what Kevin would have called beach weather, Gabbie was pleased to be invited to the American beach on the Wannsee. This meant that she and Kevin spent a lot of time there, despite the liquid Berlin sunshine that non-Berliners prefer to call "rain" for some reason. If Kevin had waited for it to quit raining like some people at the Site did, he'd never have gotten to see Gabbie, and wouldn't have gone to the Wannsee at all.

The trip to the Wannsee was a long one, if you went by bus. You had to change buses twice, but all the busses had to be on time, which was an iffy proposition. If one bus was late, that was a guaranteed 15-minute wait; 30, if your luck was bad and the second bus was early.

The above-ground part of the Berlin rail system, called the S-Bahn, had a much faster connection to the Wannsee. The S-7 line was a straight shot with no changes. Therefore, the Army's prohibition on using the S-Bahn notwithstanding, Kevin and Gabbie occasionally went by train when they were in a hurry to get to the beach.

The reason that U.S. Forces personnel were forbidden to take the S-Bahn was that some of the lines crossed the Sector border. Passengers who missed their stop could end up on the Russian side of the border. Kevin and Gabbie figured that this would never happen to them, so they chanced it. The Steglitz to Wannsee run went right as rain the first three times, but the fourth time it went wrong.

Kevin and Gabbie were talking about what they were going to do that evening. It was a Saturday and Kevin thought that he could get an early-in after he'd gotten all the tapes done. The last two Saturdays before had been pretty slow, and Fast Eddie had taken an early-in on the last one. Now it was Kevin's turn. He was sure that he would be off by 18:00 Local, which left them plenty of time to catch a show in town, or maybe a movie at the theater where Meg worked. The Outpost was showing *Three Coins in a Fountain* with Dorothy McGuire, Jean Peters and Maggie McNamara.

Kevin and Gabbie were looking at each other, and not out the window as they talked. Looking into one another's eyes is great for lovers, but not for people who can't afford to miss their S-Bahn stop. Their train stopped at Wannsee and left for Potsdam, but Kevin and Gabbie didn't notice. When they reached a decision on the movie, Kevin looked out the window of the train the see where they were. He had a sudden sinking feeling, because he hadn't seen this scenery on any of the other three trips.

Wannsee was the last stop in the American Sector, and two weeks ago Bama had missed the Wannsee stop. When he got off in Potsdam, Bama walked right into the arms of a Vopo patrol that spotted him for an Ami right away. Bama's clothes were what gave him away. He was wearing things that no German could get hold of. It also didn't help that Bama's German was limited to "zwei Bier" and "nix verstehen." Bama spent a tense day as a guest of the Russians, before he was handed over to the U.S. Military Liaison Mission to the Commander Group of Soviet Forces, Germany.

There had been a really big flap at the Site when Bama turned up in Russian hands. Kevin had done the script of Badunov and Besstrashnyj talking about an American corporal named Suedmann who had been taken into custody at the Potsdam S-Bahn station. Kevin went ballistic in his best "you've got to listen to this" fashion, waking up Fast Eddie in the process. Eddie woke up the Chief of Base, who swore like a sailor, even though he had never been in the Navy.

"He'll regret this till the day he dies," said the Chief of Base, "if he should live so long."

The Chief of Base woke up the American Military Commandant of Berlin, who was livid with rage, and threatened to put the "kibosh" on all those "make-believe soldiers" working for the Chief of Base, who thought that rules weren't made for them. The Commandant then woke up the Chief of USMLM, who commiserated with the Commandant about the poor state of discipline in what were supposedly "intelligent" units.

The Chief of USMLM went round to the Russian Commandant of Potsdam, who was getting started on what would be a wonderful hangover on Sunday. The Chief of USMLM inquired politely if the Commandant had seen an American soldier. One had gone missing that afternoon. After about five toasts to Soviet-American Friendship, Stalin, Roosevelt, Churchill and the Commandant's wife, drunk with Stolichnaya vodka supplied by the Chief of USMLM—the export kind that ordinary Russian officers like the Commandant never got to see—the Commandant admitted that he did indeed have an American soldier in custody. The Chief of USMLM politely requested Bama's immediate release, and put another bottle of export Stolichnaya on the table to seal the bargain. The Commandant asked for four. The Chief of USMLM countered with three. It would have been impolite not to haggle.

Two more bottles of vodka appeared on the Commandant's desk as if by magic. A bruised and battered Bama was turned over to the Chief of USMLM, who in turn conveyed Bama to the Chief of Base, who made Bama wish that he had stayed with the Russians. Bama was on the eight-o'clock flight out of Berlin the next morning, headed for the Zone and points west. Nobody knew where he had gone. In fact, nobody ever heard from him again, which is probably pretty much the same thing that would have happened to him, if Kevin had not scribed the tape of Badunov asking Besstrashnyj what to do with him.

The only thing that saved Bama from experiencing an extended period of Soviet hospitality was that Besstrashnyj couldn't make a decision on the question of what to do with Bama on his own. Besstrashnyj had to seek instructions from the Politburo. The reaction to Kevin's script had been faster than the Politburo's answer to Besstrashnyj's question. Kevin had done the follow-up call, which came in 13 minutes after Bama had been released to the Chief of USMLM. General Besstrashnyj told Colonel Badunov to have Bama taken to the KGB/Stasi prison in Bautzen for interrogation. From there the prisoner was to be shipped to KGB central at Lubyanka prison in Moscow. Since Bama wasn't available to be shipped to Moscow, the Commandant of Potsdam was reassigned to Sverdlosvk.

Kevin's sinking feeling had been generated by the instant replay of the incident with Bama that flashed before his eyes. This was followed by the unsettling certainty that:: one, no one would be on Swings to transcribe the tape of Badunov and Besstrashnyj's conversation about him, which meant that there was nil chance of a rescue by the Chief of USMLM; and two, Besstrashnyj would probably just use the decision he got for Bama rather than asking the Politburo what to do again, so number one didn't count. For a moment, Kevin had a wonderfully cheery vision of himself improving his command of Russian prison-camp slang somewhere in Siberia for the next several years.

"I think that there may be a problem when we get to Potsdam," said Kevin to Gabbie trying to sound calm.

"Why? We'll just walk over to the other platform and take the next train back," replied Gabbie.

"It might not be quite that easy," said Kevin, pretending to be confident. "If the Vopos check my documents, there could be a big problem. I'm not supposed to be on this train. Even if they let me go, they might report it, and that would be a ticket out of Berlin for me."

That was an alarming enough thought for Gabbie to take Kevin seriously.

"I have a plan, " said Kevin, who had been feverishly turning over scenarios in his mind. "When we get off the train, if there are any Vopos around, pretend you're mad at me. Hit me as hard as you can, and scream that I'm a drunken, no-good, son of a bitch, and that you're going right back with the next train. Then you head straight for the other platform, and I'll come along behind you grovelling, asking your forgiveness in my best drunken Berlinerisch. I figure I can sound convincing, if I don't say more than 'But, sweetheart!'"

Gabbie agreed that Kevin's drunken slur sounded sufficiently German to even fool her mother who always complained bitterly about Kevin's American accent.

The train stopped at S-Bahn station Griebnitzsee, the first station in the East. Kevin and Gabbie got out, and looked around. There were no Vopos to be seen. The two of them headed for the stairs that led down to the passage under the tracks to the Exit and the other platform back to Berlin. Kevin and Gabbie were about halfway down the stairs when a pair of Vopos emerged from the passage under the tracks and started up the stairs.

Gabbie took a swing at Kevin and hit him so hard that he fell down.

"Du besoffener, nutzloser Schuft. Ich gehe gleich zurück, ohne dich!" she screamed and ran down the stairs past the Vopos and on to the other platform.

Kevin hadn't been expecting to be hit that hard, but he staggered to his feet, and wobbled hurriedly behind her, rubbing his eye, mumbling: "Aber, Schatzilein!"

The younger Vopo asked his older partner if it would be wise to intervene, but the senior man, who had been with the force since the end of the war, and had seen more than his share of this sort of thing said "Why bother? He's no danger to her. She's more of a danger to him. Did you see that smack she pasted on him? And she'll get him off the street and sobered up sooner than we could, and with a lot less paperwork. Besides, remember that last drunk that we picked up? The one that threw up all over you."

"Yes, I get the point," said the younger Vopo, rubbing the front of his uniform blouse, as if trying to wipe off a stain.

The Vopos continued up the stairs to the south-bound platform, and walked slowly down to the end, sizing up the passengers there who were waiting for the next train. The older Vopo stopped to say "Hello" to Ilse and her granddaughter were on their way to the open air market in Potsdam. Ilse and Ilselein were almost a regular fixture on this beat on Saturday.

Kevin and Gabbie walked under the tracks and climbed back up the stairs to the north-bound platform. Gabbie continued to pretend to ignore Kevin as she walked down the platform away from the stairs. Kevin bumbled along behind Gabbie, rubbing his rapidly blackening eye. Gabbie stopped about midway down, and turned to glare at Kevin. When she saw what had happened to his eye, however, she went over to give him a hug instead.

This was the point at which the Vopos reached the far end of the platform and turned around to walk back to the stairs. It was an established routine: stairs to the end of the platform and back, under the tracks, followed by the same thing on the other side for more times than the younger Vopo cared to count. The older Vopo noticed that Kevin and Gabbie were a couple again. He was pleased that his assessment had been correct. "The drunk" wasn't a danger to the young lady.

The more he looked, however, the more the older Vopo felt like there was something wrong with the picture he was seeing, only he couldn't quite put his finger on it. He looked away to say "Hello" to Ilse and her granddaughter once again. When he looked back at Kevin and Gabbie, it hit him like a Saturday-night drunk in a bar fight. Kevin was an American. He could see it from the way Kevin was dressed. No German could be dressed like that.

"You there!" yelled the senior Vopo to Kevin. "I want to see your papers!"

Kevin held up his hand to his ear, pretending that he could not hear the Vopo.

"He's an American," said the senior Vopo to his partner. Kevin heard that.

"Run down the stairs and over to the next platform to keep them from getting away via the exit," continued the senior Vopo. "I'm going across the tracks."

The young Vopo took off for the stairs, and the older one started back up the platform to where he knew there were steps that would let him climb down onto the tracks and back up on the other side. Before the senior Vopo could get there, however, the screeching of metal wheels on the steel rails announced the arrival of the train from Wannsee. The older Vopo decided not to chance trying to beat the train across the tracks. His partner would get the American and his girlfriend via the stairs.

Kevin was trying to think of another cunning plan when the train going back to Wannsee from Potsdam announced its arrival with a toot on the horn as a greeting to the south-bound train on the opposite track.

"We've still got a chance," said Kevin to Gabbie. "Come on!"

The train pulled to a stop, with Kevin and Gabbie running towards the front of it so as to put as much distance as possible between them and the young Vopo who would be climbing the stairs at any moment. The door just in front of them slid open, and a young man in a gray suit got out. Kevin and Gabbie shot inside, and Kevin slid the door shut.

"No sense in telling that Vopo which car we got on," said Kevin.

The first of the crowd getting off the train reached the young Vopo when he was about halfway up the stairs. The young Vopo was new to the game, but he had sense enough to know that Kevin and Gabbie might try to hide themselves in plain sight by becoming a part of the crowd getting off the train. He stopped, scanning the sea of faces coming down the stairs.

The last of the flood of passengers passed by the young Vopo on the steps. It was the young man in the gray suit who had opened the door for Kevin and Gabbie. The man in the gray suit passed the young Vopo without a second glance, even though he was carrying a thousand West Marks that could have been a big problem for him, if the young Vopo had stopped him.

There was nobody left on the steps between the young Vopo and the platform. He charged up the steps as fast as he could, but he was only just in time to see the train pulling out of the station.

"Boy, can you hit hard," said Kevin, once the train was on its way back to the Wannsee station and he had started breathing again. "I'm never going to be able to live this down at the Site. They're not going to believe that I ran into a door. You're not going to tell Meg about this, are you?"

This was a logical question, because Meg and Gabbie got on thick as thieves. If Gabbie told Meg, Meg would tell Eddie, and Eddie would tell everybody. It would be in the "Pass-on Book" by the end of the Swing.

"I'll think about it," said Gabbie, giving Kevin's eye a kiss.

"You can do that again," said Kevin. "It makes it feel a *lot* better."

They didn't miss their stop at Wannsee this time, and Gabbie didn't tell Meg when they met Eddie and Meg for lunch at the beach snackbar.

"The train stopped suddenly," she said, "and he hit his head against the wall, trying to keep me from falling, the poor dear."

That, however, didn't stop an anonymous contributor on Swings from writing "Gabbie gave Kevin a black eye" in the *Passion Book*.

**Circuit 53:   11:13-11:16Z 06 June 1955
               Reel 4899**

FEMALE 1: KARLSHORST, can I have 5298 for my
    party, please? This is MOSCOW.
FEMALE 2: I'll connect you. It's ringing.
MALE 1: 5298. Finance.
FEMALE 2: Put your party on the line.
MALE 2: Hello?
MALE 1: 5298. Finance.
MALE 2: Is that you, VLADIMIR IL'YICH?
MALE 1: LEV DAVIDOVICH! It's good to hear from
    you, or did I do something wrong again?
MALE 2: It's not you exactly. It's this voucher
    for BIRCH. Most of the receipts are in
    German, and you didn't have them
    translated, which means the new boss can't
    make heads or tails of them.
MALE 1: I thought that the figures would speak
    for themselves. So many West Marks and so
    many East Marks. It's pretty
    straightforward.
MALE 2: Colonel HONEST TO A FAULT [Transcriber
    COMMENT: his real name is CHESTNIAKOV,
    which means 'honest'. See reel 4381.] wants
    to know exactly what you are spending the
    people's money on.
MALE 1: What do you mean? It's for an op against
    the Americans.
MALE 2: No, he wants to know what you bought to
    support this op against the Americans. It
    has to seem logical to him.
MALE 1: BESPOLEZNYJ never wanted this kind of
    detail.

MALE 2: That was BESPOLEZNYJ. He's the one they
fooled with the KROPOTKIN constant,
remember. This is CHESTNIAKOV, and he is
the squeaky kind of clean honest that
drives everyone nuts. Sometimes, I hate to
say it, I even miss BESPOLEZNYJ.

MALE 1: I never thought that I'd hear you say
that. It must really be bad.

MALE 2: You have no idea. So could you get me
those translations? It would make my life a
lot easier.

MALE 1: I'm not sure that they will. We outfitted
a whole snackbar to put out in front of
SPOTLIGHT, and about a quarter of the
receipts are for beer and Schnaps.

MALE 2: Just label them 'consumables,' and he
won't bat an eye. It'll just blend right in
with the receipts that we get for
'consumables' from embassy receptions.
PAVEL, you remember him, used to work with
his honor when he was a major, and warned
everybody what to put down on booze
receipts so that we could avoid a flap.

MALE 1: Thanks for the tip. I sent you all the
original receipts, so I'll just have to
make a list of amounts with a 'translation'
of what it was for. Will that do for this
one?

MALE 2: Yes, I think I can make that work. But
the next time, please include an 'adapted'
translation.

MALE 1: I'm going to have to put in a request for
a full-time translator.

MALE 2: If that's what it takes. And while I've
got you on the phone, let me tell you about
my interview with your Colonel BADUNOV.

MALE 1: Yes, do tell.

MALE 2: It was the strangest thing I've ever
seen.

MALE 1: I can imagine. My interview with him was
weird too. He asked all kinds of questions
to see how NADEZHDA and I get along.

MALE 2: That was a phone interview. I met him in person. He looked me up and down. Asked if I was married. Then said that he and his wife were dining at the Field-Officers' Mess in the Kremlin that evening, and they would expect me to join them for dinner at 19:00 Local and to bring a date.

MALE 1: I don't suppose that you had much trouble finding a date.

MALE 2: It was 17:30 Local when he said it!

MALE 1: That could have been a problem.

MALE 2: I wanted somebody very presentable. TATYANA was busy, so I had to settle for LYUBA.

MALE 1: You had to settle!

MALE 2: TATYANA would have impressed the colonel more.

MALE 1: Perhaps you're right. What happened?

MALE 2: The man watched me like a hawk the whole evening, and hardly asked a question. It was just chitchat about the weather and soccer, and where I got the flowers for LYUBA.

MALE 1: Hey, that's right. He asked what kind of flowers NADEZHDA likes.

MALE 2: I think that he was just watching how I behaved around LYUBA and his wife. Once I figured that out, I just turned on the charm. I had compliments flowing like water from a spring. I leapt up every time one of the ladies got up and helped them with their chairs. I held their coats for them. I think the colonel's wife was impressed. He apparently does not do that for her.

MALE 1: Sounds like you scored lots of points.

MALE 2: More than just points, I got the job. He says that I can expect my orders by the end of the month.

MALE 1: Great. Let me know when you're coming and I'll meet you at the station myself.

MALE 2: And it's all thanks to you. I owe you one for getting me this job.

MALE 1: What goes around, comes around.
MALE 2: That may be, but I'll see if I can make
    it come around a bit sooner in your case.
MALE 1: Thanks.
MALE 2: And see to it, comrade captain, that you
    get us the translations of those receipts.
MALE 1: The boss just come in?
MALE 2: Yes, comrade captain.
MALE 1: Well, tell him 'hi' for me. Let me know
    when you're coming.
MALE 2: I serve the Soviet Union.
MALE 1: Sure you do. Bye.
[Hang up]

The Outpost Theater

16
The Average Channel Number

"Damn army statistics," said Blackie out loud to no one in particular, in the hope of finding some fish or other to take his bait.

"What statistics?" asked Corporal Neumann, who should have known better, but didn't.

"The average channel number for the twenty-two-hundred-Zulu hour," replied Blackie, unable to believe that it was Corporal Neumann who had taken the bait. *Doesn't this guy ever learn?* said Blackie to himself.

"What good is that?" asked Neumann, displaying some indication of common sense.

"Beats me," replied Blackie. "I guess that somebody back in the world doesn't have anything better to do than dream up reports for us to send in so that he can fill up file folders with 'em."

"What a waste of the taxpayers' money," intoned Neumann, who should have seen himself as a taxpayer, but didn't. His army pay was just barely enough to pay taxes on. His mother, on the other hand, paid *taxes*, and she said "What a waste of the taxpayers' money" all the time. Feeling a sudden, uncontrollable urge to do something to help his mother, Corporal Neumann said: "We should report this gross violation of the trust of the nation and waste of our valuable, but limited resources."

Blackie started to feel a bit uncomfortable about reporting the average channel number to anyone, but before he could do anything, Corporal Neumann turned on his heel and left. Blackie went back to his position, where he could comfortably pretend that he was awake until it got to be shift change. He had barely fallen asleep, when Lieutenant Sheerluck came back into the bay with Corporal Neumann.

"Why haven't I ever heard of the Average Channel Number Report before, Schwartz?" asked Lieutenant Sheerluck in his best Officer Candidate School voice, which could be heard all over the bay. That caused a number of ears to perk up. They wanted to see how Blackie got out of this one.

Blackie blinked awake and got his mouth in gear with a speed that surprised most of those in the bay. It didn't, however, surprise Sergeant Galworthy, who was out like a light with his head in the keywell of his military typewriter, known to one and all as a "mill." He was oblivious to everything except his circuit.

"It's a new requirement, sir," said Blackie.

"I should have been informed," said Lieutenant Sheerluck in a tone that sounded like he had been personally insulted.

"Undoubtedly, sir" said Blackie betraying a hesitation that showed he was not entirely awake yet.

"Well, let's have it!" commanded Lieutenant Sheerluck.

"Have what, sir?" asked Blackie, who still had not comprehended the speed with which disaster was about to catch up with him.

"The twenty-two-hundred-Zulu average channel number," said Lieutenant Sheerluck, as if he was talking to some imbecile, who was deaf to boot.

"56," said Blackie, recovering handily.

"Thank you," said Lieutenant Sheerluck curtly, incorrectly certain that Blackie should have been rejected at the recruiting station as non compos mentis.

"Now what can you do with that piece of information?" asked Lieutenant Sheerluck of Corporal Neumann, who had no idea what it was good for.

"It provides the hour-to-hour Delta of the collection Gamma, as a part of a manpower survey, which is used to adjust equipment and staffing levels," said Fast Eddie in a stage whisper that only Blackie and Lieutenant Sheerluck could hear.

He had come in quietly behind Corporal Neumann and Lieutenant Sheerluck and been following the situation with rapt attention. His keen analytic mind had alerted him to the possibility of something interesting going on when he saw Corporal Neumann go out through the scribe bay with a face as clouded as a week of Berlin weather, only to come back through seven minutes later with Lieutenant Sheerluck in tow. Kevin could be entertaining on a Swing when he came back to earth from whatever ethereal plane he went to when he listened to tapes, but in between times, when he was off in outer space, talking to the people on the tape, Fast Eddie had to provide his own entertainment.

His penetrating analytic assessment was that this was a unique chance to blackmail Blackie, by getting him out of the hole that he had dug himself into with this newk joke. You never knew when you might need something from Blackie.

"Really," said Lieutenant Sheerluck, who had no idea what any of that meant. "And 56?"

"For the twenty-two-hundred hour, that is within parameters, and no adjustment is indicated," said Eddie, as if he knew what he was talking about.

"You should brief your men better, sergeant," said Lieutenant Sheerluck. "If this man had been able to tell Corporal Neumann what the average channel number was used for, none of this would have happened."

"Need to know, sir," came the coup de grace.

"Oh, I didn't realize. I hope that I haven't let the cat out of the bag, or something," said Lieutenant Sheerluck timidly.

"No, sir. I think that we have contained any possible damage."

"Carry on, sergeant," said Lieutenant Sheerluck apologetically.

"And as for you, corporal. That information's on a strict need-to-know basis. I'm not surprised that you didn't know," said Lieutenant Sheerluck in a tone that left no doubt that he was not pleased at being placed in this indelicate position. With that, he left as suddenly as he had come.

Corporal Neumann had the sneaking suspicion that something was rotten in Denmark, but he could not quite put his finger on what it was, and went back to the copy of *Hamlet* that he had been reading when Blackie's remark about statistics caught his ear.

Fast Eddie bent over to Blackie, and whispered in his ear. "You know you owe me one, Blackie. If Sheerluck had figured out that you were playing a newk joke on him, your dish-pan hands would have been all black from weeks of pulling burn right after KP. Corporal Neumann's one thing, but officers are another. I'll send you a bill."

Blackie only said: "Thanks ... I think"

The next time that Corporal Neumann walked through the scribe bay, Fast Eddie flagged him down.

"You know what Kevin always says: 'Reading is a prerequisite for success in this endeavor.' I think that you ought to read these," said Fast Eddie, pointing to four pieces of goldenrod six-ply on the other side of his desk.

The four pieces of paper were a series of scripts that Kevin had done earlier in the evening. They were the kind of 'fun' things that Kevin loved to turn out, but which the Fort hated to see, because they thought that they were a waste of time. Blackie, on the other hand, obviously did not share their analytic opinion of this type of script. He always came over to see if Kevin had turned out any "good ones," even though he was firmly convinced that Kevin was making all this stuff up.

He wouldn't say that to Kevin's face though. He knew when it was best to keep his mouth shut. The last person who accused Kevin of making stuff up woke up with a classified stamp emblazoned across his forehead and couldn't leave Operations until he had gotten it off. The Chief of Base would not have taken very kindly to him walking around with the words SECRET ▬▬▬▬ prominently displayed on his forehead in red ink. The first place he went when he left the Operations was the hospital, because he had taken off so much of the skin getting the stamp off, that his forehead was one big bleeding abrasion and he needed more medical attention than was available in the Site first aid kit.

"Blackie read them, you know," said Eddie.

Corporal Neumann picked up the scripts and started to read.

**Circuit 173:   16:13-16:14Z 07 June 1955
Reel 5720**

MALE 1: MOSCOW Center! This is the 253rd
    Independent Radiotechnical Regiment,
    MERSEBURG. I have a report for the duty
    officer, Captain BENDER, OSTAP BENDER.
MALE 2: MERSEBURG, I'll connect you. Who is
    calling, please?
MALE 1: This is Lieutenant junior grade NOVACHOK.
MALE 2: Just a moment, please, lieutenant.
MALE 1: Thank you. I'll hold.
MALE 3: Captain BENDER speaking.
MALE 1: Comrade captain, I have the average
    frequency report for the nineteen-hundred
    MOSCOW hour.
MALE 3: Very good, comrade lieutenant. And what
    is it?
MALE 1: 46.38 megahertz.
MALE 3: Your report is much too late, comrade
    lieutenant. It is almost a quarter past the
    hour. Does it take you that long to collect
    the data and calculate the result?! All the
    other Sites had their reports in at five
    minutes past.
MALE 1: I am sorry, comrade captain. This is my
    first time as a shift commander. I will try
    to do better with the subsequent reports.
MALE 3: See that you do. Your career hangs in the
    balance, comrade lieutenant.
MALE 1: I serve the Soviet Union
[hang up]

**Circuit 173:   17:10-17:11Z 07 June 1955
Reel 5721**

MALE 1: MOSCOW Center! This is the 253rd
    Independent Radiotechnical Regiment,
    MERSEBURG. I have a report for the duty
    officer, Captain BENDER, OSTAP BENDER.
MALE 2: Lieutenant NOVACHOK?

MALE 1: Yes.

MALE 2: Just a moment, please, I'll connect you, lieutenant.

MALE 1: Thank you. I'll hold.

MALE 3: Captain BENDER speaking.

MALE 1: Comrade captain, I have the average frequency report for the twenty-hundred MOSCOW hour.

MALE 3: Very good, comrade lieutenant. Pass your report.

MALE 1: 47.28 megahertz.

MALE 3: You've improved, comrade lieutenant, but you're still too late. It is ten past the hour. All the other Sites had their reports in at five minutes past. You'll have to do better.

MALE 1: I do my best to serve the Soviet Union, comrade captain.

MALE 3: Your best is not yet good enough.

MALE 1: Yes, sir.

[hang up]

**Circuit 173:　　18:04-18:06Z 07 June 1955
　　　　　　　　Reel 5722**

MALE 1: MOSCOW Center! This is the 253rd Independent Radiotechnical Regiment, MERSEBURG. I have a report for the duty officer, Captain BENDER.

MALE 2: Lieutenant NOVACHOK?

MALE 1: Yes.

MALE 2: Comrade lieutenant, have you ever read The Twelve Chairs by Ilf and Petrov?

MALE 1: Yes, I have, but this line is not supposed to be used for personal chitchat.

MALE 2: Just as you say, comrade lieutenant, I'll connect you, with Captain OSTAP BENDER.

MALE 1: Say, that is a strange coincidence. Your captain having the same name as the character in The Twelve Chairs.

MALE 2: Yes, it is, comrade lieutenant. Our

captain is quite a character. I'll connect
you.

[Transcriber comment: OSTAP BENDER is the
consummate conman of Russian literature, and the
hero of The Twelve Chairs. The closest equivalent
in English would be P.T. Barnum with his infamous
"There's a sucker born every minute."]

MALE 3: Captain BENDER speaking.

MALE 1: Comrade captain, I have the average
frequency report for the twenty-one-hundred
MOSCOW hour.

MALE 3: Very good, comrade lieutenant. Let's have
it.

MALE 1: 45.63 megahertz.

MALE 3: You have improved, comrade lieutenant.
Right on time. I can see that you catch on
to things quickly, but you have not
entirely mastered this procedure.

MALE 1: I do my best to serve the Soviet Union,
comrade captain.

MALE 3: Your best is still not good enough.

MALE 1: Yes, sir. … Comrade captain, may I ask a
question?

MALE 3: But of course, comrade lieutenant.

MALE 1: I don't recall the function of the
average frequency report from my class work
at the technical training school, and my
notes have not yet arrived in the
classified shipment that I sent myself.
Could you, perhaps, explain it to me?
Knowing what it is used for will help me to
motivate myself so that I can better serve
the Soviet Union.

MALE 3: But, of course, comrade lieutenant. It
provides the hour-to-hour Delta of the
collection Gamma, as a part of a manpower
survey, which is used to adjust equipment
and staffing levels.

MALE 1: Thank you very much, comrade captain.

MALE 3: Don't mention it.

[hang up]

Circuit 173:   18:08-18:09Z 07 June 1955
Reel 5723

MALE 1: MOSCOW Center! This is Lieutenant
    NOVACHOK of the 253rd Independent
    Radiotechnical Regiment. Are you the
    operator I spoke to just a moment ago who
    asked me if I had read The Twelve Chairs by
    Ilf and Petrov?
MALE 2: Yes, comrade lieutenant.
MALE 1: It is a strange coincidence that your
    captain has the same name as the character
    in The Twelve Chairs.
MALE 2: Yes it is.
MALE 1: Should I draw some conclusion from this
    fact?
MALE 2: That would be wise, comrade lieutenant.
MALE 1: This is some sort of practical joke,
    isn't it?
MALE 2: You're not as dumb as you sound,
    lieutenant. Shall I connect you to Captain
    BENDER.
MALE 1: Yes.
MALE 3: Captain BENDER speaking.
MALE 1: And when do I get the keys to the safe
    where the money is kept?
[Transcriber comment: this is a phrase that Ostap
Bender repeats a lot in The Twelve Chairs.]
MALE 3: You catch on quick, lieutenant. Your
    classmate, Lieutenant IVANOV at the 250th
    in STENDAL, reported through the zero-two-
    hundred MOSCOW hour before he caught on.
    Welcome to the fraternity.
MALE 1: Thank you … I think.
[hang up]

Corporal Neumann gave the scripts back to Eddie. "Thank
you," he said.

"I wouldn't tell Lieutenant Sheerluck about this, if I were you," said Eddie.

"No, I don't think that I will," said the corporal.

"I wouldn't do anything precipitous to Blackie," cautioned Fast Eddie. "He's got a lot more between his ears than most people give him credit for, and he can be very vindictive."

"I'll think about it," said Corporal Neumann, who then headed off to the Worst L Stand for a glass of milk.

17
Burn Detail

All the hard-copy collection at the Site was done on six-ply fan-fold paper, and the Site used an enormous amount of it. The paper was connected in long strips of 500 sheets, all folded up like a Japanese fan so that it would fit in a box. The boxes were set on the floor, and the paper snaked up out of them and through mills and teletypewriters that covered the paper with letters and numbers and words.

The teletypes ran non-stop, and consumed five reams of paper a shift. The morse operators—better known as "ditties"—pushed three reams a shift through their mills. The scribe shop—where the "Marys" worked—only used three reams a week. Before all this paper could be distributed to the six recipients whose layers of the six-ply pie were identified by a different color of paper, the carbon paper had to be pulled out of the strip and disposed of.

The local analysts who would try to make something of the letters, numbers and words on the paper, as well as the off-site recipients of the colored paper didn't want to have to deal with the carbon paper. It was dirty, nasty stuff. It, therefore, fell upon the people who filled the paper with letters and numbers and words to strip the carbon paper out of each set of six, and stuff it in burn bags.

Since it was possible—but messy—to read everything that was on the colored paper if you had access to the carbon paper, the carbon paper had to be destroyed to keep the Russians and other people without a "need to know" from learning what the Site was up to. Lieutenant Sheerluck, however, did not believe that anyone would be willing to get that messy just to learn what the Site was up to, but as if to prove him wrong, from time to time the Chief of Base brought some Russian carbon paper by for Kevin to read. All the Chief of Base's Russian speakers were in the field collecting stuff like that and didn't have time to read it for him.

There was some justice in the world, however, because the local analysts, at least the ones who were enlisted men, were required to help destroy all those reams of carbon paper that the Site's collection generated, not to mention all the other waste paper that was produced by the headshed and its administrative sections, and the miles of paper tape and the chad that the teletypes turned out in addition to the six-ply. Burning all this stuff was one of those little duties as assigned, that, like KP and latrine detail, could ruin the crease in your uniform, not to mention the smile on your face, when you had them.

Initially, "the burn," as folks called the classified destruction detail, was carried out in a small shed behind the warehouse. The shed was intended to keep the Vopos in the tower across the Shoss from seeing what it was that was going on, and the bags of classified trash from getting wet in the rain that was a fact of life in Berlin. That changed after Blackie let the burn get away from him one weekend and burned the shed to the ground, almost taking the warehouse with it. After the burn-shed fire, the burn site was a concrete pad with roofless brick walls 100 meters away from the warehouse. The bags of classified trash never got that wet from the rain that they wouldn't burn with all that carbon paper in them.

The burn wasn't inherently dangerous. The classified trash had been destroyed safely in the shed for almost three weeks before Blackie burned it down. The problem that led to the fire was the way that Blackie did the burn that Saturday. According to the Standard Operating Procedures that regulated the burn, only three bags at a time were supposed to be put in the hopper. Blackie was in a hurry and, in violation of the SOP, stuffed the thing full. Since it was a Saturday, he could go into town as soon as he was through with the burn. He didn't want to waste any time, because he was missing prime black-market hours at Potsdamer Platz, the proceeds of which he expected to finance a hot date with his moose.

The reason that the limit on the number of bags in the hopper was set at three was that the carbon paper that made up the bulk of the burn went up in a flash. It burned so fast that it almost exploded. It was this very feature of carbon paper that made it popular on Swings and Mids—especially on Mids—as the primary component of what its perpetrators called a "harmless" practical joke. Victims of this practice had another view of it. It was the ditties' version of a "kick me!" sign taped to somebody's back in high school. Blackie should have been very aware of this characteristic of burning carbon paper, as he was—more often than not—the one behind what was lovingly known as "giving someone a carbon-paper tail."

The unsuspecting victim would be approached stealthily by the practical joker with "a tail" of still connected fan-fold carbon paper, three or four sheets long, its length depending on how tall the victim was. The tail was attached to the victim in the same way as a "Kick me!" sign: with a small piece of tape and a pat on the back. The tail having been attached, it was set alight with a match. The tricky part of this operation from the practical joker's point of view was to stand well clear of the tail, because as soon as the match was applied, there would be a hot, bright flash as the whole of the tail went up in flames almost all at once. The heat and the flash were startling, but the fire was already out by the time the victim was aware of it.

So, when Blackie set fire to the hopper that Saturday morning, he should have expected an explosion, sort of like a super carbon-paper tail, but he didn't. All he cared about was beating feet as fast as possible. The roof was on fire before Blackie could say "fire extinguisher," let alone grab one of the five on the back wall. He and Detroit were lucky to make it out of the shed alive. By the time the fire department arrived, there was nothing for them to do. The shed was just a pile of glowing embers. The duty operators from inside the warehouse had broken out the fire hoses and wisely directed them at the nearest warehouse wall, while letting the shed burn to the ground. "That's the only thing that saved the warehouse," said the chief of the responding fire truck.

When the firemen left, Blackie signed the destruction log, certifying that he had burned all the classified trash that day, and left for town as if nothing had happened. The SOP didn't say that burning down the burn shed required a report to the powers that be. Blackie had a great weekend and made a killing on the black market. His 'hot' date was "as hot as a carbon-paper tail," he said, but the straight month of KP after that weekend kept him too tired to warm up again to his moose until July.

Circuit 53:   15:03-15:07Z 17 June 1955
**   Reel 7859**

FEMALE 1: MOSCOW? This is the KARLSHORST
       operator, GERMANY. Please give me 5467 for
       my party.
FEMALE 2: Connecting … It's ringing.
MALE 1: 5467.
FEMALE 2: Your party's on the line, KARLSHORST.
       Go ahead, please.
MALE 2: EVGENIJ! It's BORIS from GERMANY.
MALE 1: BORIS! How good of you to call. I was
       just thinking of calling you myself. OLGA
       has been after me to get her some more
       American coffee.
MALE 2: Consider it done, EVGENIJ. It will be in
       Tuesday's pouch.
MALE 1: Thank you, BORIS. I knew I could count on
       you. What did you call about?
MALE 2: I've got some information from PRIMROSE
       that would normally just be filed away and
       not reported. But I wanted to call you
       about it, because you said you wanted to
       hear my interpretation of things, even when
       my conclusions are not based on solid
       enough 'evidence' to be put into a report.
MALE 1: Hm. Tell me more. You know what I think
       of your conclusions.
MALE 2: You'll have to bear with me, because it
       sounds like a joke at first. Actually,
       PRIMROSE's report is about a practical

joke. The thing that makes it serious,
however, is something from a recent
conversation with an old academy classmate
about a practical joke that some of the
troops in his unit pulled on the newks
there.

MALE 1: OK. I'll keep that in mind. Tell me
PRIMROSE's joke first.

MALE 2: It seems that they use lots of fan-fold
six-ply paper at SPOTLIGHT. And this
generates lots of carbon paper, which has
various uses for the practical jokers
there. One of these uses is to give the
victim of the joke "black ears." This means
that they take the victim's headphones and
rub the muffs that go over his ears with
the carbon paper until the muffs are coated
with a thick layer of carbon black. When
the unsuspecting victim picks up his
headphones and puts them on, the black
layer on the muffs is transferred to the
victim's ears, causing them to turn black.
It's very messy stuff and hard to get off.
The victim is marked as being the brunt of
a "black ears" joke for several days, it
seems.

MALE 1: Yes. I get the idea. It's all very droll.
It just goes to show you how lax discipline
is in the American Army.

MALE 2: I wouldn't jump to conclusions, EVGENIJ,
at least not until you've heard the second
part of my story.

MALE 1: OK. Let's have it.

MALE 2: Keep in mind that the source for this
part of the story is an old academy
classmate who's the commander of the
signals collection regiment in STENDAL. It
seems that they use lots of fan-fold six-
ply paper, which generates lots of carbon
paper, which has various uses for the
practical jokers in the regiment. One of
which is to give the victim of the joke a

set of "black ears." It is done the same
way that the Americans do it. Do you still
think that this is an indication of lax
discipline?

MALE 1: Yes, but I got your point.

MALE 2: Very interesting. Isn't it?

MALE 1: So SPOTLIGHT is running a signals
collection operation?

MALE 2: Yes, that's been my guess all along.

MALE 1: You're right. You couldn't report this.
The consumers of the report would laugh you
right off the street.

MALE 2: What should I do with it then?

MALE 1: I think that you have done the only
useful thing you can do: tell me. That, of
course, and keep it in the back of your
head as you sift through the other
information that comes our way. Just keep
building your case until you can put
together enough other 'hard' evidence to
prove your conclusion to the consumers in a
way that they will accept. … And I wouldn't
mention your friend's joke to anyone else,
not unless you want to put an end to his
career. Most people on the staff would
react the same way that I did: "lax
discipline," and he'd lose his command.

MALE 2: Yes, that's a point well taken. I
wouldn't want that to happen. I won't put
it in the PRIMROSE folder then.

MALE 1: This just proves what I've always said
about you, BORIS. You're a great analyst.
And I'm not just saying that because you're
married to my sister. Tell her I said 'hi,'
by the way.

MALE 2: I will.

MALE 1: I'm glad you called. I'll be laughing
about this to myself all day. My staff will
wonder why I'm in such a good mood, but I
won't tell them. It's good to keep them
guessing.

MALE 2: Yes, I do the same thing to my staff.
    Give OLGA my regards.
MALE 1: Yes, of course, and thanks again for the
    call, BORIS. You've made my day.
MALE 2: You're welcome. And thanks for the
    advice. Good-bye, EVGENIJ.
[HANG UP]

Kevin's Headphones

18
Decisions, Decisions, Decisions

A complaint about the constant power blackouts and brownouts and what they were doing to collection, not to mention to the equipment, slowly made its way to the attention of Lieutenant Sheerluck. Although he had better things to do, like finish his dissertation, he felt that it might advance his career if he were to apply the same disciplined research techniques that he had applied to his dissertation to deciding on an answer to the question of whether or not an emergency power generator would be beneficial for the Site.

His dissertation advisor, however, had neglected to impart to him one of the key tenets of academia: avoid making decisions at all cost. If you made a decision, you might be held responsible for the consequences. There were always consequences. Even if things went right—which they did less often than pure chance dictated, because that is what happens when nobody is willing to take a chance and make a decision—credit was always given where credit was due, that is at the highest level of the hierarchy intelligent enough to claim it. This type of credit grab is not entirely with out risk, because there could be consequences for not doing it sooner. If, on the other hand, things went wrong, which they often did—because that is what happens when you avoid making decisions and leave things to chance—the first order of the day was to find a scapegoat. If you had made a decision, you might be it. It's a lose, lose situation.

Perhaps Lieutenant Sheerluck's dissertation advisor thought this information about making decisions unnecessary to then Ph.D. candidate Sherlock's success in an academic career. Or perhaps he sought to ensure the failure of Sherlock's career, for fail it certainly did. Dr. Sherlock ABD found that the "honorific" ABD is the kiss of death to any candidate for an academic position. Not being able to complete his dissertation to his advisor's satisfaction, he found himself compelled to join the Army when his funding ran out. Sherlock's advisor had applied the time tested maxim of academic indecision: "When in doubt, wait it out," and simply "undecided" Ph.D. candidate Sherlock out of his life. Not having made a decision, the things that subsequently transpired could not be considered his fault.

From the logic of this point of view, it was the fault of Lieutenant Sherlock's army recruiter, who, had he known the real significance of the letters ABD, would never have recruited Ph.D. candidate Sherlock, unless, of course, he was up against making his quota at the end of the month. But it was the beginning of the month and the recruiter had never been to graduate school, so he did not know the real meaning of ABD, and the 9539th had to put up with Lieutenant Sheerluck, which meant that it was also stuck with his analysis of the question of whether or not an emergency power generator would be beneficial for the Site.

Lieutenant Sheerluck studied the problem. He collected data endlessly. He compiled charts and tables. He looked at the question from all angles. He even went so far as to ask one of the operators about it. Asking an operator was a bit unorthodox perhaps, but he was sure that he could justify it in a footnote, or maybe he would just not mention it.

"Hey, you troop! You are a disgrace to the uniform! Shine those shoes! Get some starch in those fatigues! Do you want me to put you on KP? Do we need an emergency generator? If I see you like this again, you'll be on KP for a month!" Lieutenant Sheerluck's closing statement being one that always seemed to end any conversation that Lieutenant Sheerluck had with a member of the lower classes, known in more polite company as enlisted men. The enlisted man whom he had asked automatically replied: "SIR! No, Sir!"

The enlisted man in question, in point of fact, never listened to anything Lieutenant Sheerluck said, but he knew that "SIR! No, Sir!" was always the right answer to any question that the lieutenant asked. Nobody in his right mind wanted to go on KP for a month.

After two months, his research was complete. The proud Lieutenant Sheerluck went to the colonel the next day to present his findings. The colonel recalled that Lieutenant Sheerluck had had something to do with power generators before, but he could not quite remember what.

Sheerluck's conclusion had the logical clarity of an optical illusion. "An emergency generator is a waste of time and money. Records show that the Site has never intercepted anything when the power was down. If there was nothing to intercept when the power was down, then the Site obviously does not need a generator for those times when it is." As to the question of a power outage damaging the equipment, he replied with a question of his own" "How could equipment be damaged when it was off?" His response was that "the assertion that a loss of power can damage equipment is simply absurd."

The colonel, however, never got to the conclusion of Lieutenant Sheerluck's report. After he had encountered the word *actually* five times in the first paragraph, which made no point that he could discern, the colonel decided to place the report in circular file 13, where it would be held for possible further study as time permitted, so long as that was some time before the duty gopher came by to pick up the classified trash for destruction. Lieutenant Sheerluck had demonstrated once again that he hadn't been given his nickname for nothing. If the colonel had reached the report's conclusion, he might have done something about Lieutenant Sherlock after all.

The lieutenant's report had overlooked just one or two little things. One, the project had unlimited funding, and being able to spend more of its funding than any of the other projects with unlimited funding was the key to honor, accolades and advancement. Two, the Chief of Base had ordered an emergency generator one minute after he had read the transcript of the call between Colonel Badunov at Karlshorst and General Besstrashnyj at KGB headquarters in Moscow that Kevin had done on Swings the previous evening.

**Circuit 53:   16:02-16:03Z 19 June 1955
Reel 8001**

FEMALE 1: MOSCOW, I need 5467 for my party,
     please. This is KARLSHORST, in GERMANY.
FEMALE 2: Just a moment, KARLSHORST, please. I'll
     ring the general.
MALE 1: 5467.
FEMALE 2: KARLSHORST. Go ahead, please. Your
     party's on the line.
MALE 2: EVGENIJ, I wanted to bring you up to date
     on REDROVER.
MALE 1: Boris! It's almost as if you have second
     sight. I was just about to call you to ask
     about that.
MALE 2: Everything is in readiness, just awaiting
     your orders. We'll really put one over on
     the Americans this time.
MALE 1: Good. I certainly hope so. Why don't you
     give me a brief rundown of your
     preparations. This is too important to
     leave anything to chance.
MALE 2: Of course, Evgenij. I have my most
     seasoned operative on this one. I think
     that you know him personally. He's . . .

[Transcriber comment: The recording ended at this
     point due to an unexpected power outage.
     The conversation appears to have continued,
     however. When power was restored 7 minutes
     later, Colonel Badunov and General
     Besstrashnyj were still on circuit 53. They
     were exchanging good-bye pleasantries. I
     couldn't get those on tape, because the
     power spike when electricity was restored
     killed the recorder.]

19
Cross Words

It was a Swing like any other. Fast Eddie was working the crossword puzzle in *The Stars and Stripes*. He did them in ink, because they were so easy. Kevin was off in East Hermland, talking to the voices on his tape. That disturbed Fast Eddie, because he knew when Kevin started talking to the tape that he'd have to report it, and it was getting close to mealtime. He'd probably be late to chow again, and when you were late, all the good stuff was usually gone by the time you got in line.

He knew better than to try and guess what it was that had caught Kevin's attention on the tape. Despite the fact that he had a pretty vivid imagination, whatever he guessed would pale in comparison to what Kevin claimed was on the tape. He also knew better than to say "claimed" to Kevin's face. The picture of Lieutenant Sheerluck running around with that great big bandage on his forehead was still very clear in his mind.

"You Son of a Bitch," said Kevin.

That can't be good, said Fast Eddie to himself. Kevin rarely cursed at real people, and almost never cursed at the voices on the tape. He looked back down at his crossword puzzle. Kevin would come and get him when the script was done. "Stevenson novel" was the clue. He counted the horizontal squares: 1-2-3-4-5-6-7-8-9 letters. "Why do they have to make them so easy," said Eddie out loud, as he wrote down K-I-D-N-A-P-P-E-D.

Kevin kept banging away at his mill, stopping the tape occasionally so his fingers running across the typewriter keys could catch up with the voice on the tape. He returned the carriage violently, making the mill jump. That was usually the sign that he had reached the end of a really good conversation. He advanced the six-ply paper to the perforation that delineated the end of one page and the start of another. He thumped the perforation with his right index finger to start the tear, and ripped the page free. He didn't even wait to take out the carbon paper as he usually did before rushing over to Eddie's desk.

"Eddie, this one's gotta go, and go fast! It should have been out of here five minutes ago," said Kevin, putting the script down on top of the crossword puzzle that Eddie was working.

"What's it this time? Hannibal on Potsdamer Platz?"

"Better than that. It's a kidnapping in the Grunie," said Kevin, pointing to the place where it said "Grünewald" on the script. That was the large forest on the western edge of the American Sector.

"Give me a chance to read it," said Eddie, who figured that it would be better to get down to business, rather than going over to refresh his cup of coffee, like he'd been planning to before Kevin jumped up out of his chair.

**Circuit 39:   18:46-18:48Z 22 June 1955
                     Reel 8362**


```
FEMALE 1: MOSCOW, can I have the GRU duty officer
    for my party?
FEMALE 2: Just a moment. I'll ring them.
MALE 1: GRU Headquarters. Captain DEZHURNYJ
    speaking.
FEMALE 2: Go ahead, WUENSDORF.
MALE 2: General SERPOV, please.
MALE 1: May I say who's calling?
MALE 2: Colonel MOLOTOV from WUENSDORF.
MALE 1: Just a moment, please.
MALE 3: VYACHESLAV MIKHAJLOVICH! Have you given
    that little matter we talked about any more
    thought?
```

MALE 2: But, of course, VLADLEN MARKOVICH. That's why I'm calling.

MALE 3: Good. The defection of PEREBEZHENTSEV to the Americans was very embarrassing, and we have to do something that will be as embarrassing for them as this was for us. So, have you identified anyone that we could induce to come over to us?

MALE 2: No, no one at that level. The only ones I have whom we could <u>induce</u> to come over are some disgruntled enlisted men.

MALE 3: No, no, no. That would never do. We have to have someone of equivalent rank and position.

MALE 2: In that case, we will just have to grab someone, and make it look like he wanted to come over.

MALE 3: You have a potential candidate?

MALE 2: Colonel OBERST, the Chief of Staff for the American Commander of Berlin.

MALE 3: Yes, that seems quite suitable in terms of rank and position.

MALE 2: I thought that you would say so. I've had him under discrete surveillance and have established a pattern of movements. He likes to go horse-back riding in the Grünewald. Alone.

MALE 3: How interesting. What about the family?

MALE 2: The only way we would be able to get the family as well, would be to wait for them to drive out to the American Zone on the autobahn, and grab them 'in transit'. Every place they go in Berlin is very public, and they always have either the colonel or his driver, usually both, with them.

MALE 3: We can't wait that long. We need to act immediately to make it clear that it is a tit for tat. We need to teach the Americans a lesson now!

MALE 2: You'll sanction the operation then?

MALE 3: Yes. What day did you have in mind?

```
MALE 2: Friday, the 24th. It is the next day that
        he goes riding.
MALE 3: Very good. Do it, but send me a message
        for the record.
MALE 2: I'll get it right out to you.
MALE 3: You will have a confirmation message this
        afternoon.
MALE 2: Give my best to MARIYA ANDREEVNA, VLADLEN
        MARKOVICH.
MALE 3: Yes, I will.
MALE 2: I'll call as soon as we have him in
        custody.
MALE 3: I'll look forward to your call. Good-bye.
MALE 2: Certainly. Good-bye.
[Hang up]

[Transcriber's note: COL SERGEJ PETROVICH
        PEREBEZHENTSEV, member of the staff of
        Commander, GSFG, defected to the west on
        June 7, bringing his family with him.]
```

"Yes, I've got to admit that this looks pretty reportable," said Fast Eddie, feeding a report form into his mill, and entering a title.

SUBJECT: SOVIETS PLAN KIDNAPPING OF AMERICAN IN REVENGE FOR DEFECTION OF SOVIET OFFICER

Eddie was about halfway through typing the report when an American warrant officer with a limp and a patch over one eye came into the scribe bay. Kevin recognized him as the Chief of Base in disguise the minute he opened his mouth.

"Let me know when you tell him, so I can look for a reaction from Vyacheslav Mikhajlovich," said Kevin.

"I can't tell him," said the Chief of Base coldly.

"What do you mean 'you can't tell him'!?" said Kevin in disbelief.

"We can't tell him. It would compromise the project."

"Compromise the project!? You think that this is the only place this plan has been exposed!" said Kevin in the well-known tone of incredulity that he put on when he had to deal with an inferior intellect.

"I don't know of any other places it has been exposed except here. If I did, I'd tell him," said the Chief of Base calmly.

"So, you're going to let 'em grab this guy, pump him full of chemicals, turn him into a zombie and parade him around like a puppet, spouting anti-American propaganda?" said Kevin uneasily.

"If I have to to protect the project."

"I seem to remember something about being here to protect American lives and interests. This seems to be a pretty clear-cut case of both," said Kevin in disgust.

"I can't tell him. He's not cleared."

"Clear him!" said Kevin indignantly.

"He'd tell somebody. It would leak."

"So, you're a plumber! That's a surprise. I thought I was talking to an intelligence officer," yelled Kevin, displaying the smooth people skills that had got him put on straight Swings and out of everyone's way.

"Cut the crap, Kevin! I don't like this any more than you do, but we've got to protect the project. If they've got his schedule, and he goes out of pattern, they'd know he was tipped," replied the Chief of Base, elevating the pitch of his voice to match Kevin's.

"Screw the project! ... OK, you kidnap him. Break both his legs or something. You've got lots of people who know how to do that," implored Kevin, offering what seemed like a good compromise.

"I can't go around kidnapping field-grade officers in the U.S. Army and breaking their legs," said the Chief of Base indignantly, wondering if he could get away with having someone break both of Kevin's legs.

"It's not OK to kidnap him yourself, but it is OK to let him be kidnapped! You lost me."

"I can get into trouble for kidnapping him myself, but I can keep my ass covered, if—if mind you—he gets kidnapped. This information hasn't been confirmed via another source."

"Oh, so it's your ass you're worried about and not his. And don't give me any of this crap about 'if.' Vyacheslav Mikhajlovich wouldn't lie to me. He doesn't even know that I'm here. Or is it my ear that makes it an 'if'?"

"For Christ's sake, Kevin! Give it a rest! I can't do it and that's that."

"Give me a break! This is a real-live human being we're talking about here!"

"Human being! Since when do you care about human beings? Ninety-nine percent of all the human beings you ever come in contact with are not flesh-and-blood people. They're just analog reproductions of complex wave forms on magnetic tape. And no wonder! With your innate charm and tact, half of those voices would never talk to you again, if they ever really met you."

"Forget my charm and tact! That has nothing to do with this. This is a question of right and wrong. Keeping this guy from getting grabbed is right. Ignoring this information is wrong. I can look myself in the mirror when I shave every day. Can you?"

"I won't tell him!" said the Chief of Base, standing up. "And if a note shows up under his door warning him, I'll take away your friends. You'll never listen to another tape again as long as you live!"

The Chief of Base turned on his heel and walked away, limping on the wrong leg for this particular counter-surveillance disguise.

Kevin plopped down in his chair, and sat there for a minute, then turned around to face his tape recorder. He put up the next tape in the stack. It was Vyacheslav Mikhajlovich.

"And I thought you were an SOB, Vyacheslav Mikhajlovich, my old friend," said Kevin to the slowly revolving tape.

"Hardly," said the voice on the tape.

Fast Eddie wisely kept his mouth shut.

20
Crossed Swords

Kevin's independence quotient was permanently pegged at maximum, and when he recognized something that needed doing, whether anybody agreed with him or not, he took the initiative to make it happen. His ability to think outside the box and get results was what really set him apart from others, and the one thing that kept him on Swings, and out of the military prison at Fort Leavenworth. He put little store in other people's unsubstantiated opinions and viewpoints, when they conflicted with his own, which was often the case, and never let this deter him from doing what he thought was right.

So, when the Chief of Base said that he would not inform Colonel Oberst of the impending doom that awaited him on Friday the twenty-fourth, and cautioned Kevin not to warn the colonel, Kevin took him literally at his word. He concocted a plan to thwart the kidnapping without telling Colonel Oberst.

Kevin knew that Fast Eddie wouldn't help him. He had too much vested interest in not going to Fort Leavenworth to want to risk an unsanctioned operation with Kevin, so Kevin didn't ask him for help. Kevin just sat there scribing tapes until they ran out at about 22:00 Local.

With two hours to go until shift change, Kevin told Eddie that he was taking an early-in, but that he'd be in his room, if Eddie needed him. He grabbed a stack of copies of the East German

daily newspaper—*Neues Deutschland*—"to read himself to sleep,"
he said, and beat feet. On his way to his room, he grabbed a pair
of rubber gloves from the latrine cleaning closet.

When he got to his room, he put on the gloves, took the
issues of *Neues Deutschland* from the center of the stack—the ones
that did not have his fingerprints on them—and began to cut
individual words out of the papers. He arranged them on his rack
as he cut them out to make sure that he had all the words he
needed for his note.

GRU plans to kidnap AMERICAN officer horseback riding in the Grünewald on Friday the 24th

He only needed two more words to address the envelope. He
found them in the issue for 13 June. That had been an eventful
day.

Gehlen urgent

He put the cut-out words in an envelope, and went to bed.

The next morning, he took the bus five stops to a stationary
store, where he bought a package of envelopes with matching
stationary and a bottle of glue with a brush.

He took the bus back to the Site, where he went to his room
and pasted together his message. It was difficult getting the words
where he wanted them with the gloves on, but he wasn't taking
any chances. He even glued the envelope shut instead of licking it.

The cut-up copies of *Neues Deutschland* and the rest of the
stationary packet went into a burn bag that he delivered to the
classified trash collection point on his way back to the bus stop. It
would be burned to a crisp before he got to his next destination.

He was headed for the nearby refugee reception camp in
Marienfelde. He got off the bus and dropped the bottle of glue in
the trash can at the stop. He walked along the camp fence until he
found a bored little boy about five years old looking out through
the wire.

"Hey, kid," he said in German. "You wanna make five Marks?"

This was an enormous amount of money for the boy, who readily agreed.

"All you have to do is take this envelope to the processing center building and give it to one of the German "interviewers,"" said Kevin, holding up the crisp white envelope in a gloved hand.

The little boy took the envelope in a dirty hand that left marks on the envelope's pristine whiteness. Kevin placed a five-mark coin in the boy's other hand.

"Und jetzt schnell!" said Kevin. The kid took off like an Olympic sprinter. Kevin watched him until he disappeared inside the door of the processing center building. By the time the kid brought the "interviewer" back to the place where he had been given the envelope, Kevin was long gone.

The German "interviewers" were really all members of the Gehlen organization. They were at the camp to identify people coming from the East who had information that they could use, or who could be returned to the East to work for them. Kevin had learned that in an article in *The Stars and Stripes* that shouldn't have been printed, but had been anyway.

Half an hour later the envelope and letter were in a forensics lab. Another hour later and the report was ready. It said: post-war paper of German manufacture, German-made glue, with words cut out of three different issues of *Neues Deutschland*. No fingerprints other than the boy's and the case officer's. The envelope was not licked, but glued shut. "A sign of a professional job," said the technician who processed the envelope.

The note, the envelope and its contents were brought to Gehlen's personal attention. It was a very interesting letter, and it had been addressed to him, after all. He studied the package for a moment, and then turned to his deputy.

"It's hard to conceive of this as a provocation since it is in the American Sector," said Gehlen. "Let's put a paramilitary unit in the area. If a Russian body-snatcher team shows up, I want them invited politely, but forcefully if necessary, to remain our guests for a while. And let's not tell the Americans about this until we have more information." Gehlen was a cautious man, which is one of the reasons that he had survived long enough to reach the position of power that he now held.

That Friday morning Gehlen's "reception committee" noted two cars with East German plates entering the Grünewald in the American Sector. Each of the cars had four men in it. The cars concealed themselves just off the bridle path about half a kilometer away from where Gehlen's unit had its observation post.

Gehlen's unit formed a loose perimeter around the two East German cars, and two men in West German police uniforms were dispatched to the cars to ask the occupants for their papers. As the two approached, the occupants of the cars opened fire, killing one of the police officers, and seriously wounding the other. There was an answering hail of bullets from the comrades of the two fallen officers.

The hail of bullets ceased, and when, after five minutes, no further signs of resistance were encountered from the two cars, two more officers rushed forward to aid their fallen comrades, who were quickly taken away to the hospital.

Eight of the ten Russians in the two cars, which now seemed to resemble two over-large, black kitchen sieves, were dead. The two who had survived the initial onslaught did not make it to the hospital, after being convinced to tell the unit leader who it was that had sent them. The unit leader had fought on the Eastern Front and had a few old scores to settle.

Gehlen sent a hatbox to Colonel Molotov in Wuensdorf with a note that made his displeasure with this whole affair more than evident. It contained the head of the leader of the Russian body-snatcher team. "Captain Silnyakov," said his dog tags. The note was in very precisely polished Russian, It said:

"If you plan to grab somebody else from the Western Sectors, keep in mind that I know where you live, and if we cannot interdict the team making the 'snatch,' that I will send *your* head to General Serpov in a hatbox."

Colonel Oberst returned from his Friday-morning horseback ride unaware that he had been the target of a GRU body-snatcher operation. The ride had had its intended effect. He was thoroughly refreshed and ready to tackle the mountain of paperwork on his desk. The Chief of Base was left wondering what had gone wrong with the GRU's plan. He wondered if Kevin could have had anything to do with it, but dismissed the thought as soon as he had it.

**Circuit 39:   10:16-10:18Z 25 June 1955
                    Reel 9010**

FEMALE 1: MOSCOW, can I have the GRU duty officer
    for my party?
FEMALE 2: Just a moment. I'll get them for you.
MALE 1: GRU Headquarters. Captain DEZHURNYJ
    speaking.
FEMALE 2: Go ahead, WUENSDORF.
MALE 2: General SERPOV, please.
MALE 1: May I say who's calling?
MALE 2: Colonel MOLOTOV from WUENSDORF.
MALE 1: Just a moment, please.
MALE 3: VYACHESLAV MIKHAJLOVICH! I had expected
    you to call last night. Did something go
    wrong?
MALE 2: That's an understatement, VLADLEN
    MARKOVICH. The kidnap operation was a total
    disaster. This morning when I got up, there
    was a hatbox on my doorstep with Captain
    SILNYAKOV's head in it.
MALE 3: Lenin preserve us. I had no idea the
    Americans would react that harshly?
MALE 2: No, it wasn't the Americans. It was
    Gehlen. He sent a note.
MALE 3: Gehlen? So what does his message say?
MALE 2: It reads: "If you plan to grab somebody
    else from the Western Sectors, keep in mind
    that I know where you live, and if we
    cannot interdict the team making the
    'snatch,' that I will send your head to
    General Serpov in a hatbox."
MALE 3: He can't be serious!
MALE 2: I think he is. It's hard not to take a
    note like that seriously when it comes
    delivered with the bodiless head of one of
    your subordinates.
MALE 3: Next time, you'll have to . . .
MALE 2: There won't be a next time for me.
    SILNYAKOV's head convinced me that GEHLEN
    is serious and does know where to find me.
    It was delivered right to my quarters and

not to my office. This is hitting too close
to home.

MALE 3: You're overexaggerating.

MALE 2: I think not, VLADLEN MARKOVICH. Captain
SILNYAKOV was as cool and resourceful a
SPEZNAZ officer as I have ever seen, but
that did not help him in his encounter with
Gehlen. I'm not as young as he was, and I
don't have a SPEZNAZ team on hand either.
If Gehlen could get to him, he can get to
me.

MALE 3: Perhaps, and perhaps not.

MALE 2: I am not prepared to have my head sent to
you in a hatbox to prove my point.

MALE 3: Hm, I see your point.

MALE 2: I suggest that we forget all about
PEREBEZHENTSEV, and that we forget about
all the operations that we have lined up
for the next six months at least.

MALE 3: Perhaps you're right. I'll want a written
report with your recommendation for
inaction, and a copy of the note plus
photos of the head in the hatbox.

MALE 2: Are you sure that you would not like the
hatbox itself?

MALE 3: I think that the photos will be
sufficient. You may return the captain's
head to his next of kin.

MALE 2: How very kind of you.

MALE 3: Good day, VYACHESLAV MIKHAJLOVICH.

MALE 2: Good day, VLADLEN MARKOVICH.

[Hang up]

Kevin listened through the conversation with a smile on his face.
Fast Eddie figured that it must be some perschat with a good joke.
Kevin really liked perschat, especially when they told jokes. He
figured that Kevin would come over and tell him the joke in a
minute like he always did.

The tape stopped, and Kevin got up. He walked over and
grabbed a Recorder Repair Request.

"What was on the tape, Kev?" asked Eddie. "It looked funny."

"It was blank," said Kevin. "I'll just run this down to Howie so he can get the collection recorder fixed before another cut gets lost.

21
God Zulu

God Zulu had the undisputed last word in matters of time at the Site. His effigies hung everywhere. There were fat squarish ones on the walls and long, thin ones in the equipment racks. His effigies showed the official Site time, which, of course, was not local, Berlin time. That was "Zulu plus one." Zulu time was the time in Greenwich, England. Such civilian minds as were conscious of the use of the time at the zero meridian as a reference time, referred to it as 'GMT,' Greenwich Mean Time; but to the military, it is known as the time in time zone 'Z,' pronounced 'Zulu' in the phonetic army alphabet.

God Zulu was a central time source that sent reports of the current Zulu time to all his effigies so that they all showed the same time, all the time, any time, every time. Everything that happened on Site was reported in Zulu time so that there could be no confusion about what time something happened, unless, of course, the person filling out the report looked at his watch and not at God Zulu, and then the report showed what time it was 'local' instead of 'Zulu,' which really confused things for some people who should have known better, but didn't, because they had trouble grasping the concept of the relativity of time, which stated that measurable time only exists relative to a fixed location, usually, but not always, the one where you are. If the person you are listening to is far enough away, for example, in Moscow, then it is a different time. Moscow is "Zulu plus three."

To get around this problem of relativity, some people didn't wear a watch to work so they *had* to look at God Zulu to know what time it was. This didn't seem to create many problems for them when they were off Site, as Berlin seemed to be full of large clocks that showed the Germanically correct time, and they could always just look at them and know what time it was 'local.'

Any explanation of this profusion of clocks on public buildings and on elegant poles on street corners and at the entrance to U-Bahn stations inevitably contained two of the four Russian words known to every German who had survived 'Liberation' from National Socialism by the Russians: "Davaj chasy!" which meant "give me your watch!" in no uncertain terms, as it was usually punctuated by an arm with six or seven watches on it, waving a firearm in the direction of the supplier. Sometimes not just waving, but also firing. With all their watches shipped off to Russia as "war reparations," and resources being tight in the post-war period, the efficient, pragmatic Germans had created a network of outdoor clocks to replace their watches. It worked. Watch theft was down and people still knew what time it was, which was very important to the Germans.

Kevin had gone local in that regard. He didn't wear a watch. He also wore long sleeves a lot, so that it was not all that obvious. One day, after he had been asked what time it was local about ten times, Kevin decided that he had had enough of this and said: "Let's see." He bent his left arm inward, raising it to about chest level, grasped his cuff and pulled it up to reveal what appeared to be a naked wrist. He looked down at his wrist and said: "It's ten thirty-five and fifty-nine seconds local," having just looked at one of God Zulu's effigies and made the conversion from Zulu to local by adding one to the hour.

Blackie was the first person to be an audience to this performance. He wisely said "Thank you," and walked away without further comment. After a while Kevin got tired of this game, and made up a new one. When Detroit asked him what time it was, he said: "Let's check my wonder watch." He repositioned his arm and pulled back his sleeve, and shoved it under Detroit's nose.

Detroit should have kept his mouth shut like Blackie, but then Detroit was not as smart as Blackie, and opened his mouth and put his foot in it.

"Where's your wonder watch? I didn't take it!" exclaimed Detroit, letting his Freudian sense of guilt slip.

"It's right here," replied Kevin pointing at his left wrist. "I watch it and wonder what time it is until I can find God Zulu."

After that, nobody seemed to ask Kevin for the local time anymore.

Then there were the people who set their watches to Zulu. Kevin called this the "Zulu is always with us" watch. It was a very subtle joke, which most folks did not get, because they didn't recognize it as a pun on a post-revolutionary Communist slogan: "Lenin is always with us." That was the problem with most of Kevin's jokes; they were too subtle by half. Since any joke that you have to explain isn't funny, you can just forget that I told you, and we can get on with the story.

People who wore a "Zulu is always with us" watch invariably seemed to be late for everything when they were off Site. They kept forgetting that local Berlin time was Zulu plus one, which meant that when their watches said that it was 12:00 noon, it was really 13:00. Zulu was a 24-hour god, which only added to the confusion for those who were chronometrically challenged by the military 24-hour system of telling time. "Zulu is always with us" watch-wearers also steadfastly refused to look at the street clocks, because seeing that the time on their wrist did not match the time on the street made them feel schizophrenic, which was a misdiagnosis, since they were only really schizochronic. Even with the correct diagnosis they would not have felt any better, since they were either perpetually hungry, because they kept missing the closing time of the serving line in the mess hall, or perpetually broke, because they spent all their money on *Currywurst und Kartoffelsalat* at the Worst 'L' Stand, because they had missed "chow," or both broke and hungry. After a couple of months of that, most sensible people either switched to a 'wonder watch,' or at least took off their wristwatch when they went to work.

Sergeant Spaeter was not like most people. He clung to his "Zulu is always with us" watch like a Communist party boss to his dogma. As a result, he was always late for things that took place on local time. Not that he was particularly on time for things on Zulu time, but he was always late local, and that meant that he never got to work on time.

Sergeant Laufflaecker had once written a performance appraisal for Sergeant Spaeter that said: "This individual can never get to work on time." Lieutenant Sheerluck had signed off on it, but the company commander had bounced it back down the line with the instruction to rewrite it. If Sergeant Spaeter's performance appraisal said that he was always late, then somebody might want to know why no disciplinary action was ever taken against him, and that would be inconvenient, because someone might have to miss lunch or happy hour to throw the book at him, provided that they could lift it. So Sergeant Laufflaecker rewrote his performance appraisal to say: "Standard working hours hold no fear for this man," and all the higher-ups were happy. Now they wouldn't have to miss lunch.

Boredom being the good mother of invention that she is, one particularly slow Swing, Blackie became the proud father of a cunningly clever plan. They would hold a pool to bet on exactly how late Sergeant Spaeter would be. A fifteen-second slice of time cost twenty-five cents. A whole minute cost a dollar, and nobody could buy more than one contiguous minute. There was plenty of interest in the pool, as Sergeant Spaeter's being late got on the nerves of everybody who worked for a living, meaning the enlisted men and not the officers. If the enlisted men were late, they got written up and put on burn detail. If Spaeter was late, nothing ever seemed to come of it. Besides, betting on how late Spaeter was going to be was something to relieve the boredom. With any luck, he could keep folks on the edge of their seats for 30 minutes. With a lot of luck, somebody might win some money.

The technical arrangements were a source of entertainment for a long while. It took over half the Swing to figure out a system that would satisfy all the people willing to participate in the pool. After all, the pool represented a lot of money, in relative terms. A dollar was more than a day's take-home pay for some people on the floor. After bouncing a number of ideas off the wall, they decided to set up an electric eye hooked to a tape recorder that had a Zulu track. When the beam between the eyes was broken by Sergeant Spaeter walking through the door, the tape would stop and the last time on the tape would be the winner.

The first night that the pool ran, Sergeant Spaeter was 27 minutes and 37 seconds late, according to God Zulu. Nobody had that time, so the pot rolled over to the next night. It had been $7.75, a princely sum, especially that close to the end of the month. The next night, the pot reached $17.50. The rumor of big money to be had had brought out the big spenders, including Fast Eddie, who took two dollars worth of time slots. Just talking about where he got that kind of loose change kept people, who would have normally been asleep, awake for most of the Swing.

God Zulu judged Spaeter to be 18 minutes and 5 seconds late, which was again a time that nobody had. The next night's pot was over a month's take-home pay for some, and even Corporal Neumann took a chance, knowing that his mother would not approve. His quarter pushed the pot to $29.75.

Blackie was haranguing Kevin to get in the pool and get wet. Kevin was pissed because Blackie would not let him get on with his tape, which was a fun tape from yesterday of some personal chatter between two drunken ops, that had already yielded three true unit designators and the location of a new whore house in Rostock that Lieutenant Sheerluck had missed when he did the tape on Days. Kevin wished that they would keep Sheerluck away from tapes, and that Blackie would go away. He stuck his hand in his pocket and pulled out the solitary coin that he found in there. It was a nickel.

"It's all I've got," said Kevin.

"All right," said Blackie, who never liked to take 'no' for an answer where money was concerned. "You can have three seconds for your five cents."

"And you'll go away and leave me alone to finish my tape?"

"Sure thing," said Blackie with a smile.

Kevin thought about it for five seconds. It was only a nickel, and there was not a lot that you could get for a nickel. It would not even get him a bus ticket to Steglitz to see Gabbie.

"OK. Now get out of here and let me get back to Rostock," said Kevin, handing over his last cent.

"Which seconds you want?" asked Blackie, his pencil poised to write this piece of information down in the pool.

"What?" said Kevin, who had already turned towards his tape.

"Which three seconds you want for your nickel?" repeated Blackie.

Kevin was annoyed. He had missed the joke on the tape that the op in Wuensdorf was laughing at. *What was Blackie going on about? Oh, a time.* He looked at his Zulu effigy, which showed the time on the tape. It said "22:22:22," which is a sacred time to the true believers for it is the same numeral repeated six times, an event that only occurred twice a day. Once at 11:11:11, and once at 22:22:22. When these times were displayed, all the believers, as one man, said "Zulu!" in a loud voice, except on Days when Lieutenant Sheerluck was around, because he was not a believer, and always gave everybody hell, if they shouted "Zulu!" He didn't know what it meant, but he was sure that no good could come of it.

Kevin said: "Zulu! Twenty-two twenty-two. Now go away and leave me alone!"

"Done, oh great God Zulu," said Blackie, in reverence to the holy time displayed on the effigy of God Zulu above the tape recorder. He wrote down that Kevin had twenty-two minutes and twenty-one, twenty-two and twenty-three seconds late. 'OK, so it was only a nickel,' he thought. 'But it was Kevin's last nickel, and that had to be worth something. And what are the chances that he is going to nail the time right on the head with three seconds?'

That made the pot $32.30.

God Zulu continued to measure the march of time, and, after a while, Sergeant Spaeter crossed the threshold onto the Operations bay floor, breaking the electric eye beam, and stopping the recorder.

"Time, gentlemen, please," said Blackie in a good imitation of a British pub keeper at closing time.

Spaeter was oblivious to everything going on, like he had been the last two nights. He walked over to the coffeepot and fixed himself a cup of the dark black liquid that passed for coffee on Site. He added condensed milk (there was no fridge, so they could not use fresh) and four teaspoons of sugar. That almost made it drinkable.

Blackie went over to the "Spaeter time recorder" and rewound the tape about a foot's worth. He pressed play. The effigy of God Zulu flickered and synced up. It showed 16:22:17. It blinked 16:22:18, then 16:22:19, and Blackie had a sinking feeling. God Zulu glowed 16:22:20. *STOP!* said Blackie to himself. If the time dropped out now, they could roll the pot over for a fourth night. God Zulu chuckled. The effigy showed 16:22:21 and went blank.

"Who won?" said a chorus of curious voices, who knew that it was not one of them.

"Kevin," said Blackie, almost in a whisper.

"Kevsky?!" replied the chorus.

A crowd gathered around Kevin's position.

Kevin could have just as well as been in Wuensdorf with the op he was listening to. He did not notice a thing. The Russian duty officer in Wuensdorf walked into the room where the op was on the line. The op did not hear him, and kept on telling his story about the drunk at the corner of *Einbahnstrasse* and *Kein Einfahrt*. The duty officer reached out and pulled the plug on the conversation, and the cut ended. Kevin typed:

```
[Cut ends unexpectedly in mid joke. Transcriber
comment: suspect that the duty officer caught him
on the line perschatting.]
```

Kevin looked up, surprised to see all the people gathered around his position.

"What's up? Am I on fire?" asked Kevin, looking briskly around to see if he had a carbon-paper tail.

"You won!" said Corporal Neumann.

"Is that the prototype for the U-2?" asked Kevin.

"No, you won the Spaeter pool," said Fast Eddie.

"Oh, how much was it?"

"$32.30!"

"I may retire," said Kevin. "Give me the money, Blackie!"

Blackie counted it out like a man parting with his last cent, which it was not.

Kevin took the money and walked over to Sergeant Spaeter. "Thank you, sergeant. That was very kind of you."

Spaeter looked non-plussed. He had no idea what was going on, which was nothing new for him.

"Would you care for a beer, instead of that liquid tar that they call coffee?" asked Kevin.

"You know that there ain't no beer allowed on the floor!" said Spaeter in a loud voice, looking around. Not seeing any of the treads around, he added softly: "A Weisse?"

"Be right back," said Kevin.

When he came back he had a whole crate of beer with him, and the KGB agent who ran the Worst 'L' Stand just outside the gate was $6 richer. He wondered if he should report this, and decided against it.

Kevin handed Spaeter a beer.

"I don't get it," said Spaeter with a blank stare. "What's this for?"

"For being late."

"What d'ya mean, late?" snarled Spaeter.

"You're never on time, so we held a pool to see how late you would be, and by some strange twist of fate, I won and you get a beer."

"Won what?"

"$32.30," waving his money around in front of Spaeter.

"You mean that you won $32.30 betting on how late I would be? I want a piece of the action!" demanded Spaeter.

"Have another beer."

"That ain't enough."

"OK, complain to the captain. You want me to call him at home? Or maybe we should call Lieutenant Sheerluck. I'm sure that he would side with you, especially after I tell him how I won the money."

Sergeant Spaeter did not say a word, but went over to the crate and pulled out another bottle, and then went over to his desk and sat down to enjoy his beer. It was, after all, a Weisse.

"Hey, you didn't get no Schuss with it," complained Spaeter.

"Sure I did," replied Kevin, who walked over and poured some raspberry syrup into Spaeter's open beer from a small bottle. "Prosit!"

It had turned into a very pleasant Swing. Even the Russian ops on the circuits seemed to have come up with a beer or two or three, but it was not a Weisse with a Schuss. You couldn't beat that. And all thanks to God Zulu and the sacred time of 22:22:22.

22
Lost and Found

Kevin's unexpected windfall made him want to try out some things to do in Berlin that he had heard about, but that he had been saving for a sunshiny day. Tops on his list was the Lost and Found auction held once a quarter by the BVG, the Berlin Public Transportation Authority. The auction offered all the things lost on busses, streetcars and U-Bahns in Berlin, that had remained unclaimed for 90 days or more, for sale to the highest bidder. The auction was that coming Friday, and Kevin—only having a nickel in his pocket at the time—had originally thought that he would have to give it a pass for this quarter.

Maybe next time, he had said to himself.

Winning the Spaeter pool, however, changed all that. School was out and Gabbie could go with him. She was the one who had told him about it in the first place. Her uncle had bought a very nice watch there for only 11 West Marks. That was not quite three dollars, less than half what Kevin had spent on beer for the trick the night he had won the Spaeter pool. And though he never wore a watch himself, his father might like one. It would be a good Christmas present. Besides, he had never been to an auction before. It might be fun.

They got there at 09:11 Local, which gave them plenty of time to look over the things to be auctioned off before the bidding started at 10:00 Local. There were whole trays of watches, stacks of briefcases, a row of suitcases, a pair of skis, not to mention piles of rings, gaggles of cameras, and heaps of coats, jackets, gloves and scarves.

There were also umbrellas. Kevin could not understand how anybody could leave an umbrella behind on public transportation, since rain was a fact of life in Berlin, but clearly some people managed to do just that, as there were boxes of them. Fancy ones, plain ones, black ones, colorful ones, big ones and small ones.

Gabbie pointed out a ring in a tray of others that attracted her attention.

"Sure, we can bid on that," said Kevin, when she showed it to him. "You can bid to 12 Marks," he added in a whisper, so as not to give away their bidding budget to any competitors for the ring. That was half his planned budget for the auction. He figured that he could afford to spend as much at the auction as he had spent on beer for the trick. "More, if the watch for my dad goes for less."

They found a couple of watches that looked like they would be suitable for Kevin's dad among the multitude of trays, and then grabbed a couple of seats in the back, off to the side. From this vantage point, they could keep an eye on the other bidders.

"People-watching during the auction should be half the fun," said Kevin, as they sat down.

The auctioneer started things right on time like any other good German enterprise. His first announcement was a surprise to Kevin and Gabbie.

"Ladies and gentlemen, we have a lot of items to get through today, and the only way that we can hope to finish before we all have to go home for dinner is to sell things in multiple lots. Watches, for example are sold in lots of six," said the auctioneer.

"My uncle didn't mention anything about that," whispered Gabbie.

"We'll have to be satisfied with people-watching then," replied Kevin. "I can't afford six watches at 10 Marks apiece. Even If I could afford them, I don't know what I'd do with them all."

"Our first lot is a collection of six watches," began the auctioneer. "What am I bid for this fine group of six watches? Shall we start at two Marks?"

The price climbed rapidly to nine Marks, but seemed to get stuck there, and the auctioneer prodded the buyers to see if he could wring a bit more money out of them. "This excellent assemblage of six watches for only nine Marks, ladies and gentlemen?! That's only one Mark 50 each. Surely they're worth more than that. Even if only three of them work," appealed the auctioneer.

Kevin looked at Gabbie. Gabbie smiled back.

"No advance on nine Marks? ... Going once, going twice, sold for nine Marks!"

Kevin's first choice watch for his father was lot number 67. It was a Movado. He and Gabbie enjoyed the show that the auction provided as they waited. Lot number 66—another six watches—had no bidders, so the auctioneer rolled it in with lot number 67. "Let's start the bidding at two Marks," said the auctioneer, pointing his hammer in the direction of the 12 watches on velvet trays off to his right.

Kevin held up his hand.

"I have two Marks in the back," called the auctioneer. "Three, now four, now five, now six, now seven, now eight, now eight. ... Eight to the gentleman in the back. Any advance on eight? ... Going once, going twice, sold for eight Marks!"

Kevin had a dozen watches. "When they see me with all these watches at work, they're going to say 'Davaj chasy!',", joked Kevin to Gabbie.

"That's not funny," said the man in the next chair who had been liberated from National Socialism by the Russians and knew very well from personal experience what "Davaj chasy!" meant.

"My apologies," said Kevin in German. "Can I offer you a watch? I have 12."

The gentleman refused.

Gabbie's ring was in lot 103. It went for 10 Marks 50, well within budget, with a little left over for a snack on the way home. It had been fun, and they were both pleased with their purchases as they looked them over in the nearby café that had excellent applestrudel. The owner's wife made it herself.

Kevin wound up his watches, and they all ran, except for two, and one of them did not even have a face. It had a yellow and a blue dot with a thumb wheel to select between them, and a big knobby thing that was labeled "Steineck f2.5 12.5mm CL." "That sounds an awful lot like a camera," said Kevin, and he was right. The Chief of Base recognized it immediately when he stopped by the scribe bay to see what all the commotion was about in this usually quiet corner of his dominions.

Kevin and Blackie were having an animated—perhaps loud would be a better word—discussion about the price of watches in Berlin. Blackie was offering a buck apiece for Kevin's surplus, and Kevin was holding out for a buck and a quarter.

"I'll give you five bucks for the Steineck and the story of how you came by it," said an American master-sergeant with infantry insignia and more hair than your usual infantry master-sergeant had.

The gathering was joined by Lieutenant Sheerluck, who had been on his way to inspect the evening meal service, when his attention had been caught by the infantry master-sergeant who had just offered five dollars for one of the dozen or so watches on the desk.

"You need a haircut, sergeant! Who's your commanding officer?" demanded Lieutenant Sheerluck, saving his question about the obviously illicit trade in wristwatches for dessert.

"Lieutenant Sherlock, I will take the fact that you did not recognize me as a compliment for my disguise technique, but if you would like me to remain favorably disposed to your person, I recommend that you stand right where you are and keep your mouth shut!" said the Chief of Base, turning to give Sheerluck the same stare that he had given the geologists when they asked to drill test holes all over the compound.

Sheerluck was three syllables into his infamous "I'll brook no insolence" speech when he recognized the face of the man in the master-sergeant's uniform, and stopped midway into the fourth.

"The Steineck camera," said the Chief of Base, directing his attention to Kevin, "and the story of where you got it. Five dollars."

"Sold," said Kevin, "unless you want to bid more, Blackie?"

"He can have it," said Blackie.

"And you can have the others at a buck apiece, Blackie" replied Kevin, who was making a killing as it was. He was getting 14 dollars for what had only cost him eight Marks.

"Any why, pray tell, kind sir," said Kevin addressing the Chief of Base, "is your interest in this piece of junk worth five bucks?"

"Because the Russians are handing them out to their agents like stocking stuffers at Christmas. Now just where did *you* get it?" asked the Chief of Base with a note of impatience in his voice that did not escape Kevin's attention.

Blackie was torn between making himself scarce to avoid the carnage, and sticking around to find out what happened to Kevin. He decided on staying for the floor show.

Kevin told them the story of the Lost and Found auction, and Blackie wondered if he could get his moose to go with him for the next one. He wasn't sure that his German was up to an auction, and, besides, Trudie always brought him good luck.

Kevin quickly pulled out the receipt from the auction to show to the Chief of Base.

Seeing the price on the receipt increased Blackie's respect for Kevin. He had never figured that Kevin could put one over on him.

"If any of the pictures turn out well, you'll let me see, won't you?" asked Kevin as the Chief of Base left with the Steineck.

He did. The eight exposures on the film disc were of secret documents from the headquarters compound on Clay Allee. The Chief of Base could tell where they were from, because of the accountability numbers on the documents. He even knew which safe they were kept in, but he wouldn't tell Kevin which one it was. Not that it mattered, four days later Colonel Badunov told Kevin what he wanted to know.

Circuit 53:   15:04-15:08Z 28 June 1955
**   Reel 9227**

FEMALE 1: MOSCOW? This is GERMANY, the KARLSHORST
    operator. My party needs 5467, please.
FEMALE 2: I'll connect you … It's ringing.
MALE 1: 5467.
FEMALE 2: Your number's on the line, KARLSHORST.
    Tell your party to go ahead, please.
MALE 2: EVGENIJ! It's BORIS from Karl's.

MALE 1: BORIS! I'm always glad to hear from you.
    What's important enough for you to call at
    this time of day?
MALE 2: A PRIMROSE report that is coming your
    way, EVGENIJ. It will be on the wire in an
    hour.
MALE 1: What about it?
MALE 2: PRIMROSE reports that one of our STONE
    CORNER concealed cameras was purchased last
    Friday at the Lost and Found auction run by
    the Berlin Public Transportation Authority.
[Transcriber comment: I draw your attention to
    the fact that STONE CORNER is the most
    literal translation of "Steineck," the
    trade name of a concealed camera worn like
    a wristwatch.]
MALE 1: Hm. Tell me more, but I can't imagine
    that this is going to make me happy.
MALE 2: There is actually not anything more in
    the PRIMROSE report, but I think that it
    explains why JITNEY was rolled up
    yesterday.
MALE 1: Which one's JITNEY? Is he the one in the
    Chief of Staff's Office? One of the GRU's
    "recruitments".
MALE 2: That's the one.
MALE 1: Your reports never gave me a good feeling
    about him. I'm rather surprised he lasted
    as long as he did.
MALE 2: Me too. The tie that I see between the
    PRIMROSE report and JITNEY is that JITNEY
    lost his STONE CORNER in February, and
    since he's the only one to have lost his
    camera, the one that showed up at the
    auction has to be his. The delay between
    his losing it and it turning up again at
    SPOTLIGHT is that the quarterly Lost and
    Found auctions only sell things that have
    remained unclaimed for 90 days of more.
MALE 1: I see. So he could have actually been
    rolled up 90 days ago?
MALE 2: In principle, yes.
MALE 1: Then we were lucky.
MALE 2: That's one way of looking at it.

MALE 1: I thought that all of SPOTLIGHT's people were signals collectors and were not active on the street?

MALE 2: Yes, that's correct. This is just a case of the wrong person being at the wrong place at the wrong time.

MALE 1: Coincidence? I don't believe in coincidence.

MALE 2: I like to give our American friends a lot of credit for well-planned operations, but unless this is a piece of disinformation being fed to us via PRIMROSE, I can't see how they could have planned this.

MALE 1: Disinformation? That would mean that PRIMROSE has been compromised. Why don't you make some inquiries to see if you can confirm her information.

MALE 2: Yes, that's a point well taken. I'll see what I can find out.

MALE 1: I would hate to lose PRIMROSE now that things seem to be getting underway at SPOTLIGHT.

MALE 2: I'll check and let you know what I find out. Give OLGA my regards.

MALE 1: Yes, of course, and tell NATASHA "Hi!" from her big brother.

MALE 2: Certainly. Good-bye, EVGENIJ.

[HANG UP]

23

The Whorehouse Report

Sitting around waiting for something to happen that probably never will happen is boring. On the one hand, Kevin wanted something to happen to keep him from being bored. On the other hand, however, if what he was there to keep a lookout for ever happened—in civilian parlance it's called a war—there was a high probability that he would end up dead, because Berlin was surrounded by a numerically superior enemy force. Kevin suspected that being dead might be even more boring than Mids, which are not called the graveyard shift for nothing.

There was never anything to do on Mids. The target—like all sensible people—was asleep. Regulations, however, said that there had to be someone on duty 24 hours a day to look for Indications and Warnings of a prelude to war, I&W in the alphabet-jargon of the intelligence establishment.

The most exciting thing to do between midnight and eight in the morning was listening to the Russian commo ops, who had to keep the lines open—just in case the Americans started something—and were as bored as their American listeners were. Boredom on both sides of the line always seemed to reach its peak at about 02:00 Local. That was when the unauthorized personal chatter started. At that time of day, the Russian ops could be reasonably sure that there were no officers awake anywhere on the circuit to point out that the line was for official conversations only. It was something to do and they could always claim that it was a commo check, if they got caught.

Most folks just marked perschat tapes 'Nothing To Report' because they couldn't understand what the ops were talking about. They didn't have the Russian gutter vocabulary that you needed to follow along with the conversation. Kevin, on the other hand, did. He was one of those people who can absorb a new language like a sponge absorbs water. He read everything that would stand still long enough, including dictionaries.

He actually enjoyed listening to Mids perschat tapes. They were linguistically challenging, and he learned a lot about the people on the low end of the totem pole on the other side of the Sector border. Compared to them, Kevin felt himself rather well off, especially on straight Swings, where he could avoid the boredom of Mids, the slings and arrows of the Day weenies, like Lieutenant Sheerluck, and go to school with Gabbie.

Master-Sergeant Laufflaecker had ostensibly left him on Swings so that he could go to Russian classes at the Freie Universität during the day. The real reason was that he and the colonel had figured out that this was the easiest way of resolving the conflict of interests between the Chief of Base, who wanted Kevin to do tapes, and Lieutenant Sherlock, who wanted to have Kevin court-martialed every time he saw him. Life was much simpler for all concerned this way. The savings in paperwork alone made it worthwhile.

The greatest achievement of Kevin's fascination with perschat was *The Whorehouse Report*. Ops on Mids from all over the Group of Soviet Forces, Germany, rated the whorehouses in their area and compared notes. There were those back in the world who were of the opinion that this kind of conversation is a worthless waste of valuable collection resources. A "nasty-gram," therefore, floated up through channels from some "prudish wheel" in "forward-area analysis" that instructed the Site to stop wasting its time, ending with a snide "Haven't you got anything better to do?"

That didn't go over too well with the Chief of Base. He hated to get pinged on by the weenies at headquarters, even when they had their heads up their asses. He went to Kevin to make sure no more scripts of ill repute got sent back.

"She wouldn't know a piece of intelligence, if it bit her on the ass," said Kevin in his inimitably tactful style. He knew the analyst and was unimpressed by her. She had briefed him on his way out to the Site.

"What do you mean piece of intelligence? What kind of intelligence can there be in listening to some drunk, bored Russki talking about the last time he got laid? G'me a break!" said the Chief of Base, raising his voice to match Kevin's operatic intensity level. He had no idea who had written the message. It wasn't from his office, it was from the Fort.

Kevin reached over to a desk drawer and pulled out a working aid done on six-ply. That meant that it was locally produced. The stuff from the folks back home was nicely printed on pretty paper. This was the blue—first—copy. Keeping the blue copy was a privilege of the author. Kevin threw it across the desk to the Chief of Base.

"This is *The Whorehouse Report*. It's got the street address of every whorehouse within walking distance of almost every Russian military installation in GSFG. In most instances we know the name of the Madam, how many girls work there, and which senior officers patronize the place. It correlates covernames with locations and shows the true unit designators in some cases. No intel?! This all comes from the conversations we are now not supposed to scribe and send back. But I suppose that you've already seen this from the Fort?"

The Chief of Base hadn't seen it, and wasn't likely to any time soon, but he was very interested.

"You planning a visit?" asked the Chief of Base.

"No, but I sort of expected that you might have someone who would like to," replied Kevin.

"Why haven't I seen this before?" demanded the Chief of Base.

"Beats me. I'm just in production. Once I give it to Fast Eddie, I don't know what happens to it."

"Romeo will love this!" said the Chief of Base, more to himself than to Kevin.

"Anyone I know?" asked Kevin.

"No, but I'll send him 'round to meet you. He's a specialist in this kind of thing." The Chief of Base got up. He turned to Fast

Eddie. "Don't send any more of the kind of 'dirty' scripts that go into this back to the world, but do make sure that a copy comes to my office. I'll see it reaches the right people."

Romeo came by the next morning. His name wasn't Romeo on the visitors' list, but there was no mistaking him. He was tall and good looking, pleased to meet you and perfectly sure that you were pleased to meet him. He oozed charm from every pore. In short, a perfect case officer for dealing with the ladies.

"Wow, this is great," he said as he read through *The Whorehouse Report*. "Wuensdorf: three colonels and a general. Looks like my first stop."

"You plan to sample the wares?" asked Kevin.

"Maybe," said Romeo with a smile. "But what I really had in mind was taking some pictures."

"Bring some back for us," said Kevin.

He did. They were fascinating.

It was a big, rambling house that was down on its post-war luck. The stucco was crumbling off and you could see a line of bullet holes where someone had fired a machine gun burst diagonally across the front. It had once been a very aristocratic pink, a color that took on another connotation for its present use. The location was just right too. Only six blocks from the front gate of the caserne. Not that that mattered much to the staff officer whose car was parked out in front. He didn't have to walk it.

The Madam was an over-large, middle-aged war widow named, appropriately enough, Juliet. Romeo's charm, but, perhaps, more importantly his large bankroll, had made her a willing partner in Romeo and Juliet Film Productions, GmBH, the German alphabet soup for "Inc."

The story that she gave to Romeo when he asked about her husband was that he had been killed on the Eastern Front. When she was entertaining Russian guests, the answer to that question was that he bought it at Normandy. In any event, she was only in this line of work temporarily, until she could get together enough money to move to Bavaria and buy a farm. Without Romeo's money, it would have taken her a long time. *The Whorehouse Report* listed the prices she charged too. And Romeo paid in West Marks, which went a lot further than the East Marks the Russians paid in. The exchange rate was 4 East to 1 West Mark.

The star of the show was Hildie, short for Brunhilda. She was reserved for the senior officers—the ones with money. The description in Romeo's report did not do her justice: early twenties, five-seven, 120 pounds, brown and brown. She was very photogenic. She could have made a big splash in Hollywood, and not just in the B-movies, like the ones that Romeo was making. Rumor had it that when the operation folded, Romeo brought her out and they got married. An occupational hazard, the Chief of Base called it.

Chief of Base never would tell Kevin what they got from whorehouse operations, but he always complained if *The Whorehouse Report* hadn't been updated in a while, which seemed to suggest that there was something useful about it, at least from his point of view.

He also would occasionally regale them with stories like the one about the Russian KGB colonel who, when confronted with photos of himself and a beautiful young woman in a state of undress, asked if he could have a dozen 8X10 glossies. "Now that took brass balls," said the Chief of Base, obviously proud of his Russian opposite number who had refused to be blackmailed.

The Site never got an apology for the nasty-gram that told it to put a kibosh on the kind of scripts that went into *The Whorehouse Report*, but it did get a request for copies of the report itself. One day, right around Christmas, the Chief of Base showed Kevin a copy of *The Whorehouse Report* printed on pretty paper. Intelligence of ill repute had made it to the big time.

Circuit 121:   01:09-01:12Z 04 July 1955
**   Reel 10103**

MALE 1: VASYA, are you there? This is VOVA.
MALE 2: VOVA! How's they hanging?
MALE 1: By a thread. I drove the major over to
        his favorite whorehouse in NORA yesterday,
        Frau Heidi's place.
[Transcriber comment: 8 Guards Army is
        headquartered in NORA.]
MALE 2: How so? Sounds like cushy duty.
MALE 1: Yeah, most of the time it is, but this

time things got out of hand.

MALE 2: What went wrong?

MALE 1: We drove out to the place. It's a real classy joint. You should see it. They say that it used to belong to some big Nazi party member. Inside it's all low lights and low-cut dresses. And wall-to-wall brass. I ain't never seen so many officers outside of headquarters, and no wonder, with the prices they charge, only officers can afford it.

MALE 2: Ain't it the truth! The officers got everything, but we don't get nothing.

MALE 1: But I figured out a way to get myself a piece of the action, so to speak. Every time I take the major over there, I fill up his staff car to the brim. When we get there, I drain out all the gas, except for enough to get us back to garrison. It's a barter deal. They get the gas, and I get the ass.

MALE 2: Sounds like a great idea. Maybe I'll give it a try.

MALE 1: It worked out great till last night. Afterwards the major wanted to make a stop on his way back to garrison. Well, I hadn't left enough gas for that and we ran out on the way back. Boy, was he pissed.

MALE 2: I'll bet.

MALE 1: He said I'd have to walk back to garrison for gas. I got out and left him there steaming, but lucky for me the MPs stopped me to check my pass. I'd only gotten about a kilometer from the car. They had some gas cans in the back of their car and that got us back to garrison. The major was fit to be tied. He told me that if I wanted to keep driving for him, I'd better be damn sure that the car was full of gas when we left garrison from now on.

MALE 2: Maybe you'd better put a jerry can of gas, or two, in the trunk, just in case.

MALE 1: Yeah! He might sign off on that. I'll
        give it a try. How's life in EBERSWALDE?
[Transcriber comment: 20 Guards Army is
headquartered in EBERSWALDE.]
MALE 2: Oh, not nearly as good as it is on your
        end. My major is so straightlaced, he
        wouldn't be found dead in the local cat
        house. I got a buddy in the 35th, though,
        who drives a light colonel with a taste for
        the ladies. He says that the local dorf is
        a jumping place on a Saturday night. I'll
        have to tip him off to this gas thing.
MALE 1: Which 35th? Where's it at?
MALE 2. KRAMPNITZ.
MALE 1: Oh, you mean the 35th MRD.
[Transcriber comment: The 35th Motor-Rifle
Division, subordinate to 20 Guards Army, is
garrisoned in KRAMPNITZ.]
MALE 2: Yeah. Then again, maybe he won't be
        interested. He's been telling me that
        there's always enough staff cars there for
        the drivers to get a game of cards going.
        He always wins big, 'cause he cheats.
MALE 1: He should be careful. If they catch him
        cheatin', they'll tear him limb from limb.
        They caught a card shark here in the 79th
        TD, and he 'fell' under a tank the next
        day.
[Transcriber comment: The 79th Tank Division of 8
Guards Army is stationed in JENA.]
MALE 2: Yeah, the gasoline thing would be a lot
        safer, and how much can he win from a bunch
        of drivers! None of us has got any money.
MALE 1: Tell me about it.
MALE 2: Thank you, 8th Guards. I read you fivers
        too. End of channel check.
MALE 1: [Whispers] Say 'hi' to your lieutenant
        for me. Bye.
[Transcriber comment: The duty officer apparently
showed up unexpectedly at the 20 Guards end,
forcing the op to pretend he wasn't
perschatting.]

24
Lieutenant Sheerluck's Moose

There were rumors that Lieutenant Sheerluck had a moose, but these did not meet the standard reporting criteria for substantiated fact. The sources were the usual "a friend of a friend of a friend told me," or the almost as common "I was as close to them as from us to the perimeter fence" sort of thing. The fact that the perimeter fence was over 200 yards away, and the source was near-sighted and did not have his glasses on at the time, or that the "friend" at the end of the chain was drunk and had never ever seen Lieutenant Sheerluck before did not keep the stories from being told, but it did give the listener pause.

Then there was the fact that no one could quite imagine Lieutenant Sheerluck with a moose. Sure he was an officer. Sure he had money, and a lot more than most of the people wondering if he had a moose or not. Sure he had access to the PX and coffee and chocolate and nylons. But was putting up with Lieutenant Sheerluck worth any of that?

"Maybe he's like Jekyll and Hyde?" suggested Blackie. "We've got the Jekyll, and she's got the Hyde."

That idea was vigorously debated, and the conclusion was that there was insufficient proof for this theory. Nobody had ever seen a hint of Mr. Hyde in Lieutenant Sheerluck.

"I'd have to see it to believe it, and even then I might not believe it," said Fast Eddie, who had fairly stringent, but logically reasonable requirements for 'proof.' That's why he was an analyst.

One fine summer day, however, July the twenty-third to be precise, Corporal Neumann provided the incontrovertible proof of what no one had deemed to be possible. His moose knew Lieutenant Sheerluck's moose. This immediately engendered demands to meet the witness face-to-face. Corporal Neumann wisely did not want to introduce his moose to the motley crew of reprobates that insisted upon the opportunity to interrogate her forthwith. Inducements and blandishments were offered: money, coffee, booze, nylons, cigarettes. Corporal Neumann refused. Things escalated, and Blackie threatened to write Corporal Neumann's mother about his moose. That was hitting below the belt, and everyone knew it. Corporal Neumann weakened.

"Come on, Blackie! That's not fair. What would you do, if I wrote your mother that you did *not* have a moose?" said Kevin, who thought that Corporal Neumann at least deserved a fair fight under the Marquis of Queensbury rules.

"I'd rip your arm off and beat you to death with it," countered Blackie bravely, though no one could really imagine him doing so, especially to Kevin, who would have strangled him with a patch cord in self-defense.

"Just what I thought. So before Neumann rips your arm off and beats you to a bloody pulp with it, let's get back to the problem at hand. Finding out what Uschie knows about Lieutenant Sheerluck's moose."

Corporal Neumann was touched by Kevin's gallant defense, and the fact that Kevin knew his moose's name. He made an immediate counteroffer. Kevin—and only Kevin—could talk to Uschie, but he had to bring his own girl, and the inquisition had to pay for the date. Corporal Neumann was not as dumb as he was sometimes thought to be.

"Sounds good to me," said Kevin. "Let's see, a dollar a head should do it."

"Yeah, four bucks is OK," said Blackie.

"I meant a dollar from each of you inquisitors," responded Kevin. Come on, are you going to tell me that the straight skinny on Lieutenant Sheerluck's moose isn't worth a buck a piece?"

"Where you going on that kind of money?" asked Blackie.

"The Pavillon du Lac, of course," said Kevin. "Nothing but the best for a source with this kind of information. And besides, you don't think I'd take Gabbie to some dive, do you?"

The inquisition agreed to the proposal. Everyone trusted Kevin as an information broker, and, maybe later, they could pump Corporal Neumann for some info on the elusive Gabbie, who a number of them thought as non-existent as Lieutenant Sheerluck's moose, who, at the moment, had no name. They each forked over a dollar, including Master-Sergeant Laufflaecker, who had come in on the tail end of the deal, but was as curious as everybody else about Gabbie and Lieutenant Sheerluck's mystery moose.

Uschie spoke with a Bavarian drawl and had the figure to match. Gabbie was surprised that she had on a real dress and not a Dirndl, which she told Kevin was the national costume of Bavaria. Kevin was glad that they spoke English for Corporal Neumann, because he had trouble keeping up with Uschie's Bayrisch, which was almost thick enough to cut with a knife.

She knew which knife and fork to use, did not drink from the finger bowl, used the bread plate, chewed with her mouth closed, and was, in general, pleasant company. Kevin tried to picture her seated at the table with Mrs. Neumann, but since he had never seen Corporal Neumann's mother, his effort was not entirely successful. Considering the way that Corporal Neumann reacted to Uschie, however, it was clear that thinking along those lines was not just idle speculation. No wonder Corporal Neumann had not wanted to subject her to the inquisition. They would have had her for lunch and Corporal Neumann would never have seen her again.

The service at the Pavillon du Lac was excellent, the food was superb, the wine a choice Merlot. Uschie had Three Seasons Salad with Thousand Islands Dressing and Trout Almondine with Artichoke Hearts in a Chardonnay Sauce. Corporal Neumann had the Grilled Filet Mignon with a mixture of Exotic Mushrooms served with Bordelaise and Bearnaise Sauce. Gabbie—Spinach Salad in a Vinaigrette dressing and Chicken Cordon Bleu with fresh young peas. Kevin preferred the Veal Cordon Bleu with its Gruyere Cheese filling.

As the meal progressed, the conversation slowly turned to other German-American couples, and finally, specifically to

Lieutenant Sherlock and Marla, which was short for Marlene. She and Uschie had met in class at the Uni. It was one of those big classes that everybody had to take: Intensive Writing. Otherwise, they would never have met. Uschie was in Americanistics and Marla was studying Political Science.

They sat next to each other in Intensive Writing, but only got to know one another because of Rilke. They had both brought a copy of Rilke in English to class, and had bumped into one another in the rush out the door when class ended, each spilling her books on the floor in the process. Of course, "just like in the movies," said Uschie, they picked up each other's copy of Rilke, and had to find each other again to swap them back. Uschie's book had an inscription for Corporal Neumann in it, and Marla's an inscription for Lieutenant Sherlock. Kevin could not imagine either of them reading Rilke, not even in translation.

When Uschie and Marla met to exchange the books, they started talking about Rilke, and moved to the inscriptions, and from there the conversation naturally found its way to the boyfriends. Uschie had not known the difference between a corporal and a lieutenant, but Marla straightened her out soon enough, not that the difference made any difference to Uschie, but it apparently did to Marla. She had evidently met her lieutenant on the eighth of September, which was her birthday, so she liked to call him 'my birthday present,' which, when listening to the list of the things he bought her, made it seem like a very apt name for him. He had taken her to Harnack House and to the Pavillon du Lac, and Uschie was pleased to have earned some bragging rights this evening with her dinner at the Pavillon du Lac so that she could let Marla know that she was not the only one with a "generous" boyfriend.

"Do you think we could go to the Harnack House some time?" asked Uschie.

"That might be a little hard," replied Kevin. "It's only for officers."

"Schade," said Uschie, a little disappointed.

"Not at all," replied Gabbie. "Tell her you prefer the chocolate sundaes at the PX."

"Why haven't you ever taken me to the PX for chocolate on a Sunday?" said Uschie to Corporal Neumann, in a tone that showed that she was more than a little disappointed.

"We could go tomorrow," said a shaken Corporal Neumann.

"But tomorrow is Friday," said the incredulous Uschie.

"A chocolate sundae is not a day of the week, but a dessert made with ice cream," explained Gabbie in German.

"In that case, by all means, tomorrow," said a very pleased Uschie. Marla had never mentioned chocolate sundaes or Sundays at the PX.

At about that time the Baked Alaska arrived. It was one of the really special things that were part of the charm of the Pavillon du Lac. It took a really long time to prepare, which meant that you had to order it before the meal, but it was worth it. People who waited to order until after the meal—like people usually do for the dessert course—were disappointed. Kevin knew better, and had ordered it before anything else.

"Certainement, monsieur!" said the waiter taking the order, who immediately moved Kevin up a notch on his hierarchy of customers. Even with Americans, an order for Baked Alaska usually meant a good tip.

Two waiters wheeled an enormous cart with a huge covered silver dish up to the entrance to the dining room. The lights were dimmed. The first waiter raised the cover with a flourish. The second poured a snifter of brandy over the contents of the dish and struck a match. The whole room ooh-ed and aah-ed, as the flames leapt up, illuminating the darkened room. You could feel the heat getting more intense as they wheeled the flaming Baked Alaska up to the table. The floor show that went with the Baked Alaska, and the startled awe and envy of the other dinner guests were worth the price on the menu. The fact that the Baked Alaska was also delicious, was just icing on the cake.

"Tell her that you had a Baked Alaska," said Kevin. "I'll bet the lieutenant never got her one of these."

Kevin was right. Not only did you need to know to order it in advance, you had to know what it was called in French, since it did not say "Baked Alaska" on the menu. There it was called "Omelette Surprise."

The Baked Alaska got Uschie a lot more bragging rights with Marla, who Uschie obviously did not consider one of her best friends. When pressed to describe her, Uschie said:"pleasant for men to look at, brash, bleached-blond hair, brown eyes, an over-large mouth, about 168 centimeters tall, and one of those popular hour-glass figures: 95-70-90."

Girls always sound somewhat strangely larger in centimeters, when you are used to them in inches. Even Kevin had trouble getting used to that. He had to translate it to inches for the inquisition: about 5'7" and 38-28-36.

After finishing off the Baked Alaska, Uschie decided that perhaps tomorrow would not be a good day to have a chocolate sundae after all. She and Corporal Neumann agreed on Saturday for the sundae.

The evening concluded with a taxi ride down to the Kudamm, Berlin's Fifth Avenue, for a moon-light stroll and some people watching before the two couples split up so that the guys could escort the girls home on the bus. Operation "Dinner Out" was viewed as a huge intelligence coup by the members of the inquisition. After listening to Kevin's report about Marla, and later to Corporal Neumann's about Gabbie, they all felt like they had gotten their money's worth out of the deal. Lieutenant Sheerluck really had a moose.

Circuit 53:   10:23-10:26Z 16 July 1955
**   Reel 11137**

FEMALE 1: KARLSHORST operator. This is MOSCOW
          calling. 4371 for my party, please.
FEMALE 2: I'll connect you. ... It's ringing.
MALE 1: 4371.
FEMALE 2: Your party's on the line, MOSCOW. Go
          ahead, please.
MALE 2: BORIS! Am I keeping you busy enough.
MALE 1: Yes, EVGENIJ. NATASHA is complaining that
          I am hardly ever home.
MALE 2: Then I am ordering you to go home tonight
          and keep my sister company.
MALE 1: But of course, comrade general. To hear
          is to obey. But what about all those other
          things you 'ordered' me to do?
MALE 2: They'll keep, but NATASHA won't, if you
          don't pay enough attention to her.

MALE 1: NATASHA will be pleased. I'll tell her
that it is a present from you. Now what is
important enough to get my brother-in-law
the general on the phone?

MALE 2: The last report you sent in on SPOTLIGHT.
The one from PRIMROSE. You wanted a report
on the corporal with the Germanic name.

MALE 1: Yes.

MALE 2: His family has enough money to run your
entire operation out of petty cash. Oil.

MALE 1: Money, it seems, is out as an inducement.
Perhaps we could threaten to reveal his
relationship to the German girl to his
family.

MALE 2: My guess is that his mother would be
thrilled with this girl. The maid told
MILKMAN that all of the young women after
the son are only after his money and not
his love. Even though she may be somewhat
mercenary, the German girl undoubtedly has
no more idea about how much money he has
than anyone at SPOTLIGHT. Even with all my
resources I had a hard time finding out.
And then there's the fact that PRIMROSE
said that the girl is actually attracted to
the young man.

MALE 1: So PRIMROSE's suggestion of money seems
to be out then.

MALE 2: So it appears.

MALE 1: I'll make a note in his dossier in any
event. Thanks, EVGENIJ.

MALE 2: There'll be no hard copy, because I want
no mention of MILKMAN and his information
in any files but my own.

MALE 1: I understand, EVGENIJ. I'll just say
'money - negative.'

MALE 2: That'll be fine, BORIS. My best to
NATASHA this evening.

MALE 1: Of course, EVGENIJ, and ours to OLGA.
[Hang up]

The Kurfürstendamm

25
Kevin's Got a Screw Loose

"I've got a screw loose," said Kevin.

"Yeah, I know you've always been a bit flaky," replied Fast Eddie.

"You've got one of those little screwdrivers?"

"Oh, that kind of screw! There was one here somewhere," said Eddie digging around in the center drawer of his desk.

"My headphones short out if I don't hold my head just right. I'm getting a stiff neck," said Kevin, rolling his head around to loosen up his stiff neck.

"Here it is," beamed Eddie, holding up a small screwdriver.

"Thanks," said Kevin, taking the tail end of his headphone cord out of his right-front pants pocket, and screwing open the phone plug.

Kevin's loose screw

The screw that secured the top of the two wires in the cord to the plug, following the dictates of Murphy's Law, dropped onto the floor and rolled off somewhere.

"Why do they always do that?" asked Kevin crawling around on the floor.

"SOP," said Fast Eddie, suppressing a smile.

"No wonder! The SOP's always fouled up."

"Are you sure that it's holding your neck just right and not the torque on the screw that's making your neck stiff?"

"An interesting thought. I'll ask the screw what it thinks, if I can find it."

"What's that man doing under your desk, Sergeant Fastbinder?" asked Lieutenant Sheerluck in his usual "stand to attention and salute me, you peon" tone of voice.

"He's got a screw loose, Sir!" said Fast Eddie, springing to his feet and standing right on Kevin's lost screw.

"I know that. If I'd had my way, he would have been out on a Section 8 a long time ago, but what's he doing crawling under your desk, sergeant?"

"Looking for his screw, Sir!" said Fast Eddie, emphasizing 'Sir!' in the best traditions of military obsequiousness.

"Ah! Maybe the colonel and the COB will listen to me now and get rid of him," said Sheerluck, pronouncing the abbreviation for Chief of Base as if it were a word instead of an abbreviation, which was something only newks did. He had been around long enough to know better, but he didn't. "Do you think he could be violent?"

"He will be, if he can't find his screw, Sir!" proclaimed Fast Eddie, remembering the tedious lecture he had had to listen to the last time he forgot to say 'Sir!' to Lieutenant Sheerluck.

"Good. You keep an eye on him, and I'll go write up a report," said the lieutenant, smiling at the thought that he could finally get rid of that troublemaker who thought he could speak Russian. He did an about-face that would have done a drill team proud, and strode purposefully out of the Operations bay. Maybe if that troublemaker became violent and killed Sergeant Fastbinder, he would be rid of them both. With that pleasant thought his smile expanded from ear to ear.

Sergeant Fastbinder plopped back down in his chair and put his feet up on his desk.

"You were standing on it all the time, you bastard!" yelled Kevin demonstrating his well-polished "win friends and influence people" skills. "What did Sheerluck want?" Kevin never listened when the lieutenant talked, because he never had anything to say to Kevin.

"He's going to write a report."

"Don't send it out without QC. Remember the NAAFI tape."

"Not that kind of report! He's going to tell the old man and the 'COB.' that you've got a screw loose."

"Great! Maybe they'll get some decent headsets that don't keep coming undone all the time."

Fast Eddie didn't say that he was the one who kept coming in early to loosen the screw in Kevin's phone plug. It kept Swings from becoming really deadly dull.

"Screw yourself back together. The recorder for circuit 53 just turned on," said Fast Eddie.

Circuit 53:   09:15-09:19Z 26 July 1955
**   Reel 12761**

FEMALE 1: MOSCOW. This is GERMANY, the KARLSHORST
    operator. Could I have 5467 for my party?
FEMALE 2: Just a moment, please. I'll ring them
    for you.
MALE 1: 5467.
FEMALE 2: KARLSHORST. Go ahead, please. Your
    party's on the line.
MALE 2: Wheels up, EVGENIJ! They've gone!
MALE 1: You sound relieved, BORIS.
MALE 2: I thought that I had seen things get out
    of hand when the CG or the IG came on an
    inspection tour, but this takes the cake.
    We must have had 30,000 troops out cleaning
    the streets, painting everything white and
    hanging up banners. Then on the day itself,
    we had 'em out lining the motorcade route.
    I wonder if it was like this when the Czar
    came in the old days.
MALE 1: The more things change, the more they
    stay the same.
MALE 2: If it was a madhouse before they left,
    it's like a madhouse in the wake of an

earthquake now. Discipline was so tight
while they were here, that now it's swung
back to the other extreme. The Officers'
Club is packed and the vodka's flowing like
water. They're even handing out beer in the
barracks. That's going to be a real
disaster.

MALE 1: You're right. Beer in the barracks is
always a real mistake.

MALE 2: It'll take a week to get things back on
an even keel.

MALE 1: At least.

MALE 2: It was exciting being at the center of
things, and having all that brass around,
but I'm glad to see the back of them.
Stopping all operations just because it
would be embarrassing to himself if one of
them got rolled up while he was here was
ridiculous. Sure the Geneva talks did not
go that well, but that's all at the
political level. Down here on the working
intel level things are business as usual. I
didn't think that things were so bad that
the Americans or the Brits would expressly
want to break the rules to embarrass Nikita
Sergeevich while he was here.

MALE 1: It only takes one politician who thinks
he can make political hay out of a blown
intel operation to make our lives
miserable. They just don't realize how much
damage their political expediency does to
our day-to-day lives. That's how I got my
assignment to LONDON. They declared my
predecessor persona non grata. He had 24
hours to leave the country, so we kicked
out the British Resident here in MOSCOW. It
set our British operations back at least
six months, and I'm sure that the Brits
were no better off. All that for some
headlines in the papers that didn't even
affect the next election. We actually came
out ahead, because it told us which of our

```
         operations were blown.
MALE 2: Every cloud has a silver lining, but I'd
         just as soon not get my assignment to
         WASHINGTON at PAVEL's expense.
MALE 1: I'm sure he'd be pleased to hear you say
         so. MIKHAEL, my predecessor, was very
         philosophical about the whole thing. He
         talked about blowing up Parliament like Guy
         Fawkes, but settled for compromising the
         politician in a honey trap six months
         later. I ran it personally as a favor to
         him.
MALE 2: Revenge is a dish best served cold.
MALE 1: Yes, it is.
MALE 2: I'm off to make an appearance at the
         party, but I don't want to make it too
         late. NATASHA and I are going to the West
         tomorrow morning early to load a dead drop,
         and then we'll take in the Dahlem Museum.
```

"You're off to the party!? But I've got 27 more tapes to do before I can call it quits," said Kevin with annoyance out loud to the voice on the tape, which quite wisely chose to ignore him. "I've got an early date too. Maybe I'll see you at the Dahlem."

"Does he always talk to himself like that?" asked a voice behind Fast Eddie's left shoulder that sounded familiar, but was coming out of the mouth of an American staff sergeant whom Eddie had never seen before. He had engineer insignia and a nose that would put Cyrano de Bergerac to shame.

"Yes and No," said Eddie, surmising correctly that it was the Chief of Base in disguise. "He's not talking to himself. He's talking to the people on the tape. And yes, he talks to them all the time."

"Is this what Lieutenant Sherlock got me over here for?" asked the Chief of Base.

"I wouldn't know," said Fast Eddie, tactfully sidestepping the issue. "The lieutenant doesn't usually let me in on his plans."

"He was here earlier this evening, wasn't he?"

"Yes, he was," said Eddie, who could hardly deny the obvious.

"He said that Kevin had a screw loose."

"He did, but we tightened it back up. His headphones are

working just fine now," said Eddie, pleased to feel some solid ground under foot.

"You mean that it was a real screw that was loose?"

"Yes," said Eddie, holding up his small screwdriver.

"Lieutenant Sheerluck took it figuratively."

"I'm sorry to hear that, sir," said Fast Eddie, figuring that a little 'SIR-ing' couldn't hurt.

In the meantime, the voices on Kevin's tape said:

```
MALE 1: That should be a fun day. Are you
        lunching at Harnack House?
MALE 2: Yes, we are. That should shake up the
        opposition. They'll be wondering who we're
        meeting there.
```

"Yes, they will," said Kevin holding up his end of the conversation.

```
MALE 1: But you're not meeting anyone?
MALE 2: No, we're just having lunch. The food's
        actually not that bad. The floor show won't
        be bad either as the enlisted pavement
        artists try to figure out how to follow us
        inside the Officers' Club.
```

"Not if I can tell the Chief of Base first," gloated Kevin.

"Tell me what?" said the Chief of Base.

"He can't hear you. He's in another world," said Fast Eddie. "You'll have to wait until the tape stops and he comes back down to earth to ask him."

The tape made three more revolutions as Kevin's fingers flashed across the keyboard of his mill.

```
MALE 1: I'm sorry that I'll have to miss it. Wish
        NATASHA 'Bon appétit' for me.
MALE 2: I will. And our best to OLGA.
MALE 1: Certainly. Enjoy the 'floor show'
        tomorrow.
[Hang up]
```

The tape stopped. Kevin stood up, ripped the page out of his mill, slipped his headphones off his ears back onto his shoulders, unplugged the cord and shoved the phone-jack end into his right-front pants pocket.

"Wheels up, Eddie! Khrushchev's gone wheels-up! Get out a message blank, 'cause this one's got to go," he yelled.

Fast Eddie already had a message blank in his mill. He recognized Kevin talking to a tape as a sign of an impending reportable item. He was just waiting for Kevin to give him the report title. He typed:

FIRST SECRETARY KHRUSHCHEV DEPARTS BERLIN

"Who's your friend?" asked Kevin noticing the engineer sergeant standing behind Eddie reading over his shoulder.

"Guess," said Eddie.

"Oh, nice nose," said Kevin, complimenting the Chief of Base's make-up technique.

"What did you want to tell me?" said the Chief of Base, cutting right to the chase.

"Oh, yeah. Boris, you know, my KGB buddy in Karlshorst, and his wife Natasha are loading a dead drop early tomorrow somewhere in the American Sector near the Dahlem Museum, and they plan to eat lunch at the Harnack House to see the surveillance team falling all over itself trying to get in. He figures the team's all enlisted men. They're not meeting anybody. They're just going for the 'floor show', as he called it."

"Thanks. You always seem to have the information I need to know before I know I need it," said the Chief of Base with a rare smile.

"While you're here," said Kevin, seemingly oblivious to the compliment, "Khrushchev was talking about a 'U-2'. What's that? It wasn't in any of the working aids."

"I'm not surprised. It's classified," said the Chief of Base.

"Well, it can't be too classified, if Khrushchev knows about it," countered Kevin. "What is it?"

"You do have a point there," said the Chief of Base. "It's a type of aircraft."

"Now that's interesting. I thought it was a type of camera. He kept talking about it taking pictures."

"Did you report this?!" asked the Chief of Base, turning to Eddie with a glare.

"No, neither one of us knew what it was, and it helps to know what it is, if you're going to report something," replied Eddie.

"Now you know. Get it out right after the 'wheels up' report," growled the Chief of Base, who knew that this would make folks stand up and take notice of his project back in the world, and might even make a few heads roll. "Anything else?"

"That's all so far," said Kevin. "But I've got 27 tapes to go on the visit."

"Keep me posted," said the Chief of Base.

"I will," said Kevin.

Fast Eddie sat down to type his reports. Kevin went over and grabbed another tape. The Chief of Base shook his head and left as silently as he had come in. He'd have to talk to the colonel about tightening up Lieutenant Sheerluck's loose screws.

27
The Summer Doldrums

It was a slow Swing. In fact it had been a slow week of Swings. Nothing, but nothing was going on. The circuits all seemed to be connected to the Sphinx central exchange. Even the drunks were quiet. Gabbie and her mother were out in the Zone visiting Tante Ursula. Kevin and Fast Eddie had read three books each and had solved at least four of the world's pressing problems in their wide-ranging talks. That, however, left a couple of thousand problems over for the world's political leaders to solve and did not do anything for their immediate problem of the boredom of the summer doldrums.

On the fifth night of the set, Fast Eddie came into the bay reading the local military newspaper. "Hey, Kev, did you see this article in the *Berlin Observer* about taking the Brit Duty Train out to Braunschweig and on to London?" said Fast Eddie, folding the paper over so that the article was on the outside.

Kevin took the paper and started reading the article. "It says that the food's pretty good on the train, and, you know, I still haven't been to London," commented Kevin. "I'd like to try a pint of bitter."

"Maybe it's worth looking into," replied Fast Eddie, taking the paper back. They both lapsed into silence again. They had pretty much used up all the interesting topics of conversation in the last four days. Kevin wondered if he should brush off the tapes on the collection recorders. They had been up for so long without turning that they were beginning to collect a layer of dust. It was something to do.

It was a really long, slow Swing. So long that Kevin had to wake Fast Eddie up so he could go home to Meg. The next evening, Fast Eddie came in with a travel guide for London. Meg had decided that they were going to London, right now, before the baby came, because, if they waited until after, they would never get to London. Fast Eddie lacked Meg's instant enthusiasm and was talking the trip up, trying to convince himself that it was a good idea. He was so good at talking the trip up that he convinced Kevin that it was a good idea, even before he convinced himself.

Talking about London and all the things to see and do there took up half the Swing. There was Big Ben and the Houses of Parliament, the POSH shopping on Knightsbridge, Piccadilly Circus, a live show in the West End, the ravens at the Tower of London, and the pigeons on the lions at the foot of Nelson's Column on Trafalgar Square. The second half of the Swing was filled with talk of all the things that had to be done to get out of Berlin. There was a leave form to turn in, Flag Orders had to be requested, train and hotel reservations to be made, and not in that order. Putting the whole thing together was like an intelligence test to see if you were smart enough to find your way through the maze to the train.

And then there was Sergeant Laufflaecker, whose immutable logic reshaped their travel plans.

"You want to what?! ... You can go, or Fast Eddie can go, but you and Fast Eddie can't go. Somebody has to stay here and keep the world safe for Democracy on the Swing."

Kevin thought that Fast Eddie and Meg should go first, since it was their idea, but the actual decision of who would go first was made by the British Rail Transportation Office, when Meg called for reservations on the Duty Train.

"Sorry, Ducks, but we've only got one seat open for a Yank on that date," said the helpful Brit sergeant at the RTO.

With unflinching decisiveness, Meg put Kevin on that train, and booked places for herself and Eddie a week later. Then she sent another telex to the hotel in London that she had found in the guide book, and told them to swap the two reservations that she had already made.

That Thursday, at exactly 09:26 Local, right on time, the British Duty train pulled out of the Berlin-Charlottenburg station with Kevin on board. He spent the first part of the trip enjoying the sight-seeing. This was his only real chance to get a look at East Germany. The American Duty Train, with ruthless efficiency, only traveled at night so that you arrived in Frankfurt or Berlin early in the morning with a whole duty day ahead of you. Kevin thought that the Brits had the right attitude. He saw a Russian military convoy on the road next to the train and wondered if anybody he knew was in it.

Kevin was in the dining car at 12:00 when the train went through Marienborn. The Wiener Schnitzel was excellent. Kevin made a mental note to remind Fast Eddie that you had to pay in BAFS. The connection to the boat-train to Hoek van Holland via Hannover went like clockwork. The Channel crossing on the overnight ferry to Harwich was smooth as glass. The train pulled in to the Liverpool-street Station, as scheduled, at 07:59 Local, which in this case was also Zulu, because London and Greenwich are on the same time. Kevin walked out onto Liverpool Street to the taxi rank to head for his hotel.

"This hotel, mate?" said the cabbie, when Kevin showed him the address. "Cor Blimey, you Yanks only got one thing on your minds."

"What do you mean 'this hotel?'" said Kevin wondering if he had understood the tone of the driver's question correctly.

"It's a cat-house, ain't it? Like I said, all you Yanks can think about is knickers and knockers. During the war a decent English girl couldn't go out on the street alone with all you Yanks around!"

"A cat-house!" said Kevin, picking his jaw up off the floor of the cab. "Let me tell you who made this reservation," said Kevin.

The cabby was laughing so hard he almost ran into a bus. "That's rich, mate. And are you goin' to let 'em stay there, or is you goin' to tell this young lady where she had you shacked up?"

"I've half a mind not to tell her, but she and my girlfriend get on too well. They'd make my life miserable, if I didn't."

"Trouble and strife," said the cabbie.

"What?" asked Kevin, who was getting his first lesson in why Churchill had said "two peoples separated by a common language."

"Trouble and strife," said the cabbie again. "That's Cockney rhyming slang for wife. That's all you've got from your friend's wife, trouble and strife."

"You've got a point there, but can you help me get out of this trouble and strife that my friend's wife put into my life?" asked Kevin.

"Listen to his honour here, rhyming and all, and not wanting to go to a cat-house. I guess that Yanks can be gentlemen too when they wants to. Right, mate! I knows a little place up near Russell Square. I'll take you there."

The cabbie was right. It was a very nice, inexpensive hotel near the British Museum, and there was a great Indian restaurant just around the corner. Kevin made a reservation there for Fast Eddie and Meg for the next week. As he was making the reservation, he told the manager the story of Meg making reservations for them all at a cat-house. The manager started laughing so hard that Kevin thought he was going to fall on the floor.

"And her a pregnant lady. I can just see it now, herself walking up to the desk with her Eddie in tow to check in. It would a scared all the customers away. They'd probably have paid her to move someplace else. Listen, Yank, I've got an idea," said the hotel manger with a gleam in his eye.

The manager told Kevin that he would call the other hotel, and tell them the story, but not tell them that Kevin was going to tell "the lady" what kind of a hotel it was, or that he had already made other reservations for her. He would tell them that Kevin was going to let her check in out of spite.

"They'd believe that, Yank. They haven't met ya," said the manager.

He called the hotel, and just like he thought, they implored him to take the booking.

"But, I'm booked solid, I tell ya," said the manager into the phone.

The hotel manager had missed his calling as a conman. By the time he hung up, the other "hotel" had offered to pay for Meg and Fast Eddie's room at his hotel for the whole week.

"You've made my day, Yank. I haven't laughed so hard in a long time. I'll be telling this story at hoteliers' meetings for years.

Your room's on the house, too. They overpaid for your friends' room."

Meg and Fast Eddie thought that it was a pretty good joke too.

Circuit 53:   **07:35-07:39Z 22 August 1955**
                     Reel 17157

FEMALE 1: KARLSHORST operator. This is MOSCOW.
    4371 for my party, please.
FEMALE 2: Just a moment. I'll connect you.
MALE 1: 4371.
FEMALE 2: MOSCOW, go ahead, please. Your party's
    on the line.
MALE 2: BORIS! I'm almost surprised to get you. I
    thought that you had all fallen off the
    edge of the earth. I haven't seen any
    reporting from you for almost two weeks.
MALE 1: Good morning, EVGENIJ! I'm pleased that
    you missed us, but there is nothing going
    on. The Germans are all on vacation.
MALE 2: Does that mean that the Americans are on
    vacation too? As I recall, they don't close
    down for August.
MALE 1: They might as well. Nothing's going on.
MALE 2: What about PRIMROSE? She must have
    something to say about the Americans?
MALE 1: She probably would, if she were here.
    She's gone to visit her aunt in Bavaria.
MALE 2: Why wasn't that in a report?
MALE 1: We did not think that it met criteria.
MALE 2: Let me be the judge of that. Next time,
    be sure to include her travel plans.
MALE 1: If you're concerned about SPOTLIGHT,
    BIRCH is still reporting. He says that he
    can't afford to go on vacation if the
    Americans don't. Business was never better.
    Beer sales on the Swing and Mid shifts have
    quadrupled.

MALE 2: No wonder there's Nothing To Report.
        They're all dead drunk.
MALE 1: That's a logical assumption.
MALE 2: Can we exploit that?
MALE 1: I doubt it. We could try to blackmail a
        single individual, but not the whole shift.
MALE 2: What other information have you been
        hiding from me?
MALE 1: We noted two SPOTLIGHT-ers on the
        passenger lists of the British Duty Train.
        One went out and is scheduled back this
        week. The other will go out when the first
        one gets back. The second one is traveling
        with his wife.
MALE 2: Why the British Duty Train?
MALE 1: Apparently the food is very good and it
        connects to the boat-train for London.
MALE 2: Do you think that it is training?
MALE 1: No, it's a vacation. It's August and the
        simple explanations are usually the best
        ones.
MALE 2: You never want to give the Americans any
        credit for subtlety.
MALE 1: They generally aren't.
MALE 2: They may surprise you one day.
MALE 1: I doubt it.
MALE 2: We'll see. My best to NATASHA.
MALE 1: Of course, and mine to OLGA. You'll get
        me that assignment to WASHINGTON, if I'm
        not surprised by the Americans?
MALE 2: You're on, BORIS! NATASHA would like
        WASHINGTON. Don't disappoint her.
MALE 1: Of course not, EVGENIJ. I'll get one of
        my sources to buy me a D.C. guide book in
        the Stars and Stripes book store.
MALE 2: Don't count your assignments before
        they're hatched, BORIS. Good-bye.
MALE 1: Good-bye, EVGENIJ.
[Hang up]

28
Marx's Tomb

One of the highlights of Kevin's trip to London was his visit to Marx's Tomb in Highgate Cemetery. He stopped by to say "thanks" to the man who had set the chain of events in motion that created his job. It takes a peculiar sort of logic to think about Marx in that light, but that was Kevin for you. He could see around logical corners to make two plus two equal four, while other people were still trying to define the problem, and wondering why it came out five. It was a good job—most of the time—and he liked the irony of the idea that its purpose was to help counteract what Marx had started.

On his way out to visit the founder of World Communism, he went by Highgate Hill to visit the statue of Dick Whittington's cat. This is not a tourist attraction on everyone's list for a week in London, or even something that a lot of people know about, but then Kevin knew lots of strange things, like the location of every whorehouse in the Group of Soviet Forces, Germany, and the alternate words to the Soviet National Anthem—the ones that could get you shot—and the fact that there was a statue of Peter Pan in Kensington Garden. He had been to Kensington Garden the day before. There was a certain amount of Peter Pan in him, and he felt himself compelled to drop by and say hello to a kindred spirit.

It isn't that Kevin never grew up, though certainly he lived in a sort of Neverland. It's more like he never grew adultish. He looked at everything with the sort of wide-eyed wonder that usually only children have, which was one of the things that Gabbie always loved about him.

Having absorbed the wonder of a statue to a cat, and having confirmed that you can indeed hear the bells of London at noon from where the statue stands, he set off for Highgate Cemetery. The cemetery was empty when he got there and the seemingly undiscovered tomb was silent, but he had barely had time to take a few snapshots of the tomb for show and tell back in Berlin, when two tour buses pulled up to the cemetery and disgorged a noisy horde of Russians. The Russians descended on the tomb en masse, and Kevin was awash in Russians before their KGB minders had a chance to notice him.

"Where are you from?" said Kevin in Russian to the heavy-set woman who had just trod on his foot.

"SɪʙTʏᴀᴢʜMᴀsʜ, Krasnoyarsk," said the woman, wondering why she hadn't seen Kevin before on the boat that brought them over. All the members of the tour had won the trip as a reward for overful-filling the plan at the factories where they worked, and each delegation identified itself with the name of the factory followed by the name of the city where it was located. On the boat, they had all had name tags that said who they were and where they were from, but when they landed in England, their KGB minders had made them take off the name tags.

"The British special services will try to get this information from you while we are on their soil, but we will not make it easy for them. No one is to wear their name tags when we go ashore," said their KGB escort.

"And where are you from?" asked the woman suspiciously.

"The armed forces in Berlin," responded Kevin noncommittally.

"And why aren't you in uniform," queried the woman.

"It is not permitted to travel in uniform in a country to which one is not assigned," answered Kevin factually.

"And what did you do to win your trip?"

"I was awarded it for victories won against our class enemy on the front lines of the Cold War," said Kevin, paraphrasing a slogan he had heard on Radio Volga, the Russian AFN, neglecting to mention that, in his case, the enemy was the Soviets.

"Girls, look! A military man," said the woman gleefully, and the nine remaining heads of the SibTyazhMash delegation turned as one in Kevin's direction. Kevin had acquired an admiring audience. They could see he was well-dressed for a Russian, all his clothes were Western. And he had a German camera, which meant that he must have connections as well.

"Oh, take our picture," said a petite—well, petite compared to the others—brunette, who had long had hopes of marrying an officer, and living abroad where they had access to things like German cameras. "I'm Svetlana," she added, and the rest of the SibTyazhMash delegation tried to follow suit, but since they all tried to speak at once, Kevin didn't catch any of their names.

"With Marx's Tomb in the background, of course," said Kevin, motioning them into place for a group photo.

The SibTyazhMash delegation was followed by six more groups of ten, posing in front of the Communist Holy of Holies, but Kevin's photo shoot was cut short by a well-dressed Russian, who said: "I don't recall seeing you on the boat, comrade."

"That's because I wasn't on it," answered Kevin, sure that he was talking to one of the KGB minders. None of the real hero-of-Socialist-Labor tourists were dressed as well as he.

An increasingly heated discussion followed, ending with the KGB man asking for the film in Kevin's camera, and Kevin informing him that if he tried to take the camera or the film, his next assignment would be guarding polar bears in Siberia. It was a threat that he had heard some wheel in Moscow use once with devastating effect.

It worked this time too, and the KGB minder retired to consult with his superiors. Five minutes later, the Russians were all being herded onto the buses, and Kevin quickly found himself alone again in the solemn silence of Highgate Cemetery with the spirit of the founder of World Communism.

He took some pictures of the buses as they pulled away, followed by the KGB chase car. He took some more pictures of the tomb, walking around it slowly, looking for that unique angle that would put it into the proper perspective. Kneeling on the west side of the tomb to get the light right for a shot from ground level, he noticed a piece of paper that wasn't there before the buses came. It was a typescript with the itinerary of the tour, carefully weighted down with a rock just beneath the fence surrounding the tomb.

I've heard of leaving notes on graves for the dear departed, but I don't think that Marx knew anybody on the tour, thought Kevin to himself. Kevin picked up the paper, folded it carefully and put it in his pocket. A souvenir of his encounter with the girls from SɪʙTʏᴀᴢʜMᴀꜱʜ. It had been fun, but Svetlana was no substitute for Gabbie. He couldn't wait to get back and tell her about it, but there was no need to hurry. She was in the Zone at Tante Ursula's till Monday week.

The rest of the week was OK. There was the changing of the guard at Buck House (lots of Royal pomp and circumstance), the Food Halls in Harrod's (food for the eyes as well as the mouth), the British Museum with the Elgin Marbles (Blackie asked Kevin if he won any keepsies), and a visit to Evgenij's favorite fish and chips shop on Russell Square (he was right: the best fish and chips in town). The visit to Marx's Tomb, however, remained the highlight of the trip.

The story of Kevin's trip to London and his encounter with the SɪʙTʏᴀᴢʜMᴀꜱʜ girls soon became common property at the Site. There was even a version in *The Passion Book* that suggested a bit more passion than there actually had been. When the prints of his snapshots came back from the PX on Wednesday and got passed around with yet another retelling of the tale, it was clear to all but the most hard-up cynics in the morse bay that the version in *The Passion Book* was a fake.

The story slowly filtered its way off Site, coming to the attention of the Chief of Base and Colonel Badunov at about the same time. The Chief of Base completed his counter-surveillance run to the Site disguised as an army sergeant first class with paratrooper boots about five minutes after Kevin finished his script of Boris's call to Evgenij about Kevin's trip.

Circuit 53:   12:45-12:47Z 26 August 1955
**   Reel 18457**

FEMALE 1: Hello, MOSCOW. This is the KARLSHORST
    operator in GERMANY. Can you ring 5467 for
    my party, please?
FEMALE 2: Just a moment. I'll connect you.
MALE 1: 5467.
FEMALE 2: KARLSHORST, go ahead, please. Your
    party's on the line.
MALE 2: EVGENIJ, there's a BIRCH report on the
    way that you'll want to see right away.
    Remember our conversation about the
    SPOTLIGHT travelers on the British Duty
    Train?
MALE 1: Yes, I do.
MALE 2: There's a story going around about what
    one of the travelers did while he was in
    LONDON.
MALE 1: Don't keep me in suspense, BORIS. Give me
    the highlights.
MALE 2: The first SPOTLIGHT traveler contacted a
    Russian tour group at Marx's Tomb.
MALE 1: He what?!
MALE 2: He met a group of Russian women on a tour
    of Marx's Tomb, and took pictures of the
    whole tour group. Apparently he's
    intimately involved with one of them.
MALE 1: I find that hard to believe.
MALE 2: You'll have a full report on your desk in
    an hour.

```
MALE 1: What about PRIMROSE? I have my suspicions
        about anything that BIRCH might have
        overheard, or did he get documents?
MALE 2: She's still in Bavaria at her aunt's. And
        you're right. It is something that BIRCH
        overheard.
MALE 1: It is hard to believe that an American
        would go to Marx's Tomb for the fun of it,
        isn't it?
MALE 2: Yes, which is why I wanted to alert you
        to the report. The contact was on the 24th.
        There can't be that many Russian tour
        groups that visited Marx's Tomb that day.
MALE 1: I'd bet that there was only one.
MALE 2: I wouldn't bet against you, because you'd
        probably win.
MALE 1: I'll make a few inquiries.
MALE 2: I thought you might.
MALE 1: Yes, a few inquiries. My best to NATASHA.
MALE 2: Of course, and mine to OLGA.
MALE 1: Thank you. … Good-bye, BORIS.
[Hang up]
```

Kevin was trying to convince Corporal Neumann to report the script when the Chief of Base came in.

"You're not his regular keeper," said the American sergeant first class in paratrooper boots to Corporal Neumann, who did not recognize him as the Chief of Base.

"He and Meg are in London," answered Kevin who recognized the Chief of Base's voice immediately. "They get back tomorrow."

"How was London?" asked the Chief of Base, beating around the bush.

"I had a great time. So great in fact that my KGB buddy Boris just called Moscow to tell General Besstrashnyj about it, and this doofus won't report it."

"He's making it up," said Corporal Neumann unwisely, but innocently, because he had never connected Kevin with the classified stamp incident that sent Lieutenant Sheerluck to the hospital.

"I'll be the judge of that," said the sergeant first class, taking a copy of the script. He read through it and asked Kevin how he knew it was about him.

"Cause I ran into a Russian tour group at Marx's Tomb on the twenty-fourth, and there can't have been that many SPOTLIGHT travelers in London last week. As far as I know, I was the only one."

The Chief of Base sent Corporal Neumann to get himself a cup of coffee, and proceeded to interrogate Kevin about his meeting with the Russians. Corporal Neumann did not quite get the hint, and came back with a cup of coffee about two minutes later. This time the Chief of Base was less subtle: "Go away and don't come back for half an hour!" Corporal Neumann disappeared like a ghost. When he reappeared, 30 minutes to the second later, it was just in time for him to overhear Kevin say: "...the itinerary had Svetlana's address on it."

Noticing Corporal Neumann's return, the Chief of Base said: "He's not making it up, but don't report it. I'll take care of it." With that he took Kevin's snapshots, the boat itinerary, and a copy of the script, shoved them into an envelope, and limped out of the scribe bay. His disguise boots were too tight.

Fast Eddie would have asked Kevin what went on, but then again, Fast Eddie probably would not have been sent to get a cup of coffee. Corporal Neumann sat down at Eddie's desk and said: "I wonder what's for chow tonight."

Kevin hated to admit it, but he would be glad to see Fast Eddie back from London.

29
The 393rd Field Mess-kit Repair Battalion

The briefing book on the 393rd Field Mess-kit Repair Battalion was a work of art. It was maintained with meticulous care by the best minds on Site. The level of detail was incredible. It had a complete list of all the officers on the battalion staff, and the names of the company commanders. The commanding officer was Major Kotelek. His chief of staff was Captain Chajnik. The three company commanders—all lieutenants—were Tarelka, Chashka and Lozhka. It included a list of unit telephone numbers that was more complete than the one compiled for the Site. There was a hand-drawn detail map, showing both the garrison and the nearby village of Essgeschirrheim. The motor-pool inventory even included the motor numbers of the trucks assigned to the 393rd. In short, there was everything anyone could ever want to know about the 393rd, except the fact that it was the product of some very bored imaginations.

There was a hint of this in the names. The commanding officer's name was Russian for 'mess kit.' His chief of staff was a 'teapot.' The company commanders were 'saucer,' 'cup,' and 'spoon.' And where else could the unit have been stationed, than in a made-up German place name that meant 'mess kit'-heim. The real pièce de résistance was the unit mission description. It said that the 393rd was a cover story for a nuclear weapons storage depot. Anybody who read that should have immediately suspected that it was a fake. Aside from that, the briefing book looked just as real as any of the other briefing books on Site. It was, after all, done by the same people who did all the other Site-generated briefing books.

Lieutenant Sheerluck was not one of the people deemed to have a need to know for the 393rd. The Chief of Base was likewise not kept abreast of the current status and activities of the 393rd, which were reported daily and in great detail in the briefing book. Sergeant Laufflaecker, however, appreciated a good joke now and then, and was fully read in. It was hard to keep anything from him in any event. Things would have been just fine, if Lieutenant Sheerluck had not found the briefing book on a day that Sergeant Laufflaecker was away from the Site on a three-day pass to the Zone.

Blackie had been reading the latest installment of the adventures of the 393rd on a Mid. He had gotten so swept up in the story—so he said—that he almost missed chow, and had had to get a move on to keep from missing the culinary, social and entertainment event of the shift, so he left the briefing book lying on his position, intending to put it away when he got back. Well, one thing led to another and he never did get back to his position after chow, and the briefing book was still out when the Day weenies came in. If Sergeant Laufflaecker had been in, he would have caught it on his initial sweep of the area, and all would have been right with the world, except in Blackie's part of it, where Blackie would have been woken up to come back to work on the detail that burned all the classified paper trash as a reminder that this kind of thing was not acceptable security practice. But Sergeant Laufflaecker was not in, and Lieutenant Sheerluck found the briefing book.

He sat down to read it. It was an excellent piece of work. More detailed than any of the other briefing books he had read. He thought with pride that this was a product of the 9539th, and that he was a part of this fine military unit. He considered it such a good piece of work that he wondered why no one had asked him to brief it to the general who was due by on an inspection tour later that morning, which was really the reason that Sergeant

Laufflaecker had taken a three-day pass to the Zone on that particular day. Sergeant Laufflaecker knew that the general's tour would be an unmitigated disaster, and had made a skillfully executed tactical withdrawal that would keep him out of the line of fire.

The general arrived in the closed panel truck that was used to transport high-profile visitors back and forth to the Site without raising the profile of the Site. He was accompanied by the Chief of Base, who was dressed as the Chief of Base for this occasion. When the warehouse doors closed and the truck could no longer be seen by the Vopo tower on the other side of the Sector border, the general and the Chief of Base exited the truck, followed by the general's two aides, who had been especially cleared for the project on this occasion. The general and his entourage took the twenty-five cent walking tour of the Site, which included an outing across the Sector border underground. They were impressed by the engineering skill that had gone into the project, awed by the technology that made it run, and appalled by the uniformed denizens of the cavernous space that contained it, in other words, the people who were there to run it. Sergeant Laufflaecker's assessment of the tactical situation had been faultless.

"That man needs a haircut! That man's uniform is dirty! This floor hasn't been swept in months!" said the general's short aide to Corporal Neumann, who wrote down what the aide said with mock efficiency, wishing that he had had the good sense to work the Mid like Sergeant Laufflaecker had suggested he do. "That man's shoes need shining! That man needs to stand closer to the razor! This light fixture is covered with dust!" said the general's tall aide to Corporal Neumann, who wrote down: "Next time, listen to Sergeant Laufflaecker!" The general did not say anything. That is what he had two aides for.

When the tour was finished, the general's party retired to the small briefing room, where Lieutenant Sheerluck was waiting at the podium to regale them with the important facts about the project. He read off the information with the polished ease of a doctor of philosophy (ABD).

"The tunnel is 1,476 feet long and six and one half feet in diameter. Excavating the tunnel produced 3,100 tons of "spoil" dirt, which is stored in the basement of this warehouse building and in sandbags, lining the tunnel walls. The tunnel sheath consists of 125 tons of specially shaped steel plates, which were manufactured in the United States, shipped by sea to the port of Bremerhaven, and brought overland through the Russian Zone on the daily American Duty Train. Its 4,428 one-foot segments were bolted together in the tunnel, providing the necessary support to keep the weight of the overburden from collapsing the tunnel. Pumps that run continuously, remove 400 gallons of water from the tunnel every twenty-four hours. The tap accesses 273 wire pairs housed on three cables, from which up to 30 telegraphic and 120 voice circuits can be collected simultaneously. Thus far the operation has collected over 17,000 reels of magnetic tape, which translates to approximately 125,000 telephone conversations and 800,000 feet of teletype messages."

"That's all very nice," said the general's short aide. "But what about the product?" continued the general's tall aide.

Lieutenant Sheerluck was not ready to move on to that portion of the briefing. He still had lots of information about things like how many watts of electricity were used, how many British Thermal Units of cooling were delivered by the airconditioners and the average channel number for the 09:00 Local hour, a valuable piece of data that he had himself calculated just this morning. The general's aides' wish, however, was the lieutenant's command, so he skipped to the part of his briefing that contained his summary of the intelligence product that the project had generated. 1,475 true unit designators recovered, 1,893 unit commanders identified by name and rank, 482 garrison areas identified by place name and Army Post Office number.

"That's all very nice," said the general's tall aide. "But could the general have some concrete examples?" continued the general's short aide.

That really put Lieutenant Sheerluck on the spot. He did not have any concrete examples. "Concrete examples?" he said, stalling for time. "Just a moment." And then he remembered. He still had the briefing book for the 393rd. He would read that to the general.

"The 393rd Field Mess-kit Repair Battalion, commanded by Major Kotelek, is stationed in Essgeschirrheim. This is not the unit's true designator, however, it is, in point of actual fact, the 1292nd Nuclear Weapons Storage Depot. ... All this information was obtained directly from our collection," concluded Lieutenant Sheerluck, with pride. "Any questions?"

"Why wasn't the general briefed on this before?" asked the general's aides in unison.

"This has been our first opportunity to brief the general," replied Lieutenant Sheerluck truthfully.

The Chief of Base stood up, wondering why he had not been briefed on this before and said: "That's been very enlightening. Thank you, lieutenant." Turning to the general, he said: "There's coffee and other refreshments in the back of the room. What'll you have, general?"

The general had a Vat 69 on the rocks. His short aide had a Berliner Weisse with a Schuss. His tall aide had a coffee. They left in a benevolent mood with a tin of Russian Beluga caviar and a bottle of Russian Stolichnaya vodka each. You could not get those in the PX or the class VI. Sergeant Laufflaecker's recommended tactic had met with the success typical of all his tactical suggestions.

The Chief of Base hoped that the general would forget all about it, but he did not. A hand-penned note winged its way through an ethereal back-channel to a military-academy classmate on the Joint Chiefs' staff, asking why the general had been taken by surprise by this. His friend wrote back: "Jerr, it's really all very hush-hush, and I shouldn't be telling you this, but since you already know about the Russians, I guess that I have to tell you, so that you won't think that we dropped the ball on this one, but you can't share this with anyone else. We'll be deploying our own nuclear weapons to Germany in March. I can't tell you where, of course, but it's not going to be in your backyard." The general was pleased with this piece of information and made a mental note to go over to the Site for briefings more often. It was handy learning unusual things like that. Knowledge is power, and the general understood that very well. His wife had been pleased with the caviar.

Circuit 53:   15:21-15:25Z 01 September 1955
Reel 17777

FEMALE 1: KARLSHORST, Operator. This is MOSCOW. I
    need 4371 for my party.

FEMALE 2: Just a moment. It's ringing.

MALE 1: 4371.

FEMALE 2: Your party's on the line. Go ahead, please.

MALE 2: BORIS! A moment of your time, please.

MALE 1: Certainly, EVGENIJ. As always, a pleasure to hear from you. What's important enough to get you on the phone?

MALE 2: This is a very delicate matter, BORIS. So delicate that there will not be any written communication about it. This will be just between you and me.

MALE 1: I understand, EVGENIJ. Go on.

MALE 2: Your last report from PRIMROSE was very disturbing.

MALE 1: How so, EVGENIJ. That was just so much BS. You know as well as I do that we don't have anything like that in the forward area.

MALE 2: Speak for yourself, BORIS.

MALE 1: Oh, my God! A 'special weapons facility' in the forward area? Why wasn't I told?

MALE 2: BORIS, please. I couldn't tell you, because, if I did, I'd have to have you shot, and you know how much that would upset NATASHA, but don't think I wouldn't.

MALE 1: Not a doubt in my mind. Why are you telling me now?

MALE 2: I want you to check their security profile. If there's a leak, I want to find it! APO 07243. And be discrete!

MALE 1: No wonder you're on the phone. I'll get started immediately.

MALE 2: Only your most trusted people, and nothing in writing. Understand?

MALE 1: Trusted people and nothing in writing.

MALE 2: And impress upon them the seriousness of the matter.

MALE 1: May I tell them that I need no further sanction to terminate those who permitted this security lapse with extreme prejudice?

MALE 2: Yes, you may, but call me before you do!

```
            Otherwise there's twice as much paperwork.
            Anything on your end?
MALE 1: No, things are quiet enough here.
MALE 2: That's good to hear. OLGA wonders if you
            could arrange for some more coffee.
MALE 1: Tell her to consider it done. And ask her
            to call NATASHA. You could call yourself.
            She likes to hear from you.
MALE 2: I will. Don't call in your report. I'll
            take it personally when you come back next
            week on TDY. I can get tickets for the ice
            hockey game. Dynamo is playing.
MALE 1: That'd be great.
MALE 2: Good evening, BORIS. My best to NATASHA.
MALE 1: And to OLGA.
[Hang up]
```

"Hey, Eddie, take a look at this!" said Kevin shoving the script under Eddie's sleeping nose.

Eddie tried to pretend that he was awake, but it was a poor imitation of the real thing. He looked at the script, but was having trouble making his eyes focus. "I need a cup of coffee."

Eddie got up, got his cup of coffee and sat back down at his desk to read, what Kevin liked to term his 'deathless prose.' It was short. He read it twice.

"What am I supposed to do with this?"

"Report it," said Kevin unabashed.

"Report what?" asked Fast Eddie, wondering if he was really awake, or if this was just a dream.

"A Russian nuclear weapons depot outside of Templin."

"Where does it say that?"

"In the script."

"Oh, you wrote this for the bennie book on the 393rd?"

"Give me a break. You know I don't fake scripts."

"OK. I give up. I'm asleep and you're a figment of my imagination. You're going to tell me whether I want to hear it or not. Where's it say it in the script?"

"A 'special weapons facility' is a 'nuclear weapons depot.' It says so in the technical dictionary that the Fort sent us."

"OK. I'll bite. Where's it say Templin?"

"APO 07243 is just outside of Templin. It says so in the 'Whore-house Report.'"

"I'm sorry I asked. And just who is the source of this information?"

"General Besstrashnij at KGB headquarters in Moscow. He and Boris are old buddies. Boris, that's Colonel Badunov to you, married the general's sister Natasha."

"And you know this from ...?"

"The telephone number and a stack of other scripts I've done on these two. I recognize the voices. We're practically old friends."

"And you want me to report this?"

"Now you're catching on."

"I am asleep. Wake me up when it's shift change."

"Don't fart me off, Eddie. Write the report! If you don't, I'll have the duty officer call the Chief of Base at home and wake him up."

Sergeant Fastbinder opened the drawer of his desk, took out a message form, rolled it into his mill and began to type:

SUBJECT: SOVIET NUCLEAR WEAPONS DEPOT NEAR TEMPLIN, EAST GERMANY.

The next morning, the Chief of Base was reading the outgoing message traffic before going over to the Site to get to the bottom of where Lieutenant Sheerluck got all that bull shit that he was feeding the general about a nuclear weapons depot in the Soviet Zone. *I'll have his guts for garters,* thought the Chief of Base. The coffee was bitter. He added sugar, stirred and turned the page. Fast Eddie's report from last night was staring him in the face. *I wonder how Lieutenant Sherlock got hold of that information to brief the general with before it went out in a report. I'll have to keep an eye on that young man,* thought the Chief of Base to himself. The lucky character of Lieutenant Sherlock's nickname seemed to have been justified once again.

30
The Passion Book

The Passion Book was the name that all the people at the working level gave to what was officially designated the "Pass-on Book." It was a bound green ledger that was intended to be the place where one trick could write down information that needed to be *passed-on* to the trick relieving it; Information about what was going on and might need the attention of the folks coming on duty. The idea was that a written summary of the key events of the shift was preferable to a verbal exchange at handover, when the off-going shift was in a hurry to get off duty, and the on-coming shift was not necessarily in gear yet. It was a great idea. It had been in use for years in shift operations. Its purpose was to record notes like:

"The Wuensdorf op said circuit 53 would be down for maint till 22:30Z."

or

"COL BADUNOV asked GEN BESSTRASH to call him back before 18:00M. Save the tape for Kevin."

or

"Troop rotation is coming up and the ops everywhere are counting the days till 'the order' comes out in 'Red Star,' 'cause when that happens, they go under 100 days left in service and become double-digit midgets. The day the order comes out in the paper they'll be reading it on the circuit with breathless excitement to their buddies who haven't seen the paper yet. They will be excited because they just got to be short-timers and can start counting the days till they go home. Don't anybody monitoring live or scribing panic when they get to the part that says 'call up all the reserves'! That's standard officialese that goes in every order twice a year. It's no big deal. Kevin"

Even though there were some notes of that kind, *The Pass-on Book* invariably degenerated into *The Passion Book*, full of cross-shift rumors, intrigues and vendettas like:

"Sergeant Laufflaecker is a tread!"
"Blackie, you've got KP tomorrow. I can recognize your handwriting."

"Days was LATE!!!!!"
"Your watch was fast."
"God Zulu never lies!"

"Cpl Neumann's mother wears combat boots."
"Who wrote that? That's not polite!"

"Kevin loves Gabbie."
"I didn't know Kevin could love anyone."

"Fast Eddie's going to be a father."
"Does Meg know?"

"Blackie's moose wears chartreuse."
"And she looks good in it."

"Lt Sherlock is ███████████████ on duty"

The middle part of the note about Lieutenant Sheerluck had been heavily crossed out with a black pen, but if you held it up to the light, you could see that it had originally said "a pea-brained martinet." The annotation "on duty" was in another handwriting, added by someone who had better sense than the author of the original entry. It was not that the author of the annotation did not agree with the author of the first entry, it was just that he realized that there would be hell to pay, if Lieutenant Sheerluck saw it, and he had better things to do with his time than pay for someone else's folly. And pay he certainly would have, if Lieutenant Sheerluck had read the uncensored original text. The author of the annotation could have saved himself the trouble, though, because Lieutenant Sheerluck never looked in *The Passion Book*. He considered the narratives in the book to be of dubious literary quality, and thought it beneath his dignity to read them.

Lieutenant Sheerluck was indeed a martinet, a word that Blackie had had to look up the first time that Kevin used it, but once he knew what it meant, he had instantly taken a liking to. He felt that it encapsulated the essence of Lieutenant Sheerluck, who insisted that all the enlisted men address him as "SIR!" and don't forget the exclamation mark, because those who did would lose a half hour, listening to his, by now, infamous lecture on military courtesy, the one that Blackie could recite by memory, which was a real feat, because even Kevin, who could quote word for word from tapes that he had scribed months ago, couldn't remember past the third word.

Blackie used to like to get the lieutenant's goat by "forgetting" to put that little extra umph into his "SIR," when he had the time to listen to the lieutenant's monolog, on occasions, for example, when he was on some fatigue detail and wanted to get out of work. He would always explain it afterwards as: "Listening to ol' Sheerluck ain't as bad as painting rocks or washing windows," or whatever else it was that Blackie had been assigned to do, but did not want to do. Sheerluck was an easy target, and Blackie could set him off any time he wanted to. You would have thought that Sheerluck would have figured out what was going on—Sergeant Laufflaecker did.

"You get the lieutenant to brace you one more time so you can goof off when you should be working and you'd better give your soul to God, 'cause your ass is gonna belong to me," said Laufflaecker one day after Blackie had used his ability to tick off the lieutenant to take a break from cleaning the grease traps behind the mess hall. After that, Blackie tried to make sure that Sergeant Laufflaecker was not around before he switched on a Sheerluck break. The lieutenant, however, never did catch on.

Not only did he not catch on to Blackie's subterfuge, he never really comprehended the colonel's subtle efforts to comply with the Chief of Base's instruction to keep him away from transcribing tapes. Lieutenant Sheerluck thought that he was an excellent scribe. He was, after all, ABD in Russian. How could any of these puny enlisted men who hadn't even finished their BAs be better than he was?

He was a lousy scribe and Kevin would have loved to be rid of him. He always had to re-do Sheerluck's stuff. Sheerluck was the one who had them issue the Critic about "calling up the reserves." That's serious stuff. Wars have begun for less.

It was a Mid. Sheerluck was there to inspect the meal service on Mids as one of his other duties as assigned, but since he had some time before the meal began, he decided to sit down and transcribe a few tapes. He put one up and listened to it. *Nothing To Report,* he thought to himself and put up another tape. He listened to it and got excited. He rewound it and got even more excited. He motioned Corporal Neumann over to the position where he was working and said hysterically: "The Russians are calling up all the reserves! It's prelude to war!"

Corporal Neumann was on his third Mid, and he was tired, but he did have the presence of mind to tell Sheerluck that "I can't report on a verbal, Sir. I have to have a written script." That simple statement saved Corporal Neumann a world of grief.

Lieutenant Sheerluck feverishly typed out a gist of his understanding of the conversation, ripped it out of the mill and shoved it in Corporal Neumann's face. "This has got to go out FLASH, sergeant! They're going to war!"

**Circuit 179:   02:37-02:39Z 06 September 1955
                    Reel 18234**

GIST: RUSIANS CALLING UP THE RESERVES, DEPLOYMENT
IMINENT
PETYA EXCITEDLY INFORMS VANYA THAT HE HAS JUST
SEEN AN ORDER FORM THE MINISTER OF DEFENCE CALLING
UP THE RESERVES (PRIKAZ MINISTRA OBORNY O VYZVANII
VSEKH NA VOENUYU SLUZHBU). VANYA SAYS HE'S BEEN

EXPECTING THIS FOR A WHILE NOW. HE WONDERS HOW
LONG THEY WILL HAVE BEFORE THEY MOVE OUT. PETYA
SAYS "A HUNDRED HOURS." VANYA IS ALREADY PACKED.

If you ignored the typos, Sheerluck's gist of the tape read logically. Corporal Neumann took it seriously and started getting the Critic ready to send just like it says in the regs. He wasn't as gullible as this made him look, however, and sent Blackie to wake Kevin up. He'd read some of Kevin's amendments to Sheerluck's scripts before.

The clock had been ticking since Sheerluck finished the script. There wasn't enough time to wait for Kevin, so Corporal Neumann said the magic words: "when in doubt send it out," and ran down to the comm center with the Critic. The guys in the comm center were efficient. One minute later it was gone. Six minutes after that, all of 7th Army went on alert. Two minutes more on the clock, and all of Berlin went on alert. The next ensuing two minutes saw SAC bomber crews restricted to their alert facilities.

It was 02:09 Local, and Kevin had worked a Swing, which meant that he was asleep in his room. Blackie dragged him out of bed and down to Operations in his underwear. The tape was set up on Kevin's position. Corporal Neumann plumped Kevin down in the chair. The standard issue gray vinyl was cold against Kevin's bare legs. That really woke him up.

It was 02:10 Local. Kevin put on his headphones and started the tape. He stared blankly at the revolving reels, listening to the disembodied voices of the two Russians, who, without knowing it, had pushed America and Russia to the brink of war. He listened all the way through the cut without stopping the tape.

"I hope you gave me the wrong tape!"

Nope, that's the one," said Corporal Neumann, who ran off to look up how to cancel a Critic.

"You woke me up for this! Didn't you read my note in *The Pass-on Book*? You should have had Jimmy do it. He'd have just "nothing-to-reported" it and I could still be asleep, and could have done this on tonight's Swing. But no, you had to let Sheerluck do a tape! Where is he? I'll kill him and then we'll never have to re-do his stuff again!"

Sheerluck had gone down to the civilian duty officer to call the Chief of Base on the secure line and have him come in to learn about the Critic. This probably saved his life. Kevin was ready to actually carry out his mythical threat of strangling people who messed up transcripts with a patch cord, and probably would have, if Sheerluck had been in the scribe bay right then.

Master-Sergeant Laufflaecker came running into Operations with his steel helmet on and his sidearm in a shoulder holster. The all-Berlin alert had gotten him out of bed.

"What's this man doing in Operations in his underwear!?" said Sergeant Laufflaecker, who thought that Kevin was on alert too, and was wondering where his steel pot and sidearm were.

"He's QC-ing the tape that generated the Critic that caused the alert that woke you up," said Corporal Neumann.

That seemed a reasonable response to Sergeant Laufflaecker, but not to Lieutenant Sheerluck, who came running into the scribe bay to find out what all the yelling was about.

"And why is this man transcribing a tape in his underwear!?" blustered Lieutenant Sheerluck.

"He's QC-ing the tape that generated a Critic in accordance with the SOP, SIR!" said Corporal Neumann, who never had time to listen to Sheerluck's lecture on military courtesy.

"Oh," said Sheerluck. "He should have gotten dressed first."

"It's a Critic, SIR! There wasn't any time for him to get dressed."

"He should have taken the time. Proper uniform is vital at all times, regardless of the circumstances."

"I'll see to it right away, SIR! The cook just called, SIR! and he needs you to approve tonight's meal," said Sergeant Laufflaecker, who knew how to keep Lieutenant Sheerluck busy, when he needed to.

When Sheerluck rounded the corner on his way to the mess hall, Corporal Neumann turned to Kevin. "Quick, type up the amended script so I can cancel the Critic and keep us from going to war."

"Peace is our most important product," said Kevin to no one in particular.

"Who did the original script?" asked Sergeant Laufflaecker.

"Sheerluck," said Corporal Neumann.

"No wonder Kevin's got that patch cord in his hands," said Sergeant Laufflaecker. "Type, Kilroy!"

Circuit 179:   02:37-02:39Z 06 Sept 1955
**   Reel 18234**

NOTE: THIS IS A QUALITY CONTROLLED AMENDMENT

GIST: TROOP ROTATION IMMINENT
PETYA AT HQS GSFG IN WUENSDORF WITH VANYA AT 20
GUARDS ARMY IN EBERSWALDE

PERS CHAT: PETYA is bouncing off the walls as he gleefully tells VANYA that the order announcing the fall draft call is out. He laughs when he reads him the second paragraph from yesterday's Red Star that announces the call-up of all those eligible for service. "They'll be sorry," he says. This means that they only have 100 days left until they can move out for home. VANYA will get started on his short-timer's calendar right away. PETYA has already bought a suitcase to go home with.

Kevin went back to bed before the Chief of Base arrived. He had an eight-o'clock class to go to. Corporal Neumann cancelled the Critic. 7th Army and Berlin went back to bed. The SAC bomber crews started wandering around their bases again. The Russians, however, who had gone on alert in response to the American alert couldn't figure out what was going on and kept everybody in combat readiness until 09:30 Moscow, when the day weenies came in and told them to stand down.

The next morning, the Chief of Base, the colonel and Sergeant Laufflaecker had a conference about Lieutenant Sheerluck. The Chief of Base didn't want him promoted, but the colonel said that was the only way to get him out of the unit. The Chief of Base wanted him court-martialed and shipped off in irons. The colonel wouldn't hear of that. Before their "discussion" could elevate itself to fisticuffs, Sergeant Laufflaecker wisely suggested a compromise:

"promote" him from mess officer to permanent burn officer, and specify in the SOP that the burn can only be conducted during daylight hours. That would keep him out of Operations at times when he could sneak in to the scribe bay and do a tape. Lieutenant Sheerluck's nickname seemed to have worked again, but in reality, it was the apotropaic quality of his first name: *lieutenant*.

"And why is this man transcribing a tape in his underwear!?" blustered Lieutenant Sheerluck.

31
The Alt-Glienicke Players

Boredom is a relative concept. While the Army may think that it has the market for boredom cornered with wall-to-wall "hurry up and wait," there is nothing like a Sunday Mid shift to make you appreciate what boredom really is.

Things were quiet! Nothing was stirring, not even a drunken Russian. They were all too drunk. The Russians always got drunk on Saturday night when the treads went home for the Russian one-day weekend. Kevin said they were drinking shaving lotion and anti-freeze, but nobody believed him. He had to be making that up. The Russians were so drunk that they could hardly talk, and when they did, only Kevin could understand them, and he said that it sounded more or less like a group of Americans sounded after three or four hours at The Eden. The printer ops were playing Hot Shot with the teletypes. If the duty officer found out, he'd have a cow, but he wouldn't because he was so bored that he took an early-in.

Like the saying goes, 'boredom is the mother of invention,' and so, as the darkness thickened to its blackest just before the dawn, boredom gave birth to a fiendishly cunning plan.

"Hey, I'll bet that the Vopos in the tower across the Shoss are just as bored as we are," said a voice that will remain anonymous to protect the guilty.

"Why should they be? They've got us to watch to keep themselves entertained," said an equally anonymous voice.

"But we're not doing anything, except sitting here bitching that there's nothing to do," said a third anonymous voice, distinguished by its Chicago accent.

"We could put on a show for 'em. That would give 'em something to write home about, and then we wouldn't be so bored either," said the first voice.

"You mean like a song and dance act? I can't carry a tune in a basket with a lid on it," said the third voice.

"No, I was thinking along the lines of a one-act melodrama."

"Melodrama!?"

"Yeah. We get mellow, and then go outside and show them some drama."

"You mean like: 'All friends shall taste the wages of their virtue, and all foes the cup of their deservings.'?"

"More like: 'What art thou that usurp'st this time of night?'"

"Ah, why didn't you say so? I like a good ghost story myself."

And the anonymous bards of Alt Glienicke withdrew from the morse and printer collection bay to gather some props for their theatrical production.

Curtain. The door of the warehouse that leads to the fenced-in compound facing the Vopo tower opens with a great bang, and a lone disheveled figure runs out into the compound wailing like all the demons of hell were after him.

"Let me out! Let me out! I've got to get out! HELP!" cries the lone figure.

The bored German guards in the Vopo tower look up from their half-hearted euchre game to see what is going on across the Sector border. Helmut was losing because he couldn't stay enough awake to keep up with the cards. But even in his sleep he played a good enough game to keep him from losing too much to Siegfried, who wasn't a good euchre player at all.

The lone figure reaches the half-way point to the fence, which is the cue for the entrance of the harbingers of death. They burst through the door and into the compound. Their leader, the first lieutenant's bar on his helmet shining in the bright compound lights, raises a pistol high above his head and yells:

"Halt, halt or I'll shoot!"

The running figure continues to race towards the fence in the direction of the Vopo tower, a blood-curdling scream issuing from his parched lips. The pistol discharges. The German guards cast off the last vestiges of sleepiness as their adrenal glands kick in. The camera on the tower begins to issue a series of slow methodical clicks as Helmut brings it to bear on the action taking place on the stage below them.

The leader of the harbingers of death lowers his pistol so that it aligns with the running figure. The figure has reached the fence. The leader fires: once, twice, thrice. The figure falls from the fence in a wretched heap.

Helmut has already shot up a whole 36-exposure roll of film, normally enough exposures to last almost a week. He feverishly cranks the exposed roll back into its cassette, pops the back of the camera open, pulls out the exposed roll, drops it in the middle of their card game. He tries to load the new roll. The new roll of film jumps out of his excited hands and rolls under the table out of sight. Helmut and Siegfried crack heads as they both try to get down on the floor to find the fugitive roll of film. It is the only one they have.

The harbingers of death walk to the pitiful body at the fence slowly so as to give the Germans time to finish reloading their camera. Helmut stands up, triumphant with the roll of film in his right hand. Holding the camera firmly in his left, he inserts the roll of film, pulls out the tail, inserts it in the take up spool, closes the camera back and advances the frame and triggers the shutter a couple of times. He swings the camera around to the drama taking place below them.

Seeing that their audience is ready for the second act, two of the loutish brutes approach the corpse. One takes its feet and the other its shoulders. They pick it up and walk back to the warehouse. The door closes. Curtain.

The Alt-Glienicke players finish their beer, pleased with their successful skirmish with boredom, and rush off to clean up before the Day weenies come in.

Ten minutes later, the collection recorder for circuit 75 started up. Vopo Headquarters was calling Wuensdorf. The first reviews of the play were coming in.

234 The Alt-Glienicke Players

"I wonder who that is?" said Corporal Neumann, wishing that he had taken an early-in when they offered him one. "Where's the duty lingie?" asked Neumann of nobody in particular.

The duty lingie was wisely sound asleep behind the transcription rack. It was dark. It was quiet. It wasn't comfortable, but at least nobody bothered you back there on a Sunday Mid, and it was less expensive than playing poker in the ditty bay. His name was Jimmy. He was a semi-literate Russian lingie, who had had four years of German in high school. He also had a moose, but she only spoke to him in English, because his German was horrible, and she wanted to practice her English, which wasn't that bad, but she did think that the plural of 'moose' was 'meese.' Jimmy never told her that it wasn't.

Corporal Neumann went back behind the rack and gave Jimmy a gentle kick.

"Wake up! We've got a tape," said Corporal Neumann, wishing that he had had the good sense to be asleep.

"Is it trick change already?" asked Jimmy.

"Get up! We've got a tape," said Corporal Neumann again, wishing that he had had the good sense to take the early-in when they offered it to him.

"It can wait till trick change, can't it?" moaned Jimmy, still half asleep.

"No, you know they'll be late. It's Sunday," said Corporal Neumann, who was starting to lose his temper, not at Jimmy, but at the guys on Sunday Days, because he knew that they would be late. He had almost missed Sunday breakfast the last time he came off a Sunday Mid because they were so late.

Jimmy got up groggily, went around to the front of the transcription rack and threaded the tape. It was in German. The duty officer at Wuensdorf spoke a reasonably understandable Hochdeutsch, but the Vopo duty officer had this marvelous Saxon accent. Jimmy could understand the Russian well enough, but he could only understand one word in five of what the Vopo captain was saying. He played the cut all the way through to the end. Good thing that the Russian repeated all the high points.

Jimmy took off his headphones and turned to Corporal Neumann.

"Some Herm at Vopo headquarters who needs German lessons reporting to the Wuensdorf duty officer about what sounds like a jail break. One dead. The guards shot him. Nothing to get your knickers in a knot for, as the Brits say. Now let me get back to sleep, unless it's time for trick change, in which case I should probably stay awake so I can get into bed. That floor's hard."

"Go back to sleep," said Corporal Neumann. "It's another hour till trick change." He was disappointed that it wasn't something more exciting. "I hate Sunday Mids!" he said to himself. "They're so boring!"

Little did he realize that his boredom would have been over, if Jimmy had been able to understand a heavy Saxon-German accent. Now he'd have to wait for his excitement until Kevin did the tape on Monday's Swing. The waitress at the place that he and Gabbie liked to go for lunch was a Saxon and proud of it. The accent would be no problem for Kevin. He'd had plenty of practice with it. Master-Sergeant Laufflaecker would come around that evening to find Corporal Neumann and personally bring him his excitement, but it never tasted as good cold as it did hot.

32
The Courier Run

The people who worked as couriers seemed to live on airplanes as they accompanied classified materials from one place to another. The Site's regularly scheduled run to the courier facility at Gatow Airbase was on Mondays, Wednesdays and Fridays, just before the plane left for London. The Chief of Base did not want material from the project lying around in the courier service vault waiting for the plane. The thrice-weekly courier run was one of those "other duties as assigned" that through the grace of God, or the luck of the Irish—the Brits swore that he wasn't English—or the fact that the colonel did not have anything better for him to do, fell to the lot of Lieutenant Sherlock, Robert NMI, unit of issue: each (thank God!), first-lieutenant's silver in color.

"It'll keep him from falling asleep after lunch," said the colonel, who had just missed catching the lieutenant asleep on duty on a Day shift shortly after the lieutenant had had a particularly heavy, two-hour lunch at the Pavillon du Lac. If the colonel had caught him asleep, the Chief of Base and the 9539th would have really been rid of him, but the enchanted character of his nickname seems to have rescued him once again. The Day trick had been doing its best to maintain the kind of tranquil quiet that is conducive to sleep in the hope that the colonel would catch Sheerluck "in flagrante somnambulo" on his afternoon walk-through, but the tape ran out on recorder 13. Roxy, the tape ape, jumped up to stop it, knocking over a box of tapes, which landed on the floor with a loud bang, waking up Lieutenant Van Winkle and giving him something to be doing when the colonel came into the collection bay.

The courier run was one of those "warm-body" jobs that needed somebody capable of riding in the truck and signing his name about twenty times. It wasn't even physically strenuous for the officer in charge—Lieutenant Sheerluck—who only had to watch the two enlisted men on the detail do the heavy lifting. (A full box of tapes weighed 40 pounds.) Being the Officer in Charge of the courier run made Lieutenant Sheerluck feel rather important, because he got to strap on a belt with a black leather holster that held a .45 automatic, which the lieutenant loved to pull out and point at people to impress them with how powerful he was with a gun in his hand when they were unarmed.

The illusion of his importance did not last long; just until someone found out that he was only issued three rounds of ammunition, which were so old that they were corroded green, and that he had to sign for the magazine and each round individually. These two facts considerably lessened the threat of a pistol in the lieutenant's hand, because being accountable for the ammunition and the magazine made him loath to even try and load the weapon. He knew that, if he lost one of the rounds, he would be filling out paperwork in quadruplicate for a week, and that was a pretty daunting threat for the likes of Lieutenant Sheerluck, so he kept the three bullets in his right-front pants pocket and the magazine in his inside jacket pocket, and was constantly patting his pockets to make sure that his accountable combat consumables were still there.

The second consideration was the question of what would happen even if he managed to put the three rounds in the magazine and insert it in the weapon the right way around, which was more probable than some people considered possible. The bullets were so corroded that they probably would not chamber, and, even if they did, they probably would not go off. (Nobody ever mentioned that to Lieutenant Sheerluck, because he would probably have had them polishing the ammunition the next day, if they had.) Even if the round did go off, almost everybody assumed that they would be safe because he could not hit anything he was aiming at, ignoring the fact that he might not be aiming at them. After people followed that chain of thought to its logical end, going on the courier run with Lieutenant Sheerluck became rather boring.

Sergeant-First-Class Twelvetrees was in charge of the local courier office on the British air base at Gatow. He was friendly and garrulous. Every time you were on the detail, he acted like you were a long-lost friend, and bombarded you with questions.

"What'r you blokes shipping out here? Lead?" he asked one day, adding a new item to his usual repertoire of questions, as he lifted a box of tapes off the scales.

"Yes," said Kevin with a wink, "but don't tell anybody."

"What makes this lead classified?" asked Twelvetrees, thinking that there was no way that lead could be classified and that he could get out of lugging around all these heavy boxes that these clowns from the Site brought in for every flight.

"It's not the lead that's classified. It's the uranium ore that's inside it," said Kevin in a stage whisper. "It's being smuggled out of the East for analysis."

Twelvetrees's jaw fell open in surprise, and the bag he had been holding fell painfully on his foot.

"You should be more careful with those," said Kevin. "If you break those lead plates open, that pain in your foot will be the least of your worries."

Twelvetrees hobbled over to a chair and plopped down in it.

"Are we going to have to file an accident report?" asked Lieutenant Sheerluck. "It says in the regs that every injury that requires medical treatment requires a detailed report on a Disposition Form."

"I don't think that he is hurt that bad. Are you, sarge?"

"How did the bag come to fall on your foot, sergeant?" asked Lieutenant Sheerluck.

"I guess I dropped it from the shock of hearing what's in it," said Twelvetrees, massaging his foot.

"What are you doing talking to this man about the contents of a pouch?!" yelled Lieutenant Sheerluck. "The colonel's going to hear about this!"

"He's cleared," said Kevin in the vain hope that this would make things better.

"That's no excuse. He has no need to know," said Sheerluck who was a stickler for regulations.

"You can rest assured, Sir, that I won't breath a word about them lead plates and the uranium ore from the East for analysis," intoned Twelvetrees, coming to attention, even though the pain in his foot made him wince.

"If you do, we'll have to come back and shoot you!" said Lieutenant Sheerluck, pulling out his unloaded trusty .45, and waving it around in Twelvetrees's direction, oblivious to Twelvetrees's clearly incorrect description of the contents of the pouch.

Twelvetrees sat back down.

"Could you sign the hand receipts, sarge?" implored Kevin.

Twelvetrees stamped his signature on each of the four copies of the four pouch receipts, and initialed the stamped signatures to acknowledge that he had stamped instead of signing.

"Thanks," said Kevin.

"Here are the signed receipts, sir," said Kevin, turning the pieces of paper over to Lieutenant Sheerluck.

"Into the vehicle, soldier! You and I have an appointment with the colonel," said Lieutenant Sheerluck in his best militarily threatening voice.

They did not really have an appointment with the colonel, and they had to wait 45 minutes before he would see them. Kevin pulled out the paperback copy of Rilke that Gabbie had given him. Sheerluck picked up a copy of *The Stars and Stripes*, but could not read it, because he kept looking suspiciously at Kevin's German book, wondering if it was printed in East or in West Germany.

When the colonel finally called them in, the lieutenant gave him a blow-by-blow description of the incident, forgetfully leaving out the part about him waving his weapon around and threatening to come back and shoot Twelvetrees. The colonel listened carefully and silently, then said: "Thank you, lieutenant, I'll deal with this. You may go!"

Sheerluck saluted, did a crisp about-face, and marched out the door.

"You really told him that it was a lead-lined box full of East German uranium ore?"

"Yes, sir. It seemed better than telling him it was a box full of ten-inch reels of magnetic tape. It is almost heavy enough to be lead."

"I wish I could have seen his face!"

"He went kind of pale, sir."

"I can imagine. Was he badly hurt?"

"I think that he will be walking with a limp for about a week, sir."

"All right. I thought that we had you on straight Swings to keep you and Lieutenant Sherlock apart."

"Yes, sir."

"Then how is it that you were on the courier run today?"

"Blackie hurt his back, and Sergeant Everhart needed a 'volunteer.' I was foolishly asleep in my room after a Swing, sir."

"And Sergeant Everhart 'volunteered' you. I get it. I'll put a word in his ear. Now get out of here, and try not to make my life any more complicated than it already is. A lead box?! How could you keep a straight face?"

"It wasn't easy, sir. Luckily Lieutenant Sheerluck provided a diversion."

"I'll pretend I didn't hear you say that."

Circuit 53:   16:02-16:05Z 08 November 1955
Reel 27392

FEMALE 1: Hello, MOSCOW. This is GERMANY, the
    KARLSHORST operator. Please ring 5467 for
    my party.
FEMALE 2: Just a moment, please. I'll connect
    you.
MALE 1: 5467.
FEMALE 2: KARLSHORST. Your party's on the line.
    Go ahead, please.
MALE 2: EVGENIJ, there's a PRIMROSE report on the
    way that you'll want to see right away. Her
    EAGLE told her a very interesting story
    about some geological samples from our Zone
    that are being shipped out in a lead box.
MALE 1: Is that what I think it is?
MALE 2: I would imagine so. You'll have the full
    report on your desk in the morning.
MALE 1: I wonder what their source is? You should
    make some inquires.
MALE 2:I've already started asking questions down

south. I expect to have some answers by this time next week.

MALE 1: Maybe it's one of our former guests. Some of them did not like our hospitality.

MALE 2: That's a possibility that I was considering.

MALE 1: Insightful as always, BORIS.

MALE 2: Our friends keep me on my toes. They're always coming up with something unexpected. To give you an example, just last week we had an intercept where one guy was telling his friend that as soon as they get word that "the Russians are coming" his job is to drive into the Fulda Gap and start putting up signs in Russian that say "This way to the Voentorg" with big arrows showing the way. The joke, he says, is that they are just supposed to map out a twenty-mile circle with them that points right back across the border.

MALE 1: I know some units where that just might work, BORIS.

MALE 2: Unfortunately, so do I. But the same mind-set that created this joke is the one that found a source in the mines down south of here. That's what I have to put up with working with the Americans.

MALE 1: The British have an entirely different sense of humor, and they play the game seriously. I'll never understand why you like working the Americans instead of them.

MALE 2: The British are too straightlaced. The Americans seem more like us.

MALE 1: I had never thought about it like that. Tell NATASHA I asked about her.

MALE 2: I will. And our best to OLGA.

MALE 1: Certainly. Let me know what you hear from down south.

MALE 1: Of course. Good-bye.

MALE 2: Good-bye.

[Hang up]

33
Sunday's Mid

Kevin had wangled a Saturday off, so there was a small stack of tapes to be scanned when the Sunday Mid trick came on. Jimmy was the duty lingie. He had been out on the town with his moose Saturday night, but had to cut it short to get in for the Mid on time. That was the biggest reason that he didn't like Mids. Going out on the town before a Mid was like being Cinderella. You had to be in by midnight, or you turned into a pumpkin. Swings didn't like it when you were late, and the trick you were on with liked it even less, especially if you left them shorthanded, either for a game of cards or for operations.

They could do some pretty strange things to get their point across about you being late. The "Sergeant Spaeter pool" was one of the more civilized forms of retribution for being late. They once wrote "I'm late" on Charlie's forehead in indelible ink, and he didn't take off his cap for the whole of the month that it took to wear off. It was a good thing that Lieutenant Sheerluck hadn't seen him. You could practically hear the "Hey, you, troop! Don't you know that you're not supposed to wear your headgear indoors!" that would have emanated from Lieutenant Sheerluck's mouth, if he had seen Charlie during that month. Kevin often wondered how Charlie had managed to avoid Lieutenant Sheerluck for a whole month, but he could never worm the secret out of him

Jimmy didn't begrudge Kevin a little time off, but he did begrudge him the stack of tapes. He had hoped that he could grab an early-in, and catch the late show at the Eden. He grabbed the first tape in the stack and played it through.

**Circuit 39:   11:11-11:14Z 03 December 1955
                Reel 31620**

FEMALE 1: MOSCOW, operator. I need the GRU duty
    officer for my party.
FEMALE 2: Ringing.
MALE 1: GRU Headquarters. Captain DEZHURNYJ
    speaking.
FEMALE 2: Put your party on, WUENSDORF.
MALE 2: General SERPOV, please.
MALE 1: May I say who's calling?
MALE 2: Colonel MOLOTOV from WUENSDORF.
MALE 1: Just a moment, please.
MALE 3: VYACHESLAV MIKHAJLOVICH! It's about time.
    You have good news, I hope.
MALE 2: VLADLEN MARKOVICH, yes, I have. We
    grabbed the American and his girlfriend
    when they crossed over into our Sector.
    Actually, it was on Alexanderplatz. We did
    not want to make a scene at the crossing
    point.
MALE 3: Quite wise, I would say. They put up a
    fuss, did they?
MALE 2: Nothing that we could not handle. I had a
    team of 12 at the scene.
MALE 3: Ah, VYACHESLAV MIKHAJLOVICH, sometimes I
    think that you take the principle of
    overwhelming force too literally. 12 Men
    for a boy and his girl?!
MALE 2: Six men and six women. And you are right.
    It was overkill, but it contained events,
    and kept the public's attention of them to
    a minimum.
MALE 3: Where are they now?
MALE 2: They are at the safe house in Potsdam.
    The American is not cooperating yet, but it
    is early yet. We have the rest of the
    weekend to work on him. He'll be ready to

```
cooperate by the time they miss him on
Monday.
MALE 3: Very good, VYACHESLAV MIKHAJLOVICH. I
expect to be kept abreast of developments
as they happen. I have given instructions
to the duty officer to put any calls from
you through to me here at my dacha. MARIYA
ANDREEVNA and I will be relaxing in the
country for the next few days.
MALE 2: Give her my best, VLADLEN MARKOVICH. I'll
call when I have something new to report.
MALE 3: Yes, I will. And I expect you to call.
Good-bye.
MALE 2: Certainly. Good-bye.
[Hang up]
```

Jimmy took off his headphones and turned to Corporal Neumann. "Where's Kevin when you need him?" said Jimmy. "I've got some general and some colonel talking about an American and his girlfriend, and some fight. If Kevin were here, he'd be able to make sense of it."

"You really believe that he understands all that stuff? I think he's just making it up," replied Corporal Neumann.

"After he's got it down on paper, and I can read the script along with the tape, I can actually hear what he says they said."

"That's just the power of suggestion," countered Corporal Neumann.

"Yeah, but all those times that the Chief of Base has taken action on Kevin's stuff, the stuff Kevin said was going to happen happened."

"OK, you might have a point there."

"Why don't you go see if he's in his room," suggested Jimmy, who thought that this would be a good way to get back at Kevin for leaving him a stack of tapes. "I'll see if I can make any more sense out of this babble."

Corporal Neumann headed over to the billets, making a stop at the Worst L Stand for a glass of milk on the way. Kevin wasn't in his room, and none of the folks still awake in the billets or in Operations had any idea where he was.

Jimmy suggested giving Fast Eddie a call. He reasoned that Eddie wouldn't be out painting the town with Meg, what with Meg being eight months pregnant. He was right. Eddie and Meg were at home and asleep when Corporal Neumann called. Corporal Neumann had never known that Eddie could swear like that.

"Eddie says that Kevin was gonna take his girl shopping this morning, over in the Russian Sector," said Corporal Neumann, offering a censored gist of his phone conversation with Eddie. His mother would never have approved of him using the words that Fast Eddie used.

"Well, we won't see him again till the handover at the end of Monday's Swing. This tape can't be that important. I'll mark it for Kevsky, and put it back in the stack. He likes all this weird stuff. Why don't you see if the ditties next door wanna play some cards," said Jimmy imprudently, forgetting how much money he had lost the last time they played, and how much flak he and Corporal Neumann had gotten from Sergeant Laufflaecker the next day after Kevin scribed the tape he botched with the review of the play staged by the Alt-Glienicke Players for the Vopo tower across the Shoss.

Jimmy's luck had changed since his last card game in the ditty bay. He cleaned everybody out by the zero-three hundred hour. Now he could really afford to take his moose out on the town.

The Alt-Glienicke Players had not been resting on their laurels either. They had developed a cunning new plan for the entertainment of the guys in Vopo tower. It had been set in motion that evening, just before handover, when Detroit and Charlie had "borrowed" a jeep and driven out on the Shoss, where they faked a flat tire right in front of the Vopo tower. This was their cover for the "delivery" phase of the plan. When the Vopos saw that it was only a flat tire, they misguidedly redirected their attention away from Charlie and Detroit, who began to throw things over the fence into the Vopo compound which was guarded by large, ferocious German shepherds that had been barking at the pair ever since the jeep stopped.

The Vopos should have noticed that the barking had stopped, but they didn't. They were already back at their game of euchre. The dogs were rather pleased with the things that their newly found benefactors were throwing over the fence. It wasn't every day that they got fresh ground beef. Their three-pound supply of meat balls exhausted, Detroit and Charlie got back in their jeep, and headed for the motor pool to turn it in before it was missed.

That night, around the card table, they let people in on the stage show that they had arranged in the Vopo compound for tonight. Each of the 50 meat balls that they had thrown over the fence contained a laxative tablet. "It won't be long before the Vopos are knee-deep in doggie poo,"said Detroit with a grin.

The best seats for the show were in the Crow's Nest, where you could see the Vopo tower through the Questar astronomic telescope especially requisitioned for that purpose by Sergeant Laufflaecker through abnormal channels for the Chief of Base. Blackie, who had Crow's Nest duty that night charged ten cents a head to look at the show. Even though it was his idea, he split the take with Detroit and Charlie. There is greater honor among thieves than among some segments of what passes for civil society. Blackie, Detroit and Charlie, along with Jimmy, were the only ones who came out ahead financially that night.

34
Monday's Swing

Fast Eddie was late getting into work. The bus he was taking out to the Site had been held up by an automobile accident at the corner of Neuköllner and Kopenicker that blocked the intersection for a good ten minutes. He finally decided to get off and hoof it the rest of the way to work. He wasn't too worried to discover that Kevin wasn't in yet. He figured that Kevin had been held up by the same traffic accident.

When it got to be 17:00 Local, however, he began to get worried, and started looking for Kevin. A check of Kevin's room in the barracks found it empty, which was not too surprising, because that was its normal state. Normally speaking, Kevin would have spent the best part of the day with Gabbie, and would have been a bus before or after Eddie getting in to work. Fast Eddie considered calling Gabbie, which would have irritated her mother, Liesl, no end, but he couldn't, because Gabbie didn't have a phone, which saved Gabbie and Kevin a lot of problems with Liesl.

Fast Eddie considered asking in the ditty bay if anyone knew where Kevin was, but rejected that idea almost as soon as he had it, because Kevin didn't socialize with the ditties. He tried *The Passion Book*, but the only recent thing about Kevin was a note from Jimmy, asking Kevin to check out tape 31620 from 11:11-11:14Z 03 December.

When God Zulu indicated that it was 16:30 Zulu—that's 17:30 Local to the chronometrically challenged—Eddie decided that it was time to get serious about Kevin's absence, and flagged down Sergeant Laufflaecker when he walked through the scribe shop on his way out the door to meet his old buddy from the Gators at Club 48 for Happy Hour.

"Kevin?" replied Sergeant Laufflaecker. "No, no idea where he is. I'll check around."

Kilroy's gonna make me late for Happy Hour, he grumbled to himself as he headed towards the billets.

Eighteen minutes later, Sergeant Laufflaecker came back into the scribe shop.

"Kevin's at the 279th Station Hospital. He was in a traffic accident. The bus he was in was hit by a truck, and he and a whole bunch of the other passengers were injured. When they found out that he was an American, they carted him off to the 279th. The medic I talked to said that they were almost through sewing him back together, and that we could come get him anytime. Go get a jeep and pick him up. I'm off to the Club."

That was Sergeant Laufflaecker for you: efficient and focused on the priorities of life. Now that he knew where Kevin was, somebody else could take care of getting him back to where he was supposed to be. He'd have probably done the same thing if Kevin had turned out to be dead.

The ride back from the hospital with Fast Eddie was not as harrowing as the one almost a year ago when Eddie had rushed Kevin to the 279th following his accident in the tunnel. This time the stitches were in Kevin's forehead and not in his arm, and the bleeding had already stopped, and Sergeant Laufflaecker wasn't with them. Eddie dropped Kevin off at the Worst L Stand, and went to turn in the jeep. Kevin bought two Weisses, with a Schuss, and made his way slowly to the scribe shop, only having to stop four times along the way to explain the bandages on his forehead.

"Who would of thought that being a spy was so dangerous," said Kevin, handing Eddie a beer. "Carpe Diem!"

"Your health, not to mention mine," said Eddie, returning the toast.

"How's Meg doing?" asked Kevin, holding the cold beer against his black eye.

"Feeling ten months pregnant, and mad as a wet hen, because you woke her up at oh-three-dark-early on Sunday."

"Couldn't have been me," said Kevin defensively. " I had a fight with Gabbie, and was down at The Eden, drowning my sorrows."

"Doesn't that place ever close?" asked Eddie.

"Not that I know of," said Kevin. "I don't recall seeing you and Meg there, but then I was four sheets to the wind at the time."

"No, we weren't there. We were at home, and in bed. And it wasn't exactly you that woke us up, it was Jimmy looking for you."

"See, it wasn't my fault," replied Kevin.

"If you'd have been in your room, instead of out boozing, he'd have woken you up instead of us."

"Oh, it is my fault. I shouldn't have had that fight with Gabbie about her mother. If you remind me not to do that anymore, I promise not to wake you and Meg up at three o'clock in the morning again. I spent the whole day patching it up with her," said Kevin.

"Did the patch take?" asked Eddie, who had spent most of the day trying to improve Meg's mood.

"I think so, but I'm not sure. I think I'll know better tomorrow morning, when I see her in class. This bandage and the black eye should be good for some sympathy, maybe that'll turn the tide. Any idea what Jimmy wanted?"

"There's a note in *The Passion Book* for you to look at some tape," replied Eddie.

It took Kevin about 10 minutes to find the note in *The Passion Book* and to find the tape. He put the tape up and listened through it once, and went ballistic.

"Let's go find Jimmy, tie him up in a pouch bag, and throw him on the S-Bahn for Potsdam," said Kevin, which was an indication to Fast Eddie that he was more than a little perturbed with Jimmy. His normal reaction to a "bad" script was to threaten to go garrote the perpetrator with a patch cord.

"Come on! You can help. He woke you and Meg up in the middle of the night. Now's your chance to get even," said Kevin heading for the door.

"I think I might need a little more incentive than that," said Fast Eddie. "What's so bad about what he didn't get off the tape?"

"Yes. What is so bad about what was on the tape?" said an American MP sergeant with a pronounced southern drawl that almost kept Kevin from recognizing his voice, but not quite. It was the Chief of Base in one of his counter-surveillance disguises.

Kevin proceeded to summarize the contents of tape 31620 for Fast Eddie and the Chief of Base, ending with: "Now, let's go grab Jimmy and throw him on the S-Bahn! That GI and his girl are probably languishing in Bautzen right now, and it's all Jimmy's fault!"

"OK, I know that you're right more often than not, but that does not give you the right to stomp all over the people who've got to work with you," said the Chief of Base who was trying to maintain harmony in the operation, because that made life a lot easier for everybody.

"It does, if they're wrong. You want me to let this GI and his girl get shipped off to Siberia and killed, because my being right spreads disharmony, when I insist that people be held accountable for not taking action on it?" said Kevin who did not care what people thought about him, as long as the things that needed to be done got done when they needed to be done.

"OK, but this is an isolated incident with extreme consequences. Do you have to bust everybody's ass for the small stuff, too?" said the Chief of Base who was trying to keep his peace-maker hat on in spite of the hurricane blowing up from Kevin's direction that was trying to take it off.

"The small stuff adds up to be big stuff. The significance of this conversation does *not* hinge on just one word. It's not small stuff, it's big stuff. And you don't know how isolated it is, because Sheerluck and Jimmy are doing tapes for you, and neither one of them could scribe his way out of a wet paper bag. How many people have you lost, whom you could have saved, if I had done those tapes? Can you answer that with any degree of certainty?" said Kevin, who had a serious dislike of mediocrity, which is what ignoring the small stuff amounted to. "I've got to look at myself in the mirror when I shave every morning. I don't want my reflection asking me why I gave saving someone's life less than 110 percent of my best effort."

"I'm not asking you not to save people's lives," said the Chief of Base, recalling two operations that had recently gone bad, and ended up getting people killed. "I'd just like you to turn down the volume a little," he added, wondering if Kevin were a Russian, would he be able to turn all that righteous indignation into a recruitment.

"You turn up the volume on people's hearing aids, so that they react to my info seriously, and I'll turn down the volume on my delivery," answered Kevin, always practical to a fault.

"I'll put a word in people's ears," agreed the Chief of Base, hoping that this would not be as hard as dealing with Kevin.

"I can't fucking imagine what it must be like to be right all the time!" blurted out the Chief of Base, losing the grip on his peace-maker hat, and using a tone that indicated he did not want a smart-ass reply. That did not happen very often.

Mighty damn lonesome, thought Kevin to himself.

"If anything happens to Jimmy, I'm holding you personally responsible," said the Chief of Base. "I don't care what it is! I don't know how you foiled the kidnapping of that American colonel, but I'm sure that you had your fingers in that pie somehow, so don't go thinking up any cute tricks to get even with Jimmy."

"What are you going to do about the GI and his girl?" asked Kevin.

"I've got some strings I can pull. You get any more tapes about them, you have the duty officer call me. Anytime, day or night! You got that?"

"I got it," said Kevin and sat down to type up the script for tape 31620, and he didn't get up again until 03:37 Zulu, well past his going-home time, but there wasn't a tape left from the backlog that had been caused by Kevin not being there on Saturday and Sunday to scribe, and Jimmy, who had come in at the start of the Mid, hadn't done any of them. Kevin wouldn't let him.

Kevin called the Chief of Base three times before he finished all the tapes, and when he finally left the scribe bay he took a stack of *Neues Deutschland*s with him so that he could write another note to Gehlen. At 08:47 Local, another dirty-faced kid at the Marienfelde refugee reception camp earned five Marks. At 09:12 Local, Gehlen was reading his note, and at 11:39 Vyacheslav Mikhajlovich got a telephone call from a man with a ominously deep voice who spoke Russian with a German accent. Two hours later, the battered and bruised GI and his girlfriend were handed over to the Chief of USMLM in Potsdam. The Chief of USMLM had been at an official luncheon and could not get away from it any sooner.

The Chief of Base couldn't imagine why the Russians backed down, but he was glad that they had. Now it would be easier to deal with Kevin.

35

Christmas in Kladow

Circuit 39: **17:21-17:25Z 14 December 1955**
Reel 33592

FEMALE 1: MOSCOW, This is WUENSDORF in GERMANY.
   The GRU duty officer for my party, please.
FEMALE 2: Just a moment. It's ringing.
MALE 1: GRU Headquarters. Captain DEZHURNYJ
   speaking.
FEMALE 2: Your party is on the line, WUENSDORF.
MALE 2: General SERPOV, please.
MALE 1: May I say who's calling?
MALE 2: Colonel MOLOTOV from WUENSDORF.
MALE 1: Good evening, comrade colonel. The
   general has been expecting your call. Just
   a moment, please.
MALE 3: VYACHESLAV MIKHAJLOVICH! I was just
   getting ready to call you myself. I wanted
   to ask about our annual little "Christmas
   party" for the British in KLADOW.
MALE 2: The very reason I'm calling. We've got it
   all set up. You wanted it to be a surprise
   this year, so we moved it up to the 25th.
MALE 3: Why's that?
MALE 2: You know and the British know that we do

this every year, and for the last four
years we've done it on the 28th. The
British know this so well that last year
they had a reception party waiting for us,
with a tank, no less, so this year we
thought that we'd be early and catch them
unaware.

MALE 3: I see your point. A cunning plan indeed.
Not only do we have the element of surprise
on our side, but there'll hardly be anybody
on base that day. They'll all be on leave
or off celebrating.

MALE 2: Exactly, VLADLEN MARKOVICH. With any luck
we should, nevertheless, be able to find
someone to detain and take back through the
wire with us to make our point. I'll bet
they won't notice until after "Boxing Day."
If they don't notice by the 27th, we'll
call the duty officer and tell him to come
and get them, they've overstayed their
welcome.

MALE 3: [Laughs] Very droll! I'll bet that you
don't get to use your joke, though.

MALE 2: You want to put your money where your
mouth is, VLADLEN MARKOVICH?

MALE 3: 10 Rubles.

MALE 2: 20.

MALE 3: Done! I'll collect when I'm out there TDY
on my inspection tour in January.

MALE 2: You mean that you'll pay me when you're
out here. I might just as well go out and
spend it right now. They've got these new
German cameras in the Voentorg that I've
been looking at. 20 Rubles is just what I
needed to go ahead and buy one.

MALE 3: Don't count your cameras before they're
hatched, VYACHESLAV MIKHAJLOVICH. I've
worked against the British for a long time,
and they're not as stupid as they seem at
first.

MALE 2: We'll see who laughs last, VLADLEN
MARKOVICH.

```
MALE 3: I don't think it'll be you.
MALE 2: Care to make it 30? I'll lead the patrol
        myself.
MALE 3: I don't want to drive you to the
        poorhouse.
MALE 2: I'm the one who'll be doing the driving.
        30?
MALE 3: You're on, but only if you go yourself.
        I'll be watching the cable traffic for your
        report.
MALE 2: You'll have to wait till the 27th.
MALE 3: I've got patience, but I won't need it.
        My best to KLAVDIYA GREGOR'EVNA.
MALE 2: And my best to ELIZAVETA MIKHAJLOVNA.
[Hang up]
[Transcriber comment: I wish I could be there to
        see the look on MOLOTOV's face when his
        surprise goes bad.]
```

Kevin hit the carriage return so hard that his mill almost jumped off the table. The noise woke Fast Eddie up.

"Man, that's a good one," he said to the tape recorder, as he rolled the six-ply fan-fold up past the perforation and thumped it with his index finger to start the tear.

"What's a good one?" asked Fast Eddie, who'd been looking unsuccessfully for a reason to stay awake, and was hoping this wasn't it.

"This script," said Kevin, noisily stripping the carbons out of the fan-fold.

"I'll be the judge of that," said Fast Eddie, trying to sound officious instead of sleepy. "Let me see it!"

"It's Colonel Molotov in Wuensdorf talking to his good buddy, General Serpov in Moscow," said Kevin rustling the script as he waved it around in Eddie's direction. "They're throwing a 'Christmas party' at the British compound at Kladow like they do every year, but this year it's going to be on December twenty-fifth."

"You're making this up! You expect me to wake up enough to report this feeble fictional fantasy, generated by your blithering bumbling brain?"

"And you call yourself an analyst!? Don't you ever read anything except my scripts and the incoming? Those who don't know their history are doomed to repeat it. The 'annual Christmas party' is just another way of saying the annual incident at Kladow barracks. It's legally on Soviet territory, but the Brits have got some kind of permanent lease on it. The same sort of deal as the 'Tomb of the Unknown Plunderer' in the Brit Sector down by the Brandenburg Gate. It's officially on Brit territory. Maybe it's a barter deal: Kladow for the Tomb. Who knows? It's just one of those little things that makes Berlin unique," said Kevin, still waving the rustling script around to punctuate his points.

Fast Eddie grabbed the script out of Kevin's hand and said, "If another person tells me how unique Berlin is, I'm going to scream. We're unique! Berlin's unique! If we're all so damn unique, where's my promotion?!"

"The same place mine is," said Kevin opening a Coke to toast Colonel Molotov's "Christmas party." "Don't complain too loud. If Sheerluck heard you, the way his mind works, he might get the idea that we should be paying them for the privilege of being in this unique chicken-plucker outfit instead of in the real army."

"Arrrrggggg! I couldn't afford a cut in pay," moaned Fast Eddie, thinking of Meg and the baby. "You're right. It's just the kind of thing he'd do."

"To the 'Christmas party'!" said Kevin raising his Coke bottle in Eddie's direction.

Fast Eddie raised his half-empty cup of cold coffee and clinked it against the Coke bottle. "Damn! This stuff tastes terrible. I'm going out to the Worst L stand for a beer. You want one?"

"I'll pass. I've got an eight-o'clock at the Uni tomorrow with Gabbie."

"Whatever floats your boat," said Eddie and headed out the door. He couldn't imagine how Kevin could get off at midnight and then be up in time to make an eight-o'clock class over in Dahlem, where some Herm professor would be droning on and on about ... what did he say it was? ... Schiller, Goethe, Fitzgerald?

When he got back, Kevin was reading out loud to himself from a book of Russian translations of poems by Goethe. *No wonder they stuck him on Swings,* thought Eddie to himself. *He'd drive everybody on Days crazy. But why did they have to make me his keeper?*

"OK, Herr Doktor Professor Comrade Goethe, can we get back to the 'Christmas party' at Kladow? Tell me what I need to write in the report," said Eddie, positioning a report form in his mill.

"It's almost a tradition for the Sovs to demand 'the right to inspect their property' sometime around Christmas and send over a detachment of men with a lieutenant to breach the wire and take back any Brits that get in their way. It's their way of pointing out how easy it would be to overrun this place."

"What a comforting thought!" said Fast Eddie, who wasn't comforted. One of the few things that he liked about working Swings with Kevin was that if the Russians ever did decide to overrun Berlin, Kevin would be the first on this side of the Sector border to know about it, and would come running over full of glee to tell him, which would give him time to get Meg and the baby on the first plane out the next morning before they became trip-wire troops, or, as Kevin liked to say 'trups,' which, as he always blithely added, is the Russian word for *corpse.*

Having told him that the end of the world was nigh, Kevin would then probably run off to wherever it was that he kept this mythical stash of Russian signs that said:

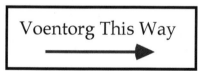

and go plant them in circles so that the Sovs were directed back across the border into their own Sector. That would give him time to go get Gabbie, he said, and they'd exfiltrate to the East, and hike out to the American Zone. As a plan, it wasn't any crazier than staying here to defend the indefensible, which is what Sheerluck would want them to do.

Fast Eddie focused his attention on the form in his mill and banged out the report. It was short and to the point. It looked much more believable in this form than in the transcripts that Kevin churned out.

It was still 10 days till Christmas, so he had marked it ROUTINE, and put it in the out-box for the next time the duty gopher made a comcenter run.

The next step was to censor Kevin's transcriber comment. The folks back in the world always sent nasty-grams about his transcriber comments, and the Chief of Base had said to "disappear" them before distributing the script. Eddie was down to the goldenrod copy, when Blackie stuck his head in the door and said, "Chow line's open."

Not wanting to let the line get too long in front of him, Fast Eddie jumped up and just beat Kevin to the door. The Swing meal was the highlight of the evening, a chance to relieve the boredom of waiting for something that probably would not happen, by going out to consume the inevitable inedible leftovers of that afternoon's dinner. Tonight's fun feast was mashed potatoes with gravy, Brussels sprouts and cube steak. It hadn't gotten any better being kept warm in an oven, waiting for it to be time for the Swing meal.

By the time they got back to the scribe bay, the duty gopher had come and gone, and with him the uncensored copies of Kevin's "Christmas party" script. Fortunately, the copies that Fast Eddie had not been able to censor only went to local consumers, like the Chief of Base, who occasionally had a sense of humor. The day he got the script was one of those times. He thought that Kevin's comment was so funny that he had Kevin decked out in a British colonel's uniform and sent him off to Kladow to invite Molotov to dinner when he came through the wire, and then invite him to defect while passing the Christmas goose.

Kevin got a big kick out of the idea, but he knew that he was going to have a hell of a time explaining to Gabbie why he couldn't come to her mom's for Christmas dinner. The invitation had been a hard-won victory in the continuing struggle between Gabbie and her mother about Kevin, and Gabbie was not going to be pleased. He couldn't tell her the truth—he had to go con a Russian colonel into defecting for the Chief of Base—and had said that Sergeant Laufflaecker insisted that he work the Swing because the baby was due any day, and if Fast Eddie had to leave for the hospital to be with Meg, then Kevin had to be on duty to keep the world safe for Democracy on the Swing. Meg was kind enough to give birth to Elizabeth on Christmas day, giving Kevin's story a ring of truth, even if it had been a fantastic fabrication.

36
Kevin and the Night Visitors

And it came to pass that while Fast Eddie was abiding by Meg and Elizabeth that night in the 279th Station Hospital, Kevin was at Montgomery Barracks in Kladow, dressed up as a British colonel, pleased that he only had to speak Russian and not English with a British accent. The real British colonel detailed to escort Kevin around all night was named Sackville hyphen Smith (pronounced Smyth and the hyphen is silent), O.B.E.. He wasn't sure that this was all really very above board, but his general had been very insistent about it, and he had to make the best of it.

"I don't care what your opinion is of a Yank wearing the uniform, old boy. We've got a jolly good show laid on, thanks to the Yanks, and they insisted on having their own man make the pitch to the Russian officer. Apparently he knows him. Hands across the sea, and all that," said the general.

"Sir! Yes, Sir!" said Colonel Sackville-Smith, with a parade ground salute.

Colonel Sackville-Smith would have been even less pleased, if he had known that Kevin was not a lieutenant, as he suspected, and not even a sergeant, but a member of what the British like to call the "other ranks."

One of the lights on the perimeter fence had been disabled in order to offer the Russians an enticing bit of shadow to conceal their approach to the wire. If they took this suggestion, it would lead them into the motor pool, where two Special Air Service teams stood ready to "invite" them to Christmas dinner. The Russians were expected at 18:30 Local, and they were right on time. That gave the SAS team leader a much better feeling about Kevin and his information.

This burned out perimeter light is more than we could have hoped for, thought Colonel Molotov. He kept thinking how easy this would be, right up until the moment that Kevin and the two SAS teams blocked his patrol's forward and backward motion.

"Good evening, Vyacheslav Mikhajlovich" said the man directly in front of Molotov, in Russian. "The Commanding General's compliments, and his excuses that he could not be here personally to greet you and your men. My name is Isaev, Maksim Maksimovich Isaev."

Colonel Molotov was taken aback. This man had just claimed to be the number one spy of Soviet-Russian literature. The man also knew his name, and, very obviously, knew that they were coming. Colonel Molotov knew that this could not be good, but he did not know how bad it was going to get. For one thing, he could kiss the 30 rubles that he had bet with General Serpov good-bye.

Kevin had thought that calling himself Isaev would be a particularly droll joke. From the look on Molotov's face, it had had the intended effect. "The Commanding General requests that there be no arms in the mess," he said.

"Give them your weapons," commanded Colonel Molotov, recalling Engels' dictum of freedom being the recognition of necessity.

"Won't you please come this way," said Kevin, pointing off to the right. "We've held dinner for you, and for your men. They'll be taken to the Other Ranks' Mess, of course. You and I will, naturally, be dining in the Officers' Mess." Kevin thought that this was a pretty good joke too, but he thought it better not to share it with Colonel Molotov, or with Colonel Sackville-Smith for that matter.

Having separated Colonel Molotov from his men, Kevin was now free to make the pitch to the colonel that the Chief of Base had prepared for him—without any witnesses. Kevin started his spiel when they brought the soup course.

"Vyacheslav Mikhajlovich, I would like to discuss a little opportunity that you have, now that your daughter and her family are here visiting you for the holidays," said Isaev-Kevin. "An opportunity that you ignore at *their* peril," added a very life-like Isaev.

Colonel Molotov knew where this was going. He had made the same pitch often enough himself. He weighed the alternatives. The positive aspects of the proposal were certainly attractive. London was not without its charms, he had heard. The negative aspects of an invitation such as this were invariably fatal.

The Chief of Base had been right. It was better to make suggestions of threats and let Molotov's own imagination fill in the blanks. The dark resources of Molotov's mind could conjure up all the tricks that he himself had used, which were much more threatening than anything that the Chief of Base could dream up, let alone get authorization to apply.

Molotov chased the nightmarish vision of his daughter's head in a hatbox from his mind by agreeing to the pitch just as the meat course arrived. It was a very tasty Christmas goose. He only regretted that his family was not able to enjoy the meal with him. It was truly excellent.

Molotov was, in fact, so pleased with the meal that he had them bring out the cook so he could compliment him by inviting him to come work in the Russian Field Officers' Mess at Wuensdorf. The cook wisely refused. Kevin took the opportunity of translating the cook's refusal to add a reminder of his own. The colonel was a bit too self-assured for his tastes.

"And please remember, Vyacheslav Mikhajlovich, that the *dead*line is 12:00 Local," said the ruthless Colonel Isaev, sending a shiver up Molotov's spine.

There were Christmas puddings that hadn't come out of a tin. There were Christmas crackers with funny hats that Colonel Molotov and Colonel Sackville-Smith refused to put on. There was brandy with cigars afterwards, which made Colonel Molotov think that if this was a preview of his new life in London, then he was going to enjoy it. At 22:07 Local, a somewhat pleasantly disposed Colonel Molotov rejoined his well-fed men for their trip back through the hole they had cut in the fence.

"It was a very pleasant evening, Vyacheslav Mikhajlovich," said Kevin-Isaev, as the colonel and his men were leaving. "I look forward to seeing you again. And bring your lovely daughter and her family with you, won't you. If you don't, we'll simply have to come and get them."

It was a heavy-handed hint, but Colonel Molotov got the point.

The next morning, Colonel Vyacheslav Mikhajlovich Molotov gave his driver the day off, saying that he needed the extra space in the car to fit his daughter and her family in.

"I'll drive myself. We're going sightseeing," said the colonel.

The driver was pleased. He had been told that he could hide from the sergeants in the colonel's quarters until the colonel got back with his family.

"And there's beer in the kitchen for you to drink. But you had better be sober enough to drive the car back to the motorpool when we return. You put a scratch or a ding on the car, and your next assignment will be guarding polar bears in Siberia," declared the colonel.

It's a good thing, however, that the colonel did not return, because the driver was falling down drunk by noon. He'd have wrecked the car for sure on the way back to the motor pool, and he would have hated an assignment to Siberia. His grandfather had been there, and had told him all about it.

At 10:13 Local, Colonel Molotov pulled up to the front gate of Montgomery Barracks and announced to the gate guard that he and his family had come to request political asylum. They were on a British military plane headed for England before anybody on the Russian side of the Sector border knew that they were gone.

Kevin thought it was a great joke, getting the head Russian body snatcher to defect, but he wondered if that would make things dull on circuit 39. It did, but Boris and Evgenij on circuit 53 picked up the slack.

Circuit 53:   14:09-14:15Z 27 December 1955
**   Reel 35763**

FEMALE 1: KARLSHORST, this is MOSCOW. Can you
          give me 4371 for my party, please?
FEMALE 2: Just a moment. I'll ring them.
MALE 1: 4371.

FEMALE 2: Go ahead, MOSCOW. Your party's on the line.

MALE 2: BORIS! I wanted to get your unofficial opinion about this GRU defection. The cable traffic makes it look like he was kidnapped, but that doesn't ring true for our British friends.

MALE 1: No, I don't believe a word of it. I think that it is all mirror imaging. He was, after all, head of the GRU's body snatcher unit in WUENSDORF.

MALE 2: That wasn't in the traffic! That makes a lot more sense. Any idea what the British had on him that could have induced him to come over?

MALE 1: Not a one. I do think that it was rather fortuitous that his daughter was here with her family. I think that this is something that he had been planning for a long time. You know how long it takes to get travel permission for family members to come out here, even for people with good political connections.

MALE 2: Yes. The approvals have to come through my office, and we do a complete files check.

MALE 1: Are you expecting some fallout from this then?

MALE 2: Definitely. There'll be frozen hell to pay, if I'm not shot first, if they can find something in the files that was overlooked.

MALE 1: I'll get a recheck of the files started on this end right away.

MALE 2: Thank you, BORIS. I'll get my adjutant working on things here. As long as they are officially calling it a kidnapping, I have some time to get the recheck done, and done right. If they stick to this story of a kidnapping, we'll be off the hook, but if they change horses in midstream, it'll be good to be a step ahead of them. I don't want them trying to pin this one on me.

MALE 1: At the very least SERPOV is going to have to retire.

MALE 2: I hope that he lives long enough to enjoy retirement.

MALE 1: You think that it is as bad as that?

MALE 2: Senior officers don't just go over to the British without leaving some potentially lethal repercussions in their wake. The scapegoat will have to be somebody more senior than MOLOTOV, and that points right to SERPOV.

MALE 1: I thought that STALIN's passing would make some difference.

MALE 2: It has. It's been more than 24 hours since MOLOTOV went over and nobody has been shot yet. I consider that a major improvement compared to the way that things were.

MALE 1: I had not thought about it like that.

MALE 2: You've been out in the field for too long where things are too relaxed. A tour closer to the flagpole would sharpen the sensitivity of your political antennae, but it would probably ruin you as a field operator, not to mention that it would not do NATASHA's nerves any good. She'll like WASHINGTON, and so will you. The game's a lot of fun there, so I'm told. It's like the real Wild West compared to LONDON, according to SERGEJ, you remember him? Two years ahead of you at the academy.

MALE 1: Yes, yes. I knew that he had a tour in LONDON.

MALE 2: And in WASHINGTON as well. He's up for his first star.

MALE 1: People always said that he'd go far.

MALE 2: He has, but he keeps complaining about being "forced" back to headquarters to work behind a desk. He says that he's got a lot of miles left in him for field work.

MALE 1: I can empathize with that.
MALE 2: So can I, but I don't say it out loud
    back here. Some of the real apparatchiki
    back here can't understand why anyone would
    want to go overseas, away from all the
    trappings of power, to some place where you
    are in constant danger from Capitalist
    entrapment.
MALE 1: The danger is part of the attraction.
MALE 2: If danger is what you want, then you
    should come back here. There is a greater
    chance that you or your career will be
    killed back here than there is in the
    field.
MALE 1: In that case, send me to WASHINGTON.
MALE 2: Where the greatest real danger is a
    recall to MOSCOW.
MALE 1: Knock wood.
MALE 2: The Americans can be real cowboys, but
    they present no actual threat to your
    physical well-being.
MALE 1: Yes, I'd told NATASHA that already, but I
    haven't mentioned the listening devices in
    the bedroom. I'm afraid she'd find that too
    unbearably icky.
MALE 2: I think you're right. Do tell NATASHA
    that I asked about her.
MALE 1: I will EVGENIJ.
MALE 2: And thanks for the info on the defection.
    I'll get the file checks started and then I
    really need to get home to OLGA. She's been
    complaining again that I'm working late too
    often. You'd think that she suspects that
    I'm sampling the SWALLOWS. Good evening,
    BORIS.
MALE 1: She should know better. Good night,
    EVGENIJ.
MALE 2: Yes, she should. I think that she misses
    the field too. We spent more time together

then than now. It was great taking her out
to fill a dead drop or make a meet. Those
were the good old days.

MALE 1: Yes, I'm sure they were. NATASHA and I
enjoy it.

MALE 2: Now I've really got to go. Good-bye,
Boris.

MALE 1: My best to OLGA.

[Hang up]

37
Rumors of War

Mids came around too often for Mike and Charlie, two of the ditties who were on rotating shift, and worked Mids six days out of every 24. The mathematics of this maniacal rotation was based on three eight-day weeks, one of which was on Days, one of which was on Swings and one of which was on Mids. This methodical circadian disruption resulted in desultory cognitive function, especially on Mids. *The Passion Book* said that this particular form of torture was used by the Russians to wring confessions out of suspects who would admit to anything after two sets just to be set free of it. Mike and Charlie figured that this was their thirteenth set of Mids since the tap was turned on. They were ready to confess, only they did not know what it was that they were supposed to have done, and their tormentors wouldn't tell them what they wanted them to confess to, so they had no hope of being taken away to a show trial, like KGB prisoners were, once they broke down and confessed. They found that particularly depressing.

The thirteenth set of Mids, combined with the full moon in the last week of February, must have had some particularly potent effect on them, inducing a sort of sleep-deprived lunacy that everybody who ever worked a Mid can understand. The full moon came on the twenty-sixth, which was the second day of the set, and a Sunday, the worst of all possible boring days of the week for a Mid.

Mike and Charlie decided to liven things up, but they livened things up a bit more than they intended. They had been working on their fiendishly cunning plan for three sets of Mids. It was a very imaginative plan, and quite funny, if you looked at it from the right point of view, that is not from the point of view of the two guards on the Vopo tower just across the Shoss that looked into the Site compound. The Vopos were Germans, who didn't have much of a sense of humor about this kind of thing anyway. They were always there, looking at the inhabitants of the compound through binoculars and taking their pictures through a telephoto lens. It was like being in the zoo.

Mike and Charlie took an old piece of stove pipe and painted it army green. They waited until things had really quieted down on the Mid, sometime after 02:00 Local, and then rushed outside with their helmets on. Mike dropped down on one knee and threw the stove pipe on his shoulder. Charlie shoved a coke bottle into the pipe, slapped Mike on the back, turned aside and covered his ears. The two guards in the tower, who had been following this stage show with rapt attention, decided that discretion was the better part of valor and jumped off the tower. They were sure that a bazooka round was headed their way.

The tower was thirty feet up. One broke both legs and the other broke his left leg in two places plus his right arm. Mike and Charlie laughed all the way back into the building. They hid the stove pipe and went back to their collection positions. They couldn't wait to tell the rest of the bay about it.

The first call about the "American assault on Tower 23" was collected twenty minutes later. It was the Vopo Battalion Commander in Berlin calling the Russian duty officer at Wuensdorf. He spoke a polished, well-educated German, clearly enunciated for the benefit of the Russian at the other end of the line, whose German was competent, but not up to following the Battalion Commander when he launched into a tirade about the Americans. The Russian had to ask the Battalion Commander to repeat himself, which only irritated him further. The substance of his tirade also escaped Jimmy, the duty lingie, who thought that it had something to do with a traffic accident.

Kevin, on the other hand—once Corporal Neumann, alarmed by the uncommonly high level of German activity on a Sunday

Mid, decided to wake him up—got it on the first pass. The Vopo
Battalion Commander said:

```
The round missed the tower hut, and detonated in
     a motor pool a thousand meters behind it,
     destroying six vehicles. Those idiots in
     the tower should have known that they had
     nothing to fear from those stupid
     Americans. They probably couldn't hit the
     side of a barn if they had to. I have a
     battalion of infantry on alert, and am
     ready to show them some real marksmanship.
```

The Russian duty officer, did exactly what any well-trained
Russian staff officer should do at a time like this, he stalled the
Vopo Battalion Commander until he could call to the next higher
rung in the chain of command and ask what to do.

```
Thank you, major. I'll pass on your report and
     your suggested response to the Commanding
     General. Please do not take any action
     until you have heard from me.
```

said the Russian duty officer diplomatically. It was clear that he
had a brilliant career ahead of him in liaison positions.

The eighteen tapes that had been collected before Corporal
Neumann woke Kevin up to scribe them, all had to do with the
unprovoked assault on the territory of the People's Republic of
Germany, but from the changing details and rising casualty figures
the voices on the tapes were reporting, it seemed like there must
have been at least ten different attacks.

```
The Americans scored a direct hit on the tower,
     killing both guards inside and raining
     burning debris down on the Schönefelder
     Chaussee, causing a 23 car pile-up.
```

said a German lieutenant, who had only just been woken up,
excitedly to an academy classmate in the next sector, who had

called, hoping that his buddy in Berlin would have the straight
skinny on the incident.

```
Twenty-three rounds were fired at one of our
     towers, but not a one of them hit it. The
     motor pool behind it, however, is a sea of
     flame.
```

said a German captain, who had been recalled from an all-night
Kneipe crawl, and wasn't quite yet what could be termed 'entirely
sober'.

```
It was intended to look like an accidental
     discharge of a weapon in the direction of
     our tower, but in reality, it was a
     cleverly executed devious plan implemented
     by the special services of the Western
     imperialists to cover up the fact that one
     of the guards in the barracks behind the
     tower had defected to the West. Two rounds
     hit the barracks, killing all 23 soldiers
     inside.
```

explained a German political officer, who instead of going through
the rain to the scene of the incident himself, had called the Russian
duty officer in Wuensdorf, and gotten hold of a Russian whose
German was only sufficient for getting lost on maneuvers, not for
explaining the developing serious situation under discussion.

The reported locations of the "attacks," however were all
identical: tower 23 in Alt Glienicke, across from the American
Warehouse compound in Rudow. Kevin had told Corporal
Neumann to call the Chief of Base at the end of the first tape. By
the time the Chief of Base had completed his counter-surveillance
run to the Site, Kevin had done all the tapes. A grumpy, sleepy-
looking American major in a rumpled uniform with quartermaster
insignia came running into the scribe shop, accompanied by
Sergeant Laufflaecker, which could mean only one thing: that it
was not a major, but the Chief of Base. Sergeant Laufflaecker would
never be seen next to a real major in a rumpled uniform.

"What the hell's going on?" asked the Chief of Base, when he saw Kevin scribing in his underwear. The last time that had happened, there'd been hell to pay, so he thought that he'd get "hell" into the conversation early this time, rather than later.

"The Germans are claiming that 'the Americans' have launched an unprovoked armed attack on the Vopo tower in Alt Glienicke across from the Warehouse compound in Rudow," said Kevin, who had just finished a tape, and was, therefore, in communication with the world of the living. "Depending on who you listen to, the tower is in ruins or is standing unscathed, and there are bodies strewn all over the other side of the Shoss, or the guards from the tower just broke their legs."

"Are you suggesting that the situation is confused?" asked the Chief of Base.

"Yes. That's a good description of the situation: confused," replied Kevin. "The Russians sent a major to the scene to evaluate the situation, but he hasn't called in yet. I hope that he'll clear things up for us when he does."

"I can clear things up a bit now," said Sergeant Laufflaecker, who had just hung up the field telephone to the Crow's Nest, where they kept an eye on the Vopo tower across the Shoss. "The tower's still standing and there are three guards in it."

"That probably means that the German major in the first tape on the incident has the best grasp of the situation," said Kevin, handing the Chief of Base and Sergeant Laufflaecker copies of that transcript. While they were reading it, the Russian major called in his report.

```
I have spoken to the two German guards in the
     hospital. They claim that they were fired
     upon by the Americans with an antitank
     rocket. They jumped from the tower to avoid
     being killed when the rocket impacted. The
     doctor assures me that there is no trace of
     alcohol in their blood. Their service
     records show no disciplinary problems, so I
     am inclined to believe their version of the
     story, up to a point. The Germans at the
     tower are unable to show me any damage that
     could be attributed to the impact of an
```

```
antitank rocket on the far side of the
tower. My assessment is, therefore, that
the Americans pretended to fire an antitank
rocket at the tower as a joke. I was not
able to ascertain if they were drunk or
not, but I am given to understand that this
is not an unusual condition at this time on
a Sunday Mid.
```

reported the Russian major methodically.

"I'll go make some inquiries," said Sergeant Laufflaecker, who had been reading over Kevin's shoulder as he typed.

"I'll go with you," said the Chief of Base, following Sergeant Laufflaecker into the ditty bay.

Mike and Charlie made the eight-o'clock plane out of Tempelhof—at least that's what the Chief of Base said—and that was the last that anyone ever heard of them again. The Chief of Base was pissed, but he presumably did not terminate them with extreme prejudice. Wherever they went, everybody figured that they didn't have to work Mids anymore.

38
The Precision Operator Head-space Adjustment Tool (ST-one)

A Precision Recorder-head Alignment tool was one of those things that no operation that used a lot of tape recorders could do without. Even though it weighed close to 60 pounds, Howie, the recorder maintenance tech, had it bolted to his work bench so that it couldn't grow feet and walk off like some things seemed to do in Operations from time to time. It was bigger than two tape decks put together, and had a big O-scope in the upper right-hand corner that showed an eye pattern when the recorder heads were aligned correctly.

You could tell what kind of mood Howie was in from across the room by looking at the O-scope. If it was off, Howie was either off duty or asleep behind the bench. If it showed an eye pattern, he was in a good mood. If it showed any of the other crazy Rorschach green ink patterns it was capable of, it wasn't a good time to ask Howie to pay you back the ten bucks he borrowed from you last Thursday (he always seemed to need a ten spot on Thursdays), or to tell him that the cook in the mess hall was making minute steaks (he was crazy about good minute steaks, and the cook never made *good* minute steaks), or to even say 'hello,' 'good-bye,' but some people always seemed to be able to fail this electronic green Rorschach test for which there were no 'right' or 'wrong' answers, just inappropriate behaviors. Lieutenant Sheerluck was one of them.

Lieutenant Sheerluck invariably set: 1) Howie off and 2) recorder repair back with 1) some inane request that could have waited until the Precision Recorder-head Alignment Tool showed that Howie was in a good mood, or 2) with some feeble requirement that really had nothing to do with Howie and could have been better handled by the duty flunky. Lieutenant Sheerluck never seemed to be able to get it through his head that even though it looked like Howie wasn't busy, he was. No, it wasn't just with Howie. Lieutenant Sheerluck had that problem with everybody.

One evening, after Lieutenant Sheerluck had been saved from being impaled on a phillips-head screwdriver by the agile intervention of Sergeant Fastbinder, and Howie saved from a court-martial by the calm intercession of Corporal Neumann, Blackie—ever sensitive to what constituted good timing for a practical joke—concocted a cleverly cunning plan. He waited until Lieutenant Sheerluck was leaving for the mess hall to check the quality of the evening meal service, and grabbed Fast Eddie by the arm, saying: "Let's go down to the chow hall and get a cup o' joe," accompanying this 'invitation' with a very obviously conspiratorial wink.

Fast Eddie, who normally would not have poured a cup of coffee on Blackie, even if Blackie was on fire, looked around suspiciously to see if he himself was on fire, or about to be set on fire, which was what any sensible person would do when Blackie made a suggestion of this kind. Blackie's association with carbon-paper tails was infamous. Blackie gestured at Sheerluck and winked again. Having determined that he was not the target of Blackie's warped sense of humor, and that Lieutenant Sheerluck was, Fast Eddie leapt to his feet, and started off towards the mess hall in Lieutenant Sheerluck's wake. Lieutenant Sheerluck was the only person on whom Fast Eddie would have helped Blackie to put one over.

Blackie stepped out rather smartly and Fast Eddie had to live up to his name to keep up. When they got within stage-whisper range, Blackie said, supposedly to Fast Eddie, but really for Lieutenant Sheerluck to overhear:

"Boy, that Howie's always in a piss-poor mood."

"Don't you know it!" said Fast Eddie, not knowing where this was going, but eager to find out.

"Yeah. He's pissed because he can't get himself one of those fancy new ST-one Precision Operator Head-space Adjustment Tools."

"How come?" asked Fast Eddie, genuinely curious to hear the answer.

"The supply sergeant won't order him one 'cause Howie's only a sergeant."

"You don't say!" replied Fast Eddie, who didn't believe a word of it.

Lieutenant Sheerluck slowed his pace to the mess hall, indicating that Blackie's practical joke had acquired its target and was homing in.

"But Howie knows what he's doing, and if he could get himself one of those ST-ones, he'd be in a good mood all the time, and the recorders would be fixed a lot faster."

"Why doesn't he go to the sergeant-major?" asked Fast Eddie, sensing that he needed to say something.

"The sergeant-major sides with the supply sergeant. They were in the *big* war together. And Howie's never going to go over the sergeant-major's head to get one, so we're just stuck with having Howie pissed off all the time and a bunch of recorders waiting to be fixed. Too bad that the brass will never get to hear of this."

Lieutenant Sheerluck came to the mess hall door and a conclusion at the same time. He would requisition an ST-1 Precision Operator Head-space Adjustment Tool. The supply sergeant would never dare turn down his requisition. He would resolve this obviously very serious flaw in the technical maintenance part of the operation. He would let the colonel know that the sergeant-major was the one who had been holding up this particular piece of progress. That would show him. The colonel would be so pleased that he could go out and buy those captain's bars he had been eyeing in the PX. It was a brilliantly conceived, cunning plan. He would put in his requisition the first thing in the morning.

Too bad for Lieutenant Sheerluck that Blackie's plan took precedence.

The ST-one Precision Operator Head-space Adjustment Tool was an old joke that was played on newks wherever recorders were used. Corporal Neumann had been sent to get one, but he never did get the joke. He took the whole thing seriously, even after he opened the box and looked inside, and saw that this precision tool was a very large stone. The supply sergeant was in on the joke and kept a *Tool, Precision Operator Head-space Adjustment ST-1, O.D. green in color, unit of issue, each, with protective case* in the back of the supply room just for such contingencies.

When Lieutenant Sheerluck showed up to requisition an ST-1 the next morning, the supply sergeant was a bit surprised that anyone would dare try a newk trick on the lieutenant, but when he tried to explain things diplomatically, the lieutenant just thought that the supply sergeant was being obstreperous in an effort to keep Sergeant Jergins from getting the right tool for the right job. He'd book no insolence from this enlisted man.

"That's enough of your insolence, sergeant! If you don't get me an ST-1 Precision Operator Head-space Adjustment Tool immediately, I'll have you up on charges in front of the colonel before lunch!"

The supply sergeant's sympathies did an immediate about-face.

"Yes, SIR! Right away, SIR!" and off he went to the back of the supply room, where he picked up a large, heavy wooden box that was painted olive drab with white stencilled lettering on the sides that identified it as a "ST ONE." He placed it on the counter with a thud.

"Careful with that, sergeant! It's an expensive precision tool."

"Just sign here ... and here ... and initial here, sir, and it's all yours."

Lieutenant Sheerluck signed the hand receipt where indicated—twice—and initialed—once—without reading what he was signing and initialing, which is never wise. He reached out to take possession of his prize, but discovered that it was heavier than it looked. The lead weights in the false bottom must have had something to do with that.

"Can you have that delivered to Operations, sergeant?"

"I'm sorry, sir. You've signed for it, and it's your responsibility now. If I take it back, I have to send it back to Frankfurt for refurbishment before I can issue it again. Regulations, you know, sir," said the supply sergeant, who knew which buttons to press to make Lieutenant Sheerluck jump through hoops.

"Very well," said Lieutenant Sheerluck, looking around for some troop to carry the thing. All the 'troops,' however, had, upon hearing that Lieutenant Sheerluck was in the area, wisely found convenient reasons for staying out of the area. Having ascertained that there was no one around whom he could commandeer, he hefted the box by its rope handles and set off laboriously in the direction of Operations.

The rope handle on the left-hand-side of the box had been cleverly installed so that one of the two knots that held it in place was only slightly larger than the hole that the rope went through. Each time the lieutenant set the box down to rest his hands and then picked it up again, the knot slipped a little further through the hole. By the time he was ready to make the last leg of his tortuous journey from supply to the maintenance area in Operations, the knot was ready to slip out of the hole. The lieutenant hefted, the knot slipped, the box fell to the floor with a thunderous thud.

This attracted the attention of the colonel, who was just coming out of his morning briefing. The lieutenant had timed things so that the colonel would see him delivering the box. Recognizing the box as one used for the transport of landmines, the colonel yelled at Lieutenant Sheerluck: "You trying to blow us all to kingdom come, lieutenant?!" Sheerluck was taken aback. He did not know that an ST-1 was explosive.

"I'll take care of it, sir," intervened the sergeant-major who recognized the box for what it was. He had invented the ST-1 himself when he was a corporal, collecting German voice on a wire recorder during the big war. "If you and the other officers will evacuate the area, sir, I'll get our specialist in these things to come and make sure that it's safe."

"Very good, sergeant-major," said the colonel. "We can't be too careful with these things."

The sergeant-major turned to the duty flunky on Days, who had a big grin on his face, and said: "Go find Blackie, and buy him a drink, but tell him he owes me. He should know better than to try and put one over on Sheerluck, I mean Sherlock."

Even though their trick had not been as successful as they had hoped, Blackie, Fast Eddie and Howie were pretty pleased with the result and were in a good mood for a week.

Some people suggest this incident was the point at which the talismanic quality of Lieutenant Sheerluck's name began to fail him. Not only had the sergeant-major called him by his nickname—something that he had never been known to do before—but he also protected Blackie from the inevitable repercussions that would have followed, if Lieutenant Sheerluck had learned that he had been the brunt of a practical joke. They view it as the thin edge of the wedge that eventually led to the sergeant-major's denouncement of Sheerluck to the colonel.

Circuit 159:   17:18-17:22Z 26 February 1956
Reel 43987

FEMALE 1: WUENSDORF, operator. This is MOSCOW. I
    need 8375 for my party, please.
FEMALE 2: That's the Commanding General's
    apartment. I have instructions not to
    connect that number without asking who's
    calling.
FEMALE 1: It's Mrs. Commanding General.
FEMALE 2: She's the one who gave those
    instructions. It's ringing. …
FEMALE 3: General GRECHKO's apartment.
FEMALE 4: NINOCHKA, it's mama.
FEMALE 3: Mama! Is everything all right? I didn't
    expect you to call.
FEMALE 4: Everything is fine, well almost, papa
    went to a secret session of the Twentieth
    Party Congress with NIKOLAJ ALEKSANDROVICH.
    NIKITA SERGEEVICH denounced STALIN from the
    podium, saying that he permitted some
    mistakes during the period he was in power
    that will have to be corrected. It's
    amazing!
FEMALE 3: How did papa react?
FEMALE 4: He said his jaw hit the floor. Can you
    imagine anyone saying anything like that

about STALIN while he was alive? Remember
what happened to Major GORDEENKO, the
little man with a big mustache, who told
that unflattering postage stamp joke about
STALIN? He disappeared the same night and
was never heard of again.

FEMALE 3: No, I don't remember him, but I know
the joke. I haven't seen anything in the
papers here yet.

FEMALE 4: And you won't. It's supposed to be a
great big secret, but it's spreading like
wildfire here.

FEMALE 3: You mean I can't tell anybody?!

FEMALE 4: Well, maybe just KATYA MARKOVNA, but
nobody else. The real reason I called is to
tell you that we will be coming home early.
Papa wants to be in his office to deal with
the consequences of this first thing Monday
morning.

FEMALE 3: That means that you won't get all my
shopping done.

FEMALE 4: There's less here in the stores, even
the special stores for the Party, than we
have in the Voentorg in WUENSDORF. I
haven't found a thing on your list, and
aunt TATYANA doesn't think that I would
have found anything next week either. As a
matter of fact, she's giving me a list of
things to buy for her in the Voentorg.

FEMALE 3: Aunt TATYANA's the best shopper I know,
and if she can't find anything, the stores
must be in really desperate shape back
there.

FEMALE 4: Yes, indeed. I'll really be glad to get
back.

FEMALE 3: Do I need to call papa's office and
tell them to meet you?

FEMALE 4: No, he's taking care of that. Just be
sure to tell the cook to expect us for
breakfast. Papa will want his usual.

FEMALE 3; Yes, mama. And tell papa I love him!

FEMALE 4: Yes, I will, and I love you too
        sweetheart. Bye.
FEMALE 3: Bye, mama. Have a good trip!
FEMALE 4: Thank you, dear. Good-bye.
[hang up]

[TRANSCRIBER NOTE: NIKOLAJ ALEKSANDROVICH is
probably Minister of Defense BULGANIN. NIKITA
SERGEEVICH is most likely POLITBURO MEMBER
KHRUSHCHEV.]

The "unflattering postage stamp joke" probably
goes something like this:
The Post Office brought out a new stamp, honoring
Comrade Stalin, and printed two billion of them,
more stamps than America prints in honor of its
presidents. Complaints, however, began to come in
from postal patrons that the stamps would not
stick to the envelopes. The KGB investigated the
factory that produced the glue used on the
stamps, and shot the plant manager who under
interrogation confessed to sabotaging the project
for the Americans by making unsticky glue. They
recalled all the old stamps, and printed three
billion more, but it wasn't long before
complaints began to come in again that the stamps
were not sticking to the envelopes. They knew
that it could not be the glue, because the
factory was now being run by a KGB general, and
when the commission formed to investigate the
matter tried to stick the stamps on the
envelopes, they stayed on just fine.

    Finally, one of the commission members had
the bright idea to interview some of the postal
patrons who had complained. He was gone a week,
and when he got back, he announced, "Comrades, I
have discovered what the problem is! The people
are spitting on the wrong side of the stamp." The
commission thought about this for a while, and
then recalled all three billion of the old
stamps, and issued four billion new, double-sided
stamps, which was an entirely new, Soviet
invention, something that the Americans did not
have at all. Comrade Stalin's portrait was on one

side under a thin, transparent layer of glue, and
the Hammer and Sickle on the other. A week went
by, and there were no complaints that the stamps
were not sticking. Two weeks, three weeks, and
the commission chairman said, "See, comrades. I
knew all along that it wasn't the glue. We just
had to get the people to spit on the correct side
of the stamp."

Fast Eddie didn't need Kevin to tell him that this one was reportable,
but that did not stop Kevin from telling him. Eddie didn't report
the joke, much to Kevin's chagrin.

39

The Primrose Path to Korea

Circuit 53:   **15:19-15:23Z 13 April 1956**
                     Reel 50836

FEMALE 1: KARLSHORST, can you connect me with
    4371 for my party? This is MOSCOW.
FEMALE 2: Just a moment.
MALE 1: 4371.
FEMALE 2: Go ahead, MOSCOW. Your party's on the
    line.
MALE 2: BORIS! I wanted to warn you about an
    up-coming "spontaneous" demonstration at
    the Freie Universitaet next Tuesday. The
    comrades plan to shut the university down,
    and it is not unreasonable to assume that
    there will be a police reaction.
MALE 1: Judging by what happened the last time
    there was one of these, that is <u>not</u> jumping
    to conclusions. But what does that have to
    do with me?
MALE 2: Your last PRIMROSE report said that her
    next scheduled meet with her case officer
    was set for Tuesday, and I recalled that
    our meet with her when I was out TDY was in
    a university building. I wanted to give you
    a heads up so that you could abort the

meet, if the demonstration will endanger
it. The police will undoubtedly be
photographing everybody in the area of the
demonstration, trying to ID the
provocateurs.

MALE 1: I'm sure that they will be, but not to
worry. The meet with her case officer is at
the U-Bahn station right under the noses of
our American friends, at Oskar-Helene-Heim.
There won't be any police or demonstrators
there,

MALE 2: How very droll. Hide in plain sight.

MALE 1: Yes. I keep rotating officers through
there to go to the American Voentorg or to
the Harnack House, so that our Friends
won't think anything of seeing one of us
getting on or off the U-Bahn there. Their
"PX" is the source for lots of the things I
send you, like OLGA's coffee.

MALE 2: You crafty devil. Combining business with
pleasure. The next time you're back, I want
you to give a presentation on this at the
academy.

MALE 1: I'd be honored.

MALE 2: It will not only be a good lesson for
future field officers, it will give me the
ammunition I need to overcome the last
vestiges of resistance to your WASHINGTON
assignment.

MALE 1: I'll be doubly honored to make the talk.

MALE 2: It will show your detractors that you are
not afraid to play in "the lion's den."

MALE 1: It's hardly as dangerous as that makes it
sound.

MALE 2: I suspect not, but if that's what it
takes to get NATASHA, and you, of course,
to WASHINGTON, then I am prepared to make
you sound like a modern-day Isaev.

MALE 1: NATASHA will be pleased to know that you
think so much of her.

MALE 2: It is not entirely for NATASHA's sake.
You are a very competent field officer, and

much, much better than the idiot whom your
opposition is backing. He's the nephew of
one of the members of the Central
Committee, I can't tell you which one, of
course.
MALE 1: You don't have to. I recognize the
description.
MALE 2: That just proves my point: you're a well-
trained intelligence officer.
MALE 1: Thank you, EVGENIJ.
MALE 2: And just to give my nerves a rest, why
don't you give me a call when PRIMROSE's
case officer gets back from his meet with
her?
MALE 1: Of course, EVGENIJ. The meet is set for
10:30 Local. That means if everything goes
all right, I'll give you a call about 13:00
my time, that's 15:00 your time.
MALE 2: Good. I'll look forward to your call. By
the way, you mentioned OLGA's coffee.
MALE 1: Of course. It's on the case officer's
shopping list. He'll be picking it up at
the American Voentorg before he meets
PRIMROSE.
MALE 2: You're efficient to a fault, BORIS.
MALE 1: That's what keeps you from getting rolled
up out here in the field where it's
"dangerous."
MALE 2: There's no need to overdo it, BORIS. That
kind of humor won't improve your chances of
WASHINGTON.
MALE 1: I'm sorry, EVGENIJ. I got carried away.
MALE 2: You should be sorry. Give my best to
NATASHA.
MALE 1: I will EVGENIJ. And tell OLGA that her
coffee's practically on the way.
MALE 2: I will. Everybody raved about the coffee
at that last reception we gave. She's the
envy of all her girlfriends. She'll be very
pleased. Good-bye, Boris.
[Hang up]

"Thank you, Boris," said Kevin, his fingers racing to get the last of Evgenij's good-bye pleasantries on six-ply before he ripped the script out of the mill.

Alerted by hearing Kevin holding up his end of the conversation with the people on the tape, Fast Eddie had a report blank in his mill.

"Hey, Eddie, look at this!" said Kevin energetically waving the script around so that Eddie couldn't focus on it at all.

"Just tell me what to write in the SUBJECT line, Kev," replied Eddie, "and we'll get this baby out of here."

"Oh, you don't have to report it," answered Kevin. "Just don't let the Chief of Base get out of here without seeing it. He's the only one who can do anything with it. Boris told me when and where PRIMROSE is going to meet her case officer on Tuesday, and the Chief of Base should go and take pictures."

"You're really sure that PRIMROSE isn't Gabbie?" asked Eddie.

"Get off my case, Eddie! If I wasn't sure, would I be tipping off the Chief of Base where to go get pictures?"

"Do not, as some ungracious pastors do, Show me the steep and thorny way to heaven, Whiles, like a puff'd and reckless libertine, Himself the primrose path of dalliance treads, And recks not his own rede," replied Eddie, showing off the fact that his B.A. was in English Lit.

"OK, Ophelia, just make sure that the Chief of Base sees this when he makes his rounds. It's a Friday, so he might be early. This is a special occasion. I'm going out to the Worst L Stand for a Weisse to celebrate. You want one?"

"Sure, why not? Mit Schuss. If we're going to take the primrose path to the everlasting bonfire, we might as well go whole hog."

When Kevin got back, Fast Eddie was showing the PRIMROSE-meet script to a light-colonel in fatigues with army-issue glasses.

The light-colonel scowled through his glasses at the beers in Kevin's hands.

Fast Eddie cringed at the thought of what would happen next.

"It's a special occasion. We're celebrating the impending unmasking of the elusive PRIMROSE," explained Kevin.

"Aw, you didn't bring me one," said the Chief of Base, oozing irony from every pore.

"I didn't know when you'd get here, and I didn't want it to get warm," responded Kevin. "Here, take this one. I'll go get another."

"Why don't you go get it, Eddie? I want to bend our friend's ear in private," said the Chief of Base. "My treat."

That did not sound promising to Eddie. He had never been sent away when the Chief of Base had something to say to Kevin before. He was gone before the Chief of Base could give him the money "to treat" with.

"If PRIMROSE turns out to be your moose, I'll have you terminated with extreme prejudice and your skeleton can replace Von Friedhofen's as the dead man in the tunnel," said the Chief of Base in the tone he reserved for extending opportunities that people ignored at their peril.

"In the first place, she's not a moose, she's my girl. In the second place, she's not PRIMROSE, and I expect an apology when you come back with the pictures of the real PRIMROSE," said Kevin who had successfully been studying the telephone intimidation technique of a number of master KGB and GRU browbeaters for almost a year.

"Let me make what I just said a bit clearer: you are coming with me to a safe house, where you will wait "safely," unable to contact your *moose* or anyone else, until PRIMROSE meets her case officer. If PRIMROSE turns out to be your *moose*, it won't be safe anymore. I'll shoot you and dump your body in the Russian Sector. Is that clear?"

"Reasonably so. You want me to finish the tapes I've got backlogged before I go?"

"No," said the Chief of Base who was tempted to shoot Kevin right then and there.

"And if PRIMROSE isn't my girl?" parried Kevin pushing his luck.

"If she's not your girl, I may send you to Fort Leavenworth anyway," replied the Chief of Base, with somewhat less conviction than his last assertion, as he began to recall some of the actionable things that had been in Kevin's scripts that had paid off, but had never showed up in PRIMROSE reporting. "You're mighty damn sure of yourself."

"I have to be. Nobody else seems to be," said Kevin, digging in his spurs.

When Fast Eddie got back with his beer, Kevin and the Chief of Base were gone. He looked around for signs of blood, but all he found was a note in his mill that said: "You talk about the PRIMROSE script to anyone, and your next assignment will be north of the DMZ in Korea." Eddie tore the note out of the mill and threw it in the burn bag. The tape and the transcript were gone too. Eddie hoped that Meg never found out that he was the one who had squealed on Kevin and Gabbie. She'd never forgive him.

On Tuesday at 10:09 Local, the surveillance team of 20 that the Chief of Base had laid on especially to identify PRIMROSE picked up Captain Lev Davidovich Bronshtein when he entered the army commissary to buy coffee for General Besstrashnyj's wife. The team shot up six rolls of film from as many vantage points in the Oskar-Helene-Heim U-Bahn station, capturing the photographic likenesses of the captain and everyone he came close to. Most of the photos were of him and the young German woman with whom he talked for approximately three minutes before they boarded separate trains.

The surveillance team broke up as planned. The six photographers went back to develop their film. The remaining 14 pavement artists split into two teams: one to follow him and one to follow her.

Captain Bronshtein and Olga's coffee took the southbound train to Potsdam in the Russian Sector, where an army staff car was waiting to pick him up. Not having a car at their disposal, the team lost him there.

The mystery woman took the northbound to Dahlem-Dorf, where she got off and walked to one of the classroom buildings of the Freie Universität. She entered room 157, a large lecture hall, at which point the team broke off contact, because the university area was awash with demonstrators and local police, both uniformed and plain clothes. This was the only sensible course of action as three members of the team had been detained by the police as provocateurs and two attacked by a group of students as police narks.

"Mark," said the team leader to his one remaining team member. "You escort Tony and Bill to the hospital, then come back and join me at the Dahlem-Dorf U-Bahn station. I'll head back there to stake out the girl. When I get there, I'll call the office and have them send someone down to get Bob, Pete and Jerry out of the slammer."

Mark rejoined the team leader at the U-Bahn station at 12:37 Local. Tony and Bill were being held at the hospital for observation. Bob, Pete and Jerry arrived there at 13:29 Local. They were accompanied by Mike and Dan, who had been on the team that followed Captain Bronshtein.

"The Chief of Base ain't none too pleased," said Mike whose grasp of the obvious showed a flash of unusual insight that surprised the team leader. Mike had his uses, but cognitive function was not one of them.

The team leader's hunch paid off and redeemed his career at 15:07 Local, at which time the team leader started breathing again. The subject had just entered the U-Bahn station. She boarded the northbound train and traveled two stops to Breitenbachplatz, where she exited the U-Bahn and walked three blocks south on Brentanostrasse to an apartment building on the eastern side of the street. The name on the door of her apartment was Marlene Schwalbe.

U-Bahnhof Oskar-Helene-Heim

40
Kevin's Choice

The team leader delivered the surveillance report to the Chief of Base in his office by hand at 19:11 Local. It would have been 18:59, but he had to type the report himself. He was a two-fingered key pounder who could hit 25 typos a minute, and sometimes more. This was one of those times. The report was short and sweet and to the point.

The team leader handed over the report and stood waiting to see if there would be any further instructions, while the Chief of Base read it. He followed the Chief of Base's eye movement down the page, and could see that he was at the concluding paragraph.

"At 18:03 Local, the subject left her apartment and traveled via U-Bahn to Oskar-Helene-Heim, from where she walked east down Saargemünder Strasse to Harnack House. She was met by an American first-lieutenant, who escorted her inside. The lieutenant's name is Sherlock, Robert N.M.I., assigned to the 9539th," ended the report.

"Thanks," said the Chief of Base, looking up at the team leader. "Drinks for the whole team on me," he added, holding out three twenty-dollar bills. The team leader took the proffered reward and left. He knew an exit cue when he saw one. The sixty bucks would make for a big party. They'd have to take some over to Tony and Bill in the hospital, he thought. Maybe some of the nurses would be interested in joining them.

The door hadn't even closed behind the team leader before the Chief of Base was on the phone to the 9539th's colonel in his quarters. "My office at 19:30," said the Chief of Base perfunctorily.

The colonel was on time. That was one of the things that had helped him make it to colonel: he knew when not to be late. He assumed that the Chief of Base was about to have one of his men shipped out of Berlin on the eight-o'clock flight next morning. It wouldn't be the first time. He had brought along the sergeant-major and Sergeant Laufflaecker. There was safety in numbers when dealing with the Chief of Base.

"I want 'em both shipped off to Fort Leavenworth," said the Chief of Base, beginning the meeting without prelude, as was his wont.

"Both?" said the colonel, who had incorrectly deduced that Kevin was the only topic of discussion at this meeting.

"Sheerluck and Kevin," said the Chief of Base, sliding the surveillance team's report across the table to the colonel.

The casual observer would have thought that Lieutenant Sheerluck's luck had run out, but the apotropaic quality of his first name had just not kicked in yet. The colonel would not hear of having an officer shipped out to Fort Leavenworth. A discreet, short-of-tour reassignment with a promotion would be fine, but Fort Leavenworth was out of the question.

Kevin, on the other hand, was not a problem as far as the colonel was concerned. "You'll get his orders cut right away, sergeant," said the colonel to Sergeant Laufflaecker.

"Begging your pardon, sir," said the sergeant-major. "While I agree that they are both idiots for violating the standing non-frat order, if the enlisted man who isolated and eliminated the threat to the Site is going to Fort Leavenworth, then you had better do something worse to the officer who was the threat, or I'll be forced to lodge a formal complaint with the IG."

The colonel had known the sergeant-major since the War, and recognized this pronouncement as a promise, not a threat. He quickly convinced the Chief of Base of the utility of heeding the sergeant-major's advice. "For one thing, it will get the project a lot of unwanted notoriety," he said.

"OK, Leavenworth's out, but I want 'em both on that eight-o'clock plane," said the Chief of Base.

"Both, sir?" said the sergeant-major. "I don't perceive any appreciable difference in their treatment with this course of action."

"OK, if Kevin dumps his moose, he can stay," said the Chief of Base grudgingly, as he recalled some of the successfully actionable things in Kevin's scripts that had never showed up in PRIMROSE reporting.

"Agreed. And the lieutenant, sir?" replied the sergeant-major.

"If I might be so bold as to make a suggestion," said Sergeant Laufflaecker. "Perhaps the lieutenant could be curtailed to afford him the opportunity of a troop command position which is the cornerstone of any successful military career. It sounds like a promotion, if you hold your tongue in the right place when you say it. I happen to know that there is a shortage of line officers in straight-leg infantry units on the DMZ in Korea."

Sergeant Laufflaecker's suggestion was greeted with approval from all quarters.

"Now for the other one," said the Chief of Base, pressing a button concealed in the kneehole of his desk.

The door behind the colonel opened, revealing the silhouette of one of the Chief of Base's more athletic team members.

"Bring him in," said the Chief of Base, and 47 seconds later, Kevin joined the august company in the Chief of Base's office.

"You can wait outside," said the Chief of Base to his muscular minion.

"PRIMROSE is Sheerluck's moose," said the Chief of Base, unwisely pausing to lend gravity to the moment.

"And you're going to apologize for calling Gabbie a moose," said Kevin whose stay in the safe house had not done anything to improve his attitude.

"No, you get to choose between your moose and your friends on tape," said the Chief of Base, already regretting that he had agreed to this proposition.

"That's not a choice," said Kevin. "Tell Boris and Evgenij 'good-bye' for me next time you see 'em."

"OK, that does it," said the Chief of Base. "Get this clown out of here! I gave him a chance, sergeant-major, but he turned it down. He's on the eight-o'clock flight too."

"I think that I have an assignment that fits the crime," said Sergeant Laufflaecker, defusing the situation. "I have an old war buddy in Personnel at HQ USAREUR, and he'll see to it that Kevin gets what he deserves."

The Chief of Base agreed, because Sergeant Laufflaecker had a long track record of good ideas. The colonel agreed, because the Chief of Base had agreed. The sergeant-major agreed, because he recognized the twinkle in Sergeant Laufflaecker's eyes for what it was.

While PCS orders were being cut, the two "guilty" parties were escorted to their respective quarters to pack. Lieutenant Sheerluck was escorted by an MP Major and two sergeants. Kevin was "escorted" by Fast Eddie, who was working the Swing as usual, but didn't have anything to do since Jimmy was scribing and not Kevin.

"The rumors of your death were, I take it, greatly exaggerated?" said Eddie after Sergeant Laufflaecker had turned Kevin over to him.

"No, it's the rumors of Gabbie being PRIMROSE that were greatly exaggerated," said Kevin, not a little displeased with Fast Eddie for having told the Chief of Base about Gabbie. When he first saw Eddie, he would have blithely strangled him with a patch cord, if there had been one handy, but he quickly changed his mind when he realized that Eddie could be of more use to him alive than dead.

"Let me buy you a Weisse by way of apology," said Eddie, noting the change in the expression on Kevin's face.

"I'd prefer that you have Meg find Gabbie in the morning and tell her that the rumors of my death have been greatly exaggerated," replied Kevin, gruffly. "And let her know that I'm being shipped to the Zone, but that she hasn't seen the last of me."

"I get the picture," said Eddie.

Fast Eddie left Kevin alone, and went to call Meg at home, just in case Gabbie dropped by "to visit the baby," in search of Kevin. He wasn't a trained intelligence analyst for nothing. Gabbie showed up just after 21:00 Local, and Meg gave her the message.

Fast Eddie had big hopes that acting as a go-between for Kevin and Gabbie would win him some forgiveness for dropping Kevin in it. He bought Kevin a Weisse mit Schuss "on account," and flowers for Meg. He knew she'd find out sooner or later. He was right. She did find out, and the flowers did help a little bit.

She didn't speak to him for only a month. It could have been worse. She'd thought about taking the baby home to her parents' when she first heard. It was a whispered conference with Gabbie three days later that changed her mind.

At Tempelhof the next morning, as Kevin started up the stairs to the plane, Sergeant Laufflaecker shoved a package into his hands. "This is for Sergeant Smith in Personnel. Don't talk to anybody else but him. He'll take care of you," said Sergeant Laufflaecker.

"Thanks," said Kevin blankly.

The package contained a bottle of Johnnie Walker Red, a bottle of Stolichnaya vodka and a note that said giving Kevin an assignment where he couldn't make use of his Russian would be a waste of all the time and money that the Army had invested in teaching it to him. "I happen to know that Sam at the 7747th Military Police Railway Security Group Detachment in Berlin is short one translator on his TO&E. Why don't you do Sam and me a favor, and send this guy to the 7747th to ride the Duty Train?" concluded the note.

Sergeant Smith would have done it without the two bottles of booze, but he appreciated Sergeant Laufflaecker's thoughtfulness in sending them. The counterfeit German tax seals on them made them safe to swap on the open market for something really useful, like a Zeiss Ikoflex IIA Twin Lens Reflex with a fresnel finder screen.

"You must have pissed somebody off," said Sergeant Smith to Kevin.

"Seems that way," replied Kevin reservedly.

"Must have been lady trouble," continued the sergeant.

"You must be clairvoyant," said Kevin.

"Tommy's always had a soft spot for young army people in love," answered Sergeant Smith. "Ever since Alice left him. If you'd have done something really heinous, he'd a' cut your orders to Hell himself and not have sent you to me."

Kevin was on the evening Duty Train out of Frankfurt, headed back to Berlin and the 7747th. He and Gabbie had lunch the next day, and together they sent a thank you note to Sergeant Laufflaecker, who came to see Kevin just before his next scheduled Duty Train trip out to Helmstedt and back.

"A word in your ear, Kilroy," said Sergeant Laufflaecker. "I'd keep a low profile, if I were you, and not go looking up any of your old buddies from the 9539th, like Fast Eddie. If the Chief of Base finds out you're here, he could make life unpleasant for the both of us. And if anything happens to Fast Eddie, I'll come looking for you."

"I get the point, sergeant. Thanks again for this assignment," replied Kevin. "You ever need anything, just let me know. I don't know what I could do for you that you couldn't do for yourself, but I'll give it a try."

"You turned out to be good folks, Kilroy. Hang on to that attitude."

Kevin's new assignment was not as exciting as life had been at the 9539th. He missed Boris and Evgenij, and he missed going to classes with Gabbie at the Freie Universität, but that was OK, as long as he didn't have to give up Gabbie. She had hit number one in his top ten listing of things he liked about Berlin. They were married four months later.

The Chief of Base never missed Kevin, because he was blissfully ignorant of what was missing from the transcripts of the conversations between the voices under Berlin after Kevin was banished to the safe house and exiled from the Site. Having Kevin transcribe the conversation on Reel 51384 would have made him very happy indeed, but Kevin didn't do it, and, as a result, he was very, very unhappy.

Circuit 158:   10:27-10:30Z 16 April 1956
Reel 51384

MALE 1: NORA, this is WUENSDORF. Channel check.
MALE 2: WUENSDORF, this is NORA. I read you
      fivers.
MALE 1: ALEKSANYCH, is that you?
MALE 2: KONSTANTINYCH, good to talk to you.
      What's all this channel-checking? Seems
      like everybody and his brother is channel-
      checking.
MALE 1: Haven't you heard? There's a fault on the
      line and we're trying to isolate it.
MALE 2: No, I hadn't heard anything. LENA and I
      just got back off a week's leave.
MALE 1: Well, the chief commo officer is going
      nuts. The CG tried to make a call and the
      circuit he wanted was down. You know what
      kind of flap that can create.
MALE 2: Tell me about it!
MALE 1: So far the problem seems to be between
      KIPs 25 and 26, and the commo chief wants
      to be sure that it's the only one before he
      gets a team out to look for the break.
MALE 2: That's mighty brave, making the CG wait.
MALE 1: No, it's not. He's a big chicken. The
      only wand to listen for the gas leak is
      broken, and he needs time to get a
      replacement in from MOSCOW. He thinks that
      there'll be less of a fuss over a cautious
      delay "to gather sufficient information"
      than over a lack of the proper equipment.
MAKE 2: That's still taking a chance. When you
      think it'll be in?
MALE 1: It's got to come through unofficial
      channels, so it'll be Friday at the

```
            earliest.
MALE 2: Good luck. Any chance of you and MARUSYA
        getting down our way?
MALE 1: I don't think so, but there's a training
        course for crypto techs being scheduled for
        here next month. Maybe you and LENA could
        come up?
MALE 2: I'll put a bug in my lieutenant's ear.
MALE 1: It'd be good to see you again. I'll see
        if I can get the message to go out with a
        request for you by name, and spouses are
        always required to accompany on trips like
        this to cut down on the hanky-panky after
        class.
MALE 2: That's smart. No spouse on site is what
        got my predecessor in trouble.
MALE 1: Yeah, tell me about it. If his moose
        hadn't poisoned him, and they'd found out
        about her while he was still alive, he'd be
        servicing a circuit to some polar bear in
        deepest darkest Siberia right about now.
MALE 2: A hard choice: being dead or being in
        Siberia. I think he made the right one.
MALE 1: Whoops! Here comes the lieutenant. Keep
        in touch. [In a much louder voice,
        obviously for the benefit of the
        lieutenant] NORA, this is WUENSDORF. I read
        you fivers.
[Hang up]
```

Jimmy had no idea what any of this meant, and his script read:

Circuit 158:   10:27-10:30Z 16 April 1956
**   Reel 51384**

```
NORA (8 Guards) with WUENSDORF (HQ GSFG)
Commo and perschat. NTR.
```

By the time this tape was QC'd in the States, it was too late for it to make any difference to the Site. Jimmy—unlike Kevin and the crusty, brusque, gruff stateside QC who redid the transcript of reel 51384—did not know that KIP is the abbreviation for Control Inspection Point, and that KIPs 25 and 26 bounded the part of the cable track that the tap was in. Kevin—who, among other things, knew where all the whorehouses in GSFG were—also knew that commo cables are filled with gas under pressure so that if there is a break in the line, the repair team can quickly find it by listening for the sound of escaping gas with a thing that looks like a wand with headphones attached to them.

That was one of the things that made doing the tap so hard. Not only did the techs installing the tap have to keep the impedance of the tap low so that it would not show up on an automated line check, they also had to keep the gas pressure in the cable from dropping.

Having put these two facts together, Kevin would have bounced off the walls until someone went down to the tap chamber to make sure that the tap was OK. The tech who serviced the tap chamber was not as conscientious and efficient as the tech who installed it, but with Kevin rattling his cage, he would have discovered the cold solder joint that took down circuit 48 and the slow gas leak that gave away the presence of the tap to the Russian who walked over it in the rain with a wand.

But Kevin was riding the Duty Train and the tech did not find the cold solder joint and the gas leak. The Russians, however, did.

41
The Voices Fall Silent

It was raining the Saturday night that they shut the Shoss down. Detroit was in the Crow's Nest, but even he could not miss the fact that the blurred streaks of light that normally floated about four feet above the Shoss on dark, rainy nights like this one had disappeared. It was normal for it to slow down to one or two trucks a minute with the occasional car thrown in for variety, but for it to go totally dark—except for the compound-perimeter lights and the spotlights on the Vopo tower—was unheard of, until at least 23:00 Local. It was only 20:00 Local and there should have been plenty of life left in the light show yet.

Detroit knew what time it was because he had AFN on and the unmistakably American voice of the announcer had just said: "It's eight o'clock in Central Europe. Do you know where your children are?" Detroit did not have any children, but he knew where he was, and he would have rather been out in the rain, looking for the children he did not have than sitting in the Crow's Nest watching trucks and cars that were not there.

There was not anybody to talk to in the Crow's Nest, and nothing to do except watch the Vopos watch you, and stare out into the dark, looking for some threat to the tunnel, whatever that might be. It was terribly boring and everybody pulling duty in the Crow's Nest dreamed of seeing the mythical floozies in the Vopo tower that Kevin had always talked about, or at least finding a threat to the tunnel, so that they would have something to do.

Detroit had the same dream as everybody else, but there he was with an indication of a threat to the tunnel that he did not recognize, so he just kept watching the darkened Shoss do nothing, and did not tell anybody.

At 20:37 Local a single Russian jeep came out of the darkness, moving at a walking pace. It was preceded by a uniformed Russian on foot, holding a long, thin stick that he swept slowly back and forth across the shoulder of the road in front of him as he plodded along in the pouring rain about ten feet ahead of the jeep. He was walking the cable track. Even Detroit could see that.

Detroit picked up the binoculars and studied the walking Russian. He looked even more disgustingly bored than Detroit was, which was a major achievement in and of itself, but the Russian did have the advantage of being sopping wet. If Detroit had been sopping wet too, he would have, without a doubt, looked more disgustingly bored than the Russian, but he was dry and sitting down to boot.

The Russian held up his hand and stopped. He didn't want the jeep to run over him and had to let them know he was going to stand still. He was right over the tap chamber. He waved his wand back and forth. He motioned to the jeep to cut the motor so he could hear better. That action also explained why the Russians had shut down traffic on the Shoss. The cable track walker would not have heard anything as quiet as a gas leak with all those noisy trucks zipping by him every ten seconds.

The drenched Russian turned around, walked back to the jeep, and climbed in. It wasn't heated, but at least it got him out of the rain and the wind. Six minutes later, the jeep was joined by a Russian two-and-a-half-ton truck.

An officer got out of the jeep, and went back to talk with the sergeant in the truck who was in charge of the digging detail. After a short conference, the sergeant got his crew out of the back of the truck and showed them where to start digging: right in front of the truck. The truck's headlights lit up the work site for them.

The officer went back to the jeep and got inside. The jeep did a three-point turn so that its lights were pointing at the truck. The extra light made it easier for the shovellers to see what they were doing.

This was something Detroit could understand. All the hours of seemingly wasted vigilance expended on manning the Crow's Nest had just paid off. The Russians were digging right over the tap chamber.

Detroit picked up the handset of the field telephone and spun the crank. A bored voice at the other end said "You rang?" in imitation of Master-Sergeant Laufflaecker's now famous greeting to the Crow's Nest. It was Corporal Neumann.

"The Russians have stopped all the traffic on the Shoss, and they're getting ready to dig right over the tap chamber."

Detroit's call to Corporal Neumann produced a flurry of activity. The Chief of Base started his counter-surveillance run to the Site. Fast Eddie wrote an imminent threat to the Site report and ran it down to the comm center. Sergeant Laufflaecker climbed up to the Crow's Nest, not so much to keep Detroit from getting lonely, as to confirm his observations. No actions as dire as those prescribed by the SOP for an event such as this could be taken on the basis of uncorroborated reporting.

"That doesn't look good," said Sergeant Laufflaecker, corroborating Detroit's analysis of the situation. As if to corroborate his corroboration, one of the Russian diggers put his foot on his shovel to push it another six inches deeper into the ground, and fell 13 feet to the bottom of the tap chamber instead.

Sergeant Laufflaecker instantly recognized the significance of the digger's disappearance, grabbed the field phone and aggressively turned the crank that rang the bell at the distant end.

"Yes," said Corporal Neumann, who recognized the sound of disaster striking that was implied by the way the bell of the field phone was ringing.

"Intruder alert!" intoned Sergeant Laufflaecker. "Evacuate the tunnel, and cut power to the lights!"

"The tunnel's been empty since Detroit made his first report," replied Corporal Neumann. "The tunnel is dark," he added, turning the key in the switch that activated a big red light at the tunnel entrance. The light said "Do Not Enter."

"Good," replied Sergeant Laufflaecker, "and get the fifty-caliber into place."

The Russian digger who had fallen into the tap chamber was out like a light and had to be hoisted out of the hole by his buddies, who first had to go borrow a ladder from the Vopos. The Russian officer sent him off to the hospital in the jeep, and then called for reinforcements on his R-105 radio.

While waiting for the colonel, two majors and four captains who would shortly arrive with more diggers and equipment, the lieutenant descended into the hole to look it over. It was a small chamber, scarcely a meter square with a heavy steel door—the kind normally found at the entrance to communications centers—as its western wall. There was a sign on the door in Russian and German that said: "No entry except by the written permission of the Commander, Group of Soviet Forces, Germany." He decided to take the sign at its word, and climbed back up to ground level to await his further instructions from his superiors.

The Chief of Base and the Russian lieutenant's reinforcements arrived at about the same time. The Chief of Base climbed out of his panel truck and the colonel, two majors and four captains got out of their respective staff cars, and climbed into the back of the diggers' truck, the only nearby place with a roof big enough to accommodate all of them at once. That did not make them very popular with the diggers who had to go back out into the rain to make room for the officers.

The Chief of Base was greeted by the coldly efficient Sergeant Laufflaecker, who recapped the situation, ending with: "We've got a fifty-caliber machine gun set up at this end of the tunnel."

"Sergeant, as much as I'd like to, we can't go shooting Russians in the tunnel. Just look at what happened when Mike and Charlie fired that Coke bottle at the Vopo tower across the Shoss. It almost started World War III. Really shooting at the Russians would take us all the way."

"As much as you'd like to, sir," said Sergeant Laufflaecker, "we can't go shootin' at the Russians, 'cause there ain't no ammunition."

"Then what's the gun for, sergeant?"

"It's mighty spooky in the tunnel when it's dark, and working the bolt on that fifty-caliber makes a really loud, scary sound that doesn't need no translation into Russian. A sane man—Russian or American—would do an awful lot of hard thinking before walking any further down a tunnel where there ain't no cover, after hearing that sound in the dark."

"Sergeant, you're a genius. If this works, you can have all the booze in my 'grease the skids' locker," said the Chief of Base.

The bevy of Russian officers climbed down out of the truck, where it had been dry, and made their way to the hole at the side of the Shoss, where it was pouring rain. The Russian colonel shined his flashlight into the hole, looked at the sign on the door, looked at his entourage, and turned to the lieutenant.

"Open the door," said the Russian colonel.

"Open the door," said the lieutenant to the sergeant in charge of the diggers.

"Open the door," said the Sergeant Makaronshchik to Private Chernenko, the biggest goldbrick in his platoon. He suspected incorrectly that the lieutenant knew something about the door that he did not.

Private Chernenko climbed down into the hole, took hold of the handle and pushed it downward. The door swung open, revealing a very dark hole.

The bevy of Russian officers climbed down into the hole and walked through the door, flashlights in hand. They were amazed at what they saw.

"A very professional installation," said the colonel. "The wire room at Wuensdorf should be so well equipped."

The Russian colonel looked at the black hole that was the opening of the tunnel back to the warehouse.

"Lieutenant, go see where that leads to," he said.

"Sergeant, go see where that leads to," said the lieutenant.

"Come with me," said the Sergeant Makaronshchik to Private Chernenko.

"I hear footsteps in the tunnel," said Corporal Neumann.

"Work the bolt," said Sergeant Laufflaecker.

"The footsteps stopped," whispered the corporal.

"A sane man," replied Sergeant Laufflaecker.

The next morning, the tunnel was front-page news in all the East German press. The article in *Time* magazine the next week was the most comforting: "It's the best publicity the U.S. has had in Berlin in a long time."

YOU ARE LEAVING
THE AMERICAN SECTOR

ВЫ ВЫЕЗЖАЕТЕ ИЗ
АМЕРИКАНСКОГО СЕКТОРА

VOUS SORTEZ
DU SECTEUR AMÉRICAIN

SIE VERLASSEN DEN AMERIKANISCHEN SEKTOR

The Army of Occupation Medal

Awarded for thirty or more consecutive days of duty as a member of the occupation forces after World War II. While in Austria and most of Germany the period of qualifying service for award of the medal ended in 1955, Berlin was legally an occupied territory until the Reunification of Germany in October 1990. This is one of the things that made Berlin a unique place to be stationed.

About the Author

The author served at Field Station Berlin in the mid-1970s, following a tour at Herzo Base in the early 1970s. He is a three-time graduate of The Defense Language Institute (DLIWC) in Monterey, California. A collection of his short stories received an award at the 2006 Hollywood Book Festival. He is a member of the Military Writers Society of America.

The illustrations were taken from documents in the public domain. The quality of the reproductions of the illustrations is a function of the quality of the originals, some of which were showing their age. Map (modified by the author) — *Berlin*, Berlin Command, 1954; Outpost Theater, The PX and The Ku-damm — *Special Services Berlin Tour*, Berlin Command, 1953; Glienicke Brücke — *Special Services Berlin Tour*, Berlin Command, 1958; Digging the Tunnel and Check Point "Tunnel" (modified) — *Clandestine Services History: The Berlin Tunnel Operation 1952-1956*, CIA, 1967; Communist Bounty Hunters — *Troop Information Fact Sheet No. 48*, HQ U.S. Army, Europe, 1961; Black Market and U-Bahnhof Oskar-Helene-Heim — *Views and Facts of Berlin*, 78th Division Special Services Office, circa 1947; RTO stamp — Berlin travel orders dated 25 June 1952; The Naked Transcriber — drawn by G.M. Richards (modified), *Everybody's Magazine*, volume 34, 1916, p. 781; T.H.E. Hill logo, Marx's Tomb, Kevin's Loose Screw, Kevin's Headphones, BAFS (modified), Dollar MPC (modified) and Army of Occupation Medal — by the author.

Want to learn more about Berlin in the early 1950s?

Then read *Berlin in "Early Cold War" Army Booklets*. It reprints a series of six army booklets on Berlin, covering the period from 1946 to 1958, two years after the tunnel was shut down. It represents part of the research that went into *Voices Under Berlin*.

The decision to reprint these booklets was based on a number of considerations, number one of which was preservation. The second consideration was that—when presented in a single volume—these booklets have a historical value that is greater than the sum of the individual booklets in isolation. They all represent a single institutional viewpoint, that of the United States Military Command in Berlin. When read in parallel, the booklets create a sense of living history, because, while the they cover the same topics of interest about Berlin, their coverage of these  topics changes as time goes by. The value added to the booklets by reprinting them in a single volume is that the single-volume reprint makes it possible to compare the texts and see the changes.

As the series progresses, the role of Hitler and the Nazis moves further and further into the background, as does the amount of war damage noted. At the same time, the relationship between the USSR and the USA can be seen to rearrange itself.

The reprint is indexed and the changes in the text from one edition to the next of the individual booklets are highlighted for ease of comparison. To help better define the historical context of the booklets the reprint is provided with a Berlin Chronology.

To learn more about *Berlin in "Early Cold War" Army Booklets*, visit: <www.voicesunderberlin.com/1950.htm>.

18718208R00180

Made in the USA
Lexington, KY
20 November 2012